# TWO RIP-ROARIN' WESTERNS BY T.V. OLSEN, WINNER OF THE GOLDEN SPUR AWARD!

## A $7.98 VALUE FOR ONLY $4.99!

### *CANYON OF THE GUN*

"What do you want here, kid?" the bartender asked, dipping his hand below the bar. But the kid stepped a wary sidepace from the bar, suspecting the bungstarter the bartender kept there. He kept his eyes directly on Ames, directly on his father's killer.

Suddenly Ames boiled up out of the chair, pushed over the table, his fancy gun blurring out and up.

Young Gault slapped his own gunbutt then, cocking the weapon and bringing it up with a clean, easy motion....

### *HAVEN OF THE HUNTED*

Taine swung suddenly to Hassard, frowning and at least half sobered. "Damn it, Egan. We all liked Melanie...."

"So did I, George," Hassard said. "Only what can we do? Besides, Kingdom's innocent. Half a dozen public-spirited citizens said so this morning at the inquest...."

Taine said with great gentleness, "Just show him to us."

"We're with you, George," a man shouted; a swift clamor broke out.

"Name the play, Egan," growled Taine.

"Get a rope," Hassard said, grinning. "I'll name it...."

Other *Leisure Books* by T.V. Olsen:
**HIGH LAWLESS/SAVAGE SIERRA**

# T. V. OLSEN

## CANYON OF THE GUN
### &
## HAVEN OF THE HUNTED

LEISURE BOOKS    NEW YORK CITY

A LEISURE BOOK®

December 1993

Published by special arrangement with Golden West Literary
Agency.

Dorchester Publishing Co., Inc.
276 Fifth Avenue
New York, NY 10001

# CANYON OF THE GUN

# Chapter One

Calem's fingers curved around the gunbutt with the easy reflex of practice, and the interval between his full-cocking the hammer and the whisper of steel clearing the waistband of his jeans was almost imperceptible. He aimed by instinct, bringing the old gun level, and then rammed it back into his waistband. He thought then, grinning a little, *That was good. Wonder what Jesse would say?*

His face sobered, and he raised a hand to his shirt pocket and dug out a few precious cartridges. He juggled them in his palm, thinking, *They should be gone all day. Why not?* Again he lifted out the gun, thumbed three of the shells into the well-oiled cylinder, and set the firing pin over the first. Holstering the heavy weapon, he turned and walked off a few steps.

At nineteen Calem had his full growth, a gaunt six feet three of it. He had shot up like wild willow in the last few years, and his big-boned frame already hinted at the beef to come. His chest and shoulders boasted more heft than his father's, and he could heave a fifty-pound feedsack into a loft six feet over his head and hardly know the effort. He had outgrown about all his clothes; turning now, he shifted his shoulders against his rough homespun shirt with a vague discomfort, but carefully, because sewing up the occasional torn seams of his exertions made an extra chore for Ma.

He eyed his unmutilated target—a tin can set on a post—like an enemy. It brought an indrawn somberness to his long bony face, not quite hardened to the lines of manhood. His eyes were gray as smoke, now faintly squinting under their heavy dark brows. Above a high forehead his shock of black hair was roached like a mule's mane. His chin was stubborn and with his full lower lip conspired to lend a hungry brooding to his expression even in repose.

*Point your gun like a finger,* Jesse had always said. *Aim by feel but give yourself that second. You ain't J. E. B. Stuart; just see you get there with the mostest.*

The gun, blurring up and coming level, sent whipcrack echoes across the silent yard, and the can leaped up and

7

bounded away into the empty breaking corral; and sighting between the poles Calem sent it another twenty feet. His third shot dropped the can, dented and twisted, into a bed of trampled mud. He lowered the gun and licked his lip and blinked against the stench of powdersmoke; he grinned again.

The rattle of the wagon coming up by the pasture gate froze Calem then, and he tore his shirt open and rammed the gun inside. Not looking around, he set off toward the tack barn with his hands in his pockets, a casual whistle on his lips. But his belly was turning hot and cold; they couldn't have failed to hear those three shots. He had learned to speak softly and mind his talk or else he would have sworn. It was hardly past noon, and most Saturdays they would lay over in town till nearly nightfall.

Ducking into the barn and its shadows, Calem pulled out the gun and jammed it into an open barrel of grain. As he stepped outside, the spring wagon was swinging past, and his father gave him a hard sideglance, his iron-colored eyes stabbing him. His gut tightening more, Calem walked slowly toward the house. His father reined up the team by the slanting lean-to near the kitchen door and climbed stiffly down. After assisting his wife to the ground, he turned wordlessly, ignoring her low anxious, "Jared," and came straight on toward his son.

Jared Gault was a tall and rawboned man, gaunt and dry and unbent, and his drab linsey shirt and homespun jeans hung on him like tattered cast-offs on a scarecrow. He was ungainly but not ludicrous; the hard strength of him thrust out at you from his deeply lined, deeply weathered face. He came to a stop and planted his run-down workboots a little apart, and Calem halted too.

Jared said briefly, "Where is the gun, boy?"

"In the barn."

Jared's big-knuckled hand made a motion, and Calem turned and tramped ahead of him. In the barn he dug deep in the feed barrel, feeling for the gun, and brought it out. Jared took it, handling it like something unclean, and laid it on a bench. He straightened.

"Where did you get it?"

"From Jesse before he lit out."

Jared's breath whistled out gently. "A good two years ago, then. And the shells?"

Calem's face was warm, and he lowered his eyes.

"Reckoned I'd missed a few time to time. My rifle gun shells would fit this one. Never heard a shot, though."

8

"I—" Calem made a loose gesture. "That place Jesse and I used to go back in the hills—uh—shot it off there some. . . ."

"Bare your back."

"Pa—"

"Bare your back, son." Jared's eyes were strangely tired. Calem met his stare a long moment and, slowly turning, peeled off his shirt and planted his palms against the wall. A shame boiled in his belly. It had been four years since Pa had used the strap. He heard him cross the barn to some harness hanging on the wall, then a rattle of dry leather, and Jared came up behind him. He shut his eyes. The first blow drew a grunt from him, and then Calem clamped his teeth and braced out nine more strokes without a wince, counting them by old habit and letting his breath sigh out on the last one. After he had shrugged carefully into his shirt and buttoned it, his father picked up the gun and said curtly, "Come along," and wheeled outside. Halting, he pulled back his arm and threw the gun. It made a bright arc in the sun and struck the sod in the horse pasture and bounced twice.

"Let it rust there. . . . Why, Calem?" There was a first break in Gault's voice, and slowly he shook his head from side to side. "Can you tell me why?"

"No, Pa."

"It's a possibility," Jared said gently, "that I told you too long ago for it to take good. A handgun ain't like a rifle, which can be took up for the use of killing your game or your varmints. Worse coming to worse, you can defend yourself with a rifle. But a man packs a sidearm is one priming for trouble when there is no goddam need." It was his strongest oath, yet infrequently used, and his face was ruddy with anger. "I rode with Quantrill and with George Todd and 'Bloody Bill' Anderson. And with Cole Younger and Frank James and his slimy little brother 'Dingus.' Him you heard called Jesse, and giving your brother that name was never my notion. I knew 'em all. They used to string Navy Colts from their belts like beads. I saw—" Jared broke off, his breathing ragged, and Calem watched him open-mouthed. "I never told you none of that, and don't mean to. All you got to mind is that I joined up a green kid and it took me a while to learn the difference between a soldier and a wild-eyed killer. I quit the band after Jeff Davis outlawed Quantrill in '63, and spent ever since burying it to my own mind. I told Jesse some of it, but I reckon not enough to make the difference."

9

"You pushed him!" Calem let it out in hot protest, saying the words at last.

"What was that?" Jared took a step and balled his son's shirtfront in a fist, shaking him savagely. "By God, that's your mother talking! Don't you ever—"

He broke off and said, "Ahhh," with a soft and bitter note, pushing Calem away. "Let it take, boy. A licking never broke the sap from Jesse, and I don't expect it will from you. Too much of me in you both. But you ain't like your brother; you got a mind and you got ears. Use 'em, and mind what I said. Let it take, Calem."

He wheeled and strode toward the house, and Calem trudged slowly after him. He knew his father was a hard man, not a brutal one; the harsh and the gentle warred in him and the mixture was confusing. *Quantrill.* Did that explain things? Calem understood Jared enough to have doubted him only once: no man could halter-break a colt with a gentler hand, yet he had dealt only a harsh and unforgiving one to his older son. Martha Gault, understanding her husband still better, had shared that doubt, and her forgiveness of him after the explosive final quarrel that drove Jesse away for good had come hard.

Still, Jess' wildness had been brash and unrepentant; there was always some girl, but that was the least of it. He'd had a talent for slithering out of that sort of trouble; it was his wounding of a drunken and belligerent cowhand in a saloon brawl that had broken his father's patience.

They hadn't seen him since, and range gossip carried only vague rumors, but they knew he was hanging with a wild bunch over by Pima Flats, not far east. Only last week one of the bunch had been hanged as a proven rustler.

Jared Gault only clamped his jaw against such talk, having forbidden Jesse's name to be mentioned under his roof.

Calem's mother was waiting in the doorway. She was a large woman on the stout side with gray hair bunned tightly on her head. Over the years some of her husband's iron had rubbed into her square, stern face. The gentleness was in her eyes, her quiet voice.

"Come in, Calem, and take off your shirt."

Jared, hoisting a sack of flour out of the wagon bed, said with a frown, "First he'll help me tote this stuff in the lean-to."

Her mouth tightened. "No, Mr. Gault. No."

Their life together was a good one, with all differences met by a measured compromise, and Jared, in whipping his son,

10

had had his way. Now it was Martha Gault's turn. Jared shrugged a wry concession, heaved the sack to his shoulder and tramped into the lean-to.

Calem sat at the table, his arms tightly folded, while Martha bathed his back with hot water which brought every welt alive till she applied the cool relief of a salve. Jared came in, took off his black slouch hat and hung it up. "There was no need to shame him so." Martha was calmly reproachful, walking to the doorway to throw out the basin water. "He's a man now, Mr. Gault."

Jared said irritably, "Then let him act the man," and sat down, leaning an elbow on the table and rubbing a hand over his face. "Damn it all, Martha."

"You push too hard, Mr. Gault," she said and compressed her lips.

They ate the dinner of beef and biscuits and wilted greens in silence. Afterward Jared took out his stubby, blackened pipe and struck a match. "You find time away from your various interests to do the chores I told you?" Calem muttered yes. Jared frowned into his pipebowl, coaxing it alight. "That's something. I do appreciate your industry, boy." He got the pipe going and drowned the match in his coffee dregs. "Cut the marketing short today so we could get to that fencing."

Martha clattered some soiled dishes into the washpan. "Blue Horse Spring?" A worried note crept into her voice. "I thought you weren't decided."

"I've put it off long enough." Jared rose and walked to the door and took down his hat. "If there's to be trouble, might as well have it done with."

Without a word she went to the east wall and lifted his rifle from its pegs. "No, Martha." Jared cleared his throat gently. "That there's looking for it. We will wait till the fence is up and see." He clamped his hat on decisively and walked out.

Calem gulped his coffee, wiped his mouth, and stood. His mother held out the rifle. "Take it, Calem." He hesitated, and she said, "Take it along. He takes a spell building a head of steam. It's gone off now."

He took the rifle, opened the breech and checked the load, and looked at her. "Take care, Calem," she said softly, and he sensed the depth of her worry.

She had reason for it. There were few fences in Coyotero Basin; good watering places were far between, and by tacit agreement the basin ranchers left them open so that no man's

11

cattle would be slacked. Blue Horse Spring lay on the line between the hardscrabble Gault outfit and Major Jeffrey Dembrow's big, sprawling Skull to the north. There had never been trouble over watering rights there because Skull's northwest range was hard by the only abundant water in the basin, Ten Mile Tanks below Mesa Amarillo. But after a band of Coyotero Apaches, reservation breakaways, had made camp near the mesa a month ago, Major Dembrow had been pushing his far-drifting stock south toward safer range and water, including Blue Horse Spring. His thirsty cattle had trampled the spring that supported the meager Gault herd to a muddy mire.

Jared Gault had not pleaded but had made his case clear to the Major. Jeffrey Dembrow, an oldtime cavalryman, had a ramrod will to match his small, hard body. His reply of "We'll see," had held a spare indifference, and his real answer had been to throw more cows into the Blue Horse area. That was when Jared Gault, a man with iron of its own sort tempered by a hatred of violence, had toyed with the notion of fencing off the spring. Now his decision was solid, making an acid test of how far the Major would go.

Calem said, "Don't worry, Ma," trying to lard it with conviction, and went outside on the lope. He jumped into the bed of the wagon as his father drove it across the yard. Stacked by the barn was a pile of fresh-cut cedar posts that had been intended for pasture fencing. Jared halted the team and stepped down, only then noting the rifle. He scowled but said nothing. They loaded the posts. Jared fetched two rolls of new wire from the barn, while Calem toted out the shovels, wire stretchers and pliers, two hammers and a keg of staples. He sat the seat with the rifle on his knees and Jared grimly hoorawed the team into motion.

Calem breathed deeply of the hot afternoon, trying to ease the knot of trouble in him. A hawk spiraled against the glittering sky; wind flattened the brown grass of the rolling flats in undulant waves, and to the north rose the red hulk of Mesa Amarillo and, beyond, the serrated dark tracery of mountains. That far range was as virgin and untamed to his mind as when his grandfather, Ephraim Gault, had tramped and trapped it with "Old Bill" Williams, Tom Fitzpatrick, Bridger and old Glass and the young Kit Carson. And he remembered the long winter evenings by a roaring fire in the Missouri farmhouse, he and Jesse hugging their knees, wide-eyed while the old mountain man told of the Shining Mountains of his youth, the big beaver kills and piles of glistening

12

"plew," the red-eyed rendezvous and ring-tailed eye-gouging *hivernants*. At which their mother shortly dispatched the boys to bed, but Jesse and Calem would lie awake for hours, whispering, dreaming out loud.

The wild flavor of it stayed with Calem, and it must have taken to a degree with Jared too, for he'd pulled his stakes, westering shortly after Gramps died. But Jared was a plodding sort of man, stolid and close-mouthed of his desires, the impractical dreamer offset by the family provider. If there was a bloodstrain of wildness in the Gaults, it had cropped out strongly in Jesse, while in Calem it was a qualified rebellion against not his father's settled ways but his rutted notions. A keen but untutored mind not yet come to terms with itself might find a restless outlet in gun practice, but it was also a thinking mind aware of duty; his father and mother, no longer young, needed his strong back—and more.

Calem started, wrenched from his reverie, as Jared spoke suddenly: "Don't think too hard of me, son. Maybe I took the wrong tack with Jesse, though I'll larrup you if you tell your ma I said so. Jess—" he paused, picking his words with difficulty—"he always had to act black when you said white. Harder you tugged, the more he shied. I was hellfire on loose women, so he took all he could find. Called a pistol the devil's own tool, so he took to one like a duck takes to water." His jaw ridged hard against its black stubble. "Had to be a way of handling Jess, but I never found it."

Jared was silent for a time, then: "I know you been wanting to cut the traces. Got an idea why you ain't too, and want to say I am obliged. Ain't forgot how a colt's vinegar boils sometime." He cleared his throat and closed his mouth, and Calem respected his embarrassment. Today had seen breaks in Jared's gruff and indrawn reserve, and these words had cost him an effort.

Shortly the wagon left the flats for humpy grass knolls. Jared negotiated the jolting wagon expertly, braking down a long flank into the muddy vale where Blue Horse Spring lay. It was a natural saucer about a hundred feet in diameter. The water, once clear and pure, was brown and roiled and stood in glassy pools in the trampled hoofpocks around the edge. A number of cattle stood about muzzling the dirty water, and these moved off sluggishly at their approach. Some yards back the caked mud had baked to a laved whiteness seamed with a network of cracks. Here Jared halted, got down and tramped through the loose mud to the spring. He

13

stared at it a bitter moment; his orders were brief and harsh, and they went to work.

They dug and sweated for two hours under the broiling sun, and Calem decided that spading postholes through slushy mud and the solid hardpan beneath was as mean a chore as he'd known. They had thirty feet of cedar posts anchored when, pausing for a breather, he saw the lone rider watching from a hillcrest. He said, "Pa," and Jared growled without looking up, "I see him." The rider soon cantered off the hill and was gone.

Calem was watchful after that, and he said nothing when two more horsemen skylined into view and came straight on toward the spring. Jared rammed his shovel into the ground and sleeved his forehead on his grimy shirtarm, waiting. The two men came around the spring, skirting the mud, and halted. Ed Grymes, the Skull foreman, said meagerly, "Boots Hostettor was riding line and seen you. Good thing for you, Gault."

The weathertracks deepened around Jared's eyes. "How you figure?"

"Save you plenty more work. Them posts is coming down."

Calem edged backward toward the wagon, and Jared said mildly, "No, none of that. Hold still, Calem."

Grymes' stare passed from Calem to the rifle on the wagon seat, and he gave a bleak nod. "Smart. No call for it."

He was a massive barrel of a man with a moon face whose bland dullness was relieved by a full black cavalry mustache. His reputation for toughness was less a bone-deep quality of his than part of the front that went with overseeing the affairs of a big outfit, and his loyalty to Skull was deep and doglike and unswerving.

Ames Dembrow said impatiently, "Let's get to it, Ed." He was Major Dembrow's only son, a wire-tempered man in his mid-twenties, slim as a whip. His mouth was hard in the way of a cruel-bitted horse's, but he was a wan mirror of his father. He wore *taja* leggings, a fancy charro jacket, and a black Spanish hat with a band of silver conches, which also decorated his fine black saddle.

Grymes rumbled, "No call to crowd it yet," as he swung heavily to the ground, his bleached eyes watchful on Jared. "Gault, we'll give you a hand."

Jared planted his feet apart, and his big fists knotted against his thighs; his answer came low and flat. "No. Them posts stay up. I had enough."

Grymes cuffed his hat back with a swipe of his fist, scowl-

14

ing at the line of posts. "Sorry about this. Thought the Major'd made it plain enough. Ten Mile Springs is too close to them Coyoteroes. After they move on—"

"Them Coyoteroes ain't touched the basin cattle," Jared broke in heatedly. "They ain't wartrailing; they want to be left alone, live their own way. That goes for me. But how long you think my cows can live on this slop? Blue Horse can't water half your herd too." He pointed a long arm. "I'll leave it open there. With the spring fenced you can water your stock a small bunch at a time. After they're in shape to move, you can drive 'em on. There's other places on Skull."

Ames Dembrow said softly, "Told you, Ed. This brush-hopper's got to be showed." He reined abruptly sideways, lifting his coiled rope off his pommel; he shook out a loop and dabbed it over a post and heeled off to take up the slack.

As quickly, Jared took six long steps, butting Grymes aside with the heel of his palm; he reached Dembrow and caught his belt and yanked sideways, dumping him to the ground. Almost in the same motion he wheeled away and slogged to the post, jerking slack into the taut noose to lift it off.

Ames Dembrow, sprawled on his side in the muck, raised his head. His hat had fallen off and his long blond hair hung over his mud-smeared cheek. His eyes blazed with bad temper, and seeing the gun come up in his fist, Calem stood rooted and dumb. Grymes spun toward Ames now, yelling, "No!"

The gunroar cut his words in half.

Jared Gault, coming about on his heel then, took the shot full in the chest, and the impact arched him backward. Falling, his body had a boneless looseness even before it struck the mud.

Calem stood in a shocked detachment, watching Ames Dembrow crawl to his knees. "Now," Ames said in a hot and shaking voice, "we're tearing down those posts."

# Chapter Two

Calem tramped out of the Coyotero County courthouse like a sleepwalking man, his mind closed to the bustle of Saturday traffic. He halted, blinking at the harsh midday sunlight, and his mother's hand tightened on his arm; she murmured, "Calem."

He said, "All right," and assisted her to the high seat of their wagon. People were straggling from the courthouse in loose groups, talking as they headed for saloons and stores. The tie rails were lined with rigs and single horses, and like others on a long market-and-court day, the Gaults' team had been unhitched and tied to the tailgate so that the horses could feed on straw in the wagon bed.

Calem walked to the tailgate to untie the team, and now a burst of laughter pulled his glance to the courthouse entrance. Ames Dembrow had stepped out, passing talk with some friends. He paused on the steps, hipcocked and wearing his dark suit with a slim grace, and took out a cigar. Briefly, as he bit off the end of the cigar, his light restless eyes locked Calem's. The arrogant humor in his handsome face hardened into open mockery as he spat out the cigartip.

Ames' young wife lagged behind him, a bored indifference in her face, and he glanced at her with a sharp word. She moved dutifully forward, taking his arm, and Ames delibertly lighted his cigar and chuckled at something a friend had said. *We're Dembrows,* his whole manner said with a hard conviction, *and we are not required to give a damn.* The party moved on down the sidewalk, talking and laughing.

Ed Grymes came out now, edging along ponderously, almost furtively, behind a wedge of other people. Martha Gault said calmly, "Mr. Grymes." Her tone was even, almost underpitched, yet it cut through a hubbub of talk. People hauled up, looking on curiously.

Grymes said unsteadily, "Miz Gault—"

"Why did you lie, Mr. Grymes?"

"No, ma'am"—he was already shaking his head—"no, ma'am," and came off the steps with his head hunched, walking swiftly to his tied horse. Swinging up, he roweled the animal away with a furious haste. The undercurrent of talk resumed as the onlookers broke up, and Calem hitched the team.

He had swung to the seat to take up the reins when Major Dembrow and his nephew Cody came out of the courthouse, apparently the last to leave. Cody had started to say something, but the Major cut him off with a lifted hand and came over to the wagon, doffing his hat.

Jeffrey Dembrow was not a big man, and his head was outsize for his body, which was blocky and compact, but his square face was stamped with the habit of command. His full face was strongly handsome, while a Roman senator might have envied his profile; his crisp plume of white hair was peaked at the temples with small devil's horns that seemed to bristle with his moods. It made a solid contrast to his black brows, arched above a single eye of flinty gray; the other being covered by a black eyepatch. That eye, with a trick way of seeming to look beyond whatever it fixed, gave him a distance and austerity heightened by the black broadcloth he usually wore, but lessened by a sensitive, mobile mouth that betrayed a driving impatience coldly restrained.

"Ma'am," he said quietly, "I deeply regret the ordeal this matter has caused you—and even the necessity for it. I would like you to know that."

"It's heard." Martha Gault kept her eyes directly on the team. "Drive along, Calem." It was an utter dismissal of Major Dembrow and whatever charitable suggestions he might offer. He stepped back with a stiff bow and turned away.

Calem set a brisk clip on the south road, heading home. A searching sideglance at his mother showed him a stern composure in her face, her hands folded on the lap of her black dress. Her forty-five years of living had never offered her an easy lot, and absorbing the fact of Jared's death could only strengthen her care-tempered dignity. Calm and dry-eyed since the first shock had spent itself, she had gone through the motions of a service, a funeral, an inquest and now an open hearing as a matter of course. Because Calem knew that her callous if simple acceptance was anything but unfeeling, it awed him a little.

For him, unable till now to shake the strange numb unreality of the shooting and all that followed, it was only beginning. He had a memory like a bad taste of how he had only stood, dumbly unmoving after Ames Dembrow rode away, until Ed Grymes had stirred him with a brusque order. Together they had lifted his father's body to the wagon and he had driven it home, feeling like an observer in a bad dream from which there was no pinching yourself awake. That tough and vital Jared, who should have been good for his own father's fourscore and five, was suddenly a broken and lifeless lump in the mud had made no sense at all. Maybe it was only a vacuum of personal helplessness, of apathy reinforced by taking for granted that justice would be done and all of it was out of his hands.

Today the court hearing had shown otherwise, and now like a forming crack in the dike of bewildered disbelief, anger was trickling through, black and bitter and scouring. Ames Dembrow had good reason for his bland cocksureness, and knowing only this, Calem let the mounting fury have its free, unreasoning way with his thoughts.

The five miles rolled behind them without talk until they turned through the pasture gate below the house. Martha shaded her eyes, peering toward the porch. "Seems we've company. Reckon a neighbor come to pay his respects."

Calem muttered, "Took him long enough," and then hauled up the team abruptly, his heart lifting to his throat. The man sitting in deep shadow on the porch had stood, and now with a slack negligence he stepped off the porch. Calem said softly, "Ma," and heard the sharp catch in her breath.

Letting out a whoop, he rein-whipped the team into a run. "Calem," she protested, "don't drive so—oh, Jess. Jesse! . . ."

An hour later, sitting at slack after-dinner ease and picking his teeth, Jesse Gault was saying, "That's about it, Ma. I cut the dust out of Pima Flats without delay soon as I got the news about Pa from this drifting man. Sorry to miss the funeral."

Martha's eyes glowed with a softness that Calem hadn't seen in a long time. "It's all right. You're home, Jesse."

Jesse selected a nut from a table-centered bowl and cracked it between the heels of his palms. "Sure, Ma." He punched Calem lightly on the arm, chewing and grinning. "Boy, you sure enough grown a damn foot." The old deviltry filled his dark eyes, and except for a veneer of cool assurance he hadn't changed by a jot. His long saturnine face beneath his roached black hair was smooth and unlined. A faint white scar showed in the deeply weathered skin of his forehead, and his left ear was thickened by scar

18

tissue. Otherwise he was the old Jesse, slim and hard, with a lazy grace about him, and Calem felt a surge of warm feeling. Jesse was back and now, somehow, things had to be all right.

"So you testified at a hearing today?" Jesse tilted back his head, tossing the nutmeat into his mouth. "How she go, boy?"

Calem's warm moment went cold, and his voice thickened with resurging wrath as he talked. "He said Pa grabbed his rifle after knocking Ames off his horse. Like Ames had no choice, and that's how it goes in the record."

"I can't believe it," Martha said quietly. "Ed Grymes helped Calem bring Jared home. He told me himself how it had happened, and it wasn't easy for him."

"Look, Ma, Ed is Skull ranch. So is Ames, and the Major's whelp into the bargain. Hell, it's sewed up." Jesse tilted back his chair, grinning with a hard wisdom. "The word of the Skull foreman against a two-bit cattleman's grieving son? Take it to trial and any good shyster will have tall medicine out of making Cal all unwrought by Pa's death. Grymes is not a bad sort for all he's stupid as an ox, but he's Skull and that comes first."

Martha said heatedly, "Don't talk like that. There has to be a way, Jesse."

"Look, Ma." Jesse cracked another nut, scowling. "You don't live in the world the preacher tells about at Sunday meeting, the one you want to believe in. You're in the real one where right and wrong don't mean worth a damn." A faint jeer touched his lips. "You want to find out what you don't have the belly for, you people, take it all the way to trial and watch a man guilty as hell walk free." He popped the nutmeat into his mouth. "That's if you could get it to trial."

"No," Martha said softly, stubbornly. "That's your world, I know, but it's not mine. I can't accept that Jared's killer will go unpunished. There has to be a way."

"A way," Calem echoed bitterly. "There's one way for sure, and it's past time someone said it."

He saw the small shock in her eyes, and then Jesse said swiftly, "He don't mean it, Ma," as he stabbed a hard finger against Calem's arm. "You listen, boy. Go after that Dembrow now or ever and you'll kick up a wildcat that'll tear you apart."

"I can take him," Calem said hotly. "I can handle a gun with you, Jess! You ain't seen me!"

19

"I don't want to," Jesse said coldly. "That's my style, maybe, but not yours. If something happens to you, what'll happen to Ma? You think on that!"

"All right, it's your style! You take him—you hadn't no plans on staying around anyway, Jess, that ain't your style either. So you take him and drift!"

Jesse stood swiftly and stalked to the window, staring out. His voice came tight and hard. "All right, I'll say it. I didn't want to, for Ma's sake, but I will. My old man's dead, and you know how much that meant to me? It meant I could come home and see my mother." He leaned his hands on the window frame, breathing heavily. "I took his switch lickings and his hard talk for rough on twenty years, and if there was a kindly word in any of it, I don't recall it. I don't hate him no more, fact I don't feel a damn thing. Happen otherwise, I might not sit about on my hands, but that's how it is." He dropped his arms and turned, shaking his head. "I didn't want to say that, Ma."

"Neither of you could help the way you was," Martha said tiredly. "Born or made, Jess, there's nothing a body can forgive in that. I'm as glad, if it'll stop more killing. I'd as lief leave Jared's killer to God, come to that. You, Calem, you listen to your brother."

"What about our water rights?" Calem demanded. "Skull will hold Blue Horse now, and where'll we water?"

Jesse said acidly, "You reckon bracing Dembrow will help that?"

Calem ducked his head stubbornly, biting his lip. Jesse moved back to his chair, lifted a foot to it and leaned his elbow on his knee, gently shaking his finger. "You hear me now, and hear good. You and Ma sell the place for what you can get and head back to Missouri. We got family there, and they'll help you get a fresh start." His voice hardened distinctly. "But get shed of your damfool notion or I'll trim it out of you."

"I'd like to be back with my own," Martha said wistfully. "Coming to New Mexico was Jared's want. But he put so many years, so much work into this place, and I feel—"

"Look at the facts," Jesse said impatiently. "If you hang on here, the Dembrows will crowd you out. Even with good water, Cal couldn't work the outfit alone."

"No. But you, Jesse?"

He gave a wry shrug. "You know me, Ma. I gather no moss."

"I know." Martha Gault sighed. "Well, Bart Renshaw—

he owns the place next ours on the south—wanted to buy us out a while back. Maybe . . ."

She talked on, the words washing distantly over Calem's head. Again he saw Jared lifeless in the mud, and he saw Ames Dembrow's light mocking eyes. He squeezed his fists beneath the table till they were bloodless. *I won't let it go by, Pa. By God, I won't.*

Jesse smoked three cigarettes through, listening and interjecting occasionally; then he swung to his feet. "Come on, kid. I ain't seen the place in two years; how about a last look around?"

Calem shook his head tightly.

"Well, I got a few memories laying around, not all bad ones. Reckon I'll take a ride." He picked up his hat, and then catching his mother's sharp eye, chuckled. "Don't fret, Ma. My foot ain't that itchy. I can stay around anyway till you and Cal pull out."

He left the house, and shortly Calem heard him ride away. He pushed back his chair then and stood, as Martha said gently, "Son, don't brood on it now. You do think a sight about things, and given time you'll think deeper. No matter how bad it seems now, that will pass and you'll see your life ahead of you and know Jess was right."

"Sure, Ma. It's all right." He scrubbed a vague palm over his jaw. "Better change my clothes and get to fixing that pasture fence."

He went through the parlor to his room and changed from his stiff cheap suit into jeans and shirt. Then he dug a worn gunbelt and holster and a small handful of hoarded cartridges out of hiding. He stuffed them in his shirt and left the house, whistling. Reaching the horse pasture he ducked through the fence and sauntered along inside it, now and then leaning his weight to a post as if testing it. Presently he spotted the old gun in the grass where Jared had thrown it, brightly blued in the sunlight except for the flecks of dew rust. Putting his back to the house he bent in one swift casual motion and scooped up the gun, ramming it in his belt. Straightening then, careful not to look toward the house where his mother might be watching, he passed an idle glance over the south end of the pasture which was cut off from the house by the tack barn. The big lineback buckskin Jared had always used for a saddle mount was grazing there.

Calem continued along the fence, not hurrying, till he was past the corner of the barn. He ducked in through the rear door and took Jared's rig and rope from the saddle pole, sweating in his haste. Five minutes later the buckskin was ready, fretting at the bit as Calem led him toward the south gate. Once more he was in full view of the house, and as he opened the gate, heard the sharp lift of his mother's voice: "Calem—Calem!"

He didn't look back. Vaulting to the saddle, he heeled the buckskin into a stretching run on the town road.

# Chapter Three

Cody Dembrow stepped from the China Cafe and halted on the sidewalk to light his cheap cigar; he stepped to the edge of the walk and teetered there on the high heels of his run-down cowman's boots, thumbs tucked in his vest pockets. Cody was a big man of twenty-seven, his chest and shoulders heavy with a quilting of muscle that strained the seams of his old suitcoat. His face was broad and ruddy, crowned by a stiff cap of close-cropped blond hair. It was a pleasant face, though bland almost to indifference, finding a kind of negative redemption in his deep-lidded eyes which lent an expression both sly and sleepy.

He half-turned, hearing the door of the cafe open behind him. Jeffrey Dembrow stepped out with his daughter-in-law, his arm bent with a stately courtesy where her hand rested. "I'll bring the buggy from the livery barn, my dear," the Major was saying. A burst of laughter rolled out behind him; the Major's snowy brows drew together in a frown as he glanced through the half-frosted front window at the counter inside, where his son was joking and roughnecking with some town friends. Then he gave Cody a curt nod. "Ready to leave, or would you prefer to drink the Silver Belle dry with Ames?"

"I'll go home with you, sir."

"Stay with Trenna, please, and I'll bring the buggy here from the livery barn, and your horse as well."

Cody watched his uncle quarter across the street at an angry walk. Ordinarily Cody would be assigned a chore like mount-fetching, but at the moment deeply offended by the apple of his eye, the Major had no wish to wait in earshot of Ames' raucous exuberance. Full of high spirits after the inquest, Ames had not shared their table in the cafe; he had joined his friends with loud and occasionally foul talk.

Cody gave Trenna an appraising glance; her face gave no hint of her feelings. Ames' wife, like any of his string of thoroughbred horses, was a sleek fine animal, tall and full-bodied in a blue serge habit that set off her skydeep eyes. A matching hat jauntily topped her pale hair; her slim heartshaped face was serene except for the shadow of discontent marring its full mouth.

Cody hadn't stirred, and now Trenna stepped to his side and took his arm; her look was chiding. "Not noted for gallantry, are you, my friend?"

Cody smiled faintly. "Is that what you want?"

Her hand tightened on his arm. "You know better," she murmured. "No, I'd settle for some simple attention. It's the first time in two months I've been in town. I wouldn't be now if it weren't court day for the Dembrows and we-all had to put in an appearance to publicly demonstrate our solidarity behind Ames' and Grymes' lying testimony."

"Now," Cody said dryly, "don't tell me that Ames told you he and Grymes were lying."

She gave a short, deprecating laugh. "Ames tells me nothing. You saw that Gault boy testify. Didn't it occur to you he was telling the simple truth about what happened at Blue Horse?"

"I couldn't say."

"You mean you won't. You never commit yourself till you see your way, do you, Cody?"

"No."

She laughed quietly. "I watched young Gault's face when Ames and Grymes gave testimony; that boy is wound up like a watchspring, and some of it broke through then. Ames, after all, is perfectly capable of killing a man in cold blood—or hot. Oh yes, they were lying."

That could be, Cody thought almost indifferently; Ed Grymes was enough scared of Ames to cover for him. "Do you care?"

"No more than you." Her blue stare behind a wisp of veil held a disturbing intensity, and he had a vivid memory of the first time he had seen her, a percentage queen in a trail town where he and Ames had been on a cattle-buying trip. Ames had brought her back to Skull as his bride. Her poise, diction and aristocratic beauty let Cody concede her a good background, but she had obviously taken a long slip. Still, a beautiful and cultured woman who could fit the role demanded by Major Dembrow of his son's wife was rare, and Ames, whose tastes ran to high-class bordellos, would not be inclined to look far. Trenna satisfied the Major's standards outwardly, and he'd never questioned the rest.

Still holding his eyes, she said softly, "He'll be in town all day. We can have the whole afternoon—the usual place."

Cody hesitated; the challenge of her vivid allure was

strong, warring with his innate caution. She was a bored and restless woman, and he understood her resentment. Ames kept her virtually locked away, as he would any prized possession. She could have anything she wanted, but a dozen expensive ball gowns that she could wear no place meant nothing. From the first Cody had recognized her as his own kind, and living under the same roof had made an attraction inevitable. But their secret meetings were few and far between, confined by Cody's careful nature. The honor of his household was a thing the Major took for granted, as he took his own honor; it was a vague conviction of Ames' suspicions that underscored Cody's growing unease about the clandestine affair. And he shook his head.

She whispered, "Coward," but they fell silent as Ames came out of the cafe. He halted behind them, and Cody felt the back of his neck prickle under Ames' stare. Ames said nothing, and the three of them watched the currents of life along the street while silence stretched thin between them.

Cody felt a swift relief as the buggy rattled upstreet from the livery barn. The Major halted the matched bays; Cody assisted Trenna to the high seat by the Major, then stepped behind the vehicle where his saddled horse was tied. The Major shot an impatient glance at his son. "You can fetch your own horse."

"Not just yet," Ames murmured. He stood hipshot, working a toothpick in the corner of his mouth. "You take Trenna home, Pa. I want to make big medicine with Cody over to the Silver Belle."

"As you wish." The Major clucked the team into motion, and Cody felt a shadowy anxiety in Trenna's swift glance at him before the wagon rolled on. Without another word Ames started across the street; Cody followed, a deep worry thickening his throat now. He left his sorrel at the Silver Belle tierail where one other mount bearing the Skull brand stood. As they went through the batwing doors, Ames said curtly, "Get a bottle and join me," and headed for a far corner table.

A cool gloom and a stale memory of whiskey and stratified smoke clung to the long high room, deserted except for the bartender and Frenchy Duval, who broke off their idle talk as Cody moved to the bar. The Silver Belle was a cowman's watering place, unfrequented by the Saturday town crowd of family men. It would come to life tonight when the cattle crews hit town to tie knots in the wildcat's tail.

Frenchy Duval gave a polite nod. "You will have the drink on me, my friend, eh?" Duval was gaunt as a wolf, with a pinched face and slitted saffron eyes. His black hair was done in a thin queue down the side of his head, and he contrived to wear his shabby range clothes with a trace of Gallic elegance.

Cody shook his head. "Maybe later. A bottle, Len. Skull credit."

Duval briefly turned his yellow stare on Ames and nodded his understanding. *He sees a sight more than he lets on*, Cody thought, remembering all he knew of Duval. He was a Cajun who had punched cows on the Louisiana side of the Sabine; later he had run with a gang of border rustlers down near Brownsville, Texas, where he had three known killings to his credit. Here in Coyotero Basin he had handled more than one minor range dispute for Major Dembrow that never reached court. His air of wolfish danger was enough to quell a dispute, and today an uncertainty of public sympathy in the Gault killing had prompted the Major to bring Duval along to town.

Cody carried the bottle and a pair of glasses to the rear table, toed out a chair and sat. "Pour me a drink," Ames told him stonily, and he poured it. Ames took his drink, then drew a long nine from his vest pocket and bit away the end and said, "Give me a light." Cody struck a match and held it. "Now," Ames exhaled deeply, "I would admire to hear exactly what you're cooking up between you."

"Trenna?" Cody said carefully. "She wanted to talk was all. No harm in that."

"I wonder," Ames murmured, his eyes squinted against the smoke. "I call it a pure caution, what-all the two of you find to talk about so frequent. Yes sir, now that could be a case."

"Ames, there's nothing there—"

"Shut up." Ames had closed his fist around the bottle, and the knuckles were white. "You walk too goddamned soft for my taste, Cody, and you always have. I haven't forgot what a sly bastard you was when we were kids, only you've got so sly you don't show it. Sly enough so I judge you'll keep your place, and what I seen was Trenna's notion. But a likely word to the sly—you're on sufferance at Skull, always. Being kin gives you a few privileges, but one word from me'll break you to thirty-and-found, and don't you by God forget it."

Cody dropped his gaze to the glass he was turning be-

26

tween his fingers. The brassy taste of hatred was so strong in his mouth it almost sickened him, festering because he could never betray it by word or expression. It wasn't only that he, the illegitimate son of Major Jeffrey Dembrow's dead sister and an unknown father, had grown up a charity ward to his uncle's sense of brusque duty. The countless arrogant, bullying slights by his cousin Ames made a bitter etching in his memory. It had been that way since they were boys, when Ames had found that Cody, aware of his tenuous position, could be baited with small torments in the way a boy could bait a docile and uncomplaining dog. Ames was the origin of his hate, but it extended almost as strongly to the Major. For years he had worked furiously for a gesture of affection or approval, only to meet his austere uncle's total, absent indifference.

Cody was never quite sure why he stayed on, doggedly accepting a daily ration of slights and flaunted contempt. Part of it was the rut of simple habit, and he supposed that a man's knowledge of his bastardy could foster an obsession for real roots. Skull was the only home he knew, and perversely enough, that he wore the hated Dembrow name lent him a proprietary feeling toward the place. A feeling marred by the brooding fact that as things were, he belonged to it and not the other way around. . . .

He lifted his eyes, meeting the goading mockery in Ames'; he thought, *There's more than one bastard at this table, but I'm the patient one. And one day I'll take you by the short hairs, cousin.*

Behind him the batwing doors rattled on their rockers as someone came in. Cody saw a visible start in Ames' eyes, and they narrowed slowly. Cody glanced backward over his shoulder as Frenchy Duval murmured, "Well, well."

It was the Gault kid, standing big and lean with his feet apart, and there was a wild and wicked light in his eyes. He wore a long-barreled conversion Walker in a tied-down holster, and there was a tension in his long arms. *He means business,* Cody thought narrowly, and when the kid put his stare on him and said flatly, "You. Get off away from him," Cody obeyed. He stood, carefully pulling back the skirt of his coat to show he was unarmed, and stepped aside.

Gault moved deeper into the room along the bar, keeping his eyes on the whole room, and stopped half-facing the bartender and Duval, who slid his wise glance from the gun Gault wore to the pure mulishness in his young face, and said softly again, "Well, well."

"What do you want here, kid?" the bartender asked mildly, dipping his big freckled hand casually below the bar. Cody remembered the bungstarter he kept there. But the kid stepped a wary sidepace from the bar, keeping his direct glance on Ames. Looking at Ames, seeing his mouth slightly open and his palms flat on the table, Cody thought, *He never expected this from a ragheel ranch kid.*

Frenchy Duval, his gaunt length slack against the bar, folded his arms with a quiet chuckle. "Why don' you ask him what he wants, Ames, eh?"

"Sure," Ames said softly. "Sure." Cody watched his cousin's hesitation fade to wary calculation, and then to grinning mockery as Ames said: "How about it, Frenchy?"

The Cajun put all his expression into a minute shrug. "Don' ask Frenchy; ask the boy." At Ames' swift glance, he lifted the corners of his mouth. "What you want of me, eh?"

"Not a damned thing. Sit tight."

"Ah no—" Duval leisurely turned, his arms still folded, and sauntered to the far end of the bar. "A bullet don' go always where she should. I will stand here, I think."

"You better," Gault told him.

Duval's voice shook with laughter. "Very quietly, my young rooster, but your neck will get wrung all the same—"

From the tail of his eye, Cody saw Ames' hands tense on the table. The kid's glance whipped back as Ames boiled out of his chair, heaving over the table; his fancy gun blurred out and up. Cody saw young Gault's hand slap his gunbutt, cock and bring up the heavy weapon in clean, easy reflex, taking a fleeting instant for aim as Ames sent off a wild bucking shot. Then Ames dived behind the upended table.

Cody knew then, with a peculiar and brittle clarity, how it would go, seeing the kid's wrist sinews tense for the solid jolt of squeezing off his shot, and seeing splinters fly from the table angled on its side by a broken leg. Cody saw Ames' face above it dark and contorted through a haze of powdersmoke. And Ames had not shot again. He was trying to get his feet under him, and now his hand stabbing out blindly struck the table and toppled it aside. Still on his knees, Ames hugged his hands to his chest and with a long, gurgling sigh, fell on his face.

It might have been five seconds before Gault, staring, remembered Duval. He brought his gun jerkily to bear, but the Cajun was still slack-postured against the bar. Slowly

28

Duval straightened, and walking to Ames, bent and turned him on his side. Afterward he looked at the ragged hole in the tabletop. He said softly, "You are a great fool, my friend, but that was shooting."

"Don't try anything," Gault said in a high, strained voice.

"No, my young buck." There was no laughter in Duval's face now. "I have no fight with you. But soon Major Dembrow will give the order; there will be many men on the hunt. I have seen such things. Now you will run for a time, but we will meet again."

Gault sidled to the door, shot a quick look over the batwings, and backed through them. Cody heard him cross the walk and scramble into his saddle, putting his horse in a dead run for the south end of town. A flurry of voices, lifted in curious excitement, was already gathering.

Stepping over to Ames, Cody saw that Gault's shot, fired through the table, had taken him in the center of the chest. He glanced at Duval, who shook his head and said, "I would not have believe' this. Once I had the shooting game with Ames; he was good. Ver' good. Still he lost his head. The kid is a fool, but he was steady."

Cody nodded, his eyes speculative. "I'll handle things here. You ride after the Major and Mrs. Dembrow."

Mention of Trenna made him realize that her problem was solved, or part of it was. He almost smiled then. Part of his too.

# Chapter Four

Racing toward the town outskirts, Calem heard a shout and saw Bill Macavey, the town marshal, leaving his office at a waddling run. But Macavey's shout and his tub-bellied shape washed against Calem's senses in an empty blur, and then he passed the last building and lined onto the road, the thrumming of the buckskin's hoofs hammering in his temples like padded blows. For a straining mile he held the pace, fighting the thick burning in his guts. Finally, feeling it boil in his throat, he tight-reined the snorting lineback to a halt. He almost fell from the saddle, going on his hands and knees, and threw up. He thought, *Jess could have said how it would be,* and gulping, was sick again.

Shortly he took up the reins and shakingly mounted and rode on. He hadn't gone a half-mile when he made out a rider coming at a hard run across the flats, the tan dust roiling up in his wake. Calem halted again, and drew the Walker and laid it against his thigh, waiting. In a minute Jesse wheeled his slobbering black up beside him. "What happened?"

When he had the story, Jesse said bitterly, "All right, don't sit there. Follow me."

Calem said sickly, "Where?"

"Not home, they'll look there first. Our old place in the hills."

Jesse led out as they left the road and angled southeast toward the dark timbered slopes that skirmished Coyotero Basin on the east. Calem watched the stiff angry set of his back for many minutes, and finally Jesse fell back beside him. "How was it, kid?" A tight harshness strained the corners of his saturnine mouth. "You like the taste of it?"

"Jess—"

"Shut up." A gusty breath left Jesse, and he shook his head. "You ain't cut from the same cloth as me, and you just had a taste of what that means. You think you know the rest too, but you don't. Kid, you don't know the half of it."

He reined savagely out ahead once more, and they pushed

30

into the deep hills. They forced their way through tangles of catclaw and manzanita that clung to the first rocky slopes, and then plunged into deep timber, putting their horses along a dim trail. Shortly they debouched onto an open clearing facing a granite cliff down which a mountain stream gushed in sheets of creamy spray and gathered in a deep pool before wending its way to the lowlands.

Here they dismounted. Calem's legs felt rubbery, and he sat down abruptly on a rock and watched Jesse water the animals. He led them into a narrow well-grassed notch that thrust back deeply into the cliff, and returned presently carrying their saddlebags. Without a word he began to ascend the rock slide that fronted the lower cliff. Wearily, Calem got to his feet and followed him. The slide was steep-pitched, and rubble cascaded away beneath their boots. Halfway up, Jesse edged onto an abutting ledge which leaned above a vertical drop, and worked along it hugging the wall. After a few yards the ledge broadened and then sharply terminated, its rounded lip curving back into the cliff.

About four feet below the liprock was an opening less than a yard in diameter. They had discovered the cave years ago while hunting hereabouts, and it became a secret retreat where two boys could cache their small possessions or camp of a night. The entrance was invisible from the facing side of the cliff and from directly below. It penetrated at a side angle into the solid rock, and from below a body could see it only by hugging the cliff a good distance away and craning his neck. The one way of ingress was to let yourself bodily over the ledge while someone held your wrists, feel for the hole with your feet and worm yourself in. You reached up and supported your partner as he precariously lowered himself by gripping the liprock.

They did the old maneuver easily, and then Calem struck a match. They negotiated a low narrow tunnel on their hands and knees, turned a sharp angle of it and came into an arching, sand-floored cavern. Jesse opened a saddlebag and took out a candle which he stuck upright in the sand. Calem lighted the wick as the match singed his fingers; he swore and dropped it.

"The old place," Jesse murmured as the sallow light flickered over the rugged walls. "How long, kid?"

"Six years. Never could get in here by my lonesome."

Jesse grunted, digging his heel at something covered by dirt. He chuckled as he unearthed a corroded knifeblade. "My

31

old 'Barlow', sure enough. Always wondered where I misput it."

The bleak shape of the present faded momentarily in thoughts of a shared past, of long and carefree summer days playing and hunting, of swimming bare-butt in the icy pool, of the nights by a roaring fire down below cooking the grub they had packed or shot or snared, of the hours of talk in the dark cave snug and unworried in their blankets fancying all breeds of nocturnal menace and knowing they were high and safe from all.

Jesse sank with a grunt on his hunkers and settled his back to the wall. The bad light made a gaunt limning of his long face, as he sifted tobacco into a paper. "Have yourself some rest, Deadeye. You're like to get precious little of that later on."

Calem eased down beside him. "Jess . . . what now?"

"We wait." He jerked the drawstring of his Durham sack with his teeth, dropped it in his pocket, and rolled and sealed his smoke. "Ma saddled up and caught up with me after you took out. Told her I'd bring you back tied to your saddle—alive, I hoped—else if it wasn't best we show up, to wait a day and come here. She knows the place."

Calem gnawed his lip. "Jess, you reckon she'll be all right?"

"They won't hurt a woman, that's what you mean." Jesse leaned down to the candle and puffed his cigarette alight. "This'll cost her all the same, and it's your doing."

Calem dropped his head against his knees. A wave of remorseful misery swept him; his blind action had blundered them all into a trouble whose form he hadn't vaguely seen. Now as it took stark outline in his mind, he felt sick all over again.

"Hell," Jesse said. "It's done now. We ain't fixed to go on the dodge, so we'll sit tight and wait on Ma. She'll have grub and news. Then we'll ease out nice and quiet, if. If a lot of things."

Calem muttered, "You don't need to. I'll make out," aware that it qualified as a sulky little-boy statement.

"Shut up," Jesse said thoughtfully, sighing out a streamer of smoke. "We can't go west across the basin, Skull territory, which leaves north, south, east, and all points between." He stretched out his legs, crossed them, and scowled at the wavering candle flame. "Some rough travel north of here, desert and mountain, and damn little settlement. But Mercyville

32

across the mountains has a strong police force, which could be useful in your case. How about it?"

"You asking me?"

There was ice in Jesse's grin. "*You're* on the dodge now, remember?"

Calem said nothing for a while, then shifted his back against the rock. "Can they find this place?"

"Sooner or later. Look, kid, we can't stay here. Ma could fetch us grub, but sooner or later they'll put a lookout on the house so she can be followed. Take them a while to think of that, but sure as sunrise they will. Well. Make up your mind."

Calem said numbly, "North, then," and stretched out on his side, hugging his arms. He let his breathing go lax and even, and pretended to sleep. He heard Jesse's shirt rasp on the rock as he stretched and yawned. He could almost feel that dark and sardonic gaze, and then Jesse said softly, "You poor, sorry bastard. You'll learn the rest of it soon enough. . . ."

There was nothing to do but sleep and wait, and Calem found both almost impossible. He jerked fitfully awake at any slight sound, sweating, staring into total darkness—the candle having been snuffed against future need—while Jesse snored on. This was an old pattern for him, the lying low and the waiting, but Calem could only sprawl in nerve-strung wakefulness and stare into the dark and wrestle with the unavoidable question: how right had he been?

To a man raging against the wanton murder of his father, a natural retribution should seem clear-cut in its balancing of the scales, but even if he settled the rightness of the act to his mind, how did he write off the consequences? He had only to think of Ma to wish, in a wash of bitter remorse, that he could turn back the clock. But where was the right of seeing Pa's killer go free as the wind? If right could be wrong, black could be white, and Jesse, with his elemental guideline of cynical expediency, was closer to the reality of things. For Jesse, outside of his loyalty to mother and brother, the answer would be as clear-cut as another man's black and white. If your trouble was a small one, step on it; if a big one, run from it.

No, Calem thought stubbornly, you got to live by and for something. If there's no such thing as right or wrong, it can't stop a man worth his salt from living like there was. You got to start with that much, or nothing is worth anything.

Which answered no large questions, but eased his troubled

mind with the thinking on it; the thought drifted, and he slept as dawn sent its first pale glow into the cave mouth.

He woke to a hand shaking him by the shoulder, and rolled over blinking against the dimness of the cave. "Wake up, kid," Jesse said. "I been up three hours on the watch, and Ma's here."

Calem scrambled through the tunnel. Bracing himself in the entrance, he heaved the saddlebags Jesse passed him onto the ledge above, and they aided one another's ascent to it. Martha Gault was waiting below, and within a minute they reached her side.

She murmured, "My boys, my boys," holding them both, and Calem realized with dismay that she was crying. He'd never seen that, even when Pa . . . *but now it's all gone for her and your doing.* With the thought came a fresh pang of remorse. She had known hard times all her life, yet the part of living filled by Jared and her sons had been good, and now it was all gone.

She summoned her old briskness. "Now, boys, have you decided on what's to be done?"

Jesse told her the plan, and she said worriedly, "Do you know that country, Jess?"

"I can hold a line by the sun and stars, Ma, and three-four days should bring us over the mountains to Mercyville. I know it's due north of here, and the law there ain't owned by old Major Dembrow."

"Good. I brought you blankets and grub." She nodded toward the sack slung from the sidesaddle on the jughead roan standing nearby. "Jerky and hardtack. You'll be making no fire, and you won't be disposed to no long stops. Hope you boys are appreciative of this. Been some long living since your ma rode that blamed rig."

Jesse smiled. "What-all since yesterday, Ma?"

She shook her head soberly. "Nothing good. After you went after Calem I hitched up directly and drove to town. Heard about the shooting, learned what I could and got back home near nightfall. Old Man Dembrow was there, and his crew was going over the place. Didn't faze me, knowing Calem had got away and you boys 'ud meet on the road and come straight here. Got Pa's rifle and sent the lot packing. Set out for here this morning whilst it was still dark, case Dembrow had a man watching the place."

"Good thinking," Jesse said, and shook his head grimly. "That old gimlet-eyed sidewinder. He'll never quit."

34

"I reckon not," Martha Gault said calmly. "I don't excuse the man, but I know his feeling right enough. Ames was a rotten potato, but that's no never mind to a parent. Pinned his hopes on that boy, and he's lost him."

*That was for me,* Calem thought miserably, and lowered his eyes.

Jesse said, "Ma, you didn't raise any Skull men coming here?"

"I'd a turned back then," she said tartly. "No, but you bet they're out in force hunting the basin. Another thing, Dembrow's put old Abel Sutter on the scent, and that's bad."

"Sutter? Is that old wolfer still batting around?"

"Last night he was with Dembrow, going over our place like a coon dog."

"That's bad, right enough," Jesse muttered.

The knowledge of old Abel Sutter dogging their trail was a cold breath on a man's spine. Sutter, the son of a mountain man and a Yaqui squaw, had developed the uncanny senses of the animals he had spent a lifetime trapping. Usually he kept to himself in the hills, now and then coming in to collect the scavenger bounty Major Dembrow paid, and to buy his meager needs: salt, tobacco, and rifle shells. It was said Abel Sutter could study a week-old track and tell you all except the critter's color, and this too if he could locate a hair or two. And Calem remembered when a neighbor's well went dry and how, after a dozen futile shafts were sunk, Sutter was called in. He had simply pointed, "Dig there," and ten feet down water, plenty and pure, was found. "Smelled it," Sutter had said laconically. Or he might have analyzed details in the landscape, but nobody had questioned the explanation.

"Was hopeful," Jesse said bleakly, "we could start after dark and get clear of the basin without being picked up. Now, no point in waiting. Once that damn Injun cuts the sign we made yesterday or Ma's today, it's purely a matter of time, which we got none to lose."

He headed for the notch where their horses were. Calem started to follow, but Martha said: "Let Jess take care of things. Want you to hear good what I tell you now."

"I—don't know what to say, Ma."

"It's done," Martha said matter-of-factly. "Got to reckon with things as they are. No need your worrying for me. Plenty of kin in Missouri who'll see I don't lack, and I'm strong enough to hire out for my keep once I'm settled again.

35

When you're free of this, you can join me there or not, up to you."

"I will, Ma."

She said sternly, "Don't give your hasty word. A son's beholden only as there's a need, and I can make my way. You got a life to make for yourself." She reached up a hand and smoothed back his unruly forelock, the gesture filled with a sadness and a compassion. "My poor boy. You've chose a bitter way to get your growth."

"Was I wrong?"

"Man who killed your father should have hung, and you give him a chance he didn't deserve. No. I worried a spell about what it might do to you, was all." She glanced toward Jesse as he led the horses from the notch to water, and lowered her voice. "Watch out for him, Calem. Keep him with you as long as you can."

He was openly surprised, and she said: "Yes, he's the older, but in years only. Got myself little sleep last night, puzzling how it is with the two of you. You're the boy'll always make your own way, once you find your growth. It's Jesse needs something more, and he always will. Don't know as it was Jared's fault or a born lack in the boy. I'm inclined to think both, and I can't see the end of it, but I'm afraid. Try to keep him with you, Calem."

"I will," he began, then amended humbly that he would try.

They filled their saddlebags to bulging with most of the stores Martha had packed, caching the rest in their blanket-rolls. She had brought Jared's rifle and saddle scabbard too, his old canteen, and all the cartridges she could find for Calem.

"We'll backtrack out of these hills," Jesse said brusquely, "then swing north along the edge of the basin. Ma, you ride out ahead of us till we're clear of the brush. Give a holler if you see anything. No telling but they're close on this place already, and we'll have to run for it."

"Take care, boys." She held Jesse a moment, then Calem, and she was close to breaking again. Jesse assisted her to mount, and she put the jughead across the clearing and was lost to sight in the trees.

"All right, kid. I'll lead out, and we'll go easy."

Mounting, they moved into the trees along the game trail. Calem sat bolt upright, his reins moist against his palm, while Jesse rocked to his horse's gait at a careless slouch. It might have been a game to him, except for the restlessness of his eyes conning the sun-mottled glades. Presently, the trees thinned away; they climbed to high and rocky ground where deep brush flourished, well-broken by the trail. As the brush too gave way to open country, they caught an occasional glimpse of Martha, always keeping a good hundred yards to her back.

Calem's breathing eased when he saw the first rolling sage flats of the east basin, and as they came down the last slope, Jesse halted and raised in his stirrups and waved his hand. Martha responded, and Calem lifted his hand and let it slowly settle to his pommel, and his throat tightened up. He did not look again as Jesse quartered off along the slope, northward now.

They rode for a steady hour, and as the terrain roughened once more, found themselves close to Horseshoe Gap, a deep irregular pass that cut through the north basin ramparts. It would take them into the Arrowhead Breaks, a lonely and sterile region of sun-blasted rock that marked the atrophied spine of an ancient mountain range.

Hard by the gap, Jesse swung offtrail and skirted a ridge that thrust up like a knotty gray fist. Its far side mellowed into a gradual incline, and here he left the saddle. He said, "We'll have a look from above," and taking a pair of Army fieldglasses from his saddlebag, swung up the ridge like a mountain goat. Calem followed more slowly, panting and sweat-drenched when he achieved the summit, and threw himself down by Jesse. They were belly-prone on a shelving ledge over a steep drop. Jesse braced his elbows and trained his glasses on the hilly sweep of a rock-studded flat they had crossed.

Calem saw his shoulders stiffen. "What is it?"

"Something I saw move. And there again, by God. A horse-backer, sure enough."

"How many?"

"Just the one, I think. Wait a while."

The rider was hard to make out on the neutral slope, but straining along Jesse's line of sight, Calem shortly saw him move across the brow of a hill. "He getting down?"

"Yeah," Jesse said bitterly. "Him all right, Sutter. Knew he'd cut our sign somewhere, but I never figured he would breathe down our necks this soon. Would reckon he'll make sure we're pointed north through the gap, then ride to fetch the Major and his boys."

Jesse edged back off the rim on his hands and belly so as not to skyline himself, and then pulled half-erect. He handed

Calem the glasses. "Wait here and keep flattened down. Keep them glasses steady so's you won't catch the sun."

Calem opened his mouth, but Jesse was already gone, scrambling down the ridgeflank. Calem raised to his elbows and sighted in the glasses. In a moment he caught the old wolfer in the act of mounting up after checking the ground.

Sutter was a small man, desiccated and weather-stained by years of desert sun and wind. His greasy elkhide leggins were worn smoothly black, and his oft-patched calico shirt was threadbare and faded. His face was flat and gaunt and scarred, the muscles of it so prominent that it resembled a flayed mask, except for the stirring of his gray-whiskered jaw on a tobacco cud. His eyes, even in the shadow of his battered hat, were as blue and clear-cold as pond ice. Sutter rode toes out, heels gently flailing, like the Apaches he had once tracked for the Army.

Jesse's boots scraped softly to his re-ascent, and bellying down and inching up by Calem again, he found a bracing rock for his rifle.

"Jess?"

Calem's voice sounded shrill to his own ears, and Jesse said with a peculiar flatness: "He'll get us killed if he stays onto us. I don't aim to wait on him. Won't get another chance like this. Shut your mouth and don't bat an eye."

He took the glasses from Calem, sighting again. Calem's heart triphammered against the rock while the slow seconds dragged into minutes. Sutter, not dismounting again, rode slowly and saddle-bent to scan the ground. He was within easy sighting now, and Jesse's rifle barrel ground gently on the rock as he aimed. Then his sweating cheek left the rifle stock; he swore irritably. Abel Sutter had reined up, his head tilting erect, and horse and man became motionless as statues.

*Couldn't have seen us,* Calem thought, and then remembering old Jourgenson's well, felt his spine crawl even as his mind rejected the thought. As slight a thing as a telltale flick of his pony's ears, for the animal and man were like one, might have alerted Sutter. Something for sure, since he reined his mount sideways to turn back.

Jesse fired, as the horse came around full-flank to his sights. The paint went down, its forequarters smashed by the long rifle slug, and Sutter, yanking his rifle from its boot, twisted free of the stirrups. He balled his body and hit the stony ground rolling. Almost before he was on his feet, as the clap of shot echoes died off, he was lunging away. Jesse shot again, dusting the wolfer with powdery splinters from a flat boulder as he dived behind it.

"Most I hoped for at this range was to put him afoot," Jesse observed as a rifle spoke by the flat boulder. The paint horse had been thrashing in the rocks, and its struggles ceased. "Well, that old horse meant a lot to him. It is hell or high water for us now, far as he's concerned. Meantime he is laid up good in a stand-off, and he can outlast us. Seeing we've earned us a little time, let's get down off of this and ride."

# Chapter Five

They left the breaks the next day, after crossing shattered ridges, pushing through tortuous arroyos, and leading their mounts down or up treacherous slides of rock. The third dawn found them climbing the fairly regular upgrade formed by an arching saddle between several peaks. Jesse called a halt, after a rough climb to the highest dip of the saddle.

Calem was glad to step down and hold the drooping, lathered horses while Jesse ascended to a flinty spur and trained his fieldglasses on their backtrail. When he had clambered down, his face was grim. "I counted six. They made good time. Old Sutter likely knows this country like the lines of his hand. Followed the good trails while we felt our way through and run ourselves up box canyons."

Calem said in a parched croak, "How far behind?"

"Three hours, or four." Jesse wrapped the strap around his field glasses and jammed them in his saddlebag. He uncapped his canteen, rolled some water in his mouth and swallowed it. "Sooner or later they will sure-hell overhaul us, and I'd a sight rather it was after we reach yonder peaks." He added, "If we got to stand and fight, good cover will narrow the odds," in a tone indicating that the odds would still be bad.

Calem surveyed the far sweep of mountains to the north, darkened baseward by a cling of heavy timber, soaring into snow-veined pinnacles. These were the peaks of his grandfather's lusty times; there was no thrill in their proximity. The ruthless pace Jesse had set had etched a strained exhaustion into every fiber of Calem's body, and his nerves screamed for rest. He looked at Jesse, whose grimy face was a gaunt, alkaline mask relieved only by a black smudge of beard and the slitted paleness of his eyes. Calem ran a tongue over his cracked lips, knowing he looked no better. His mouth was gritty, and his eyeballs grated in their sockets; he felt as if the tissues of his body were sucked clean.

Between them and the first green foothills lay a scorched and naked arm of rock-broken desert. Though they had conserved their water, one third-canteenful was all that remained to carry them to the first water, wherever it might be. Hard pursued, they dared not lay up till night relieved the heat which laid its flat dead hand on a man's body and mind.

Jesse soaked a corner of his bandanna from his canteen and swabbed out the caked dust from his horse's nostrils. Calem did the same, and took a smooth pebble from his pocket and stuck it in his mouth, nursing it for a ghost of moisture. He said: "Jesse—we best state it plain. Water is the big problem."

"Sure." Bleakly Jesse shook his canteen. "Never make it on what's left between us, but I'm gambling we'll hit water before . . ."

When he did not finish, Calem put in, "We had sure ought to. Why, Jess, there's always watering places if a body knows 'em."

"Sure, sure," Jesse said irritably. "Might be one right under our feet, eh? Wager that damned Sutter knows every water clear to the mountains, and if so, it's more edge for them. Nothing for it, and we ain't buying any time here."

They took their plodding way down the far side of the saddle-shaped pass, and by noon left it for the barren country below. It was a cruel and heat-blasted desolation, laced by catclaw and mesquite and more kinds of cacti than Calem had ever seen. Stretches of baked, crack-seamed flats were interspersed by scattered reaches of jagged, clustered rocks that formed weird, monolithic shapes against the sky and threw grotesque shadows with the deepening afternoon.

Bringing up the rear, Calem found himself looking back repeatedly, straining his eyes for a sign of the pursuers. In the past two days he had learned about the nerve-strung state of a hunted man: a haunting and gut-deep fear that blotted out a man's character and convictions with a terrifying ease. Jesse had lived with it before this, and yesterday Jesse would have killed Abel Sutter without warning, without a second thought. *And I would of let him.*

The knowledge brought home to Calem his naked and vulnerable ignorance of life, of himself. Was becoming case-hardened against all better feelings the real key to survival? He thought doggedly that this was Jesse's way, not his, as even Jess had admitted: *You ain't cut from the same cloth as me, kid . . . you don't know the half of it.* But he was learning fast, and he wondered whether in spite of everything Jesse's price for naked survival could become his own. Already he had let plain fear and not a moral measure of

41

the act against the stakes govern him; how many times could a man forswear his moral qualms and his deepest nature go unchanged?

The afternoon was far gone, the flat sunslant painting the rocks dull orange and making deep maroon shadows, when a wink of pale green foliage ahead caught Calem's eye. The buckskin pricked up his ears at the prospect of water, and followed the bay as Jesse kicked into a lope. They crossed a low ridge and dipped onto its far side. Below was a shallow seep rimmed by a greenery of willow and scrub cottonwood. Calem reined up and piled out of his saddle in a hurry, and Jesse said sharply, "You hold on. I'll try it." He came off his saddle, moved stiff-legged to the edge of the seep and stretched out on his belly. He dipped up a double handful of water and tasted it; his face screwed into a wry grimace and he spat. "Minerals. Might be sound water could a man gag it down, but first it would bind up his jaw. Hell!"

He rocked back on his heels, and picked up a twig and twirled it between his fingers. "The gamble was that we find water soon. Well, this is it, and it's no good." He paused to isolate his next words. "The way I see it, we got one chance. It's pushing a hard pace while the sun dries you out that uses up water, and we won't last another day on what we got. We had best keep on the move tonight and lay up tomorrow first sun. Tomorrow midnight should see us deep in the mountains. Be water aplenty then. Will mean a long while getting there, but at least we will."

Calem stared at him. "Jess, you said yourself they're three, four hours behind us, and likely they have cut it to one or two by now. If Sutter knows of good water, they're in a sight the better shape, not to say their horses. They'll overhaul us in short order, then—"

"With horses," Jesse cut in softly.

"Sure with horses."

Without another word Jesse rose and stalked to his black; he stepped into the saddle and reined around and kicked into a lunging climb of the ridge they had just crossed.

"Jesse!"

"I ain't crazy, Cal. Come along and I'll tell you while we ride." He dropped downridge in the direction from which they had come. Swearing under his breath, Calem caught up his reins, mounted, and swung after him.

While they rode and Jesse talked, the light faded swiftly from the land, and only its memory welted the far sky like a vast bloodstain. The rocky scape took on a muted purpling, and its harsh outlines lost substance in the thickening dusk. The desert became alive with small sounds, strange rustlings of brush and a coyote's bay and the hoot of a great horned owl coasting on silent wing as it scanned for prey. Finally, some two hundred yards to the south of them, Calem saw the orange glimmer of a fire.

This was as near as they could get horseback without alerting the camp. They dropped off their mounts and settled on their hunkers, and waited for the camp to sleep. Jesse was counting on the relaxed vigilance of Dembrow and his men. For his quarry to backtrack and counterstrike should be so unexpected that even an ex-military man might easily forego the field habit of posting a night guard. The audacity of the plan and its element of surprise were the best augurs for success; otherwise it seemed so foolhardy that sickly tension had left Calem hollow-bellied long before they spotted the fire.

After what seemed a young eternity Jesse said meagerly, "Time to move," and came to his feet heel-grinding a ciga-rette he had rolled and not lighted. On foot leading the horses they moved in, carefully avoiding rocks. The moon's silvery disc was half-full tonight, bathing out tortured con-tours of rock, making pale and ghostly exposure where it touched and fathomless shadow where it did not. But Dem-brow's men within the rim of firelight would be nearly blind, looking toward the outer darkness.

Presently Jesse raised his hand for a halt. They were near enough to make out a half-dozen blanketed forms around the fire, its light caught on the murky glint of a spring to which Abel Sutter's lore had guided them. There was a plot of grass and scrub timber, and a horse picket line was stretched between two treeboles.

Jesse motioned with his finger, making a half-circle which indicated they would sweep wide and get south of the camp, enabling them to push the horses north. They moved for-ward again, this time halting a scant twenty yards beyond the firelight. Jesse passed Calem his reins and sat down, and worked off his boots. Afterward he went on alone, ducking noiselessly from rock to rock, then going down on his belly and crawling the remaining distance.

Abruptly a man came bolt upright in his blankets. Calem waited, holding his breath. The man was Abel Sutter of course, but what had alerted him? Then Calem realized how the horses had ceased their usual restless noises. They had heard Jesse or caught his scent; for Sutter this single break in the night's pattern was enough.

Jesse had melted into the ground shadows, and belly-flat and motionless he was as good as invisible. Sutter was on his feet now, rifle in hand; he glided warily off from the fire. *He can't be sure without he can see in the dark.* Calem's spine tingled; a man could be sure of nothing where Abel Sutter was concerned. The old wolfer sank to his haunches just beyond the firelight, his faint outline an aching blur in Calem's eyes.

It seemed a long while after the horses had resumed their normal stirrings that Sutter rose and paced back to his blankets, evidently concluding that a scavenger had disturbed them and passed on. Calem lost track of time waiting for Jesse's next move which did not come till Sutter had apparently relaxed in sleep. Now Jesse slithered with infinite care to the nearest tree securing the picket rope. Without raising his body he thrust a quick-flashing knife between knot and bark. Twisting on his belly, he inched back the way he had come.

The freed horses increased their restive stirrings, again rousing Abel Sutter, this time at once. He came to his feet in a turning motion that shed his blankets; he cocked his rifle as his eyes swept the night.

Again Jesse froze in position, and for a coldly uncertain moment, Calem's hand tensed around his gunbutt. Sutter would fire at the first hint of sound, and Calem knew that to give Jesse a chance he might have to kill the wolfer. But he had underbid Jesse's resources; suddenly Jesse half-lifted himself and let go with the blood-chilling shriek of a cougar.

Instant panic rushed over the standing horses. Starting to bolt, they entangled themselves in the severed rope but only momentarily; the end horse slipped free and the others followed one by one, thundering away into the night.

Sutter had whipped up his rifle at once, pumping shots at the source of the shriek, but now he wheeled at a stiff lope after the escaping horses. Jesse was on his feet now, coming toward Calem in a sidling half-run, at the same time opening up with his pistol, trying for Sutter while the chance offered itself. But Sutter was already swallowed by the darkness, and cursing, Jesse sprinted to Calem's side and snatched his reins and vaulted into saddle. "Come on—come on!"

He put his horse in a heedless run after the stampeding remuda. Calem's fleeting glimpse of the camp as they passed showed it in utter pandemonium. He had a vivid impression

44

of Jeffrey Dembrow in the firelight, his white hair awry, his stocky legs planted apart.

Moments later came his crisply barked orders; a spattering of gunfire broke out behind them, and Calem thought, *They can't see us but they hear us right enough.* He bent low to the buckskin's mane, and then a rifle spoke off to their left. He saw the wink of muzzleflash and heard Jesse shout and return fire. That would be Sutter, and he knew from the drift of pounding hoofs ahead that the entire remuda had eluded the wolfer and he was turning on the marauders. These things made chaotic splinters of sensation and thought, and then all of it, the camp and Sutter and the sporadic crackle of gunfire, was behind them. There was only the rake of brush along his legs and the cool rush of air along his clammy face. They were on an open flat flooded by rock-fretted moonlight and ahead of them raced the Dembrow remuda, a silver haze of dust bannering up behind it.

Jesse shouted, "Hyah, hyah," and pulled flank-on to the animals, crowding them toward a rambling wall of cliff. He meant to box the herd, Calem realized, and came abreast of the remuda on its other side. They pointed the horses into a shallow cleft indenting the base of the tortured scarp and successfully milled them to a blowing, lathered standstill.

Calem sidled the buckskin back and forth to keep the animals confined, thinking that Jesse had been right: one daring blow had broken the pursuit; now they had only to drive the horses ahead of them a ways, then turn them loose. It would be dawn before Abel Sutter could start tracking them down, and by the time they came on the horses, Jess and he would have a safe margin of many hours on them.

Turning to his brother, he saw with horror that Jesse had folded across his pommel, both hands gripping his left thigh above the knee. A dark spreading stain soaked his pantsleg, and when Calem's voice pulled his glance, the moon on his face showed the drawn tightness of shock and pain.

Calem made a move to step down, but savagely Jesse shook his head. "Never mind. Hold them horses." He paused, drawing deep, shuddering breaths as he mustered effort, then heaved a leg free of stirrup and stepped carefully to the ground. He eased himself onto his buttocks, grunting, and pulled his knife. Grasping his thigh tight above the wound, he slit his trouser leg.

Calem said numbly, "Sutter?"

"I reckon. Only one not shooting blind, wasn't he?" He

felt gingerly around to the back of his leg. "So I'm lucky for a change and she went clean through. Old lead in a man's gizzard acts up now and then."

The wound was deep enough, but did not appear otherwise serious, the bullet having taken him through the big muscle slightly front and well to the side of the bone. Yet it could prove a fatal blow to the advantage they had seized. The injury would slow their pace and take its savage, inevitable toll of Jesse's strength. Jesse said between his teeth, "Dig out that sack of flour and that clean spare shirt of yours, and toss them down here."

Calem did so, without leaving his saddle. Jesse dug into the flour, plastering great handfuls of its cool whiteness over both openings of his wound, and it caked the blood at once. "Will help some, though I'll leak plenty more if we're long in the saddle and no help for it." He tore the shirt into strips for compresses, knotting them into place around his thigh. He stuffed the flapping trouser leg into his boot and taking up his reins, inched to his feet. He took hold of the stirrup and worked the foot of his sound leg into it and heaved himself across the saddle, grunting with the agony of effort. For a moment he was bowed over with pain, then his voice came curt and crisp:

"All right, let's haze them out."

They loose-herded the remuda north along the base of the scarp, Calem keeping a worried eye on Jesse. For a time he held erect, rocking precisely to his horse's gait. Calem watched for the dull slackness to take him, then reined over to him and took hold of his reins, saying, "Let go," and when Jesse obeyed, "You're about done. We got to lay up."

Jesse roused himself with a sighing effort. "Not on my account. Ride on if you want."

"Shut up, Jess. No more talk like that."

"They ain't wanting me."

His face was polished with sweat, and his breathing carried a husky note; he was plainly in no shape to go on. Calem's own body ached for sleep, and his eyeballs burned in their parched sockets. Dembrow and his party, stranded afoot, would not be coming up fast, and for both of them a few hours' rest was a grim necessity.

Ahead he saw a sparsely grassed bench with a rim of moon-whitened boulders. Here was a natural breastworks, and a little graze for the horses. Calem pulled up beyond the boulders and swung stiffly down. Jesse had started to cant sideways in the saddle, and Calem caught his slack weight and eased him to the ground. Then he threw the rigs off the horses and hobbled them on the grass under the trees. He spread his brother's ground blanket and laid him on it and spread his own tarp and blankets above him. Jesse's teeth were chattering, and he would be burning up with fever soon, Calem knew. All he could do was keep him warm and give him of their precious water. Shaking out his coiled rope, he folded its length twice and started for the Dembrow horses standing tiredly nearby. He broke into a run, swinging the doubled rope, and with hoarse cries hoorawed the animals to a run, scattering them.

Afterward he settled himself in the rocks, his rifle tucked in his folded arms, but sleep was slow coming in spite of his exhaustion. The whole situation, the judgments and actions to take, was transferred suddenly to his shoulders, gripping him with an uneasy strangeness. By the time he was growing drowsy, Jesse groaned for water and he roused himself to fetch it.

He passed the night that way, occasionally breaking a dozing vigil to tend Jesse as he sank into fever and delirium. Most of it was incoherent babbling, but a few words came through concerning a girl named Florie, and once he called, "Ma," with a lost, wrenching note. Recalling Martha's words—"Jesse needs something more"—Calem wondered what was Jesse's real need if his hardened self-sufficiency were a mask. Maybe for some men there was no answer. When you came down to it, the only thing on which all men agreed was the need for survival. . . .

With that thought, he found himself toying on the idea of taking Jesse's advice, leaving him and pushing on alone. Yet the unwritten law of the country, to give help when it was needed, might be written off in Major Dembrow's present temper. He and the men with him knew Jesse from years ago, and they knew the reputation he had garnered since. Even if the Major's personal fury did not extend to Jesse, there was reason to suppose that the pursuit party, coming on him, would simply leave him to die. And Calem discarded the notion with no doubts.

# Chapter Six

At the pearly light of first dawn, he breakfasted off a handful of jerked beef and a meager swallow of water, and prepared for the trail. Jesse was feverish but sluggishly rational as Calem changed the blood-soaked bandages, using another shirt for the job. He hoisted Jesse into the saddle and, taking no chances, lashed his wrists to the horn and secured his ankles by running a rope under the horse's barrel.

Losing no time, he mounted and led out, threading the rocky upheaval of the desert floor. By now the gently rounded foothills below the saw-toothed range to the north seemed tantalizingly near, but at this snail's pace it was still most of a day's travel to them. His frequent, worried backglances at Jesse showed his head rolling slackly on his chest, and it came to him that even this idle, jogging pace could start the wound bleeding afresh.

Soon Jesse's sagging form was hunched deeply over his pommel, and when Calem said his name, there was no response. He halted and fell back by his brother's stirrup, feeling a dismal nudge of fear. Jesse's eyes were glazed over, and his whole trouser leg was soaked with blood. Calem kneaded his sun-cracked lower lip between his teeth, staring across their backtrail, hesitating. The sun was starting its slow climb, and a new day's heat already simmered in the air. Calem lifted his canteen and shook it, and then scanning about, saw a squat *bisnaga* cactus growing between two rocks.

In Jesse's condition a day in the saddle would probably finish him, but to lay up now would whittle precious hours from the delay last night's coup had provided. Yet there was no choice, and he felt a leaden thrust of despair. No use deluding himself that Jesse could survive long in these circumstances; he needed more than what ignorant care Calem could give, and they were unknown miles from any habitation.

Then he heard the rifle shot.

Its ringing, not-distant crack brought him motionless, disbelieving, listening to a pulse of echoes die away. Dembrow? Not this close and not this soon.

He reined the horses over to an outcrop spur of rock; he stepped down and untied Jesse, easing him to the ground. He threw off gear and spread ground tarps and blankets in the warm scanty shade, and made Jesse as comfortable as possible.

He climbed atop the spur and shaded his eyes against the blaze of a young raw day. If there were an army out in that desolation, the waste of jumbled rock could have concealed it. The teeming life of desert night had withdrawn, and all was unstirring silence now. Once he saw a chuckwalla skitter beneath a rock, and a carrion bird sailed lazily along the high currents.

Calem's spine crawled strangely, and he thought, *Now it's nerves,* and came down off the spur as Jesse gave a faint, heaving groan. It sounded like "Water," but there was no recognition in his glazed stare. Calem lifted his head, tilted the canteen to his lips and this time let him finish the water. Then carrying both canteens he moved over to the *bisnaga,* settled on his hunkers and plunged his knife into it near the crown. Careful to avoid the barbed spines that would work into the living flesh they hooked, he carved a ring-shaped cut around the barrel cactus and pried off its top.

He filled his hands with wet pulp, made hard fists and squeezed it out drop by drop into the canteens. After long aching hours of this he would have a small supply of something qualifying as liquid. He dully wondered if it mattered now, but it was something to occupy his attention while waiting for Major Dembrow. . . .

Squatting thus, he dozed on the thought, his hands relaxing. The sound of grating rock snatched him to alertness. A shadow falling across the cactus yanked him around, pivoting on his heels.

"Don't start up like that again, mister," the boy said, "or I'll blow you clean apart before you bat a winker."

The sun was in Calem's eyes, and it took him a confused instant to realize the boy must have come up unseen on the far side of the outcrop. He stood slight and stiff atop the rotted abutment, a Winchester long rifle tucked against his side.

Calem blinked to focus, only then realizing that the sun and the boyish brusqueness of the young voice had deceived him. This was a girl, not much past twelve, he thought, almost lost in a patched and oversize duck jacket and slouch hat. Her eyes were blue and fierce and solemn in a thin, sun-darkened face; she held the rifle with a negligent competence that warned him to make no move.

She said quietly, "You just stand so," and descended the spur as nimbly as a ground squirrel. "Now," she motioned with the rifle, "you set a saddle on that buckskin and be quick about it."

Calem found his voice. "You aim to steal a horse?"

She said flatly, "I need him," as if it explained everything. "You do like I say."

Calem stiffened his shoulders in the odd, dogged manner of his father. "I don't reckon I will."

"But I do." Her eyes narrowed, making faint sun-wrinkles at their corners; she cocked the rifle. "Boy, you move now."

Calem measured the distance between them with his eyes and knew she could drop him before he covered half of it. From the look of her, probably she would, too. But a wild stubbornness was in him now; he had been goaded too far and too long, and with no doubts at all he hunched his head and started toward her.

The rifle roared, almost in his face it seemed; he felt a sharp tug at his hat. He halted, not looking at the fallen hat, letting his stare lock the girl's in a wordless clash.

"Go on."

"I will! You better believe that!" Savagely she cocked the rifle again, and he wondered if the tremor in her unyielding voice were fury or desperation. "Next time I will!"

Calem hauled a deep breath and stated walking again. Three yards from her, he saw the rage and protest rise in her face and knew that if his refusal to obey did not crowd her to decision, panic might. She began, "I warned—" and not waiting then, he drove his toes against the earth, pistoning his legs, and came into her in a low lunge, grappling her around the waist. The rifle exploded above his head, and the barrel came down in a slashing arc across his back, wrenching a painful grunt from him as they fell together.

She was wiry as a colt, and for twenty furious seconds he had his hands full as she tried to brain him with the rifle, then with a rock, sputtering, "Goddam you, I'll kill you!" He did not want to hurt her, but he nearly yielded to impulse before he straddled her on his knees, pinning her wrists against the small of her back. After a writhing moment she relaxed with a panting sigh, twisting up a dirtsmudged face. "Let up, boy. Let me up now."

There was pure venom in her look, and he grunted, "Not much, without you stay quiet."

"All right."

Holding her wrists one-handed he picked up her rifle and only then released her. She retrieved her hat, lost in the scuffle, and came to her feet beating the dust from it. Her unevenly cropped hair was cut short in a boy's crude waterfall, and she glared through the pale, sun-bleached tangle of it, then tossed it back. She was well over twelve, he realized now, though her generous mouth and pugnose enhanced a childlike quality. But like many girl-women of a small, sturdy build she carried a surprising fullness at hip and bosom, this not at once apparent in her shapeless duck jacket and dress. The skirt was fairly short, coming to just below the knee; though her high deerhide leggin-moccasins covered her decently enough, it was a curiosity to see a white girl dressed so.

"Suppose you say why you want that horse so all-fire bad?"

"None of your damn business." Her nostrils flared faintly, and clamping on the hat then, she glanced abruptly at Jesse. "What's wrong with him?"

"Shot. Look, miss—"

"I'm Charley Jacks. That's to say Charlotte Lee Jacks." She made a wry grimace. "I make it Charley; you too, y'hear?" She shuttled her bird-quick glance from Jesse's face back to his. "He your brother?"

Calem nodded wearily. "I'm Calem Gault, he's Jesse. Listen—"

"My pa could fix him up right enough."

That gave a sharp tug to his fine-crowded hopes. "Your pa. Is he far away?"

"A few miles." She tilted her head vaguely toward the southeast; she set her fists on hips, a small frown touching her brow. "Mister, I surely need that horse. Reckon we could dicker about it?"

"Maybe," Calem said cautiously. Meeting anyone at all in this Godforsaken waste was unexpected enough; meeting a strange, mercurial waif of a girl like this one was downright baffling. Probably she was someone's nameless woods colt; no proper father would let his lawful daughter run out of harness so, and she could use a halter on that evil tongue. "Maybe, if your pa knows doctoring, we could make a deal. My brother needs looking to, and soon."

She laughed shortly. "You ain't asking much."

Calem stared at her a dismal and weary moment, thinking

that there was an idiotic quality to this talk. and indeed to the whole situation. He supposed being tense and nerve-frayed lent reality a nightmarish hue; he couldn't shake the feeling that he might awake at any moment in his own bed at home. He blinked, mustering himself for the effort of speech. "How's that?"

"My pa needs help for himself, that's how. Why I need your horse. You hear a shot a while back? Me. Had to kill the horse. Rode him too hard and busted a leg for him, which was a fool thing. We got no other."

"We was talking," Calem said a little unsteadily, "about your pa."

Miss Charley Jacks fingered a long scratch on her cheek; she looked off toward the broken heights southeast, and while she talked on, he caught the shades of emotion that colored her voice. They were not easy to pick out of the peculiar flatness of her tone. As she told it, she and her father lived alone; they owned and worked a gold diggings, and yesterday her father was in the tunnel when a shoring timber collapsed. His leg was pinioned, and after a night of wrestling with debris, she was unable to free him. This morning she had saddled their one horse and started for Mercyville. It lay a good day's ride beyond a saddle of peaks, but it was the only place to find help. Only her haste had crippled the bay, and shortly after shooting it and pushing on afoot, she'd spotted their horses in the lee of this rock and had stolen up to take them unawares.

Calem eyed her wonderingly. "Didn't it occur to you to ask for help instead of throwing down on us?"

"What kind of ninny you take me for, mister? My pa is pinned by a big timber which is holding up a lot of loose rock. I cleared away part of the rock, but did not dast dig more for fear of bringing down the whole shebang and burying him. Only way to free him without moving more rock is to raise the timber and the rock with it. I couldn't budge it, but might be three-four men could." Her light, appraising stare held a quiet contempt. "Mister, one man and his stove-up brother ain't no use to me."

"Be that as it may," Calem said grimly. "You want my horse and I'm in a position to name terms. You ain't."

She considered for a moment, then shrugged. "Well, then."

"Can't give my brother decent care out here. You lead me to shelter and a bed for him, and the horse is yours. Loan of it, I mean. I'll stay by Jess and see to your pa's needs too,

52

till you get back with them Mercyville fellows." He hesitated. "Does he really know doctoring?"

"Pa? Said so, didn't I? Say, how 'bout my rifle?"

"I like to got brained with it once—"

Again her nostrils flared. "We made a deal. Boy, that better come to more meaning than talk, or you can keep your damn horse and the whole kiboodle and choke on it."

Calem nodded once, resignedly, and handed the rifle to her. Charley Jacks favored him with a stiff glare, but then gave a ready and willing hand as he set to packing the gear, and helped him tie Jesse in saddle again.

On foot, they set out southeast by the sun. The buckskin was still strong and brisk-stepping, yet showed the slow wear of the grueling trek. If he kept his promise to the girl, her streak of impetuous temper and the urgency of her need might mean the buckskin would share her horse's fate; she would not spare it on the sixty-mile-or-so ride to Mercyville, and that worried him. Even now, not trusting her with the buckskin's reins, he let her lead the bay with Jesse lashed to the saddle. She walked beside him at a free, tireless stride for all her diminutive size. And presently she remarked: "What you-all running from?"

Calem gave her a wary, startled glance, and she said dryly, "Maybe your brother done the job on himself, huh? Or you did?"

Calem's instinct was to dissemble, but she had guessed this much rightly. "Some men following us. Looking to nail my hide, not his, but it went the other way."

The girl stopped in her tracks. "Listen. Pull up." He did, and then she said flatly, "Suppose you say what kind of a jackpot you have come from? Maybe we want no mix with it."

Her frank eyes were like blued gunsteel, and he shifted uncomfortably. "I killed this man's son—"

"What I want to know, was he looking at you when you fetched him?"

"Square in the eye."

"That's all right, but—" Her small frown held, and she slightly tilted her head. "They on your trail? Close by?"

"We lost 'em a good ways back yesterday."

As they moved on then, Calem felt a tinge of shame for the lie, and uneasily now, he wondered if there were some bitter significance in his sudden glibness. A few short days ago he would have stammered and flushed over an untruth. For all, it seemed, that a man's conscience could sway against fear and desperation, these had a way of battering aside scruple and will. And desperate for help, afraid of her rebuff, if she were aware that his enemies would be close on his trail shortly, he was willing to more than lie, Calem knew. *It's for Jess, and not like the choice was so all-fire personal.*

# Chapter Seven

During the last leg of their flight, he and Jesse had held wherever possible to the flatter and lower country. Now the girl was leading him in a deliberate way toward higher ground. Ahead lay a long, wavering line of vaulting, canyon-broken ridges, which in fact he had widely skirted earlier. As the terrain roughened, the climbing sun flooded it with a broiling fury; waves of mind-dulling heat danced off every tilting rock surface. Toiling up the first rocky ascent, Calem felt his lungs start to labor; his vision grew spotty and aching.

Miss Charley Jacks bounced up the precipitous lift of a massive scarp like a nimble goat; now and then she had an ingenuous curse for the bay because it stumbled or shied. Calem was about to warn her against the reckless pace when, slowing of her own accord, she led the way onto a narrow ribbon of ledge. He saw that it was actually a trail that angled in a mounting terrace along the sheer upper wall of this cone-shaped formation, following its slow curve out of sight. It looked like a deep natural fault in the scarp, but here and there were signs of chipping and flaking, the work of primitive long-dead hands.

Miss Charley moved carefully now, speaking softly to the bay, feeling out its every step with her own. The rimrock was notched with gaps where huge chunks of crumbling scale had sloughed away into a sheer drop of hundreds of feet. As they climbed around the steep-mounting curve, the trail narrowed steadily till an unreasoning fear touched him that it would pinch off altogether, boxing and stranding them on this high, cramped shelf. Their horses' right stirrups scraped along the wall, dislodging pebbles that trickled over the rim. Clammy sweat distilled on his belly and back as he put his whole attention to negotiating past a bulging shoulder of cliff, and then a thin sigh left him. The trail widened out just ahead, and the crowding wall itself tapered off in a gentle grade that formed the far side of the conical ridge.

Now they were within the pocketing heights, and the slope below plunged gently away to a small valley half overgrown by a surprising luxuriance of scrub timber, accounted for by a stream which wound like a sparkling snake under the soft green of fringing willows.

Miss Charley Jacks said, "There it is."

"Where?" He saw no cabin or sheds, and the trees were too low and sparse to conceal a layout.

She said flatly, "Look high, jughead," and without more ado led off on the faint trace of the old trail as it continued downslope. Calem hesitated, sweeping his glance across the dipping basin. This terminated on its east side in a long incline running straight up to the base of a bare flinty ridge that rose sheer for a good thirty feet to a thrusting bulge of rimrock. Beyond that, apparently, lay only the brassy sky and a monotonous series of more dun-colored ridges.

Mystified, he followed the girl down to the valley where they angled through the timber, crossed the stream at a shallow fording, and came to the valley's east end. A clear spring that was the source of the stream bubbled from the rocks there, and Calem's throat constricted with a violent sudden thirst. But the girl, not pausing, tackled the long boulder-strewn incline. It was laced with smaller rubble that cascaded away in small chuckling slides.

A long sore ache was settling into his legs as they neared the base of the ridge where the slope had its terminus. And abruptly then, he understood. The dwelling, almost invisible from beyond a few yards, was literally a part of the ridge-flank. Wind and weather had scored a large, horizontal niche into the softer rock that formed the lower ridge. A single curving wall that made a rusty blend with the rock had been built across the niche to form a room; and Calem recognized it as the work of Indian hands. He'd seen such cliffside structures before, with their half-round facing walls of small stones mortared together by a strange red cement even harder than the stones. Prehistoric men had built them as vaults for the dead and sealed them off. But this one had been built for the living; a narrow wooden doorframe was set in the rocks, its puncheon door hung by rawhide hinges and camouflaged by a red stain the hue of the rocks.

"Canyon back of the ridge has plenty grass and water," Miss Charley told him. "We kept the horse there. Best your animals be cooled off and watered and get a rest. I'll take 'em to the canyon and tend them while you fetch your brother inside." She held out her hand and, after a moment's hesitation, Calem surrendered the reins. He unsecured the ropes and eased Jesse into his arms, and while Miss Charley removed the saddles and other gear, carried him inside.

The single room was surprisingly spacious, with the sides of the niche forming the floor and ceiling and back wall. Two small windows, hardly more than wood-framed portholes with wooden shutters, flanked the door. The shutters were flung wide to admit dusty sunshafts that partly relieved a dim gloom. But the real relief was the earthy coolness here. There was furniture of the crudest sort, meager but substantial: a table and a bench made of rough narrow puncheons, and a pair of equally makeshift armchairs with rawhide weave seats. The table was set for two, he noticed, and in the middle stood a blackened pot full of a cold, greasescummed stew, never touched. The big stone fireplace was flanked by shelves which held pantry goods and a few battered utensils. A single wooden cot stood in one roughly angled corner of the niche. From the careless litter of clothes and gear around it, this must be the father's bunk. He supposed that the other rear corner, where a curtain made of jutesacks sewed together had been stretched wall to wall, formed the girl's own compartment.

The exposed bunk was covered by a faded and ragged patchwork quilt which would be little the worse for bloodsmears; he laid Jesse on it and straightened his legs, then looked around for water. He found it in a huge clay *olla* set deep in the cool shadow by the back wall. He drank deeply and greedily, and water had never tasted better. Filling a tin cup for Jesse, he held it to his lips, letting some dribble on his chin, but provoked no response now. Jesse was pale and drawn under his whiskers; there was an inert looseness to his body, and a chill of real fear ribboned through Calem's belly. The bleeding might cease now that Jesse was unmoving, but he would need some competent help and soon.

Miss Charley came in; she moved to his side and studied Jesse, her pugnosed face grave and still now. "He pretty bad, eh?"

"Bad enough. Now let's see where your pa is."

She hesitated a bare moment, then shrugged. "Why not? Want to let your horse cool off some before I set out. There's time."

"Whereabouts is this mine?"

For answer she moved over to the curtain, nodding him to follow. She lifted the smudged cloth and ducked under it. Puzzled as he followed her, Calem found as he had guessed that this was her personal cubicle. There was a cot and a wall peg with some clothes hung on it, and a shelf con-

57

taining toilet articles and a few gewgaws. A second jutesack drape, till now concealed by the first one, hung across the back wall. Before he had time to wonder at this, she stepped over and lifted the second hanging.

It covered a timber-cribbed opening, he saw, and beyond yawned a black tunnel that appeared to penetrate into the ridge. He understood then that this dwelling had been deliberately and laboriously planned to conceal the mine entrance and tunnel. A mine that had to boast a fine strike to justify this elaborate concealment of the diggings . . .

"Pa?" Miss Charley called into the darkness. "You all right in there?"

"A course I ain't, dammit," crackled a voice diffused by hollow echoes. "Not pinned like a goddam—*hah!*" The voice exploded in a hollow, racking cough which ended in a wicked curse.

"He's all right," she told Calem, then called: "Pa, you light that lantern now so's we can get to you."

After a moment a match was scratched alight, making a sulphurous flare far down the tunnel. It died to a low flame which a moment later grew on a lampwick in a wide pool of light that reached into the passage, picking out the straight rugged walls and timber cribbing. Gingerly, Calem followed the girl inside, ducking his head under the low beams. The air in the tunnel was as cool and clammy as a slug, and a stale-sweet odor of decaying wood clung to it. They picked their way into the fan of light, and she dropped to her knees beside the lantern.

The man was sprawled belly-up as the fallen timber had pinned him, half-twisted on his braced elbows and peering up irascibly. Some water and food had been left within his reach.

He was about fifty, a gaunt bantam of a man who would probably not top a hundred and twenty pounds sopping wet, but even flat and motionless there was something vibrant and restless about him, as if he were muscled with bunches of taut wires. He was, Calem guessed, as tough as cactus inside and out. His long bleached blond hair was like old hemp; his face was like an aging elf's, round and ruddy, but there was nothing elfin about his eyes. They were the color of wash-faded denim, and they looked old as sin, more shrewdly calculating than any eyes Calem had ever seen; he wondered if this were an illusion made by lampcast light and shadows.

"You hurting at all, Pa?"

"Goddlemighty, girl, what you think? Man my age takes the cold cramps in his bones has got every ailing since age five acting up. Can't feel a thing in the legs though, which is worrisome. You fool girl, you ain't brought but one man."

Miss Charley said, "Two," and launched into an explanation which did nothing to sweeten Ethan Jacks' disposition. Meantime Calem dropped to one knee by the downed timber, laying a hand on it, feeling its heavy solidness impregnated by dampness. He wondered fleetingly where Jacks had obtained such timbers—not from that scrub growth in the valley below.

He saw that the supporting stull of this massive overhead beam had given way, probably from a disturbance of the tunnel flank where Jacks was test-pitting. Most of the stull projected from the heap of rubble which had plunged from above, barely missing the miner. The overhead timber had not missed; it lay diagonally across the tunnel, half-blocking it; the upper end had slipped its stull, but had wedged against the tunnel wall, and so was prevented from dropping farther. The lower butt had plunged nearly to the floor, embedding itself in the loose earth and rubble which had tumbled over Jacks' legs. Had the butt caught them innocent of the insulating earth, or had the beam not gotten hung up on one end, the weight and impact would have crushed flesh and bone to a jelly. The timber was massive and solid of itself, and still supported a burden of rock that had been the roof. For a number of sizable boulders had fallen and a huge one had wedged itself between the wall and the beam's topside, an immovable weight. Apparently it had rendered the timber immovable too, as Calem verified by testing his strength on the timber, leaning with both hands.

"Was squatting under her," Ethan Jacks said. "Jumped when she give just in time, only not quite."

Calem said, "You move your legs?"

"Right one anyways. Left one's caught square under the point of weight. No break that I can tell. No pain without I pull hard. Not moving her without timber is moved first though."

"You try digging away this loose stuff?"

"Told you before," Miss Charley said with an acerbity that matched her sire's. "Get the wax out, bub. I tried cleaning off the rock and like to brought the whole tunnel down on him."

Calem braced a palm against the block-shaped key rock that wedged the timber down, sizing it, and she said disgustedly,

"You'll never budge it, bub, and you'll pull down all that rock behind it if you do."

Ignoring her, Calem said, "How about digging under your leg?"

"Tunnel floor is solid rock here." Jacks watched him a dry, curious moment. "You propose to flood the place and float her off, boy? You figure to witch up some water? Heh?"

Calem, his patience about played out from the acid needlings of this pair, said thinly, "I'll wait till I get my growth." He pointed to the space under the hung-up end of the timber. "Look. Room enough for one man to get his back and shoulders under; that's the only way it will ever lift."

Ethan Jacks rasped a palm over his stubbled jaw. "Mebbe so. What you say, Charley?"

"One man ain't enough," she said coldly. "Time we quit jawing and I forked that horse. You keeping your word, bub? Damn, you better!"

"If it comes to that," Calem said. "But you better consider something else." He looked directly at Ethan. "Seems someone went to a sight of bother, building that room smack against this tunnel to hide it. If your girl fetches a posse from Mercyville, it will spill the beans. This here is a lonely place, only the two of you, easy pickings for any tough nut. How you know you can trust these Mercyville men?"

"How we know we can you?" Miss Charley countered flatly.

"I'm only one anyhow," Calem said, his irritation deepening at her persistent antagonism.

"Good thought. Don't be so damn sudden, girl." Jacks' shrewd eyes gleamed, eying Calem. "Good shoulders on him. Mebbeso."

"Worth a try," Calem said, and nodded at the girl. "She has got to lend a hand like I tell her."

Miss Charley scowled; Ethan rubbed his beard again, saying, "No feeling in the one leg. Pinched-off nerve. Another full day and night while you fetch help'd be too long, Charley. Like to lose a leg, of which I need both. As lief take the gamble and let Gault make his try." He added with a snap, "You do what he tells you, hear?"

She knit her brows, biting her lip; Calem met her angry stare with his face composed against a sick worry. Jesse needed the help of skilled hands, and if Jacks' were only half-skilled, he'd have a fighting chance. But he needed tending now, not tomorrow.

60

Miss Charley gave a slow, grudging nod. "Reckon a lot of men would be no help. All right."

Calem laid hold of the fat stull projecting from the rubble and worked it carefully free. He selected a cake-sized rock and set it near Ethan Jacks' thigh close to the big timber, and thrust the stull end between the down-angled beam and the rock. Using the latter as a fulcrum, he leaned tentative weight on the stull. Dust sifted from the roof. The stull made a lever that would add strongly to his own effort.

"You get on that," he told the girl. "Put your weight to it when I tell you." He moved to the low gap under the upper timber, and flattening his bent back along it, said, "Now," and exerted slow force, lifting. He heard the gritty grind of rock on rock, and felt a faint, shifting lurch in the ponderous weight. "Try to move," he said.

He heard a grunting effort, and Ethan said, "Dirt moved some. Legs don't."

Calem's back was tight-braced and straining, and now he sucked breath into his lungs and sighed, "Again," and reached for a wellspring of power he wasn't sure he owned. His muscles shuddered with strain; the breath congested in his chest, and his head felt ready to burst. He heard the sudden rattle of falling rubble, and Miss Charley cried, "Careful! You make it, Pa?"

After a moment Ethan grunted, "No feeling in my goddam legs. Been buried too long. Lend a hand, girl."

Calem told her, "Go ahead," and felt her let up slowly on the lever. Now the full weight of the timber was on his back, and he could only brace himself shudderingly while a surge of blood darkened his eyes and his muscles screamed for release from the bone-deep ache of exertion. And then he was aware that Miss Charley was back on the lever; the weight eased slowly. Not able to turn his head, he gulped, "Is he out?"

She said yes, and now by agonizing inches they let the timber gently settle till the end struck solidly against the wall and was braced there. He dropped his shoulders, holding his breath; a little more earth and rock fell, and that was all. His legs went rubbery as he crawled from under the beam, and he simply sank to the ground, sweating and shaking and wondering how he had done it.

# Chapter Eight

"You two give a hand," Ethan said, "and I can walk."

With the girl on one side, Calem on the other, they hoisted him to his feet; Calem carried the lamp in his free hand 'as they maneuvered down the tunnel.

He judged that Ethan had not dug the tunnel nor raised the massive shoring timbers by himself. Yet he and his daughter appeared to be alone. If others had been involved with these two, where were they now? It was not the sort of speculation that rested easy in a man's craw.

By the time they reached the tunnel exit and came into the big room, Ethan was able to move by himself, limping slightly. He hobbled around rubbing his thigh, and said with a grudging nod at Jesse, "Say you want me to look to him?"

"Yes, sir. Your girl has said you know doctoring."

Ethan gave a wheezing chuckle. "Can tackle a case of colic or gallsores with a fair knowing hand, sure enough. He don't look like no horse or steer to this child."

*An animal sawbones.* Calem favored Miss Charley with a tired glare. She was standing by the window, her rifle again in hand; she met his eyes with a cool and impudent malice. "I fancy critters above a hellsmear of people I have met," she observed. "Pa, I give my word, so you look at him."

"You got no business committing me," Ethan said testily. His pale blue eyes were bitter-cold with suspicion as they shuttled from Calem to Jesse.

*Like he was seeing us both dead if he had his way,* Calem thought. *He must have him quite a strike here.*

"Pa!" she said sharply. "You hear me now. You could have lost a leg easy as not, you said so yourself. Maybe even died, but for this here man. You owe him a proper favor."

"Ain't said I didn't," Ethan said surlily, staring bleakly at Calem. "One thing. Want you both out of here by day after tomorrow." Not troubling to disguise his reluctance, he moved to the cot.

The flesh of Jesse's leg, as Ethan bared it, was swollen and discolored, and the wound was a livid purple around the edge. "Bullet went clean through, that's something. Best cauterize. Clean him up, Charley, whilst I heat the iron."

Ethan got a blaze going in the fireplace, and while he was occupied, the girl set out clean rags and sweet oil and a basin of water. Her hands were quick and competent, even gentle, as she bathed the wound; Calem stood by, feeling ten thumbs' worth of useless awkwardness. There was really nothing for him to do, and he edged over to one of the windows; he was surprised to see that the sun had canted high to the south, and it must be close to midday.

This posed a sharp reminder of Dembrow, who by now might well have caught up with at least some of his stampeded horses. Calem's jaws ached with a hard compression; as sure as sunset Dembrow would be closing the distance between them, and no telling how close he was by now. If not for Ethan Jacks' suspicion he might have left Jesse here and pushed on alone. A moment later it occurred to him that after what had happened with the horses, Dembrow might not be satisfied with only Calem Gault. He also began to worry that in his anxiety to get help for Jesse he might have brought danger and an unwelcome involvement to the Jackses. Yet, struggling with bitter uncertainty as to his next move, he said nothing.

The fire had died down; the banked coals glowed under a fine layer of ash. Ethan rummaged through a tray of cutlery and selected a steel carving knife; he thrust the blade into the cherry coals. When the wooden hilt began to smoke, he wrapped a rag around his fist and pulled it out; the dull-glowing blade steamed against the air as he carried it to the cot. "Your brother's arms, Gault. You, Charley, take aholt on his ankles."

Jesse was mumbling in quasi-awareness; his face had a dead pallor about the black slur of his beard. Calem drew his breath and leaned hard as Ethan lowered the blade. Jesse's body arched against their hands and his eyes flew open, varnished with fever. His breath sighed in and left him in a scream. Ethan said meagerly, "Turn him over," and after doing so and leaning again, Calem felt his guts wrench with the hiss and stench and trailing, muffled moan. And then with relief felt Jesse go limp under his hands.

"Sit down, bub," Ethan said, "before you fall down."

Calem was glad to sit down. He went slack on one end of the bench and watched Jacks cleanse and bandage the seared thigh. He decided that, horse butcher or not, his daughter had not exaggerated the skill in Ethan's small sinewy hands.

Phlegmatically Ethan finished the dressing and, leaving Miss Charley to clean up the mess, went past Calem to a rickety washstand and filled a basin from the small water *olla* there. He said waspishly over his shoulder, "you can stay over tonight, tomorrow. He better be fit to ride day after, because you're driftin' then."

Calem stared at his big hands flat on the table, feeling in the wash of reaction a bitter worry flavored with guilt. He could not stay here and expose these people to the danger his presence meant, but could he desert Jesse? *The day after!* Jesse would not sit his saddle for a good week. . . .

*You got to tell them the truth,* he thought, and swung restlessly to his feet; he rammed his hands in his hip pockets and began to pace. *They won't be happy with it, but they would find out when Dembrow comes anyhow. If I can get 'em to care for Jesse before I push on, that's better than nothing.*

Then, moving past one window port, he glanced out and froze, his heart almost stopping. The open port commanded a clean view of the slope below and the timbered valley, and beyond that the conical ridge he and Jesse and the girl had crossed to reach here. And now at once he picked out the riders jogging in a slow file around the curve of the ridge, coming off it down the long approach to the valley. For a cold long moment Calem did not believe it; he realized then that more time had elapsed than he had known, that Dembrow's driving fury to run him to earth would only be inflamed by knowing that one half of his quarry was disabled.

Miss Charley said, "Pa," in a breathing whisper, yanking Calem's glance around. She was standing by the other window staring out, and now she wheeled toward him.

"Them men. They the ones?"

"Yeah." Calem felt the color rising into his face under her merciless gaze. "I reckon I knew they was coming."

"I reckon you did." She turned abruptly to her rifle leaning against the wall and arced it around to bear on him as she swung back. "I ought to shoot you," she hissed. "By granny, I ought to save them the job!"

Ethan Jacks came to the nearest port, muttering, "What the old Billy Hell," and peered out. His slight form stiffened, and Calem felt his wicked glance then. But he did not take his own eyes off Miss Charley. Her rifle was level with his belly, and this time, her eyes blazing with a pale anger, she looked ready and willing to shoot; he was careful not to stir a muscle.

"Pa," she was almost inarticulate with rage, "them men is after him. He said he had shook them off and here they are not an hour hindmost! By granny—"

"Quit that cussin'," Ethan said curtly and, still looking at Calem, jerked his head toward the door. "Get out." Calem held stubbornly still, his feet apart, and Ethan yelled, "You hear me? Light a shuck. Drag it. Slope. Hit the trail!"

Miss Charley said ominously, "You better do it, bub," shifting her rifle slightly.

Calem looked from one bleakly hostile face to the other, and said resignedly, "All right, but my brother will need care. They're wanting me, not him."

Ethan said, "That's too goddam bad," with what seemed close to a wicked relish.

"No, that's suitable," the girl said abruptly. "We owe him one life, no more." Ethan growled under his breath, but she did not look at him. Her eyes were hard and unrelenting on Calem; she motioned with her rifle at the door.

Calem moved to the door and opened it; he scanned the flinty slopes all around, gauging his best chance. To saddle and ready a tired horse and make his way off the slope before Dembrow was on him was out of the question. He would stand a slightly better chance afoot, retreating deeper into the brutal, barren country he had seen to the east. In that broken wilderness even Abel Sutter could not hold the track of a lone man bent on losing himself. There, horses could not follow the trail he would set; a man could somehow live off the land. . . .

Obscurely he knew this was the desperate, driven mental state of a man with his back to the wall, but he did not hesitate. There was no time to think about it. He turned back into the room and picked up his saddlebags dumped beside the door, slinging them across his shoulder.

Then, as he straightened, Miss Charley flew in front of him; she slammed the door and shot the bolt, almost dropping her rifle. *"No.* Don't you step out that door, bub."

"You crazy, Charley?" her father shouted. "He done his best to fob off trouble on us! You buying it?"

"No help for it." Her young face was a shade pale, but she did not sound excited, only positive. "I won't see no man thrown to a damn pack of wolves. Right's right and wrong's wrong, and that is wrong. I know that much, Pa, so don't say different. He's staying."

"Hell he is!" Ethan swung violently toward the wall where

an old Henry rifle lay across pegs, but her hard low, "Pa!" brought him up short.

When Ethan turned, the rifle was centered squarely on him. His face worked like seamy dough. "You raised your hand against your pa. You should of been learned a woman's place, by God."

"Like you learned my ma?"

Ethan's faded eyes flinched; he muttered, "No call for that. I have got your good in mind."

"I ain't going to argue about it," she said with an utter finality. "I don't give a rap if these men pull a mountain down on us. We ain't sending him out there to be killed. You say more on it, and I'll hate you forever."

Her manner was artless and simple and fierce, implying a startling and primitive innocence. It was as if she had never heard of filial respect or womanly meekness or moral compromise, and not knowing, simply spoke her mind and made her stand, and go hang to the consequences.

"Damn girl," Ethan said in a haggard way, and turned back to the port, his stiff-humped back eloquent of the rage knotted in him.

Calem went to the pile of their gear and dug out Jesse's fieldglasses and, lifting his rifle from its saddle boot, returned to the window. With Miss Charley crowded beside him, he trained the glasses. By now the riders were pushing through the scant timber, and he could see the hunched, wizened form of Abel Sutter in the lead, bent low in his saddle to study the ground. As they left the timber close by the slope, Sutter straightened and looked up at the ridge; at once he reined back beside Major Dembrow and spoke, and the Major raised his arm for a halt. Sutter had spotted the "dead house" and had guessed the truth at once.

Calem held his glasses on the Major, who was listening to the tracker now. Dembrow's whipcord breeches and linen shirt were discolored with filth; a white stubble rimmed his jaw, which was ridged and jutting with an inheld tension. His one bleak and frosty eye showed nothing. Calem moved the glasses along the men ranged behind him—Perc Tucker, Severo Cortez, and Wash Breed, all top hands and handy men with guns, all with a tough, unquestioning loyalty to their brand—and bringing up the rear, Frenchy Duval and Cody Dembrow.

Briefly, curiously, Calem let the glasses linger on the broad face of Dembrow's nephew. Everyone knew that Cody was kin from the wrong side of the blanket, but that told nothing. Always a cautious air clung to Cody's manner, and while he blended like a desert lizard into any situation, a man could sense more behind his sleepy, deep-lidded gaze than Cody let on. Now he had joined the consultation, and while the Major might well be arguing for a direct frontal charge up the bare slope, Cody was no doubt advocating a more circumspect action.

"Stand away," Calem muttered to the girl, and settled his rifle barrel on the sill. He aimed and shot, and dust puffed from a rock a yard from the nearest rider. It made up their minds in a hurry, and they piled from their saddles and scrambled for the shelter of boulders.

Ethan said wickedly, "Now what did that get you?"

"Time, maybe." Calem scrubbed a palm over his sweating forehead. "What you're thinking, I could of dropped him. About why he's after me, I'm in the right, if that makes any difference."

"It don't." Ethan spat through the port. "Man who minds his own stays out of trouble."

Calem clamped his jaw on further talk, staring downward. About a half-minute later Abel Sutter stepped out to sight; he held both hands over his head, his rifle in them, and a white silk handkerchief that was doubtless the Major's fluttered from the barrel.

"What's that for?" Miss Charley said with interest.

"He wants truce talk." Ethan rubbed his knuckles along his whiskered jaw, thoughtfully. "I wonder would he abide by that thing if a man went out?"

"He would," Calem said unhesitatingly, thinking of the Dembrow honor.

Ethan gave him a swift, sly look. "That so. Who you say was on the right side of the fence?"

"Well, he thinks he is."

Ethan snorted, "Don't we all," and tramped to the door. "Can maybe dicker 'em out of something." He sounded almost tractable, and Calem felt an instant wariness.

As Ethan tramped down the slope, Abel Sutter catfooted upward to meet him. They met halfway, two undersized men, each beaten by his own harsh way of life to a rawhide mold. They talked for a long while, and Calem's grip began to ache around his rifle. But his feeling now was one of vast impatience; oddly he felt at last a strange calm freedom from overbearing tension. He had turned finally at bay, seasoned by the cold fatalism of a hunted man, ready to face whatever came.

67

The two broke off talk and split apart, and Ethan tramped hurriedly back. After entering, he barred the door by sliding a small timber into two brackets that were bent iron spikes anchored to either side of the entrance. Then he went to a shelf, took down a stone jug, shook it next to his ear and uncorked it and pulled deeply.

"Pa, what did he have to say?"

Ethan lowered the jug and eyed her with a kind of benign hostility, then drank again and slammed the cork home with the heel of his palm. He seemed to be extending the moment with a secret pleasure. "He says Major Dembrow says to send out these Gaults and we won't come to injury."

"After you straightened him out on that," Miss Charley said coldly, "what then?"

"Says they will take 'em the hard way if need be." Ethan drew his sleeve across his mouth, a sly malice filling his glance at Calem. "What else he said, you killed the Dembrow boy in a way made it as good as murder."

Ethan seemed to relax and expand with the liquor; he grinned slowly. "What this Sutter said was this Dembrow's foreman seen it and claimed Dembrow's boy defended himself agin your pa. An even break."

"I seen it myself. I say otherwise."

"All right," Ethan said cheerfully, as if the matter were of no account. "Sutter says he tracked you all the way and he figures the hurt man with you is your brother; he allus had a swagger to his sign. Reckons it was him, this Jesse, that shot his horse, too. I asked him why he figures all this. Says because this brother of yours is a known outlaw and knows the tricks."

Feeling Miss Charley's alert stare, Calem said lamely, "He has skylarked some."

"Skylarked!" Ethan shook his head with an explosive chortle. "Well, that do beat all."

"Anything else?" Calem said coldly.

"He says to tell the one shot his hoss that he don't need to worry about Major Dembrow hanging him. Says he means to call his own turn on that boy."

Ethan moved toward the curtained alcove that hid the tunnel, and entered it. Calem sank onto the bench, rubbing his eyes. A tired disgust washed through him. He was sorry to embroil these two Jackses, at least the girl, but what else could he do? This fortlike place gave him a slender chance; out there he would stand bare-handed against six guns.

Another thing that troubled him was the hint of a sly

satisfaction behind Ethan's manner after his talk with Sutter, and he thought with an increasing unease, *Suppose they made a deal of some kind?* All he could do was wait and watch.

Mingled with a deep distrust of Ethan Jacks was his worry for Jesse and a concern for when and how Major Dembrow's next move would come. Dembrow had come a long way, and now that his quarry was cornered, would he simply wait and starve them out? *I wouldn't,* Calem thought, and he knew with conviction that neither would Dembrow.

# Chapter Nine

Through the long day Calem let the girl have the care of Jesse, who tossed and raved in a high fever. He was aware that he had little of his father's fine curative touch for ailing things; with experience and maturity his big awkward hands might develop the deftness they lacked, but for now, he knew, he could serve in best capacity by mounting guard at a port. That meant simply keeping an idle eye on the slope below against any move by Dembrow.

At least they were well-prepared for either a drawn-out siege or a sudden attack. Miss Charley had told him that a good store of food had been laid in, and plenty of water too. The dwelling itself was built snugly within a niche of the ridgeside, shielding them to the sides and rear; an attacker could come at them only from the front.

Calem was still convinced that the Major, already galled with impatience and further fretted by hours of waiting, would be edged toward a dramatic move before long, and he tried to think how it would come. With only five men to back his play Dembrow would not launch a suicidal charge across fifty yards of open slope to reach the dwelling. *Not by day, but what about tonight?* But tonight the moon would be full, and even with a heavy cloud cover, men rushing the slope would be highlighted all the way.

Calem put his face to the window and craned his neck to see the looming rimrock that curved out in a generous overhang, providing shelter from above. It seemed solid, and probably nothing but a charge of giant powder could bring it down.

Several times as the hours dragged on, he almost dozed. He had slept in fitful, nervous snatches since this long flight had begun, and now with his body inactive, the toll of grinding exhaustion was catching up. His eyes burned and throbbed from staring at the flinty glare of the slope.

His thoughts drifted; he jerked to full wakefulness at Miss Charley's quiet, "Come eat now. I'll watch." He saw that twilight shadows filled the room, broken by a dance of light from the fireplace where a stew was bubbling. Its savory

70

odor filled the room, but though he hadn't put away a solid meal in days, Calem was not hungry. His head ached, and there was a strange buzzing in his ears.

He glanced down the boulder-laced incline, now blurred by the gray web of dusk. He could see a ruddy play of firelight around the Dembrow camp, set well off from the base of the slope, but the blaze itself, along with the men and horses, was hidden by a great abutting shoulder of rock. The camp was a long rifle shot from here, but the Major and his men were too seasoned hands to take chances.

Calem surrendered the rifle to Miss Charley, and afterward got a bowl and ladled hot stew into it. He ate slowly and without appetite. Shortly Ethan Jacks emerged from the tunnel which he had not left in hours, filled a bowl for himself, and took a chair at the table opposite Calem. His face was almost bland in its sly calm, and again Calem had the sense of worried distrust. *Maybe he is putting it on to make you worry.* Yet the elaborate trouble that Ethan had gone to in camouflaging his mine indicated that he might go to desperate lengths to keep its secret from outsiders. While the Gaults remained here and Dembrow was camped on his doorstep, the secret was in danger.

Ethan did not say a word through the meal, and after noisily spooning up the last of his stew, again entered the tunnel. Calem could not finish his bowlful, and the room seemed to sway unsteadily when he started to rise. He sank back on the bench, rubbing his face, and then felt a hand on his shoulder.

"You go on," Miss Charley said gently, "and get all the sleep you want. I'll stand watch."

He looked up at her, and her small face was full of a tender gravity, the underlip pouting in the way of a concerned mother's. Somehow this, with his awareness of clogging weariness, seeped through him like a sudden weakness. He felt like a long-frozen man starting to thaw; his eyes began to smart and he fumbled for the words and then, not trusting his voice, nodded dumbly.

He fetched his bedroll and spread his blankets out on the clay floor by the cot; he sat and tugged off his boots, watching Jesse. At last, he thought thankfully, Jesse was resting well. His profile, erased of its tight lines in sleep, seemed incredibly boyish even under a black smear of beard. Suddenly he remembered a time years ago when Jesse had stolen in late to the room they shared, and how, getting up still later in the night, Calem had lighted the lamp and

71

seen this same sleeping face, fresh and untroubled and serene. Later yet he had learned that Jesse had come in late from skylarking with a town girl. Grinning at the memory, then sobering with the thought that on his account Jesse now lay hurt and helpless, Calem felt the surge of old affection. *I'll stay with him like Ma wanted, maybe even point him right. I swear I'll try.*

He stretched full length on his blankets. The fire had burned low; its dim glow curved along the girl's half-turned cheek as she sat quietly by the port, the rifle across her knees. A warm breeze from the aperture feathered along his body, and soon he slept, deeply and dreamlessly.

In one of the semi-wakeful periods that come to even a heavy sleeper, he felt distinctly the sharp tug at his belt. He stirred, groaned, and rolled on his side; he heard a boot grate along the floor only inches away, and it was this sound that brought him finally and fully awake.

Ethan Jacks was about six feet away, and backing off farther. Calem's six-gun which he had taken was slack in his left fist; another pistol in his right hand was trained watchfully. Seeing Calem's eyes open, he rasped softly, "Don't you bat a winker. I have got both your guns, and your brother's. My girl's, too."

He backed over to the window, and Calem saw that Miss Charley no longer guarded it. Their weapons were heaped on the floor by the wall, and Ethan laid Calem's pistol by the others.

"Reckon you made a deal with Sutter," Calem began, and Ethan hissed: "Shut your mouth!" He shot a swift glance at Miss Charley's curtained-off alcove. "She is sound asleep. Told her I would stand guard. No reason she should even know till long after you've went." He waggled his pistol gently, the light washing wickedly against his eyes. "You wake her now and I'll blow a hole through you that you couldn't plug with a fist. You going to?"

"No."

The lantern from the tunnel stood on the floor, its flame bright and steady, and now Ethan picked it up and carried it to the door. He had to set it down, while holding the pistol on Calem, to free a hand for lifting the bar that secured the door.

Outside the wind was sharp; a hard gust promptly caught the freed door and swung it against Ethan's arm as he stood half-turned, almost throwing him off balance. He instinc-

72

tively dropped the bar to grab at the door, and the thick timber clattered on the packed floor.

There was a moment's silence as Ethan froze in place, and then came Miss Charley's sleepy, "Pa?"

"It's all right," Ethan declared harshly. "Dropped my rifle. Get back to sleep."

She did not reply; there were small stirring sounds and then the curtain was thrust quickly aside. She looked almost lost in a long heavy nightgown, much like an aroused, querulous child. As her glance passed to Calem and back to her father, understanding hardened her eyes to alertness.

She said between her teeth, "I might have known. So you'd stand watch while I got some sleep, would you? You—"

"I had enough of your sass," Ethan snarled with a harried exasperation. "You get back in there."

"Not much." She moved deeper into the room, hugging her arms; she nodded angrily toward the two brothers. "How much is a gold mine worth, Pa? One life? Two lives? Or maybe three—mine too?"

"Goddam it, now you hush that talk! You ain't going to be hurt; I am seeing to it now." He arced the pistol in Calem's direction. "With them two gone, our necks is safe. I ain't letting us get shot to pieces on their account. We don't owe 'em a thing. Time you stood by your pa for a change."

She took a step toward him, her voice low and fierce. "How much did you owe my ma? She never asked for nothing but a decent way to live. Speak of that, how much you reckon I owe you for being pa to me?"

"There ain't no sense to such goddam chatter."

"See how much sense there is to this." She straightened one arm, pointing at the guns on the floor. "I am going to stop you, Pa. Else you will have to kill me as sure as you are killing these two."

"All I got to do is lay this gun acrost your head," Ethan snarled. "And by God, I will."

She gave him a strange, wondering regard. "Why, you surely would. But happen that didn't stop me, you would shoot me to keep your gold safe. Ain't that so?"

The warm draft plied the dying fireplace coals to fresh life; the guttering flames highlighted the murky strain in Ethan's gaunt face. "No. You are way wrong. You don't know, that's all."

He bent and seized up the lantern, and moved it back and forth across the open doorway. It would be seen plainly from the camp below, and this, Calem knew, would be his signal, pre-arranged with Abel Sutter, for the Skull men to move in.

In the pressure of savage desperation, he was ready to discount all odds, even the handicap of his prone position, and make a lunge for Ethan. The bitter foretaste of defeat was in his mouth, for Ethan could gun him before he was on his feet. Yet his muscles gathered and tensed for the try.

But Miss Charley moved first, rushing on her father with the quickness of a young tigress. Catching his gun arm, she fought it down with all her weight.

Calem swarmed to his feet and took two half-diving steps. He caught Ethan solidly in the short ribs with the point of his shoulder and heard the wind gush from the smaller man's lungs as he went down. Calem and Miss Charley fell with him; after a moment of furious struggle, Calem rose with the gun in his fist. He heeled the door shut and settled the bar in place. The lantern dropped by Ethan had landed miraculously upright, unbroken. Calem picked it up and doused the flame, and moved quickly to the wash basin; with it he drenched the live embers in the fireplace. As the last cherry glow expired and the room ebbed into total blackness except for moonlight shafting through the ports, he heard the girl move quickly to his side.

Calem bent groping along the floor till he found the rifles, and he passed one to her, saying, "Get to the window." There was a soft groan in the darkness, and he added, "He hurt much?"

"No. You bumped his head on the floor is all." Her voice was grim. "He better stay out of our way." Her bare feet whispered away across the floor, and Calem pressed his face to the port.

The strong relief of moonlight bathed out every detail of rock and brush on the uneven slope, and he saw no movement along its whole length. But the campfire had been extinguished, and Calem thought, *They are watching down there all right; they seen the signal, but they know the idea went wrong. Question is, will they come on now or not?*

His moving glance came to fixed attention now on a dark mass of brush near the base of the incline. Had it moved . . . or was he seeing things? Almost at once another clump of brush made a distinct stealthy movement along the ground for a good two feet, moving upslope. Behind it he picked out the prone form of a man, just as a third clump shifted forward.

Calem kept his gaze in aching focus, hardly daring to

blink. One by one he isolated the six men in their various positions on the lower hill. Three of them had gotten nearly halfway, this before he had spotted the first betraying movement; the realization brought a wash of clammy sweat to his body.

Dembrow could not have been certain beyond a doubt that Ethan's true intent was not to close a trap on himself and not the Gaults; tolled onto the open slope by Ethan's signal he and his men would be plain targets for the rifles above. Taking no chances, he had put an idea of his own in motion, and it had nearly taken them totally unaware. The human eye tended not to look for what it did not expect to see; men sprawled belly-flat to the angle of slope behind mobile brush shields could snake upward in silence with few and unobtrusive movements. Even these might easily have escaped detection in the fitful moonlight till it was too late. Had they gotten near the shack, a concerted rush might have taken the defenders almost before they could get off a shot.

Not knowing if Miss Charley had the danger pegged, he whispered a warning, but she cut him off: "I seen them. Think I'll tickle 'em out of that."

She fired, and one tangle of brush gave a violent lurch. A moment later a man leaped up, and her second shot merged with Calem's. The man tumbled back, and his body rolled slack and inert down along a pale slab of angled rock and came to a stop. Now a confusion of yells and shots made bedlam of the night. Major Dembrow's voice crackled out, calling a charge, and orange stabs of gunflame broke the dense ground shadows.

They were coming on the climbing run now as Dembrow threw caution to the wind in his effort to salvage the attack. Calem heard bullets pock the 'dobe walls; two seared air through the port inches from his head. The near slugs and the screaming ricochet of one filled him with a fear for the girl and Jesse.

One man was within twenty yards of them, running low and pumping shots, wildly emptying his magazine. Calem's slug caught him in mid-leap as he bounded over an obstructing rock, and he fell with an odd, turning grace. At the same time Miss Charley beaded another man who dropped to his knees holding his arm.

The charge was broken.

But it was Cody Dembrow's voice, not the Major's, that now hoarsely called on them to fall back. The Major did not countermand the order. Calem watched the wounded man move downslope after his companions, stumbling as if in exhaustion.

For a long time they stayed by the ports, passing only a few bare words. And finally, certain that the attack was past, Calem wearily located the lantern and thumbnailed a match to flame, and lighted it. The racket had aroused Jesse to a loud delirium, and Calem went to check on him.

He was burning up with deep fever and sweating profusely; next would come the alternating fury of wracking chills. At least the fever was on him in full tide, which meant that it had to break before long, for better or worse.

Miss Charley had stayed by the window, but turning now, he saw her watching her father steadily, and her bluesteel eyes were implacable. Ethan sat at the table holding his head between his hands, his stare bent sullenly downward.

"Didn't want you getting shot," he muttered. "I could of settled it without shooting."

"You was thinking of your damn gold," she said without inflection. "Offhand I can't think of when you thought of anything but. Now you hear what I'm thinking of. I'm leaving you, Pa. If we get out of this alive, I am leaving for anywhere I can, so it's away from you."

Ethan Jacks' squinted gaze lifted slowly. His face was like a brown and desiccated mask with brittle eyes, and he said at last, "All right. Do what you goddam please. I ain't going to stop you."

Jesse moaned in his fever for water, and Calem's eyes sought the big water *olla* on the floor. He saw that it was broken in several large pieces, the puddling wetness broadening in a muddy stain across the hard dry clay. A downangling ricochet must have found it—and all the water that remained to them was a few tepid quarts in the small *olla* on the washstand.

Calem felt the sure, instinctive fear of a man raised in a region of little water and knowing what the lack of water meant. All Dembrow had to do now, if he only knew it, was wait out a few days. By that time the punishing heat survived on a bare dole of moisture would leave them too weak to fight off even a daylight attack.

# Chapter Ten

Cody Dembrow squatted on his heels by the fire and filled a tin cup from the blackened coffeepot. Drinking, he watched his uncle over the rim of his cup. The Major was pacing back and forth, his head bent, hands clasped at his back. *Like a damned little Napoleon,* Cody thought, but he wondered. . . .

To the world, even to those nearest him, Jeffrey Dembrow had always presented a hard and passionless face. A true cattleman of his time, his given word to another white man was his bond. The way he had built his ranch and fortune, by moving onto Indian treaty lands and bribing politicians to have the boundaries refixed, only made him bolder, not more ruthless, than the rest. It did not account for the shell he wore around his emotions.

But there had been his wife: latter-day gossip said it had been a love match from the first between the young cavalry officer and the general's daughter, and a determination to build a great thing for his bride had decided Jeffrey Dembrow to resign his commission. He had begun afresh with family influence and his own driving will; he had seized and borrowed and bribed, and his blunt answer to renegades, rustlers and squatters was a rope or a bullet.

Two years after their marriage, a year or so before the orphaned Cody had come to Skull, the young wife had died in childbirth. And for Jeffrey Dembrow then, there was only the son she had given him and the ranch she hadn't lived to see grow and prosper. Partly these things had filled the bitter void, but also they had channeled his fierce energy into the single-minded ambition of making Skull ranch a power in the territory, one that would pass into Ames' hands and his sons' after him, a dynasty of Dembrows unbroken. . . .

Perc Tucker stirred, and a grunt of pain left him; he was sitting upright against a rock, cradling his thickly splinted and bandaged arm against his belly. The arm was broken at the elbow, and Tucker grimaced with the agony that a slight movement cost him. Still he was lucky. Wash Breed and Severo Cortez also had been in last night's charge up the slope, and had not come down. From here you could see their bodies sprawled as they had fallen.

*We could all have got smoked down if I hadn't give the order to back off,* Cody thought. *How far will he carry this?* He knew the answer: Calem Gault's bullet had shattered a Dembrow dynasty, and that driving, insensate energy of the Major's would not let him rest until Gault was run to ground, no matter if many died for it.

Frenchy Duval leaned against the broad slab that sheltered their camp, his legs crossed, idly whittling at a mesquite branch. He whistled thinly through his teeth, occasionally peering about from under his brows without raising his head. Nothing fazed Duval; he took his orders and bided his time. His lean, relaxed grace was like that of a large indifferent cat inscrutable to the world.

"Major," Tucker-husked.

Jeffrey Dembrow came about on his heel and regarded the man a long moment as if he found difficulty concentrating on him. He said finally, "Yes."

"Wash and Severo died for the outfit, Major. You ain't going to just leave 'em lay out there."

"Later," the Major in a soft tone that brooked no argument; as he spoke he resumed his slow pacing, a stocky man whose face was a haggard-eyed mask. The ravages of time and ambition had never noticeably marked him, but a few days of grief and driving fury had aged him incredibly, Cody thought.

The Major halted and lifted his head as Abel Sutter dropped to view around an abutment of sandstone. The shriveled wolfer paced noiselessly into camp, squatted by Cody, picked up the boiling coffeepot in a calloused hand that was impervious to heat, and poured himself a cupful. Sutter had come on the besieged hill from behind to reconnoiter the shelving rim above the 'dobe shack.

Jeffrey Dembrow said impatiently, "Well? Can we get above them or not?"

Sutter pulled at his coffee before answering. "You kin get on the rim all right, Major, but that fort of theirn is snugged into the cliff. Man dropped a plumb line offen the rimrock, she would fall a good ways out from the base, away from them shooting ports. Gives them too good a angle of fire."

The Major's one dead eye burned on him. "So that if a man came down on a rope from the rim, he would be shot off it before he could get near the wall?"

"Might work loose a chunk of that rim and bury 'em, but she is fixed pretty solid."

"That was a barbarous observation, Sutter," Jeffrey Dembrow said coldly. "How well do you think they are provisioned?"

"They ain't no telling. Being so far from a settlement, I would hazard that little gent has laid in a good grubstake, though he might be stretching end of it, all we know." Sutter pointed at the gushing spring nearby. "Track shows they take up their water from there. A goodly climb, so they likely carry a good deal at a time. They could be fixed a long spell on both counts, but they ain't no telling."

The Major came slowly around, hands clasped at his back, to face the fire; he said in a harsh and peremptory voice, "Cody."

"Sir?"

"I want you to ride back to Skull. If you start now, you should make it before sundown tomorrow; you can travel back by the cool of night and be here before noon next day. Bring Ed Grymes and the entire crew. And something else—" The Major seemed to weigh his thought, his eyes squinting nearly shut. "Bring dynamite, Cody."

"There's some in the tack barn, left over from that roadblasting job."

"Bring it."

*The wind is up,* Cody thought, *and he has the smell of blood in his nose.* He tossed away his coffee dregs, set down the cup and rose, walking to his saddle.

While he was cinching it on his sorrel, Frenchy Duval came over carrying two canteens, Cody's and his own. "I have filled these. You will need them both, I think, eh?"

Cody nodded, and Duval fastened the canteens to the saddle, eying Cody across the horse's withers. "The Major pushes ver' hard," he murmured. "He pushes too hard maybe."

Cody said noncommittally, "Maybe," and toed into stirrup and swung astride.

Duval cocked his head, shutting one eye thoughtfully. "More men will die. It is plain. I wonder who will be the last."

Cody felt irritation at the hint of enigma, of matters unsaid, that frequently lurked behind Duval's words. "What's that meant to imply?"

"Why, the last shot may not be fired at the young Gault. Maybe at the Major, eh?"

Duval was merely needling him with some peculiar and

personal notion of amusement, Cody supposed. He gave the gunman a bare nod and rode out from the camp, quartering south.

Leaving the ridges, he made good time on the flat barrens while the late dawn still held the heat bearably low. He traveled steadily all that day and well into the cool evening before making a night halt. He broke camp before true dawn, and holding his sorrel to a strong but not killing pace, reached Coyotero Basin by late afternoon.

The cook's triangle sent its tinny clamor through the velvet twilight as Cody rode into headquarters and dismounted, stiff- and drag-footed, at the corral. He walked the horse patiently up and down, unlimbering his own muscles. The bunkhouse windows were lighted, and the crew would be at supper. Cody was hungry, but almost at once his glance was pulled to the lighted windows of the main house parlor, and he forgot hunger. In a few minutes he would see Trenna Dembrow, and how much he really wanted to surprised him.

Ed Grymes came from the bunkhouse at his rolling, thick-bodied gait; he gave Cody a surly nod, saying in an odd, slurred voice, "Heard you ride in. Where's the others?"

Cody briefly explained his mission, his easy tone blandly masking his contemptuous dislike of the Skull foreman. Grymes had been with Skull from the start, filling his boots as the Major's right-hand man, but there was no real bottom to him. His loyalty to the Dembrows had been his life; and later, like any tired old dog wanting only to lie out his days in the sun, fearful of losing his place, he had curried favor with Ames, the son and heir, by covering up his many raw escapades from the Major. Yet Cody had to wryly admit, *Maybe we're not so different, Ed and me.*

Grymes' broad face was stamped with worry. "You have got the kid pinned in this place? No way out?"

"Not as I know of," Cody said dryly. "Ed, you tell the crew I'll give them four hours to get shut-eye; then we are heading out."

"Tonight?"

"Major's orders."

Grymes gave a surly grunt, wheeling away; he almost stumbled, and Cody thought with conviction then, *Why he's drunk.* Usually Grymes was a hard drinker off-duty, but only then, and he carried his liquor well. *Something is eating in him for sure. Now I wonder. . . .*

Cody turned in the sorrel, watered and grained him, and afterward headed for the main house. It was an old rambling fieldstone-and-'dobe affair which had housed Spanish grandees. He paused on the veranda to bat the alkali from his clothes and run a bandanna over his boots, then went in. The *sala* was a low room filled with dark heavy furniture and shadowy corners not touched by the lamplight that played on the bright woolen tapestries adorning the walls.

Trenna Dembrow sat in an armchair reading; she looked up in surprise and rose with a small, uncertain gesture. Cody said mildly, "I'm alone," as he shut the door behind him. "Could use something wet and ring-tailed."

"Welcome back," she smiled, moving toward the liquor sideboard. "Where is the Major?" Even under the mourning black she wore, she moved with a feline, full-bodied grace, and the warm tones of her face belied the prim bun in which she had done her pale hair. *The grieving widow.* Cody thought ironically. He scrubbed a palm over his unshaven chin; he briefly explained, and said then, "Reckon I had ought to clean up."

In his room he lighted the lamp and poured water into a basin. He peeled off his shirt and undershirt, scrubbed himself with a sliver of lye soap that seemed to take off as much hide as dirt and sweatsalt, then scooped up water and laved its wet coolness over his head and shoulders. It cut his exhaustion, and he was toweling himself briskly when Trenna came to the doorway. "I brought the drink here." The undercurrent of her voice was like a sibilant purr.

Cody sprawled at ease on the bed, his boots crossed, sipping the drink. She had brought him a cigar too, one of the thin pale brown Havanas that Ames had favored, and she held the match. A pleasant euphoria stole over him; he wanted to draw out and savor this moment, drinking Dembrow whiskey and puffing one of Ames' cigars lighted for him by Ames' widow. But Trenna's manner disturbed him; she stood with her hand on a bedpost, slowly twisting her palm on it, and something alert and feline in her gaze made his spine prickle.

"What is it?"

"We needn't pretend with each other," she said softly. "We know how it is with us. But one thing, Cody. I will never make a demure or docile little woman for any man. I have to burn hard and bright or I will go out entirely. I warn you now—don't try to lock me up as Ames did."

Cody considered, inhaling the fragrant smoke and letting it out; then he shook his head. "No, I'd never do that. I'd trust you with a free rein. Till I found I had cause not to.

81

Then I wouldn't lock you up, I'd break your pretty neck."

"Why—I believe you would." She leaned above him with a small fierce smile, and he put aside cigar and drink, and pulled her down to him. The perfumed softness and firmness of her yielded and clung; her hands at first gentle became tense and taloned. The stirrings of sound in her throat chipped dimly at the edge of his consciousness which all-resided now in the working hunger of her mouth. Finally she threw back her head, her eyes hot and heavy-lidded. Her smile was moist and tremulous. "If you could do what you said to me—then you can do what else needs doing, now."

He frowned, his fingers working on her soft arms. "What?"

"You can kill a man." She leaned into him whispering, "Think of how it will be, only the two of us. Or rather . . . Skull ranch and us."

Cody blinked. "The Major?" His scowl deepened; he pushed her away and swung slowly to his feet. "How long have you been thinking like that?"

"When I remembered that you are the Major's one surviving blood relative," Trenna murmured. "While I am Ames' widow—who could contest our joint claim?"

"Have you seen his will?"

"Who but Ames would be the heir? Ames is dead, and he hasn't made a new will."

Cody watched her face steadily, her skin deeply colored with excitement, her eyes bright and feverish, and he thought wryly, *A man misses a hell of a lot in a woman till something brings it out.* And he said: "Now how do I stack up alongside Skull ranch?"

"Don't be a fool." Trenna's voice was an angry outlash; she wheeled away a few steps, then turned on him impatiently. "I was thinking of us, and yes, Skull ranch—why not? Why else would I put up with Ames Dembrow, let alone marry him? Why have you bided your time here, hating them, swallowing your pride, if not hoping for a windfall? Don't deny that the idea has crossed your mind!"

"Maybe," Cody said. "Maybe it has, but a man can cover plenty of ground between thinking and doing."

"Cautious Cody," she gibed. "Or would afraid be a better word?"

Cody gnawed his lip, his thoughts narrowing. Often and restlessly he had toyed with the same idea, but never while Ames was alive in more than an idle and formless way. *But now there is only the Major.* "An old man," he muttered. "He won't live forever."

"He's not quite sixty. We could grow old ourselves waiting for nature to take its course; meantime what would we have?" Her skirt rustled to her quick step; she pressed against his arm, her voice a brittle hiss. "Do you think that he would consent to his bastard nephew taking his precious son's place with his son's wife? He's already enshrined Ames in his mind, and he would disown us both. I'm not waiting, Cody, for you or for a windfall. There are always greener fields for a woman while she keeps her face and body—they do not last forever."

"A man's neck," he said dryly, "can snap in just one second. They hang you for murder."

"Only if you let them catch you. Cody, those Gault brothers don't intend to give up; they will fight until they're dead. There will be plenty of shooting before you take them, and in the confusion a stray bullet could find the Major as easily as not."

He stared at her a long considering moment. "That could be a stiff risk."

"But worth the stakes." Her words were soft and breathing. "The men will think the Gaults got him—or say the bullet took him in the back of the head, who can say with certainty who fired it or that it was not an accident? When will you get another chance like that? Will you be scared, Cody? Will your hand shake?"

"I reckon everything has its price."

"Everything. But the terms can be very lenient." She breathed deeply, flushed with her victory. Her hands lifted, fumbling with her hair, and it fell in a whitegold mass to her shoulders.

He smiled faintly. "I only have four hours and I could use some sleep."

"Could you?" Trenna glided to the commode, and softly pursed her lips over the lamp. "Or are you being cautious again? We needn't be cautious now, Cody." She blew gently, and her voice sank with the lampflame.

# Chapter Eleven

The one or two hours of sleep that Calem had achieved before the attack came had not even blunted the edge of exhaustion. Though half-drugged for want of rest, he stayed on guard by a port till a cold murk of false dawn crawled across the world. Then he started, to find Miss Charley shaking him by the shoulder.

"You was sound asleep. I'm rested enough and I'll take over."

Earlier Calem had insisted that she get her sleep; now he gave only a dumb nod and groped through the paling darkness to his blankets. He lost consciousness within five seconds of stretching out. But the strain of a long night's violence and vigil made his sleep a restless pattern of gray dozings and fitful dreams.

When he came awake, again with a start, his head ached and there was a sour taste in his mouth. A mote-flecked gauze of midday sunlight patterned the floor; he smelled food and his stomach turned over. He got blearily to his feet, feeling the discomfort of stale, slept-in clothes, and started for the washstand. Miss Charley was by the fireplace stirring a simmering pot of beans, and she said without looking around, "Don't waste water, bub."

Calem groaned, remembering. He moved to the nearest port and stared dismally out at the empty slope and the shouldering slab that shielded Dembrow's camp. "You should of woke me."

"No need," she said brusquely. "A look-see down there now and then'll do for daylight. Sit down. I'll pour you some Triple X, and grub'll be on directly."

Calem had already noted that Jesse was sleeping peacefully, and checking on him now, found that his fever had broken. There was a fresh dressing on his thigh. Calem sat at the table and accepted the steaming coffee Miss Charley brought him. He nursed the scorching metal cup between his calloused palms and drank most of the scalding liquid. It was black and strong, and he felt better already.

"Thank you for changing the bandage. He looks a heap better."

"He'll do." She brought the bubbling pot to the table, holding it by a stick thrust under the bale handle. "One of them rode out after dawn. Across the valley and over the ridge. I studied him with your glasses. Big man with light hair."

*Cody*, Calem thought, and scowled into his cup. "He'd be going to fetch help. Major'll want more men."

She brought plates and forks and set the table, then sat opposite him before putting her hard turquoise eyes on him. "How long, do you reckon?"

"Depends, but I'd guess they will push." He ladled a generous helping of beans onto his plate. "A few days anyway. Anything else happen?"

"Only they sent that little old Sutter man up with his white flag asking could they take down them two we got last night. I said all right and a couple of 'em toted down the bodies. That was all." The faint pucker lines of a frown clouded her tan face. "That surely sets rough in a body's craw. You and me, we shot that one together."

"I shot somewhat before you," he said quickly.

"Maybe you missed. I made the mark all right." She lowered her eyes, turning her food slowly over with her fork. "I'm still hungry. Ain't that something?"

The alcove curtain parted and Ethan Jacks entered the room from the mineshaft, and took his seat with a bloodshot look at Calem. He filled his plate and began to eat, and there was no more talk.

Calem turned his thoughts to the dilemma that still faced him, trying to weigh and assess every angle. Dembrow could not know that a chance bullet had wiped out most of their water supply, or he might be willing to wait the few days necessary to give thirst its way. With abundant water they might have withstood a siege of indefinite duration, rushing tactics and all. *They won't try that again, not after last night, leastways just so. But it won't matter in a few days when we are too weak to fight them off.*

He considered the possibility of slipping out by darkness, getting his horse, and making a running break. That would at least toll Dembrow away from the Jackses, who might otherwise share his fate. Dembrow would not purposely harm a girl, but she could easily be hurt or killed before the last fracas was done. This fact alone almost crowded Calem to decision.

Several other considerations dampened the idea. Dembrow would almost surely post a night guard against such a contingency, and the alarm would be sounded at once; again he would be running ahead of the hound-keen senses of Abel Sutter, this time with only minutes between himself and the enemy. Even so, he might have accepted the risk for the others' sake. But Dembrow's ultimatum, as Ethan had received it from Sutter, included Jesse as well as Calem. And Jesse was in no condition to make the break. . . .

Calem had no doubt that Ethan had conveyed Dembrow's message accurately. The Major was simply restating the old law of clan vendetta. Blood to be paid in blood, and not merely the individual but all his male kin must render payment, the bloodline destroyed. Calem's own forebears had lived by that code for generations; a whole branch of the Missouri Gaults had been wiped out to a man in such feuds, and the legacy of bloody recountings his father had given him made a raw mark on his memory.

No. Even the danger to two people who had no stake in his quarrel, a reluctant and cantankerous man and a fiercely idealistic girl, could not outweigh his duty to a brother. The blood-feeling was deep in his own bones, and he could not leave Jesse alone to certain death.

"Ma'am," Jesse's weak drawl abruptly broke the silence, "I would 'preciate a cup of that java."

Turning his head, Calem saw with surprise that Jesse was fully awake. His color was good and his eyes were alight with dark impudence. Calem rose and went to the cot, his throat thickening as he took the hand his brother held out. "Jess . . . you look fine."

"Man most always does," Jesse said gravely, "when he is not used to being waited on by no angel and about to have the pleasure."

Miss Charley had come over with a cup of coffee. "I don't truck with a lot of fool taffy, mister," she said flatly. "It is known to melt on a hot day. Here." She thrust the cup into Calem's hands and returned to the table.

Jesse blinked a couple of times and had nothing to say as Calem, grinning, lifted his head and tilted the cup to his lips. For Jesse, that had to be a seldom reaction from a girl.

While his brother drank the coffee in sips, Calem described the situation. Jesse was attentive during the telling and asked a few questions, and then he yawned. "I 'vow, still weak as a half-drowned cat."

"You get some more sleep. Plenty time for talk."

Jesse nodded and sighed deeply; he shut his eyes, and soon his breathing grew deep and even. Calem stood by the cot for a while, looking down at the drawn and sleeping face. Once again the crushing hopelessness of his dilemma thrust home; it would be days before Jesse was in shape to move, and by then . . .

Ethan Jacks gave an irritable, hacking cough as he choked on a wrong-way mouthful. *You greedy old son of a bitch,* Calem thought in a sudden and unreasoning anger. *That girl must have had a fine ma, else her ma knew a better man than you.*

He felt a swift shame for the thought; besides, Ethan owed him nothing but trouble, considering what he had brought to Ethan's doorstep. But somehow it galled him to watch the miner noisily wolfing down his food in an obsessive sweat to get back to his damned tunnel.

*The tunnel.* The idea seemed to grenade full-blown into Calem's mind, and with an impact that left no room for doubt or hesitation. Instantly he crossed the room and ducked through the two curtains into the mineshaft. He found the lantern on a stull-achored peg by the entrance, and lifting it down, wiped a match alight and let the yellow flare pick out his way as he moved deep into the shaft. Reaching its end, he made some rough calculations in his mind's eye. He had not seen the far side of the ridge where shack and tunnel were sunk, but the ridge was not a sizable formation. Gauging the tunnel's length now, he thought with a mounting excitement, *It can be done.*

Footsteps grated over the littered floor as Ethan came down the tunnel into the lantern light, blinking and glaring his querulous suspicion. "What'n hell you up to?"

Calem said, "How long you reckon it would take to run this shaft clean through the ridge?"

Ethan continued to blink. He scratched his whiskers and muttered, "By God," and stepped past Calem, digging his fingers into the hardpan wall. He hefted a gob of soil in his fingers as if weighing the possibility. "By God," he said again.

"How long?"

"Depends what-all we run into. If nothing worse'n hardpan, say six yards to the outside, a couple-three days. But there's plenty rock in this stuff."

"We can work shifts," Calem said quietly. "Day and night till we're through. The Dembrow man that went after help should be over three days fetching it, there and back. By then my brother will be fit to ride. Our horses are in the canyon back of this ridge; allowing Jesse's hurt will mean slow riding, we got a good chance to make Mercyville if the Major don't size things right in a hurry."

Ethan scowled. "This tunnel ain't the safest place to roust about in, rotten timbers and falling rock. And we got no exter timbers to shore up as we dig."

"I'll dig alone if I got to," Calem said grimly. "And you won't stop me, old man. I ain't happy about fetching my trouble to you people, but it's fetched. I'm getting me and Jesse out alive happen I can, and you would do well to think on helping us on our way soon as can be. Before Dembrow rushes the place with a small army. Awhile after we're gone you can call to him we have got away; he can look back of the ridge for the tracks. He won't wait to settle with you since we're the ones he wants."

"He or some of his men are like to be back," Ethan snarled. "The way I have this place set up, they can guess about the gold. But I ain't got a choice outside kicking your ass down the hill first chance."

"You tried that once," Calem said coldly. "You got no choice at all. You going to help me?"

Ethan spat at a rock. "When that colt of mine takes a notion in her, there ain't no argufying. Otherwise I would 'low to get you one way or t'other. All right."

The bulk of the labor fell on Calem's shoulders, and he could put in a four-hour stretch of swinging a pick or heaving rock and hardly know a twinge. But he soon found that prolonged stints of heavy work left Ethan Jacks retching with fits of deep, shuddering coughs. It was apparent that he was a desperately sick man.

Considering that, and the fact that he must by now have accumulated a large hoard of nuggets or dust from his strike, he could surely afford himself a better life for what time he still had. Evidently the unalloyed greed of getting, and that alone, held a pure domination of the man. As yet Calem had seen no sign of gold, but the whole shaft was heavily test-pitted and he supposed that Ethan had exhausted some considerable sweat and cunning in finding and caching his metal.

Foot by foot they extended the tunnel, the stubborn hardpan yielding steadily to pick and shovel. It was a bitter and frustrating job that had to be tackled slowly: the dislodging of a key mass of earth or stone might cause them to be buried alive. They repeatedly ran into huge chunks of obstructing rock. They carefully, patiently dug around these and worked them free, and lifted or rolled them out of the way; Calem could hardly budge some of them.

Jesse appeared to be on the mend; he ate a little food, wanted as much water as could be rationed him, and got a great deal of sleep. At his request his cot was moved beneath one of the ports where, by being slightly propped up, he could maintain watch during his wakeful times. This, by sometimes relieving the need for Miss Charley's presence, enabled her to help with the digging.

By afternoon of the second day Calem was becoming aware of the biting strain of unremitting labor and snatched meals and too little rest. Ethan had just come back on the job after six good hours of sleep, and Miss Charley told Calem to quit for a while. "You'll be bedded down sick as your brother if you don't get a long sleep."

Calem shook his head; there was no time for more than snatches of sleep, but he returned with her to the shack for a hot meal. Jesse was asleep. Calem straddled a bench and tiredly leaned his head against his palm while she brought him coffee and beans and biscuits. Afterward she poured a cup of coffee for herself and sat opposite him, studying him with the merciless candor that at first had made him fidget. Now it seemed so natural to her that he barely noticed.

"For all you are homely as a rail fence in a mud storm," she said presently, "you got a hell of a pretty brother." Calem almost choked. She frowned as if considering the import of her words, then shook her head. "What I mean, you have got a plain kind of face." She promptly shook her head again, saying honestly, "Nope. It's homely. It is nice homely, what I mean to say. Sure like to watch it. Can't fancy your brother's face even if he is fine-lookin'. Just something about the two of you. So almighty different, even though a body can't miss you're brothers. It's sure funny."

Calem ate in silence for a full minute, and then said, "You come here with your pa after your ma died?"

"Shucks no, boy." She chuckled, an odd throaty little chuckle that it somehow tickled him to hear. "I hardly 'member my ma; she died a long time back. Old pa, he was allus a restless scamp, I 'member that right enough." The stormy little frown lines touched her brow. "'Mandy allus said that he drove her to her grave. Seems likely when I think on a lot of things. 'Mandy said that Ma just wore out following Pa's will-o'-the-wisps across the West. Reckon

89

she meant the mother lode. He was allus tracking down one story after t'other trying to locate the mother lode."

"Who is this 'Mandy?"

She said that Japh and 'Mandy Starrett had been an elderly couple who were the last citizens of a deserted mining camp where bonanza had come and gone. Ethan Jacks had left his ailing wife and small daughter with them. Shortly afterward Addie Jacks had died, and little Charlotte Lee had been raised in a remote, burned-out glory hole by an old couple too slowed and mellowed to discipline her. Of Ethan she had seen practically nothing over the years; he would drop in from nowhere without warning, buy a few supplies at the Starretts' trading post, and be off again on the heels of a fresh rumor.

About a year ago Ethan's wanderings had brought him to the isolated camp of an aged Mexican whom he found dying of cholera. He had cared for the man, easing his last moments. In gratitude, before he died, the Mexican had directed him to an aging, yellowed map hidden in his belongings which, the old man said, told the location of a lost mine in the territory, probably the northernmost of the old Spanish gold workings. At one time, when the Comanches began raiding heavily in the district, the Spaniards had their Indian laborers camouflage the mine entrance by building the facing wall of a prehistoric cliff tomb across it. Then they had cleared out with their jackloads of dust and nuggets. The Spaniards had never returned to their concealed mine; war came and in its wake the territorial cession to the United States.

One of those Spaniards had been his *patrón*, the old Mexican insisted; he had died a broken man in Old Mexico, tired and discouraged, certain that the *Yanquis* would only rob him of his mine if he came back to reopen it. He had left the map to his faithful servant who had come here and scoured the ridges for many months, but had not yet found the hidden mine when he had fallen ill. Then, Ethan Jacks had suggested, wasn't the map false? No, but a man needed younger legs to clamber among these ridges; he needed undimmed eyes to locate an almost invisible façade in a ridge which was only an imprecise cross on a map.

After burying the dead man, Ethan had found the mine in a few days. Then he had visited Starrett's post to buy supplies. It had been a long while since his last visit; Japh Starrett had died and 'Mandy had allowed she would return to her old home in the East and take Charlotte Lee with her and raise her to be a lady.

"I wasn't going to be no lady, I can tell you," Miss Charley said with satisfaction. "Oh, I was grateful to 'Mandy and all, but I said I would go where my pa went after this. Pa, he groused some about that, but after all's said, I reckon he was feeling a touch lonely."

Calem scraped up his plate. "Seems I heard you offer to leave him last night."

Miss Charley raised her tawny brows. "You're damned well told I mean to leave him. Old Japh and 'Mandy, they learned me what's right and what's wrong. Pa and me don't see things the same atall, and I have figured what 'Mandy meant, how he killed my ma by not giving a damn. I can make my own way in some city."

"Well," Calem said, and paused to finish his coffee. "You know, it is bound to be a sight different for you in cities."

"I reckon so. You ever been in one?"

Calem thought a moment. "St. Louis. We passed through St. Louis going West. I was a tad, and I remember the street lamps most. *Electric* street lamps, they was."

"Sure enough? What's those?"

Trying to explain, he appreciated his own mind as a storehouse of civilized knowledge, despite his blank areas, next to hers. It was her lack of everyday facts that he took for granted which surprised him most, things like *McGuffey's Eclectic First Reader* and grace before meals and who was the first U. S. president. Her interest was lively and unflagging, and he needed to mention no fact twice. Still her innocence of social cautions was enough to land her in a peck of trouble in civilized places and keep her there.

Calem smothered a yawn as he stood up; he said abruptly, "You know your pa has got wasting consumption?"

"No. What's that?"

"All that coughing, you didn't make nothing of it?"

She shrugged. "He allus coughs. What's wrong with that?"

"Well, there was an uncle I remember back in Missouri coughed that way. He had a consumption which he died of."

She was silent a long moment, her eyes lifting with a fierce grave honesty then. "Reckon I got to think about this."

He was starting for the tunnel when she said, "You best sleep a few hours."

He shook his head, saying, "Can't allow the time," and half-turned as he spoke. His eyes passed casually across Jesse's face and snapped back with a fine sense of shock as

91

Jesse swiftly shut his eyes. An instant earlier they had been wide open, even though he was motionless, his breathing deep and regular as if in sleep.

It had been no moment of drowsy half-waking, Calem knew; there had been a total, animal alertness in that look, and he thought, *He tried to cover that he was listening. But why?*

If it were Miss Charley's talk of the rich-bearing mine that had taken Jesse's attention, the answer to why he was feigning sleep was as unwelcome as it was obvious. The thought came to him with an intensity of conviction of which he was not proud, but which he could not shake away either.

# Chapter Twelve

When he returned to the tunnel he found Ethan in a blue temper, staring at the fresh excavation and cursing in a bitter, savage, monotonous tone.

"What is it?"

For an answer Ethan raised his pick and hammered it into the tunnel end. There was a solid clank of metal on rock, and the pick fell away without scoring. "We run smack into a dead wall, that's what."

The great rock slab was nearly level across its face, extending wall to wall and floor to ceiling, as they found by knocking the loose earth from its surface. It was a bitter blow to their hopes, perhaps a total block to more progress. Since the boulder was too large to move, they could only attempt to find the shortest way past it, over or under or around, and hope that the impediment did not prove fatally time-consuming.

Calem found, by striking off great chunks of earth to either side, that the block curved inward on the right side. He began doggedly to dig, burrowing out a low narrow corridor along the flank of the slab. To proceed farther he had to wedge his body into the passage and, with no leverage to spare, hack awkwardly with his pick at the gravel-laced hardpan. As it fell away, Ethan, squatting directly behind him, scooped up the dislodged earth in a pan and fed it backward into the tunnel.

This was slow and grueling labor, and a clogging weariness dragged at Calem's muscles. Each exertion began to cost him a conscious effort, and he wondered if the slab would ever end. A bitter discouragement deeper than any he had known yet settled in his belly. How long had they been at it already, and how much of their precious margin of time remained before Cody Dembrow returned? He felt on the verge of collapse, yet he dared not quit for even an hour. *One more hitch as mean as this block-up, and we're done for sure.*

"You goddam fool," Ethan burst out. "Watch what you're doing!" He almost upset Calem, diving his hands between

Calem's boots to paw wildly at the fallen earth. He brought up a piece the size of a marble taw and rubbed it on his sleeve. He raised it in a trembling hand, the light catching its dull sheen. "See what you almost made me lose, goddam you? That's *gold!*"

Calem blinked and drew a gritty sleeve over his sweating forehead. He saw his hand was trembling, and suddenly all the exhaustion and harried temper in him let go, snapped his patience like a tenuous, drawn-out thread.

"My life," he said thickly, "is a sight more important to me than your damned greed. Don't you whine to me, old man."

Ethan scrambled to his feet. He pulled a flat canvas pouch from his pocket and dropped the nugget inside, restoring the pouch to his pocket. Then he picked up a shovel and fisted it in both hands, snarling, "You dirty pup, I'm of a mind to wallop some manners into you."

Calem promptly emerged from the passage, gripping the pick, feeling the feral urge to smash at something. "Come on, old man. Show me some manners!"

Ethan backed off slowly, his wiry body sunk into an agile semi-crouch. "You touch a hair o' me and I'll split you wide open!"

"You go ahead and do it anyhow!"

"By God, I will!"

"Well, what you waiting for?"

"By God—!"

Over their shouting came a quick rush of feet, and then Miss Charley, flushed and furious, pushed between them. "You stop that right now! I never seen such a set-to over nothing." She wheeled on Calem. "You ought to be 'shamed of yourself, a big fellow like you picking on a little old man." Snatching the pick from his hands then, she gave him an angry shove toward the tunnel exit. "You ain't in no fit way to work. Get up there and cool off. And get some sleep, you hear?"

*"Little old man?"* bristled Ethan, and his voice brought a little sand and pebbles sifting down.

She swung on him, her eyes metallic. "Don't you dast lift your voice at me ever. I won't have it."

Ethan was sputtering like a chain of Chinese 'crackers, as Calem wearily passed out of earshot, trudging up the tunnel. But as he neared the exit he became, quite suddenly, alert and listening. The sounds as of someone rummaging about in the room ceased then, and an instant later he heard the

94

cot creak. *That was Jess,* he thought in amazement. *He is up and about.* And then he knew the real answer: *The gold for sure. He was hunting for old Jacks' cache.*

Calem felt a sickness heighten the mild dizziness of his exhaustion as he stepped into the room. Jesse was sitting up and looking idly out the port; he gave his ready smile. "Hi, kid. How's it go?"

"Poco-poco." Calem stepped to the other port; he looked out at the rocky slopes and ridges where the afternoon heat hung like a shimmering veil. "Jesse, I hope you can sit a horse in a day or so."

"Hope so," Jesse said laconically. "Fetch me a drink, will you, and a smoke?"

It was a bitter confirmation. *Sure I will, just as if you couldn't get about.* He brought a cup of water, and Jesse's makings. Then he sat on the bench, set his elbows on his knees and laced his fingers together, grimly determined that the time had come to square them away. "Jess, I want to talk."

Jesse drank sparingly of the water, then began to fashion a cigarette. "Talk away."

"I been thinking about after we got out of this. I mean way after, when we have shook Dembrow off and can worry about something else."

Jesse nodded absently. "Like what?"

"Well, like where can we go from there. I had thought you might have an idea or two."

"Hell." Jesse expertly shaped and sealed the smoke. "You go find Ma, and I'll go back to . . ." He gestured vaguely with a match as he thumbnailed it into flame and touched it to his cigarette.

"I guess there's no need to say it," Calem agreed dismally. "I was hoping you would want to stick by."

Jesse waved out the match, squinting at him with a wondering irony. "Why, I thought it was clear. Don't go trying to make me over, Cal."

"Jess—damn you! Don't you ever think ahead?"

"A man always does, and I read the trail sign a long ways back." Jesse's eyes pinched half-shut against the smoke. "Some place there's a knife or bullet with my name on it. A man follows his nature, and it ain't a question of knowing. I may be stoking fodder for old Satan, but I mean to burn my own way till then."

Calem said flatly, "Time comes even a fiddlefoot has got to take root."

95

"So much for yours," Jesse said irritably. "Now leave me to mine, will you?"

"Hell," Calem said, his frayed temper snapping again. "You never done anything a lick of good, not even yourself. Ma, I never seen her take a thing but grief on your account. I'll grant you stuck by me a while—"

"You don't need to," Jesse cut in. "You pulled me through the desert, that squares it, by God, so don't think you'll tell me my business!"

"I won't again," Calem said tautly, and came to his feet. "So long as your business don't touch these people. It's on my account you're here, and anything bad coming of it is on my head too. I know why you was rousting about before I come in; I ain't forgetting it, so you better not."

Jesse's gaze darkened; he said very softly, "I won't, boy, you can bet on it," and snapped his cigarette to the floor in a shower of sparks. He rolled on his side, presenting his back.

Calem tramped to his bedroll and stretched out, throwing an arm over his eyes. He should not, when he was desperately in need of rest, have undertaken a crucial talk with Jesse. Yet, though he told himself that the damage done by the hot exchange could be undone in a cooler moment, he had the sinking sense that they had crossed a shadowy line of no return. That the talk had marked the end of something. . . .

Sleep came imperceptibly, even as he was thinking that he would not sleep now. A sleep that was deep and dreamless, with all sense of time and urgency blunted. He came drowsily and pleasantly awake, and was fully alert before he remembered and sat up with a start.

It was morning, and the smells of frying bacon and fresh coffee grabbed at his belly. He was not only fully rested but more ravenous than he had felt in days. Ethan, glowering at his food as he ate, did not look up as Calem sat down and Miss Charley brought his plate of food.

"You should of woke me long ago," he said gruffly. "This ain't no time to catch up on sleep."

"You wasn't in no shape for much else," she said tartly. "Pa and me got plenty done meantime."

He only nodded and bent to his plate; otherwise in argument he would have to look at her, and because he suddenly wanted to, he somehow could not. For the first time she had put on a right sort of dress made of a blue-and-white-checked calico. The skirt only hinted demurely at the flaring hips, but the bodice stressed the swelling breasts, confining the straining contours of them in a way which indicated that the dress, though bright and new, had been sewn for a younger girl. The tangle of her short hair had been combed out to a smooth palegold and tucked back of her ears by a blue ribbon. With the sharp contrast of her golden-brown skin and eyes of gunsteel blue, she hit a man's eyes about twice as hard as a girl who was merely pretty, which she still was not.

He caught Ethan shuttling looks between Miss Charley and him, causing him to brace himself for another waspish display. But strangely, Ethan looked more thoughtful than outraged.

When he and Ethan went together into the tunnel, Calem found that substantial progress had been made in his absence. A deep passage now curved entirely around the blocking slab and continued a full yard behind it. For a while they worked steadily, Calem whacking at the hardpan with careful strokes of the pick while Ethan scraped out the loosened earth, both freezing to immobility whenever a clod of earth or a trickle of pebbles fell from the sides or from above, which was often. At any moment a whole section of the unshored wall might collapse without warning.

"Enough for now," Ethan said before long. "Come on out."

"No time."

"No time, hell!" There ain't over a yard to go by my calc'lations. We don't want to bust out by daylight, and she won't be dark for hours. Come out of there. Got things to say."

The two of them worked back to the original tunnel area where there was plenty of good safe shoring and room to stretch. Ethan sank down on his spare haunches and produced a stubby pipe, motioning Calem to a rock. He sat down, leaning on the pick.

When he had his pipe going, Ethan said truculently, "I decided. Ain't safe for Miss Charley and me here even after you're gone. Them yahoos you led here know of the place and have figured by now that something like gold is the reason for it."

Calem stared at the ground in the pool of lantern light. "Reckon it's time I said I'm sorry, though you won't give a damn about that."

"Don't be so goddam sure of yourself," Ethan said testily, and Calem looked up in surprise. "Time you got something straight in your head. Ain't but one thing under the sun means a whoop to me, and that's her. My girl." At

Calem's openly skeptical look, he nodded grimly. "The other night when they come up the hill and you handed her a rifle, she could of got killed. You think of that?"

Calem lowered his eyes. "I did afterward."

"I thought about it then, and plenty since. It had been in the back of my mind, but it hadn't stuck so hard till then, knowing she could be hurt or killed." Ethan's pipe had gone dead, but he made no move to relight it. "I follered the rainbow for most of my life, and now I found the pot of gold, it don't mean a damn thing but one. It can do for Charley, give her a grand living, good schooling too if she wants it."

"Grand living?" Calem was skeptical still. "You had a chance to give her just a good life, her ma too, plenty of chance. It's like she said, you never cared for nothing but yourself. Ain't that so?"

"It's so. Had my reasons for changing. I'm dying, Gault." Ethan mechanically tucked away his pipe. "Last year over on the Yellow I got shot by a claim jumper. Bullet is still in me. Went through my lungs and is so near my heart the sawbones wouldn't go after it. Told me a blow, something sudden like that, could kill me. Then I got consumptive. Only a question of time, and I want enough gold to see her fairly off." He shook his head. "That's all of it, Gault. Gold don't shine for a dying man. But I have put away enough now that we can afford to pull out. We'll go with you."

Calem was puzzled. "Seems you might better wait till we are gone and Dembrow after us. You got every reason to want to get shed of us."

"You know the word of God, Gault?"

Surprised by the oblique question, Calem said slowly, "The Good Book? Hope so."

Ethan frowned, leaning forward and crossing his arms on his knees. "My girl is shy as a colt on knowing the world. She is wild, sure enough, but like a fawn is. It is like she never ate of that fruit the Book tells of, and if somebody she fancied told her something it would be gospel to her." Ethan shifted on his haunches. "I can make her well off, but I won't be around long. Sooner or later there will be a man. Wrong man could get her into a peck of trouble and nobody to stop it. Nobody but the right man, that is. Reckon you see now."

"No."

Irritably Ethan spat over his shoulder. "Goddam it, I am saying you're the man, Gault. I been watching you. Handle yourself choicely well, and it is plain you still believe in

God and goodness. There ain't never too many like you, so I am speaking out plain. I want your promise. Watch out for her, Gault. Take care of her."

Calem said, hedging, "She wouldn't hardly like that, you know."

"Not off anybody, no," Ethan snapped. "That dress, though. 'Mandy Starrett made her that one nice dress a spell ago and she never wore it. She wore it for you, boy, to set herself off. You're 'most of an age with her; like calls to like, and that's as it should be. If there was ever a strong thing between you, I know you would do right by her. All I want to know now, do you like her well enough to see after her?"

"Yes sir, I—I guess I do. But I got nothing to give her."

"Gold will take care of that. You take care of her."

Calem shook his head in bleak negation. "No. It ain't no good. There's Major Dembrow, and there will be hell to pay when he catches up. I can't promise anything, knowing that."

"Suppose you never had to meet him? Suppose you knew that?"

"I don't hardly see no way around it."

Ethan thumbed back his wreck of a hat. "I got a way maybe. Nor'east of here about a half-day ride there is a good piece of wild mountain country that ain't been touched except by Injuns, mountain men, surveyors and a few drifting men like me. A good ten years ago I was back in there and came on a great wide canyon with cliffs all around. Ain't but one trail to the bottom. There is plenty woods and grass in there, and good water. Plenty game, even stream fish. Struck me that with a few needs like shells and salt, a man could live in such a place for years and never be found out." He paused. "But you wouldn't need to stay there past two-three months till things quieted down. Then you could pull stakes for anywhere you had a mind to."

Calem said nothing for a full thirty seconds, turning the idea over carefully. Ethan's proposition dovetailed with an increasing reluctance he had felt about going on to Mercyville, and there, with punitive law at his back, waiting for Dembrow and the showdown. He had already felt the gray distaste of embroiling the Jackses in his trouble; involving still others was bound to result in killing. Or he might forestall the final clash by running, always running, one step ahead of a man whose tenacious passion would let him bide his time for months, perhaps for years, while he hired detectives to track down Calem Gault wherever he went, under whatever name. Ethan had offered a way to cut off the relentless pursuit, swiftly and surely, and postpone a showdown for good.

But he said: "That Abel Sutter, he can track an ant to its hole."

Ethan's denim-colored eyes glinted. "Can he track a bird? I can lead him over stretches he can't pick sign on because there won't be none."

"It sounds good, sir. Thank you."

"Got no thanks coming. I'm seeing to your neck on my girl's account."

"Mr. Jacks, I am curious on one thing. You have talked like you expect to be leaving her shortly."

"Man in my shape could any time, told you that." Ethan had started to rise, but now he sank back on his haunches. "Hell. You're right. I will see you to the canyon, then push on. Last my girl will see of me. Best that way."

"Sir, that is a mistake," Calem said bluntly. "So is not telling her about your condition."

"How you know that?"

"She wouldn't of said she was leaving you if she knew. She ain't that kind. She is the kind would want to know. She wouldn't thank you for keeping it from her."

Ethan grimaced as if he had bitten into something sour. "You heard what she thinks of her pa. Whatever she wants, I ain't got it to give. Too late to find out."

"What she wants," Calem said slowly, "is to know her pa is got a feeling for her. What you got to give is time, the time you got left. Was I you, I would spend it with her. Let her know you ain't the man you was. She would want to know that too, more than anything."

Ethan looked shaken; he said, "Damn you, Gault. No more o' that." He stood briskly, hefting his shovel. "We will bust the tunnel through when dark comes. I can get us out of here then without being caught out. You got two horses. We will put your brother on one and take turns riding the other."

Calem had been worried about the horses. "Surely hope Dembrow ain't found them."

"No fear of that. The canyon back of the ridge where they are is hid good, plenty water and grass. They will be rested and feeling sassy." Again Ethan's gaze was hard and shrewd as he fastened it on Calem. "I will turn the gold over to you before we split company. But mark you this: that brother of yours wants the gold. Has been scrounging about looking for it every chance. Got a feeling he would kill me for it. Might even kill you for it, Gault."

"No," Calem said coldly. But after a moment as the words sank in, he added almost angrily, "Anyway I'll be watching him."

# Chapter Thirteen

Cody Dembrow, heading up the bulk of the Skull crew, rode into his uncle's camp at sunset. They were a tired and temper-edged lot as they offsaddled by the seep and walked their horses up and down before watering them. The ranch cook had accompanied them leading a pack animal laden with supplies, and he promptly set to unloading his utensils. Cody assigned a couple of men to remove a bulky case from the back of another pack horse, then tramped over to where Major Dembrow stood.

The Major was bareheaded; a warm twilight wind toiled with his white hair, and there was something tense and implacable in his stance. He said in a clipped and dispassionate way, "The dynamite, Cody."

Cody motioned toward the pack horse the two men were unloading, then fell in behind the Major as he walked over. "Careful with that," Cody told the men sharply. "You ain't handling Roman candles."

They gingerly set the case down, and the Major bent over, peering at the stenciled letters across the top: *Danger—High Explosives. This side up. No. 1 Dynamite—1¼ x 8 in. 50 lb.* "I got some blasting caps and fuses in my gear," Cody said.

"I know nothing about setting off dynamite," the Major said curtly. "But I have a use for it now. You've handled the stuff."

"Sure." Cody paused, glancing up at the loaf-shaped ridge where the cliff dwelling nestled under a heavy overhang. "You want to pull that rim down?"

"As I've said before, no," the Major snapped. "I don't want to bury them; I want to take them alive if possible. I want you to blow in the front of that stone shack."

"I won't need fifty pounds of dynamite to knock down a little mortared wall," Cody said dryly.

The Major's hand made a chopping gesture of impatience. "How much?"

Cody paused, considering. "Can't get near enough to set a proper charge so the explosion is contained. Still, if a man got above them on that ridge, fused a charge and dropped it by the wall—I reckon one cartridge might breach it and not hurt anybody inside much. That's maybe, Major. A proper set one would blow them to kingdom come, that's for sure."

"The chance they take by refusing to surrender," Jeffrey Dembrow said. "However, before you drop the charge, I'll call out my intention and give them a final opportunity."

Abel Sutter had sidled noiselessly up beside them. He tipped back his hat, snuffling the air like a hound; he said, "Be rain before long. Aplenty of it."

"Tonight?" the Major demanded.

"About midnight."

Jeffrey Dembrow rubbed his chin. "A heavy overcast of clouds should be of considerable help. We'll wait till then."

Cody unsaddled his mount and carried his gear off to one side. He spread out his soogans, tugged off his boots and, stretching out, folded his hands back of his head and let all his muscles go slack. He watched the last tinge of twilight give way to full night that dyed the sky to deep indigo and gave a solid shape of blackness to the land. The men had built up a half-dozen small fires and sat in slack clusters around them.

Over by the cook's fire the Major sat tailor fashion with his foreman, Ed Grymes, and now Cody caught the abrupt, harsh lift of his uncle's voice: "Damn it, Ed, what do you mean by it's not too late to turn back?"

Grymes stirred uneasily on his haunches. "Nothing, Major. 'Cep'n I would purely hate to see you get in trouble on this account. With the law, sir, and that's all I meant to say."

The Major's answer was sharp with irritation, and following a crushed silence Grymes rose and walked to where his gear lay. He opened his blanketroll almost furtively, took a flask from its folds and uncapped it and drank deeply.

Grymes had not drawn a wholly sober breath in these two days on the trail, and by now Cody could think with certainty, *Yes sir, a conscience-killer for sure*. He had a fair idea why, remembering Trenna's conviction that Grymes had lied for Ames to cover up the real manner of Jared Gault's killing. Grymes, a simple man, was usually guided in his actions by a code of starkly defined ethics, and granted that Trenna was right, these had to be goading him fiercely. Idly Cody wondered whether Ed would finally crack and tell the Major the truth. Not that it would matter, if he knew

Jeffrey Dembrow. Calem Gault, whether extenuated in the act or not, had killed the Major's son, and to that there could be only one answer.

The rising moon turned a face of bland serenity to the rocky scape, making indefinite patterns of outline and detail. The calm clear night and the cool unstirring air made Cody wonder if Sutter had been wrong about the storm. At this stage it would make no difference; the Major was bound to determined to write off the Gault brothers tonight and God's own wrath would not stop him.

Cody covered the thin smile that fluted his lips, by pulling a cigar from his vest pocket and clamping his teeth on it. He too had a man to kill, and getting his chance meant abetting that man's interests up to a point. . . .

How would it be, putting a bullet into the one who, as far back as memory reached, had put the clothes on his back and the food in his belly? The thought was not pleasant, but since he hated the man, not intolerable either. Yet, weighing all things, even the self-admission that Trenna's direct solution was not entirely novel to his pattern of thinking, he knew that she herself had cinched the matter. Once Trenna was in a man's system, the drug of her blended into his feelings and thoughts till he could no longer separate them in his mind. Knowing what she wanted, he also knew against all misgiving what must be done.

Yet his deep streak of pessimistic caution made him scowl over an obvious dilemma. No matter how adroitly he handled it, the Major being struck down by an unknown hand would automatically open three avenues of speculation: accident, a Gault bullet finding its mark, or a possible motive among those in the Major's own party. If Cody, the next of kin, were in a too-convenient spot when the fatality occurred, no matter that nobody could prove a thing, the inevitable stain of suspicion would follow Trenna and him all their lives. Besides, he was no gunman.

*Then hire one.* The thought nudged him as he struck a match for his cigar so that he only stared at the match then, watching it burn down. Of course; hire a man for the job and make a foolproof alibi for himself. *But who?*

He let his gaze idle across the groups of crewmen, their rough, bearded faces sallowed by dancing firelight, giving each man in turn a brief or prolonged study. There were some tough hardcases in this lot, and all them were held by money and not by loyalty to Skull or the Major. A man had to care about his crew to inspire loyalty, and the Major did not. He paid gun wages for possible gun jobs—a man understood as much when he hired on.

He must choose his man with care, Cody knew; he could not discount the danger of a wagging tongue or some judicious blackmail later on. He needed a solid understanding in advance with the man he approached. His gaze touched Frenchy Duval and rested there.

The Cajun was sitting with four others, joking with them. His grin was white and startling in his dark-skinned face, a grin that had always made Cody think of a wolf baring its fangs. Perhaps Duval was no more than a human wolf; there were men like that, living for the next time they could savor the smell of blood, and an element of danger made it sweeter. Things had been fairly tame for Duval since his coming to Skull. *A long while between times for him,* Cody thought, and then: *Well, what do you care? He won't get cold hands and botch it.*

The savory odors of food and coffee were filling the still air, and the men began filing past the fire, filling their cups and loading their plates from the Dutch oven.

"You better get some rest, Uncle Jeff," Cody drawled.

Jeffrey Dembrow was drinking coffee by the fire. He said, "Rest," and gave a hollow and bitter laugh. He pitched the rest of his coffee into the fire, gave a curt shake of his head as the cook held out a plate of food, then walked off a short distance to stare into the night.

Cody ate unhurriedly, and as he finished and stood, caught Duval's eye and tilted his head toward the shadows beyond the firelight where the spring was. Gathering up his few utensils, he tramped down to the water. He squatted, scoured his plate with sand and rinsed it in the murky water. Duval moved up beside him now, squatting to wash his own utensils. Not quite looking at him, Cody murmured, "The Major will shake down a hornet's nest when he catches up with young Gault. Lead hornets. Can't say who might get stung."

Duval's narrow shoulders shook to his silent chuckle. "Ah yes, even the Major, eh? How long you and her take to come to this, eh?" He raised a hand swiftly. "Soft, my friend; nothing to make the fuss on. Frenchy misses not a thing. It is my business to watch and know. The others, these clods, they guess nothing."

Cody forced a smile. There was an obvious advantage to confiding in a man who had already guessed the truth. Shrewd and unscrupled, Duval had no cause but himself, and a habit of sniffing out every crosswind to that end. He also, Cody suspected, had an infinite talent for gauging how his assessments could be bent to his own use.

"You can see why the idea has me bothered, Frenchy," he murmured. "If an accident should happen to the Major and a man who stood to gain by it were close to him at the time, folks might wonder. A man has got to think of them things."

"But yes, I understand this concern of yours well." Duval delicately stroked a finger over his mustache. "On the other hand, if a man who could not gain by this so-unlucky accident chanced to be close, nobody would think twice, eh? Still for being so close then, I think he too must gain. Ah, a great deal."

"Whatever he wants, so long as I can stay sure of him. A man like that would know too much."

Duval gave a small, expressive shrug. "A man, even one like that, cannot stay on the move forever. The years cool the blood and give him an eye for the main chance. This oaf Grymes. Skull ranch deserves a better foreman."

Again Cody's thin smile. Later Duval might find he wanted still more, but that could be dealt with in its good time. For now he had considered it a good bargain; Duval would make a useful and competent right hand when Cody came into his own at Skull. Being equally involved, they could trust each other absolutely.

"I couldn't agree more," Cody said.

"Ah. And I wager that if you owned Skull you would replace him with a deserving man."

"Why, I'm sure of it."

"So am I." Duval chuckled, his teeth a chalky glimmer in the dim light. "So am I, my friend. . . ."

# Chapter Fourteen

Well after darkness had settled, Calem Gault and Ethan Jacks attacked the last impediment of earth and rock that barred the tunnel's end. Within the hour they had broken through, the loose surface soil collapsing into the tunnel and baring a ragged patch of cobalt sky.

There was no time to lose, for earlier they had spotted Cody Dembrow returning with the rest of the Skull crew. Now, with all of his men at his back, the Major would surely not delay another night.

Calem and Ethan returned to the shack, where Miss Charley had all the gear they would take packed and ready. Now she went ahead through the tunnel to fetch the two Gault horses from the little canyon back of the ridge where she had left them. Ethan, fussing like an old woman, told Calem to help his brother while he, Ethan, took care of a tag-end or two still hanging fire. Calem guessed that those tag-ends involved the Jacks cache. Ethan's lifelong prospector's instinct, narrow and suspicious to the last, would not let him betray even a cache place that he would never use again, despite his self-proclaimed intent of turning over the store of gold to Calem.

Helping Jesse out of his bed, Calem assisted him into the mine passage. Jesse muttered between his teeth, "Damn old miser," as he edged gingerly along holding his game leg stiff.

Calem said nothing. He knew, from what both he and Ethan had deduced concerning Jesse's sly and abortive search for the gold, that his brother's leg was fairly mended. He was feigning the degree of lameness still hampering him, and Calem could only accept this knowledge with a bitter patience.

When they emerged on the far side of the ridge, and he had eased Jesse to the ground, Calem stretched his arms and tipped his face to the night sky, savoring the good taste of freedom after the days and nights in the confinement of the shack and tunnel. He noticed that a cool wind had dipped off the ridges. Masses of dense clouds were building

107

darkly along the horizon and were scudding rapidly ahead of the wind; soon they would obscure the moon overhead. The air had a fretful and oppressive texture, forecasting the violence of the coming storm. It might have worked to Major Dembrow's advantage had they remained; now the reverse would be true.

Presently Ethan emerged from the tunnel toting his and Miss Charley's belongings. He dumped them to the ground, saying tersely, "All right, Gault, you and me'll fetch yours out," by which Calem knew that the gold had already been transferred to Ethan's person or possessions.

One trip back sufficed to bring out his and Jesse's things, along with a bait of grub that Ethan had thrown together. As they left the tunnel for the last time, Miss Charley appeared leading the two horses. In a few minutes they had gear and supplies cinched in place. With Jesse and the girl mounted on the horses, they left the ridge for a deep gulf of shadows that yawned below. By now the sable clouds were massing overhead and the moon was lost; but Ethan had no difficulty picking out his way across the stony scape, down black steep washes and around lofty spurs of rock. Calem guessed that he had mapped a back door through the broken ridges long ago, against any chance emergency.

It seemed a long time before they came onto a fairly regular belt of open slope, and Ethan took an easy way along its gentle grade. He opined that the rock-laced route they had just negotiated would throw off that breed tracker. Calem, walking beside him, silently doubted it; and then Ethan added, "But that hellsmear of a storm that is building will wipe out our sign anyways."

Glancing over his shoulder at Jesse and his daughter riding a good dozen paces to their rear, he lowered his voice. "Got a bad feeling. That damn' brother o' yours. Listen. I hid gold in one o' your saddlebags."

"Mine—"

"Shush your loud mouth," Ethan hissed fiercely. "Yours. Save me handing it over later—and with him looking on. He won't never guess you already got it unless you bray it out."

Calem said with an uncomfortable lack of enthusiasm, "You been calling my brother some hard things in front of the fact, old man."

"All right, you wait on the fact," Ethan said grimly. "Just mind you don't give him your back meantime."

On the heel of his words came a flat and not-distant boom, followed by a deep reverberation that trembled the

108

earth. It had the kind of ground-quaking quality that sometimes came with nearby thunderclaps, but there had been no lightning.

Then Ethan grunted, "Dynamite. He wants to make sure of us in the worst way. Means he will know shortly we're long gone."

The first fat drops of rain began as they forged into the teeth of the wind, Ethan pointing them northeast toward the big canyon where they would lay up for as long as seemed necessary to throw Dembrow off the Gaults' trail. And now, as they struck across open country, the storm began in earnest. Calem and Jesse had their slickers and Ethan had fashioned a pair of canvas ponchos for himself and Miss Charley.

When they halted to don their waterproofing, Calem thrust his slicker at the girl, saying almost roughly, "Here, you'll be better off in this. Swap you."

"I don't need no favors."

His jaw hardened. "I am looking out for you from here on, and we might as well get straight on how it's to be. You wear this."

Sitting horseback she stared down at him, her eyes squinted against the wind. "I ain't your lookout. I never asked to be." She spoke quietly, without the lashing anger he had expected.

"That don't make no difference." He continued to hold out the slicker in his fist, and finally she took it and silently passed down the poncho.

The rain slashed in milky sheets against their bodies as they pressed on; despite the poncho Calem soon found himself soaked as the saturated air sent damp fingers probing to every dry inch of clothing and skin. Even in slickers, he knew, Jesse and the girl must be nearly as drenched. But the discomfort of cold and wetness was nothing to the welling relief of certainty that their tracks would be eradicated by the torrents of rain. Let Ethan have his brag of throwing off the pursuit; Calem was only sure now of the throwoff. Held to a slow pace by two of them being afoot, they could be swiftly overtaken but for the rain. If the storm lasted only an hour longer, they would have covered enough distance to safely discount even the likelihood that by fanning out trackers Dembrow could pick up the trail when the rain had ceased.

After a while that earlier feeling of exultance passed off like the belly-glow from a shot of whiskey. The first windy plummets of rain ebbed into a steady downpour that it seemed would last forever. The unvarying buffet of drumming water through long hours of feeling out your way in a slate-colored oblivion of rainy darkness ate like a drug into your plodding body and mind, and the chill of a pounding wind taloned into your soaked carcass till your flesh went almost gratefully numb.

It must have been close to false dawn when the last pelting gusts slacked off and Ethan called a stop on high ground, close by a dense motte of young pine. Here they offsaddled and picketed the horses, then set to scouring up dead wood. The fire was built in a sheltered pocket girdled by trees and boulders, and with the dry heartwood from a deadfall they made it big and roaring, for all were half-frozen, their teeth chattering. They had wrapped any spare clothes in the ground tarps lashed with their soogans, and these had kept fairly dry.

While the girl slipped behind a rock with her small bundle, the men shed their wet clothes and changed quickly. Ethan said, "We'll .split the watch. You want to toss for the first?"

Calem shook his head. "No, I'll take it."

Jesse, who was spreading out his tarp and blankets, glanced at them. "I'll sit up a spell."

"I don't reckon you will," Calem said. "There's your leg. It'll want all the rest you can get."

Their glances locked, and the hint of a smile grooved the wry corners of Jesse's mouth. *He knows,* Calem thought. *Let him sleep on it.* For his own part, he didn't think there would be much sleep tonight.

Ethan was not slow in yanking off his boots and rolling into his blankets, and he and Jesse were both asleep apparently at once. Calem spread out his tarp by a rock, wrapped himself in his blanket and settled his back to the rock, rifle across his outstretched legs.

Miss Charley returned to the fire and propped her wet dress, together with her long leggin-moccasins and an unmentionable or two, on sticks near the flames where the men's clothes were likewise placed. She had changed to another, but dryer, short-skirted dress; her legs and feet were bare, and the flames made a rosy smoothness of the pale flesh. He felt uncomfortably warm; he looked at the sky, then at the ground.

Leaving the fire, she came directly over to him, making him look up. She was holding out the slicker. "I'm obliged," she said tonelessly, but there was a curious frown on her

110

brow. Unhesitatingly she let the slicker fall, then dropped to her knees beside him, leaning fully into him as her face dipped to his. The young lips came hard into his; her mouth felt dry and awkward, but soon parted with a caressing succulence. The rifle fell aside unnoticed as his hands dropped to the skirt and felt the warm roundness of her flexed sturdy thighs, the hard smooth curves of her bare calves, while she knelt.

She promptly clouted him across the head, though not very hard, and came to her feet in a spare motion. "That's all," she said matter-of-factly. "I was curious about something." Going to where her blankets were, she spread them a proper distance from the fire, stretched out with a lazy, feline yawn, and covered herself. "G'night. Keep a good watch." She placed her back to him and tugged the blanket over her head.

Calem shook himself and picked up his rifle. The wild millrace of his heart had slowed, but his hands were still shaking. He felt dazed and stupid, and it was too late to ask what she had been curious about.

He had not intended to muse, since once he began woolgathering sleep usually came quickly. But with Charley Jacks' hot sweet kiss still provoking the fantasies of warm immediacy, he did muse. He soon dozed too, and the rifle slid groundward and his head bowed against his knees.

A savage, muffled curse shredded the mist around his brain; he came to confusedly, blinking against the fitful flamelight. It took him three full seconds to realize that Ethan and Jesse were tussling together on the ground, thrashing and grunting. Even as Calem lunged upright, he saw Jesse's fist, weighted by a pistol, rise and fall in two swift, down-clubbing blows. There was a single choking sound as if a man were reaching for his last breath; then Jesse rose, his lips peeling off his teeth as he swiveled around with the pistol leveled. But the muzzle had not come to bear on Calem when the latter's rifle froze him in place.

Calem said, "Throw it away," and Jesse, with a crooked smile, tossed the gun into the rocks.

Miss Charley had scrambled out of her blankets to reach the still form of her father. He was limp, with a crumpled waxen look, as she shook him, then laid her ear to his chest. "There ain't no heart," she whispered, turning a white face toward Calem. "I think he is dead."

Jesse's smile began to fade. "Hell, he couldn't be."

111

"You lay out flat and face down," Calem said. "Hands behind your head. Do it now."

Jesse's eyes searched his brother's face; whatever he saw there made him obey without more words. Only then, Calem moved to Ethan Jacks and stooped down to verify the girl's words.

"Jess. Where you hit him."

"Hell, I rapped him on the chest once and on the jaw, was all," Jesse said angrily. "Let me look."

Calem came very slowly to his feet, feeling the girl's intent eyes but not meeting them. "That's wrong," she said with a soft insistence. "He can't be. I meant to tell him I was sorry for what I said before. I didn't mean that about leaving him. I got to tell him."

Calem was looking at the handful of Ethan's belongings scattered around, his rucksack lying open where Jesse must have dropped it when Ethan had caught him rifling the contents. Looking at the girl, Calem shook his head. "His heart was fixed to go any time. He told me himself. Never wanted you to know."

She made a little throaty sound; she came around with the agility of a young animal, going after the rifle that lay by her tarp. Calem, expecting this, reached the weapon in time to pin it with his boot. She whirled to her feet, beating her fists against his chest and screaming, "Just because he is your goddam brother!"

He did not argue; he barely hesitated before bringing his big fist around in a short sharp arc that ended behind her left ear. Without a sound she went limp. He caught her and lowered her to the ground, keeping his rifle awkwardly trained on Jesse.

"Get up," he told him, and Jesse edged cautiously to his feet.

Oddly for one long moment another scene of long ago passed before Calem's mind's eye, not with the flickering uncertainty of most boyhood memories, but with the vividness of yesterday. On the night that their grandfather had died on the Missouri farmstead, the large brood of his children and grandchildren had been gathered weeping or silent at his bedside. And Aunt Willa had said softly, "Now he's safe with Jesus." It was Calem's mother, stung by grief too, who had said sharply, "How do you know that, Willa? Because he was your paw?"

Martha Gault was a quiet farmwife, but now and again Calem had seen her rebel against the simple black-and-white

112

judgments of her people. Of course Gramps had been a blasphemous, tippling old heathen to the very last, but Martha had not meant that; she had simply undercut the clannish conviction that your own kin were on the side of the angels no matter what. It was, as Calem had found, one of the hardest convictions to shake.

You could grow almost to manhood with a brother and bear witness to his all-around helling, even hear confirmation of it from his own lips, and still a part of you would not believe. For of all the people he knew, a man knew his kin the least, accepting only what he wished to concerning them.

Martha Gault had worn no blinders where her elder son was concerned; she had the gift of seeing the people she loved in a cruel white light and not loving them a jot less because of it. She had seen the irremediable drift of Jesse's whole life clearly, and had warned Calem at their parting. Now, fully understanding, he felt something die in him, hard and forever.

"I'm going to ride out of here," Jesse said gently. "You'll have to kill me to stop me, and you ain't got the guts for it."

"Likely not. You'll ride out presently, all right."

"You think you'll take me to trial, you mean. Think again."

"No," Calem said tonelessly. "Not that. You'll ride out alone."

Jesse's thin, jeering smile formed. "So you'll turn me loose. I gave you credit for 'most no guts, and you got even less."

"You could be right," Calem conceded slowly. "A man can't shoot his brother, or let someone else shoot him, or take him in to maybe get hanged. Law might not allow it was an accident, where I'd allow you that much. I am. There's still what you tried to do, rob a man, and him dead because of it." He paused. "What I aim to do, Jess, is bust you up in a way you'll never forget."

"With what?" Jesse nodded at the rifle. "You'll notch my ears and bust a couple kneecaps for me, huh?"

"No." With a violent motion, Calem swung the rifle by the barrel, sailing it into the darkness.

Jesse's lips twitched with wicked amusement. "You can't do it, Cal. This ain't no kid toe-the-line, and that's all you know. I learned more tricks than you ever thought of."

"Watch yourself," Calem said between his teeth, and shifted his body and moved in, squaring off. Jesse danced away, flicking a couple of jabs at his face, feinting to cover the sudden upswing of his foot in a vicious kick. Calem twisted so that it missed his groin, but found his thigh with a numbing impact. He staggered awkwardly in trying to follow Jesse's dancing form, and Jesse gave a low, confident laugh. He wove close in a tight, dodging pattern, feinted at Calem's belly and drew his guard low, then slashed at his face.

Calem felt gristle crunch in his nose; his eyes watered with red pain, and then Jesse's knee lifted into his belly. Calem pitched forward, bent with the agony of it, then floundered onto his hands and knees. He could not avoid Jesse's swinging boot as it met his jaw and flung him on his back. Calem's teeth met in his tongue-edge; he tasted the metallic hotness of pain and blood, and he rolled sidelong too late as a second kick caught him in the ribs. He gulped for breath and almost choked on it, toppling again on his back, and saw the raised boot descending to savage his face. He caught blindly and twisted with the strength of hurt and rage.

He heard the thud of Jesse's fall and the grunt of his driven breath; Calem rolled half-erect reaching dimly for sight; the saffron flicker of the crackling fire swam and caught steady. He and Jesse were on their feet at the same time. Calem rushed him and locked his arms in a brutal hug around Jesse's trunk, and felt him arch with the pain, gagging. He hooked a knee behind Calem's and threw his weight to bring them both down, at the same time trying to land atop him. Calem let his body twist with the fall, and Jesse was on the bottom as they struck. The impact, and Calem's tightening hold, crushed the breath from Jesse; he flailed both fists against his brother's neck. Calem ducked his head and doggedly took the pummeling, and put his full power into the hold, his shoulders bunching like a young bull's.

Jesse's body strung tight to his retching gurgle, and his blows became feeble pawings. *I could break his ribs,* Calem thought dimly, aware of a bitter mastery now, and slowly he relaxed his hold. He pulled back and got a knee under him, laboring for breath. Jesse writhed feebly, and the feebleness was part sham; abruptly his fist lashed out and caught Calem in the throat. Calem set his teeth and came upright with Jesse's shirt doubled in his fist. Jesse's next panicked swing missed, but then he connected with a hard left that rocked Calem's jaw. He took the blows squarely, letting it fuel his anger afresh.

Spraddle-legged, he gave a brutal jerk that choked Jesse down to his knees, and twisted, watching the handsome face

114

darken with congested blood as he vainly yanked at Calem's wrist. Now Calem drove his fist down in a full-armed smash, and then let go. Jesse slipped onto his side and rolled on his face; he braced his hands and pushed slowly to his feet. Reeling for balance, he spat blood and teeth; there was a mad glaze in the eyes that pounced on Ethan Jacks' rifle protruding from its saddle boot.

He made a diving lunge, landing on his belly and a half-doubled leg that happened to be his bad one. He shouted with the pain, but his hand closed over the gunstock and dragged the weapon free. He rolled quickly to his haunches in the same instant that he brought up the rifle, levering it.

Calem came swiftly in on him with two long steps, and as the second one took his full weight, brought his other leg up in a full-muscled sweep. His boot toe took Jesse directly under the right wrist as he worked the rifle; Calem heard the audible snap of bone breaking. Jesse's cry mingled with the roar of the rifle, as, angled upward by the kick, it discharged with the muzzle inches from Calem's sleeve. He winced with the bite of powderburn as the bullet grazed past his arm.

Jesse stumbled to his feet, his eyes wide and glassy, and Calem caught a handful of his hair and sledged a brutal hook into his jaw. Jesse fell against the trunk of a pine, his head rolling limply on his shoulders, and his knees started to fold. With an insensate lack of mercy Calem slashed a final blow at his bleeding face, and felt flesh tear; his fist skidded wetly off Jesse's face and crashed solidly against the tree. Pain splintered up his wrist and arm; he had dislocated a knuckle.

He kept his feet in the ragged pain of it, cuddling his hurt hand against his chest. Through eyes squinted nearly shut, he watched Jesse's sagging fall as he slipped down along the trunk to his knees, then pitched on his face.

Feeling his own legs starting to hinge, Calem dropped unsteadily to his haunches, his head hung and eyes shut, waiting for the pulsing hurt of his slipped knuckle to recede. He looked up at a sound, and saw Miss Charley sitting upright holding her jaw. Her eyes touched him with a steely puzzlement, then moved to Jesse who lay with his head turned. Her gaze widened on the wreck of his face.

"Sorry," Calem said hollowly. "I had to hit you. Couldn't have his blood on your hands." She said nothing, and he extended his injured hand, holding the index finger stiff. "Grab that and pull hard."

Mechanically she tugged. There was an instant of blazing pain that yanked a grunt from him as the knuckle was set. His whole hand throbbed with every beat of his heart, and it would be swollen like a balloon before long, he supposed. He would not be able to hold a gun with that hand, at least to fire, for days, and he did not want to think about that.

He crouched as he was, fighting the deep shock of various pains and gutted anger, while Miss Charley, at his direction, saddled Jesse's horse and tied on his gear. Afterward she stood watchfully by, her eyes hard and dry, as Calem awkwardly loaded his brother into the saddle. Jesse started to cant sideways, but caught himself; with his sound arm he struck Calem's bracing hand away. His right arm dangled uselessly with a broken wrist. He fisted the reins savagely, his bloody lips lifting off his broken teeth as he reached for words which came as a harsh whisper.

"I'm going to kill you for this, kid. Look sharp. I'll see you again."

Coughing shallowly, he slowly turned the horse and, half-bent across his pommel, rode south into the wet bleak night.

# Chapter Fifteen

Cody Dembrow was brought out of a blank, restless fog of sleep by the cook banging a ladle on a skillet. Sitting up in his blankets, he cursed under his breath as he rubbed a hand over the unshaven scrub of his jaw. The murky light presaging dawn was only now giving way to chill red streaks of sunrise on the distant peaks as the men, grumbling to wakefulness, stirred out of their soogans.

Cody sat on his soggy groundsheet and tugged on his boots. He swore again, aware of the strain that was building daily in him. He had a cold preconviction that even after last night's fiasco the Major would refuse to admit defeat, though it seemed that the Gaults had this time made certain their escape.

For Cody too the night's work had gone sour. In their brief talk by the spring, he and Duval had made a simple but explicit plan. When they rushed the hill, Duval would be somewhere at the Major's back. Watching for an opportunity after the shooting began, he would place his bullet, taking care to finish his man with one shot. Later the killing should not be greatly questioned, when during a heavy exchange of gunfire anybody's accidental slug might have done the work. And, since several men might die in the charge, the way of one man's death should not be scrutinized too closely so long as the onus of suspicion did not touch Cody, the one who stood to benefit.

That danger was already minimized since Cody would be atop the ridge setting the dynamite charge that would launch the attack. He had done so, arming himself with cartridges and detonators and a coil of fuse, then skirting around the ridge to ascend its flank. The Major had called out an ultimatum to the defenders, warning them that a refusal to surrender meant that dynamite would be used. When there was no answer from the darkened shack, Cody had applied detonator and fuse to a single cartridge and dropped it over the rim. It was sufficient to cave in a section of the mortared wall, and at once the Major and his men had swarmed up the hill.

But there was no shooting and no need to shoot. The interior was deserted, and in a few moments discovery of the mine tunnel and its extension to the far side furnished the explanation. The inmates had made good an escape, and the storm was already erasing whatever trail they might have left. . . .

The men were shuffling past the Dutch oven, ladling food onto tin plates and filling their cups from the big cowcamp coffeepot. Cody had a belly full of moths this morning; he passed up the grub after the others had taken their helpings, but poured himself a cup of the hot black brew. As he hunkered by the fire sipping it, he let his narrowed gaze flicker to the Major who, pacing up and down, had touched neither food nor coffee.

Losing the Gaults so cleanly after coming within an ace of having them in his hands had been a blow, but it would not stop him from insensately pursuing his search, however hopelessly. They might spend days trying to pick up a fresh track.

Meantime Cody was faced with the unwelcome job of recasting his plan; he hadn't a notion of when or how a fresh chance might offer itself, and he could only shape his action to the opportunity.

Duval sidled up with his empty cup; he squatted by Cody and reached for the coffeepot, murmuring, "What now, my friend, eh? You change the mind perhaps?"

"Not likely," Cody said quietly. "There'll be a right time, fella. Watch me and you'll know."

Duval grunted and rose, moving away. Cody nursed his cup between his hands, brooding at the dawn-misted flats to the north. Thus he was the first to see the rider appear across a brow of ridge and come at a slow jog toward the camp. Cody threw out the dregs of his cup and came to his feet.

"Uncle Jeff."

The Major came around on his heel as Cody pointed; he studied the steady approach of the rider, but gave no order. The men exchanged glances, then went on eating.

Within a couple of minutes the man was near enough to recognize. Cody frowned, unable to tell much except that he was slim and young and dark. His right arm hung limply as if from an injury, and his face looked as if he had lost a fracas with a meat-grinder.

Abel Sutter broke the silence meagerly. "That there is Jesse Gault. I 'member him right enough."

118

At once the Major's gun came up, the sound of its cocking brittle in the crisp morning air. Jesse Gault reined in a good ten yards off, lifting his hand palm out. He husked, "You let that off before you hear me out and you could be damn sorry, mister."

"I may take that chance," the Major said with a peremptory snap. "Unless you can explain why you were fool enough to ride into this camp."

"In a minute." Gault slung a leg over his pommel and dropped in a fluid motion from his stirrup to the ground. "I need a cup of java first."

"Get it then."

Gault walked unhurriedly to the fire, bent and lifted the coffeepot. Cody, squatting close by, gave him a thoughtful study. There was no trace of swagger about Jesse Gault, only a latent feel of lobo meanness. Gault was the genuine article, Cody thought, a bad character of a seasoned toughness; a man learned to recognize that kind. He lacked his brother's size, being slender and of average height and heft, with a lean, nervous tensile strength about him. His features were Calem's honed to a fine-chiseled sharpness, a handsome face now battered and drawn with pain and ugly with temper, particularly the eyes which held a chill arrogance that his beating must not have lessened. He wore no gun, Cody noticed, and his saddle boot was empty.

Gault filled a cup and drank half the near-boiling liquid, then said abruptly, "Want my brother, don't you? I can tell you where he is. Better yet, take you there."

The Major's answer was clipped and unhesitating. "Why? You've helped him from the first, incidentally giving me a good deal of trouble. Why this about-face?"

"Look at this face. See this arm? That's why."

The Major slightly lowered his pistol. "Your brother did that? You've quarreled then."

"Leave it at that." Gault finished his coffee, flicked the dregs out and dropped the cup in one violent motion. "I can take you to him."

"I may find him without you. I owe you a debt too, Gault. I am tempted to collect it on the spot."

"You won't, though." Gault smiled, and the smile was not pleasant. "You'll never find him without me, and you won't take the chance you can. He's the one pulled the trigger on your boy, not me, and he's the one you really want."

"Very well," the Major said coldly. "My guarantee of your

119

safety after you've told me his whereabouts—is that your price?"

"That's part." Gault lifted his good hand, closing the fingers into a slow fist. "The rest is, I want a gun and the first shot at him when you find him."

The Major regarded him strangely. "Why," he said softly. "You hate him more than I do."

"You can give odds on it, pop."

"My word, then. Out with it. Where is he?"

Gault told of the verdant canyon toward which Ethan Jacks had been leading them, and Abel Sutter put in then, "I know the place, most of a day's ride from here. This Jacks was right enough if he said a man could live in that canyon for as long as he took a mind. Major, you would have plumb lost him there."

The Major's eyes narrowed. "You say that only the girl is now siding your brother, that Jacks is dead. How did he die?"

"He had him a bad heart." Gault snapped his fingers. "It went like that." He moved his limp arm, wincing. "Can anyone here set this wrist?"

The Major said nothing as he pursed his lips, staring at Gault, then he nodded in decision. "All right, be ready to move out in five minutes. Take care of him, Sutter."

While the grumbling men hurriedly finished breakfast, Abel Sutter set Gault's wrist with slender sticks for splints and tied it up. Without a word of thanks, Gault made a sling of his belt, then switched his dark look on Cody. "How about that gun?"

"I got an extra," Cody admitted, and got up and went to his gear, digging out his spare revolver.

Standing to one side like a withered wraith, Sutter said with a peculiar flatness, "Who was it shot my horse?"

Gault smiled, and a vicious note thinned his voice. "If it was me, old man, what you aim to do about it?"

The old tracker's eyes glinted ice-blue in his flayed-looking face. "That's an answer," he said meagerly, and walked noiselessly to where his saddle lay.

In a few minutes they rode out in a loose group, pointed northeast toward the high, rugged breaks below the deep folds of the near peaks. Sutter rode a steady lead, and the Major held behind him, heading up the others.

Quite suddenly Jeffrey Dembrow fell back beside Cody who was riding slightly to his left rear. He produced his fine cigar case and, to Cody's surprise, held it out. After a

120

hesitation, Cody selected one of the tan Havanas and tucked it into his vest pocket.

"I'll save this."

"Better if you'd get used to it." The Major had placed a cigar in his mouth but did not light it; his manner was preoccupied, and presently he said, "I've been meaning to talk to you for some time. No point putting if off. You've thought, no doubt, that I've been unnecessarily hard on you, Cody. I have been, but not without a reason." He took the cold cigar from his mouth, and Cody felt the touch of his iron-gray eyes. "A man owes his blood something, Cody, and you and I have the same blood. I have never ignored that fact, even when Ames was alive; I had always intended to see that you would have your part in whatever I have built. Now that Ames is dead and you and I are the last Dembrows, the time has come to speak frankly."

Cody said guardedly, "I've never felt slighted, sir. You took me in and gave—"

"Yes, yes, all of that," the Major waved his cigar with sharp impatience. "I also worked you as hard as any common hand from the time you were ten, nor am I insensible to the humiliations you've endured at Ames' hands. Or of your working like a dog while he loafed. But Ames—Ames was my son. You understand that his rights were incontestable, while you had to prove yourself to me." His stern voice softened a trifle. "No man can help what he is born, Cody, but neither can a man evade the circumstances of his birth. The world will not have it otherwise, as cruel and unjust as that may seem. And because of what you were born, I needed to be sure—you had something to prove to me. Do you see?"

"I think so." But Cody was not sure that he did, and in his shaken unease at this unexpected speech from a man for whom his ingrained hatred had become habit, he could feel only blank confusion.

"Well, you've weathered the storm in every way a man could hope. There'll be no more of this second-man role, Cody. You'll have to learn how to wear good clothes, how to order a good meal, how to smoke a good cigar." He fumbled for a match, and Cody quickly struck one and held it to the Major's cigar—then lighted his own.

"Skull will be yours when I'm gone," the Major went on. "Of course Trenna will be provided for—a good-sized annuity and a home at Skull for a lifetime if she wants it." He paused, puffing thoughtfully. "A thought you might consider. Trenna is still a young and most desirable woman; I

121

should think she'll marry again. And you'll be wanting a wife before long, Cody; you'll be well able to afford one now. It could work out very well for you both. After a decent interval, of course, and if she should prove agreeable."

Cody could only manage to nod, and while they rode on in silence, his mind swam with a conflict of feelings. The Major always meant what he said, and the unshakable proof that he had made a complete and final acceptance of Cody was his candid suggestion concerning his son's widow. He had stepped quite literally into the place vacated by Ames.

The hour was still cool, but Cody found himself sweating. Could he go through with what he had planned, after this? He must decide now, before they found Calem Gault and the golden chance was gone forever. Did the Major really think all the bitter years could be wiped out by one grandiose gesture? Could he really be that blind to the hatred that had cankered in his nephew for as long as he could remember?

But the deciding factor, when it came to Cody, came as certainly as death. By her own word Trenna would never wait for nature to take its course and the Major might live another twenty, even thirty, years. *She wants it all and she wants it now.* Then with a cold footnote of self-honesty: *And so do I, by God.*

# Chapter Sixteen

Ethan Jacks had told Calem enough about the way to their destination so that, holding a course by the sun and bearing a few key landmarks in mind, he was confident of his direction. When, toward mid-morning, they angled onto a high, sage-stippled tableland, he knew that the canyon was close.

Now and then he gave the girl a worried look. She had said scarcely a word since they had buried her father; he did not like her dull silence or the frozen blankness that had blunted the piquant vitality of her young face. The lively gamin of a girl he had gotten to know had gone; a stranger looked out of her eyes.

Her father's death had brought the change, but how deep it went he did not know. He did have a fair idea that in some obscure way she was blaming herself because the last intimate words that had passed between Ethan and her were bitter ones. That was as wrong as could be, he thought, but he sensed too that for the time he could say or do nothing that would help.

He put his attention solidly to the business of getting them to the canyon that now, according to all signs, should be just ahead. They left the tableland and crossed one timber-shaggy hill and then another, where they angled onto a dim game trail.

The discovery quickened his pulse, for this had to be the trail which Ethan had said would, if traced north for a few hundred yards, lead them directly down into the canyon.

They followed it onto a gently tilting bench where giant fir flourished and only a fine mottling of sunlight touched the needle-fall ground. The parklike area was nearly free of underbrush, and the trail switchbacked indifferently around treeboles and other obstructions. They came to a frothing creek which cut steeply through the bench and forced the trail to a right-angled turn along its bank. They had followed the water-course only a brief distance when the bench terminated in a gradual fallaway of land that was the first dip into the canyon. The game trail followed the creek as it

123

poured into the gulf, and unhesitating, Calem led off down it, he afoot and Miss Charley on the horse.

As the dip steepened, Calem had a clear view of the canyon floor, and it took his breath away. The gorge was bottlenecked at this end, but beyond that it grew to a width of several hundred yards, and he could not see the far end. The soaring, almost vertical walls were crowned by beetling overhangs, and sunlight colored the upper heights of sandstone and limestone with waterstain streaks of iron and salt. The racing stream sparkled over vivid rocks and chattered here and there into short rapids. The dip choked to a narrow slit, and the dense young fir climbing its flanks were bark-wet from the rise of pearly mist. This laid a clean, odorous sweetness in the air, and his senses absorbed it pleasurably. As they neared the bottom, the stream spilled into a creaming gush of rainbow-veiled falls, and they put the horses carefully down its rocky bank and tackled the last descent to where it ended in an overgrown outwash fan.

From above Calem had seen that the canyon floor was mostly lush, open meadows laced by timber mottes. Now he saw that the grass was deep and luxuriant and, because the rising sun was only now wiping back the shadows in this cliff-girdled cleft, glistening with dew which shook down to their passage.

He took the lead, forgetful of everything else in his burning eagerness to explore this pocket paradise. The stream wound away downcanyon, now and again losing itself in thick stands of cottonwood, box elder and ash, and it was fed at various points from springs or by trickles from the upper heights. Sometimes it eddied into deep still pools, and where there were shelving rocks he watched for trout. Once he spotted the granddaddy of them all, thick as a man's calf and longer than his arm, fin-batting against the streambed gravel. Stopping to listen, he found the brooding, awesome stillness and solitude broken only by a hum of bees and a soughing of wind from upcanyon.

Calem's first excitement was crystallizing into a vague form now, and he worked back and forth in erratic zigzags, studying the sunswept lay of meadow and timber with a practical eye. As well as plentiful grass, he took note of sheep-fat and antelope bush and other plants fine for stockfeed. Under the rim hard by the west end, he came on a steep notch in the cliffs that was almost obscured by clotting thickets. He rode partway into it, breaking brush, and found that it widened suddenly into a broad pass that led north across fairly regular terrain. The brush could be cleared, and a well-laid charge at this shallow ridge or that narrow passage would slough away enough rock to make an easy trail. . . .

Back in the big canyon he studied with more care a site he had idly reconnoitered, close to one flank but well out of danger of falling rimrock. A tight log house here would be cool in summer, warm in winter, with a fine view of the creek and the lower canyon. Almost before he realized what he was doing, he had picked up a sharp stick, preparatory to marking off the dimensions of a cabin.

Then, with a wry grin at his own thoughtless' fervor, he dropped the stick from a hand that was almost too swollen to hold it. He could move the recently disjointed finger with a little effort, but it hurt like the devil; he had torn cartilage, and he would have to manage left-handed for days.

Kneeling by the streambank, he plunged his throbbing hand into the chilly waters, letting go a sigh at the instant relief. Almost guiltily he glanced at Miss Charley whom he had almost forgotten. She stood by the horse, fingering the reins. She had apathetically followed his exploration without question, and her expression was an incurious blank.

"Been woolgathering," he said lamely, making a circling gesture. "Got thinking how a man might settle smack here in the canyon and run a few head. Providing he set his sights in a modest way, he could make out fine. Plenty of big timber for building, plenty game for that trail, trout in the crick, and a man could scratch out a truck patch and pack in suchlike few things as salt and flour and sugar he would need. Grass and water to suit, and no want for riders on drift lines with just a few cattle inside these cliffs. No pocket, brush or potholes for them to get boxed or hung up in."

From him this was a whole lot of talk, and it had the effect of getting the girl's half-attention; she stirred her shoulders and looked around. She said without much interest, "How you going to get cows in and out of this?"

"That little side pass. A few charges of giant powder choicely laid would open her up. You could haze out a batch of growed stuff now and then and drive to Mercyville, which has got a railroad."

She gave a small indifferent nod and he frowned, thinking, *It is time we cleared the air.* "Sorry I had to hit you back there. Couldn't let you kill him. It ain't only he's my

125

brother. Killing your pa wasn't his intent. He couldn't of knowed about your pa's heart."

"Neither did I," she said in a dull voice. "He never told me. He could of told me that and things would of been different; I wouldn't of said I was leaving him then. Why didn't he tell me?"

"He didn't know how, I reckon." Calem stood up, gingerly drying his hand on his shirt. "It surely wasn't because he hadn't a feeling for you. All the gold he took out was meant for you. He told me so, but he never knew how to say it."

She raised eyes, narrow with disbelief. "Why would he tell you that?"

"Because he wanted me to see after you when he went. He would have left us after we reached this canyon. He didn't figure to burden you none."

"That makes it all the worse." She turned, pressing her face against the horse's mane. "I pushed him clean out of my life at the last."

"Look here," he said brusquely, coming over to her. "Look at me now. You want to start setting blame, blame me ahead of anyone. If I hadn't got Major Dembrow after me, we wouldn't have found you. Or say you're the one found us—if you hadn't, your pa might have died then pinned like he was. You want to go way back, if he hadn't took that bullet next to his heart first place, a little thump on the chest wouldn't of finished him." He frowned, trying to form the gist of the idea. "Miss Charley, a body just can't hold himself to account for what he didn't know. So don't you."

She raised her face, but said nothing as she plucked absently at the horse's mane; finally she shrugged. "Whatever the cause, it don't matter now. He is gone, and all the talk won't change that. If he needed me, he was the only one who did."

"I need you." The words left him without hesitation or thought; even when he realized what he had said, there was nothing to think about. He had stated a simple truth, surely and instinctively, and he only wondered at his slowness till now in grasping it.

He watched her eyes, seeing for a moment something besides the dullness of despair. But then she shook her head. "I reckon not. Sure is nice of you to say so, though."

"I ain't just saying it," he said angrily. "But I surely don't know how to make you see it, that's plain."

Again the hint of tentative aliveness quickened her smooth

126

expression, though her voice was doubtful. "Maybe you better just say it, Gault."

"Well." He ducked his head and rubbed his neck, digging his heel at the ground. Finally he arced a hand about him. "This place is made to suit for someone who don't fancy town living or town ways." That much of what he meant to say came easily enough. He had really made the decision, if unconsciously, at first sight of this canyon; a man took such a feeling deep into his bones where it became a part of him. "I feel mighty strong on this canyon."

"Sure is pretty here," she said without expression; she was giving him no help.

"It won't be nothing without you."

"We got to stand front of a preacher."

"Well, sure," he said stiffly. "What did you think?"

"You got a ring or something to pledge me?" He shook his head and she came to him, raised on her toes and kissed him solemnly. "That'll do for a pledge. No, you keep your big hands to yourself. I like them is the trouble, a sight too well. We'll just wait."

That would be for a while, he judged dourly, as he intended remaining in the canyon until he could be reasonably sure that Dembrow had given up the search. The time would not be wasted; he could fell and trim logs for their future home with Ethan's hand-ax and perhaps get a start on the actual building. Later they could get what carpentry tools they needed from Mercyville.

But he wanted to set up immediate camp elsewhere in the canyon, with an eye to security. The chance of anyone coming here might be practically nil, but he was taking no chances. He had reconnoitered enough of the canyon to ascertain the ideal site for their temporary bivouac. A giant chunk of the rimrock had collapsed long ago, forming a low ridge of massive rubble at the base of the north wall. Now overgrown by thick brush and scraggly young firs, it seemed made to order. The brush would lend good concealment, and from the slight elevation they could command a fair view of much of the canyon, including the descending trail at its mouth. At least they would spot anybody coming into the canyon before being seen themselves.

They moved onto the rise and began to ready the camp. With the hand-ax Calem slashed down some saplings and fashioned a pair of half-shelters for them, using his catch-rope to lash the poles together and thatching each with leafy slashings.

127

Deep in the afternoon he was dozing on his blankets flung over a springy bed of boughs, hat tipped over his eyes. Miss Charley aroused him with a vigorous shake. "I seen something on the rim, so I looked with them glasses of yours. Here."

Calem took the fieldglasses from her hand and trained them on the canyon terminus where the trail was, at once catching the colored stipples that were men and horses moving downward through the black-green of heavy foliage that almost masked the long descent.

He was aware of Miss Charley's intent gaze on him, and now she said quietly, "Them, huh? Couldn't be nobody else."

Calem lowered the glasses; he tasted the stunning acceptance of what his eyes verified, and yet, not wanting to believe it, could not begin to grope for the why or how of Dembrow being able to follow them here.

The canyon that should have been a refuge had become a trap; it formed a sheer-walled cul-de-sac at this end, and the one brush-grown defile which he had marked earlier as an ingress-egress for cattle was very near the other end where Dembrow's party already was. In any case, an ex-military careerist like Dembrow would have any potential escape routes spotted and covered within minutes; common sense told Calem that much, and he promptly discarded the idea of escape.

He also realized, with a terrifying sense of discovery, that he could find in him no real wish to run any more. His first reaction had been the feel of overwhelming hopelessness that keens into despair; if against all odds Dembrow could somehow track him here, what was the use of trying any more? Yet already that feeling had ebbed into a wolfish determination.

Live or die, he was through running. It made his next move easy to decide. What his mind—or that part of it which housed the God-fearing conscience of Calem Gault— shrank from was not fear, but the utter ease with which decision came.

Somehow he must kill Major Jeffrey Dembrow.

It was another chilling glance into the submerged brute that was the essential man, bringing home to him with a shocking insight the truth that he was finally, at bottom, of the same stuff that he hated in other men; he found a kinship in Jesse's amoral instincts and in Dembrow's rapacity. And he knew with equal certainty that, if he survived today to resume the ingrained patterns of his thoughts and ways, this moment, this insight, would always stay vividly with him. . . .

Miss Charley's gaze held steady on his face. "Same as before," she said softly. "We got us a wall at our backs."

Calem lifted his eyes to the rimrock above them, and he shook his head. Not quite the same, as soon as Dembrow thought of sending men to circle onto the rim and fire down on them. And sooner or later he would, if he could not take them from the front. The chance that he could not was good, for the dense screening of brush and rocks on this shallow rise might enable two people to hold off men who would have to cross a bare slope to reach them. Only the advantage would be a short-lived one.

"My gramps—he was a mountain man—used to say when you're attacked by Injuns, shoot the leader first. May stop the rest."

Miss Charley nodded her calm understanding. "You reckon to get you a leader?"

"Best chance I see of that is finding him before he finds us."

He told her what he had in mind, and she nodded with a grave reluctance. "I don't like it much, but two of us can maybe bring her off."

"You stay here where they won't find you," he said flatly. "And I don't want no argument about it."

# Chapter Seventeen

With a last well-stressed admonition to the girl to stay where she was and lie low, Calem came off the short slope at a loping run. He plunged into the overgrowth of young firs that began just below the rise, and worked up-canyon.

He had no definite plan beyond lining up Jeffrey Dembrow in his gunsights. That meant getting dangerously close to his man, for with his injured right hand he could not handle a rifle; the best he could do was manage his old Walker pistol with an awkward and unpracticed left hand.

He moved at a swift trot where the forest was free of underbrush, and where it was not, broke brush with a heedless impatience. He kept as much as possible to the concealing timber, leaving it only where the trees thinned into grassy stretches, quickly crossing these. Only when he was quite close to the head of the canyon did he slow and make his way carefully. Here on the lower canyon floor he could not see the oncoming riders, but they must be close now, and they would be cautious in their approach.

Calem came to a break in the timber where, by dropping prone behind a deadfall, he had a concealed view of the stream and the old game trail that meandered along its bank—the likely approach for a man working downcanyon. He slipped out his Walker and braced the muzzle across the deadfall's mossy trunk, squinting down the long blued barrel. He judged that with a steady eye and a firm hand he could kill a man at the closest point on the trail, where the stream made a deep curve this way. Then he would fade with all haste into the timber and hope the Skull crew, shorn of leadership, would give up. A forlorn hope perhaps, but his only one.

He waited, his heart thudding against the earth. The first inkling he had that his idea had gone awry was when two men, moving at a low crouch, came afoot into sight through a gap in the timber beyond the stream; they were quickly swallowed again by the trees. Then a crackle of brush somewhere at his back alerted him to other men working through this same timber. He waited tensely, but the sounds faded away as the men went on past, missing him by many yards.

The Major plainly had no intention of riding boldly into a possible ambush; he had split his men into small parties that were flung out and infiltrating gradually downcanyon, covering and searching a good deal of ground as they went.

But where was the Major himself? Even if he knew, evading the small group of Dembrow's men to get near him would be a ticklish job. Now he heard more men on foot entering the motte where he was laid up; his spine crawled unpleasantly at their nearness this time. Rather than lay up here till he was found, why not boldly hit the open and continue his search for the Major?

He gathered himself and made a short run across the open; he made the high stream bank and slid down it on his haunches to water's edge, crouching there while he scanned up and downstream for a shallow fording. Then the muttered voices of men moving his way reached him. Lifting his eyes till they barely topped the bank, he saw two of them come into sight of the trail upstream. They would be on him within a minute, and caught between the streambanks, he couldn't break for cover without being seen. There was only one thing to do, and Calem did it. Jamming his gun under a matting of grass, he slid almost noiselessly into the water, letting it close over him neck-deep like an icy cloak.

The wicked chill of the high country stream wracked him to the bones as he waited; when the voices of the men were almost above him, he submerged his head completely. Peering up through the water he saw the men's refracted images pass by along the trail. When his lungs seemed ready to burst with stale air, he lifted his head barely above the water, hugging the bank.

The pair had halted a ways downstream to converse, he knew from the low-pitched voices. Their words barely reached him, but he recognized them as Cody Dembrow and Frenchy Duval.

". . . and locate the Major," Cody was saying quietly. "We'll split up here. I got to be with Grymes or some of the others when it happens."

"You are sure the Major he went that way, eh?"

"Dead sure, and he was by himself. Ed Grymes and a couple others were scouting in that direction too; watch out for them. There won't be another chance like this, Frenchy, so get going."

There was no more talk, and now Calem dared raise his

head enough to see that the two of them had parted company, Cody moving on downstream while Duval cut at right angles into the trees. Though making little sense of what he had heard, Calem had gleaned one solid fact: follow Frenchy Duval and he would find Jeffrey Dembrow. He left the water and scaled the bank. Pausing only to retrieve his pistol from the grass, he started into the timber after Duval.

The gunman was stalking through the trees like a gaunt wolf; Calem stayed well to his rear, just in sight of him. There was something amiss here, dovetailing with the cryptic speech that had passed between Duval and Cody, but that troubling notion was only a vague undercurrent below Calem's own burning preoccupation.

Duval had neared the canyon's north wall when he pulled to a stop at the fringe of a clearing. For a moment he was stiff and intent, and then he swung aside. He glided along behind the thickets that hedged the clearing and was quickly lost to sight. Calem halted uncertainly, but then moved up beside the clearing. He gave the humpy, rock-strewn meadow one quick glance, then dropped down on his haunches to avoid being seen. The stocky form of Major Jeffrey Dembrow was plodding at a dogged, tired walk across the meadow. He was almost at its center, not twenty yards away, and he was a clear target.

Calem fingered the long pistol laid across his knees, but did not raise the weapon. In this moment the troubling fact of Duval's stealthy circumnavigation of the clearing, shifted to the forefront of his mind, and suddenly he understood. Duval's behavior matched his own, which meant that Duval was here for the same reason. The gunman was circling behind the thickets only to select the choicest spot from which to fire a deadfall shot. *But at the Major?*

The answer to his disbelief came in the high crack of a rifle from the brush some yards away.

Calem heard the audible grunt of the breath smashed from Jeffrey Dembrow's body as the slug's impact drove him head foremost in a stumbling fall. He rolled over once, pawing feebly for his fallen rifle, and got it. His rollover had carried him onto his belly and face behind a low outcrop of crumbling rock. Weakly he levered the rifle as another shot sang off the outcrop.

The man who had ruthlessly dogged his trail was pinned and helpless and probably dying, but Calem's taste of bitter satisfaction was brief. If Dembrow were killed by the Cajun,

132

and Calem were the only witness, he would be blamed for a murder he had not committed. *Maybe that's what they want!*

Simultaneously he realized how a swift bold gamble might twist this situation to his advantage. At this point he had almost nothing to lose, and with that thought he made his move.

He broke into the open, running low and hard toward a deep-worn gully that cut across the stony meadow. He covered these few yards braced for a bullet at each straining step. But none came, and he hit the raw cutbank and skidded down it on his back and crouched at the bottom, panting. Duval must have been too surprised or puzzled by his action to fire.

Calem scrambled on his hands and knees along the crooked pebble bed of the dry wash, working deep into the clearing. He had taken note of a bend which angled close to the Major where he lay sprawled behind the outcrop. Reaching the bend, Calem raised himself by careful degrees until he could see the wounded man lying with his legs pointed toward the gully. A great crimson stain had spread across the soiled back of his linen shirt, and his rifle lay slack in his hands; his head had slumped onto one bent arm, and he was unconscious, Calem saw.

He clambered from the wash and, flopping on his belly, crawled to the Major's side. Instantly Duval laid down a quick close fire that chipped splinters from the outcrop; his angle of fire was poor. Tugging and rolling the Major's inert slack body with him, Calem worked back to the lip of the cutbank. Two of Duval's bullets kicked dirt against his legs before he pushed the Major over the bank and then followed him.

Now, with the two of them cut off entirely from Duval's fire, Calem lay for a moment regaining his breath. He heard an abrupt outbreak of shots from the east, and had the sickening thought that some of the Skull men had found, and tried to reconnoiter, the rise where Miss Charley was hidden, only to be met by her rifle. *They don't know it's her and not me shooting.*

If only Duval's shots would pull a few of them back here. Able to handle only a pistol, Calem could not match the Cajun's fire.

Again cautiously lifting himself, gun in hand, he scanned the irregular hedge of thickets that bounded the south side of the meadow. He gave a rigid attention to the place where the smudges of powdersmoke had betrayed Duval's hidden gun, alert to any telltale sound or movement.

The groin-knotting seconds passed into long minutes. Calem's hand ached around his gun and a wash of sweat stung his eyes. Leaning his chest against the cutbank, he carefully wiped the sweat away, using his injured hand. He was far past fear, but he wondered how long a man could live with the sheer gut-deep weariness that no longer seemed to ever leave him for very long . . . *where was Duval?*

*He has to be up to something. All you can do is wait and hope you see what is coming before it happens.*

Now the noise of hurried voices and the breaking of brush indicated that the Skull men were coming on the run, drawn by Duval's shots. Calem felt almost a relief, though he could not be sure that even his having aided the Major would improve his situation. They were coming from the east toward his back, so Calem pushed wearily away from the west bank to face the opposite way.

Even as he started to turn, he caught a whisper of quick steps across bare earth. He stopped in mid-movement, trying to isolate that sound from the distant commotion made by the approaching Skull crew.

So suddenly that he was taken wholly by surprise, Frenchy Duval stepped into sight from around the sharp bend down the gully. His steps were lithe and stealthy; his gun was held ready. Calem was already half-facing that way, and now recovering, he finished his turn in a desperate haste as he brought up his gun. His heel turned against a rock and his wild clawing for balance upset him entirely; falling, he landed close to Jeffrey Dembrow's limp body.

The sudden drop saved him as Duval's bullet smashed into the raw earth of the bank above him. Sprawled on his side facing the Cajun, Calem had no conscious thought of his gun being pointed. Yet it was, and he shot in a kind of reflex.

The high-angling bullet took Duval under the jaw and wrenched his head on his neck with almost the snapping force of a hangman's noose. He turned like a toe dancer, his body still arched from the shot, and toppled face first against the gully bank. The tension left his body and he slipped down in a sidelong roll. His arms straightened and twitched.

It had been a neat ruse, Calem thought. While he had riveted his attention on the spot where the gunman had last fired, Duval had swiftly slipped back through the timber, and come onto the meadow at Calem's back. Dropping into the gully as Calem himself had done, Duval had come up quickly on his blind side. Luckily Calem had turned then.

He stepped over to Duval and picked up his pistol. Despite an ugly head wound, the Cajun might still be dangerous.

Major Dembrow groaned and stirred, but Calem gave him only a scant glance. By now the Skull men were in sight, starting across the meadow. Ed Grymes lumbered in the lead, and he boomed an order for them to fan out.

Calem shot into the air then, lifted his voice in a shout: "Mr. Grymes, don't come any closer. This here is Gault. I got the Major with me. You come after me, he will get the first bullet that's fired."

Grymes came to a dead stop, raising a thick arm to halt the others. "How we know you got him?"

Calem hesitated, then bent and scooped up the Major's fawn-colored Stetson and waved it high. "See this?"

"I see it. Could mean he is already dead."

"No, he is hurt. But he'll be dead soon enough without you keep your distance."

Grymes growled, "What do you want, kid?"

"Ten minutes. I need to talk with the Major. He has got to hear me out."

Belatedly he remembered that Grymes, who had lied about the way of his father's killing, had every reason for allowing him no time to persuade the Major otherwise. He braced himself, half-expecting Grymes to give the order at once to charge the gully.

Surprisingly, Grymes only nodded, saying gruffly, "Ten minutes. Then it's root hog or die for you, Gault. All right, boys, pull back to the trees."

Calem glanced over at the Major who was flat on his back, his eyes wide open and focused on Calem now. Grunting, Dembrow fumbled for the pistol still holstered at his belt. Calem dropped to one knee beside him, drew the weapon and tossed it out of reach.

The Major's one eye held bitter fire; he whispered, "Finish the job. That is more your style."

Calem dug out his bandanna. "I ain't the man who shot you."

"As you didn't shoot my boy?"

Calem motioned at Duval's crumbled body. "That's your man. I dragged you into the gully after he shot you."

The Major's lips twisted as if on the edge of acid denial; then his eyes clouded as his gaze touched Calem's hand, swollen and discolored. His gaze flicked back to Duval, and he said abruptly, "Where is your rifle?"

"Left it behind. I can't hold one."

"No, I shouldn't think so," the Major said softly. "It was a rifle that fired at me. Frenchy was carrying one, but where is it?"

Calem, occupied with stanching the flow of blood as best he could, gave a shrug. "Likely you'd find it back in the bushes where he shot at you. It would of just been in his way when he sneaked up on my back."

"But you got him?"

"Yes, sir," Calem rocked back on his heels. "Major Dembrow, I want you to listen."

Dembrow gave a savage shake of his head. "I don't understand this, Gault. I don't understand you. Why help me?"

"To save my neck," Calem said coldly. "I could of killed you myself. Maybe I will be sorry I didn't. But I wanted to handle this another way bad enough to take a chance."

"Chance?"

"That you will listen to me once. I told the truth about how your son gunned my pa, whether or not you want to believe it."

Jeffrey Dembrow held a hand tightly over his right chest where the bullet had emerged; sweat stood on his forehead and his whiskered jaw was ridged with pain. "Boy, that is saying that Ed Grymes lied under oath. You expect me to believe that of a man who has been loyal to me twenty and more years?"

"Loyal or not," Calem said stubbornly, "it happened the way I said."

The Major watched him through half-shuttered eyes. His stern face was masked against any betrayal of pain, but did not quite wall off his self-struggle with the unrelenting obsession that had driven him for days: "It was a fair fight with Ames," he muttered. "He was my son and you killed him—but even so."

"Yes, sir. It was fair. I went after him for sure, but I had a strong reason."

"I am thinking of two things," the Major went on; he grimaced with a twinge of pain, and his voice sank to a whisper. "First that your action in helping me was not that of a moral weakling, as which I would designate a liar, under oath or otherwise. Also you have given me back a life, my own, for the one you took, my boy's. I cannot ignore these things. I will give you a fair hearing. Was that Ed Grymes you called to before?"

136

"Yes, sir."

"Hail him again; say that I want to see him."

Standing, Calem cupped his hands to his mouth and called to Grymes. When the foreman's deep-throated answer came, Calem shouted, "The Major says come over here, but let me see you throw away your guns first."

He expected at least a token objection from Grymes, but again the man surprised him. Without a word Grymes stepped into plain view, and discarded both his rifle and handgun. He plodded across the meadow holding his hands out from his body, and reaching the gully, made a clumsy descent of the cutbank. His startled look shuttled from the Major to Frenchy Duval, and back again.

"Duval tried to kill me," the Major whispered. "Young Gault saved my life. We'll attend to the wherefores of that matter later. Just now I want you to tell me again how Jared Gault died. Exactly as it happened, Ed."

Ed Grymes' head dropped till his chin touched his chest. He cleared his throat gently. "Major, that hurt of yours should be looked to proper." His deep voice trailed and he sighed, lifting his eyes. "I reckon it had to come out. I tried drinking it away, but that ain't no good. Ames lied, Major, and so did I. Gault never had a chance. It happened the way the boy here told it."

"In the name of God," the Major breathed. A deeper pain than any that was physical roiled in his face. "Why?"

"Ames said if I wanted to keep my place at Skull I would toe the line like he wanted."

A shadow fell across the dry streambed, bringing Calem's gaze around and up. Cody Dembrow stood above the cutbank, a gun in his fist; he said tightly, "Throw it down, boy."

Calem let his gun thud to the ground, feeling a dour disgust for his carelessness. Cody had come alone, but had he crossed the meadow with the whole crew, Calem would have been too absorbed by Grymes' confession to have noticed.

Cody dropped to the bottom of the gully, at once swiveling a sharp glance on the prone form of Duval. The gunman's eyes were closed; his hands were clutched to his chest and his breath was a stertorous sigh.

"You can put that up, Cody," the Major said tersely. "Duval shot me. It was Gault who prevented him from finishing the job."

"Frenchy?" Cody's face held a thoroughly bland amazement. "Why you reckon for?"

Of course he wanted to tell the Major of the intrigue between Cody and Duval, but Calem let the impulse die. Jeffrey Dembrow's sense of fair play was already restraining incredulity on a fine leash where Calem Gault was concerned. And Cody, who had not put his gun away but only lowered it, might react unpleasantly.

"That will keep," the Major said. "I want to hear Ed out. Ed, you might have told me the truth after Ames was dead. Why didn't you?"

"I was as skeered of how you would take it." Grymes' massive shoulders lifted and fell. "I can't live with it no more. Now it's out, anyways."

"Cody," the Major husked. "You and Ames spoke together just before his death. Did he confide in you at all about the Gault killing—anything—?"

Cody started visibly; he was caught off-guard, kneading his lips between his teeth as he watched Duval through narrowed eyes. Though the breath was rattling in Duval's throat, he was still alive, and Calem thought. *He might have enough left to talk some yet. Wonder what it is between them?*

Cody said, "No, sir. Nothing."

The Major nodded as if in a trance, his eyes strangely dead. "As you say, Ed, now it's out, all of it. Your blame, Ed—and mine." He grimaced again as pain shook him. "Not only this, not only what I've done to you, Calem Gault, or even what my boy did to your father. Started long before that. All signs plain for a long time . . . never let myself see 'em because . . . didn't want to. Ames . . . bad . . . he was bad . . . my doing. . . ."

Grymes said urgently, "Major," but Jeffrey Dembrow's eyes had closed and he gave no response.

"Ah, what a pity," came Duval's quiet croak. He had pulled himself partly erect, his back to the cutbank; he coughed as the effort of speech brought more blood pumping from his throat. "He did not have the time to ask you about why I shoot him, my friend, eh?"

Cody's nostrils flared as his gun, held in his hand by his side, began to arc up. Duval's hand, lax on his thigh, rose with a sunglint racing along metal. The double-barreled pocket pistol almost concealed in his fist blasted twice.

Cody stumbled as one bullet, then the other, took him within a two-inch-wide circle above the heart. The second shot knocked him backward, but he could never have known when he hit the ground.

# Chapter Eighteen

Duval thought he was dying, and in the next few minutes he told enough to bring some sense out of his scheme with Cody. Assassinating the Major, he said, had been an idea hatched by Ames Dembrow's young widow in collusion with Cody. By this time the whole crew was gathered in the gully around the two wounded men and the dead one, all of them listening in still-faced silence to Duval's explanation.

To Calem's question, one of them dourly reassured him that Miss Charley was unhurt; in fact all of the men had withheld their fire on realizing that it was the girl alone, not Calem, doing the shooting. Her rifle was still making it warm for them when, hearing the continuing gunfire from this direction, they had headed back upcanyon.

Abel Sutter had finished his examination and dressing of the unconscious Major's wound, and now he announced that Dembrow would be fiddle-fit with a proper herb poultice, for which he had seen the makings hereabouts. Then Sutter turned his attention to Duval, after a minute remarking, "Lead missed yer backbone an' big vein clean's a whistle. Allus had the feeling you was born to hang." Sutter lifted his blue-bright eyes to Calem then, saying inscrutably, "Seen your brother yet?"

Calem frowned, uncomprehending. "What do you mean?"

"He's about. He come into camp this mornin' and told the Major where you was. Come here with us. He is in a powerful sweat to see you decked out for six foot of earth."

Calem felt the bone-deep shock of realization; he should have seen at once that Dembrow could never have found the canyon by chance, that Jesse's savage venom would carry him this far. Beaten and brutally marked, Jesse would do anything to salvage his wild pride; stripped of only that much, he would be nothing.

139

Calem passed a narrow-eyed glance across the still faces of the crew, then mechanically gave the surrounding timber a wary scrutiny. If Jesse were not present, he had to be skulking somewhere about, simply biding his time. Some residue of old memory rose in angry, illogical protest against the whole idea: *He can't hate me that much—not Jess!*

Still he kept a careful lookout as, without a word, he left the group and headed alone at a fast walk across the meadow and into the timber. Damn Jesse. Miss Charley would be waiting at the canyon's end, wondering what had happened, and he was impatient to be reassured that she was all right.

Minutes later, as he broke from the last skirmish line of trees onto the rocky base of the rise, he called out to her. She stepped into sight above and started down to meet him. She had a determined grip on her rifle, but now as they met halfway up the rise, Calem saw that her face was set and pale and the rifle stock was slick with blood.

"You all right, boy? I waited like you said, but I was getting some worried."

"Never mind about that—you been hit."

"Shoo, it ain't nothing."

He took her by the hand and rolled back her blood-soaked sleeve. Her strong pale forearm had been deeply furrowed from wrist to elbow; she would carry an eight-inch scar there, and he only hoped that that was the worst of it. "Can you move your fingers all right?"

"Shoo, yes. Told you it ain't nothing. An old bullet glanced on a rock and cut it up some. Them fellows was shooting plenty close for a little spell."

*"Cal. Down here . . ."*

The well-known voice washed like a breaking wave against his ears; he heard himself say, "All right, Jess," before turning his head till Jesse Gault's smiling face touched the edge of his vision.

He stood at the bottom of the rise close to the heavy timber belt which had shielded his silent approach. His fractured wrist, bulkily bandaged, was in a crude belt sling. His other hand was cocked on his hip above his jutting gunbutt. He smiled handsomely, but the effect was gruesome.

"I needed a chance to get you alone, Cal," he said. "You got to know who's giving it to you."

Calem thought, *No, Jess,* as Jesse's hand dipped and came up with a back-hammered pistol. The thought was almost

140

dispassionate; he felt like a man whose muscles had gone to numb jelly on the tail end of a falling nightmare where the ground is slamming up to meet you and you have to wake or die. The feeling was sustained, trancelike, as the shot crashed out, as Jesse heeled over and went down on his face. He braced one hand on the ground, trying in a terrible effort to straighten his arm and roll himself over. He succeeded only in turning his head; then, as his glaring eyes filmed to a gray blank, the arm went limp.

Abel Sutter moved out of the trees like a shadow; he balanced his rifle in the crook of his arm as he bent over the body. Calem came stumbling down the rise, but stopped yards above the place where Jesse had fallen. There was no reason to hurry. His eyes were stinging, and he bit his lip till he tasted blood.

"Figured he was waiting for a chance like this," Abel Sutter said. "So was I. I follered you and seen him laid up. I hung back till he made his play."

"You want me to thank you?"

Old Sutter's eyes gleamed. "No point, even was you so minded. He killed the best friend a man ever had, but I had no hanker to swing for evenin' the score. I needed me a reason. When he pulled on you, I had it."

"I sure hope you found it worth it." Calem's throat felt hot and choking. "I hope you found it worth all of that horse of yours he killed."

Sutter eyed the ground for a judicious moment, then spat quietly. "No, I reckon not. Boy, your brother wa'n't even worth a good hoss."

In all of his fifty-eight years, Jeffrey Dembrow could not remember speaking words of regret or apology to any man. In a way that single attitude was both the core and the symbol of his iron pride.

He had gone his way too long to change, the Major knew. Even now.

Strapped firmly down at a supine angle on a pole-and-canvas travois lashed behind his horse, Dembrow let his gaze pass from face to face, as if the answer he sought might lie in one of them.

He was impatient to return to Skull for, among other things, the pleasure of sending his beautiful, murderous daughter-in-law packing back to the saloon from which Ames had taken her, and without a cent to her name. He had never been deceived, as they must all have thought, about Trenna's background, which he had had thoroughly investigated; he had merely wanted to see her mettle fairly tried before passing judgment.

Now he knew. She was not fit to be mistress of the Skull he had built for a wife whom the long years and mellowing memories had left framed in his mind as a prototype of unblemished perfection.

*Ames—Cody—Trenna. All the young ones, they are all gone. What is there left for Skull—or me?*

For a moment the shape of his future, the stark and sterile aloneness of the years that remained, tightened his throat; his lips stirred in a curse and then he pushed the reflection into the safe background of his thoughts.

Almost in a silent cry for reassurance his glance sought the thick, stolid face of Ed Grymes. *It's all right, Ed,* he had said of Ed's frightened lie. No need to tell Grymes that his familiar, thick-headed person was Jeffrey Dembrow's last human anchor, one that, as sorry as it might be, he dared not let go. He needed Grymes close at hand as much as Grymes needed the ancient security of Skull. . . .

Jeffrey Dembrow looked at the others, at Duval with his hands tied to his horn and his bandaged throat muffled in a dirty scarf, at Abel Sutter with his stubbled cheek bulging placidly to a working chaw, at the crewmen mounted and watching the Major while they waited for the order to move out.

That time had come, now that he had passed the brutal siege of fever and delirium and was somewhat rested and on the mend. He could delay no longer, and still he could not give the order . . . not yet.

But he could not say the other words either, the ones that he had never said and never would say.

He looked at the two of them standing off a ways. The tall, big-shouldered youth with the gentle, always-brooding eyes of woodsmoke gray, and a shock of black hair lapping down across the high brow of his homely, rugged face. The girl beside him, a head and a half shorter, sturdy as a young pine, the tanned grave pugnosed face livened by the steel-bright eyes and crowned by a pale sun-blaze of tangled hair, tomboyish yet somehow more perversely feminine because of it.

142

If you were a sentimental sort, you would hardly keep from getting a smiling catch in the throat, he supposed, just looking at this ragged and rustic pair who could not be ostensibly, physically, more strangely matched. And yet in those ways that outshone the rags and bumpkin crudeness, so rightly matched. He saw the self-sufficient strength that would bow to nothing, the unflinching and lonely courage that had made do against the bitterest odds he could offer them, and with these things, the splendid and resilient youth that would always hope and fight for a better tomorrow no matter what the odds of now. Jeffrey Dembrow saw, and he knew respect and something else that he had not felt since he was a small boy. And that was shame.

He was seized by an impulse to do something, anything, for these two admirable young people, and the discovery brought a wash of relief; perhaps he could loosely skirt around the other things that would be too hard to say.

"Gault." His voice had a metallic scratch. "I want to—I would like to do something for the pair of you. I do not mean as a payment or an amends," he added quickly. "It is just something I would like . . ."

His voice slowly trailed as he watched Gault's young face, its expression of reserved neutrality hardening so that there could be no doubt. Dembrow felt chilled.

Gault said in a polite and distant tone, "Thank you, sir. No."

"But you have nothing except the clothes on your backs. Surely—"

"Miss Charley's pa left us a good deal of gold. We'll make out fine." Gault shifted his feet; he tucked his thumbs in his belt, his gray eyes very steady. "Maybe I should say it plainer. That ain't the reason." He paused. "We just don't want anything from you, sir. Not one damned thing."

Not from the man who had relentlessly hounded him; the flat repudiation stung, but Jeffrey Dembrow could understand. Yet he had failed to pass off what he hated the thought of saying, and his jaw shook with the thought: *I've got to, now.*

"There is one thing you will have to take, young man." After a heavy pause, he cleared his throat. "My apology. For making the offer. For all else that has happened. Will you accept that much?"

Gault hesitated; his head dipped in a brief nod.

The Major leaned his head back; he said, "All right, Ed, let's get going," and at Grymes' order, felt the shift of his travois in motion as his horse responded to a tug on its lead rope. The Major wearily closed his eyes to the sudden rattle of hoofs, the creak of leather and the rough lift of men's low voices.

It had not been half hard to say, he decided.

# HAVEN OF THE HUNTED

# CAST OF CHARACTERS

### LUTE DANNING

This owlhooter had studied military tactics and dreamed of a chance to apply them.

### JIM KINGDOM

Though a Tennessee man, he'd fought for the North because he wouldn't betray his principles.

### DOUG KINGDOM

Jim's brother rode for the South with Quantrell, because he liked a bloody brawl.

### MELANIE HASSARD

She wagered her life for the love of a reckless renegade.

### TORY STARK

He had a wild laugh, a dude manner, and a hair-trigger draw.

### INCHAM

He rode his emotions like a tight-reined horse.

## CHAPTER ONE

LUTE DANNING, watching from the fly-blown front window of Red Rhuba's saloon, was the first to see the giant stranger riding into Dry Springs about sunset. Lute felt the stir of mounting excitement as he watched the man step from the saddle and tie his saddle horse to the tie-rail in front of Rhuba's. From the back of his packhorse, he untied an empty tarp.

The stranger ducked under the tie-rail, the tarp folded under his arm, and crossed the single shallow-rutted street, flanked by its tar-paper shacks, to McNamara's general store. As he stepped up on the boardwalk to enter Mc-Namara's, the massive-shouldered, square-framed height of him was straight and erect in the fading light, and Lute had his moment of fleeting doubt. He's bigger than I remember, Lute thought. A lot bigger. But it had been since before the war ended that he'd last seen Doug Kingdom, and Kingdom had been only seventeen, perhaps, less, then.

Lute walked back to the bar and ordered a bottle of whiskey which he carried back to the table by the front window, from which he could command a view of the whole street. Lute shifted his fat short bulk restlessly and poured a glassful of whiskey, downing it.

Afterward, he tilted his dirty horsethief hat to the back of his balding sandy-haired head and reflected bleakly on the two years that had fallen since the end of the war, when with others of Quantrell's guerrilla band he had attempted to surrender to United States troops only to be driven back with gunfire—to outlawry. The ruthlessness of Quantrell and of Bloody Bill Anderson was still a live and fearful thing in '65, the debacle of Lawrence, Kansas, in '63, a fresh horror in the minds of North and South alike.

Too early in '65 to forget how Quantrell had scourged borderline towns of Northern sympathizers and rebels alike, burning, looting, and murdering, regardless of the codes of warfare. And when Appomattox came, the legacy of hatred and fear that the guerrillas had reaped turned back on them and drove them to lair like hunted beasts, sport for the guns of Yankee patrols. The broken remnants of Quantrell's raiders were scattered; some, like Jesse and Frank James and like Lute Danning and like Doug Kingdom, to become wanted men west of the Missouri as well as east of it. . . .

Lute broke from his gray musing as Kingdom stepped out the doorway of McNamara's, the tarp, bulging slightly with a slender quota of supplies, slung over a shoulder. He moved back across the road. With the heavy, drag-footed gait of a man too long in the saddle, he walked to the tie-rail and surveyed it briefly, gaunt face expressionless. For a moment he stood that way, motionless, and then Lute saw why. Kingdom's two horses, which he'd hitched there a few minutes before, were gone . . . .

From his position at the table by Rhuba's front window, Lute saw that DeRoso was standing on Rhuba's boardwalk, his narrow, gangling-jointed frame loosely erect as he leaned with one shoulder against a gallery-supporting pillar.

DeRoso was seventeen, pimply-faced, and straw-haired, with a Colt's .44 strapped ostentatiously low against the thigh of his frayed butternut-striped trousers. Lute also noticed Kingdom's gaze raking up and across the walk, settling upon DeRoso.

Kingdom studied the boy briefly, then said mildly, "Where's my horses?"

DeRoso said blandly, "What horses?"

Their voices carried plainly to Lute through the open door. He saw Kingdom's obsidian gaze flatten—then grow seemingly blacker with the acceptance of an irrevocable something. Only Kingdom's voice as he spoke, still watching DeRoso, held a fathomless patience. "I'm going in for a drink."

"Maybe you'll find them in the bottom of your glass," DeRoso said slyly. Damn him! Lute thought.

Kingdom's face did not alter. He said gently, "I will be out in five minutes. If they're not here, you'd better not be."

Before DeRoso could say anything more, Kingdom had stepped up past him and through Rhuba's doorway. Kingdom paused briefly on the doorsill, his massive upper frame blocking the door space entirely, and eased the tarpful of supplies to the floor against the wall. Then he had his look around the room, his gaze settling with brevity on Lute by the window and moving to Red Rhuba behind the rough bar paralleling the right wall of the small room. Kingdom walked ponderously over to it, and Red ceased the dumping of dirty glasses in a hogshead half full of water of a dubitable gray cast, and put his big freckled hands on the bar. He was a stocky loose-jointed young man with a heavy flame-red thatch of hair falling in a great cowlick over his forehead. His kindly blue eyes regarded Kingdom questioningly.

"Whiskey," Kingdom said. "I'll take the bottle."

Red set a bottle of Mountain Brook and a glass before

him, said cheerfully, "Count your own drinks," and returned to the glasses.

Kingdom carried bottle and glass over to the farthest table by the wall, toed out a chair and slacked into it, morosely pouring a drink; and Lute, who was watching him from the side, covertly studied him now in rising puzzlement.

His face was weathered to a deep mahogany where a week's ink-black beard stubble did not sworl in into rough obscurity, a face which seemed to have aged far beyond what was warranted by the three years since the war, Lute reflected. Yet it was the face of Doug Kingdom as Lute remembered it, to the deep-socketed obsidian eyes and the high-bridged nose. But the greatest physical inconsistency was the man's size. Doug was always big and strong, but his strength had been channeled into an intense nervous energy, barely restrained. This man was built like a blacksmith, big with a bigness that was all over, though with an unproportional concentration of weight through chest and shoulders. Yet this could be the added development of maturity, and much of his apparent height an illusion caused by his great breadth.

He carried no gun, and Lute marked that as strange, strange for Doug Kingdom. . . . He was wearing a calico shirt, a black Stetson, wear-cracked boots, and blue army trousers, rusty with age, with the canary-yellow stripe of the United States Cavalry down the outseams. Lute noted in particular the trousers, and he noted too the mild amusement that briefly relaxed the man's straight mouth as he observed the fly-specked chromo of J. E. B. Stuart which hung over the backwall behind the bar. A Yankee? Lute wondered; yet the man's summer-soft voice when he'd spoken to Rhuba was distinctly Doug Kingdom's voice with its Tennessee backwoods drawl.

Lute's round cherub's face was beginning to show his troubled confusion, and when Kingdom glanced up suddenly to see Lute still regarding him fixedly, Lute looked down, blushing. He reached for his drink, downed it, and began to rise to walk over to Kingdom, then slacked back into his chair.

Don't be a damn fool, Lute thought in self-disgust, and had again put his hands on the table to rise when DeRoso slouched in through the doorway and started toward the bar. Lute tried to catch his eye with a warning glare; DeRoso didn't notice or pretended not to. He bellied up to the bar, his gun butt banging loudly against it, and Red looked up from stacking glasses beneath the bar.

"Whiskey," DeRoso said, "and I'll take the bottle."

Red deliberately finished stacking the glasses, and Lute saw the stir of anger in DeRoso's face. Lute realized that DeRoso's words were exactly the words Kingdom had used, that DeRoso was not yet through baiting the big man, and that Red saw it too.

DeRoso stopped in front of Kingdom's table, bottle in one hand and glass in the other. Kingdom looked up from his own glass, his expression—one of no bitterness, only deep, deep patience—not changing at the sight of DeRoso's mocking, reckless face.

"Want a drink?" asked DeRoso.

"I've got one," Kingdom said. "Did you fetch the horses?"

"Mind if I sit down?"

"There's other tables. Did you fetch my horses?"

DeRoso studied him a moment. "It's good whiskey," he said, extending his bottle toward Kingdom.

Kingdom leisurely slouched back in his chair, lifting one leg and doubling it, so that he could rest the heel on the edge of his chair, and Lute thought resignedly, here it comes.

Kingdom said pleasantly, "You might ask the bartender to loan you his towel."

DeRoso set his bottle gently on the table, scowling. "What for?"

Kingdom said, still pleasantly, "To wipe behind your ears. They need drying."

Lute watched them, powerless to stop what happened. He saw the swift, pale fury lash DeRoso's face to violence as he dropped the glass, saw the downward slash of hand toward holstered Colt. As he grasped the gun, Kingdom's foot raised from the chair and drove savagely into the rim of the table top, so that it skittered violently into De-Roso; a shout of pain was driven from him as it pinned his hand against his gun butt, numbing the hand beyond use.

Kingdom was on his feet, skirting the table in two strides and doubling up the front of DeRoso's greasy buckskin shirt in his massive left fist while his right palm slapped DeRoso twice with cracking reports, and on the second slap Kingdom let go of him, so that the blow staggered him backward the width of the small room, half stunned and fighting for balance. He lost it and fell heavily on his back by Lute's table.

From his back DeRoso clawed awkwardly for his gun with his left hand, and as he pulled it and was dragging it to a level, Lute came out of his chair. He took just one long step to bring his heel down on DeRoso's wrist, driving it to the floor, grinding down once, savagely, so that DeRoso's fingers splayed out with the pain of it, and his hold on the gun was gone.

Lute bent down, angrily jerked DeRoso to his feet by his shirt front, and booted him toward the doorway. DeRoso caught feebly at the doorjamb in passing, but his numbed fingers were unable to gain purchase and he tripped over the doorsill and fell to one knee on the walk. He came upright, whirling to face Lute. He was shaking with rage, his yellow eyes hot and savage with it. He said in nearly a whisper, "Don't ever do that to me, Lute."

Lute slapped him across the face, crowded him up hard against the saloon wall, DeRoso's collar doubled up in both hands. "Know who you were salty with?" Lute snarled.

"Let go, damn you!"

"That was Doug Kingdom, friend."

DeRoso's jaw went slack with surprise, and Lute, seeing it, slowly relaxed his hold.

"Kingdom," DeRoso said in a dazed way. "That's Doug Kingdom you told me about? One with you and Quantrell . . . ?"

"Him."

DeRoso's hands shook as he straightened his shirt. He said, "My God. He could of killed me."

"I wish to hell he had," Lute said bitterly. "Good God, do I always have to change your diapers? Who talked you off the day that Red River bunch was going to hang you for brand-blotting?"

"You did," DeRoso said sullenly.

"Who else would of stepped for you that time the Dallas gambler was going to shoot you for cold-decking him?"

"No one," DeRoso said sullenly.

"And I expect to be leveled with. Walk soft around Kingdom; else, don't walk. Or he'll fix you so you won't." Lute paused. "Where's his horses?"

DeRoso didn't reply for a moment, regarding the ground surlily. Then he said, "Around back of the saloon."

"Bring 'em back here," Lute said flatly, and without another word turned and stalked back into Rhuba's, pausing by his table to pick up DeRoso's gun. As Lute straightened he saw that Red had laid a shotgun across the bar and was leaning his elbows on the bar, silently watching him.

"This ain't Dallas," Red said finally.

"You won't have no more trouble off him, Red," Lute said mildly.

Red musingly dropped his gaze to his shotgun. "That's right, Lute," he agreed negligently.

Lute glanced at Kingdom, and seeing that Kingdom was watching him steadily, walked stiffly over to the table.

"Long time, Kingdom," Lute said, and watched the mild shock of astonishment at being called by name wash across Kingdom's passive face. The doubts, the suspicions, tided back on Lute, and he thought cautiously, Play it cozy.

He waited, watching Kingdom's face with care, seeing the immobility veil it again. "Long enough," Kingdom said.

"You remember me?" Lute said doubtfully. "Lute Danning? With Quantrell . . ."

"Sure," Kingdom said. "Sure, I remember you."

He nodded toward the chair opposite him. Lute pulled it up and eased into it, now as always, choosing his words. "You didn't get my note up north, Doug—Dallas?"

And this time Lute could have sworn the man gave a visible start; yet Kingdom's dark and withdrawn face was so placid he must have been mistaken. . . . Odd, in Doug —this colorless reserve . . . .

"I passed through Dallas on the run," Kingdom said idly. "The marshal had me move. I was an unsavory influence."

Lute said, "You would be," with a grin. He felt relief. This explained Kingdom's surprise and his first lack of recognition. He had come to Dry Springs by chance, not following the note.

"This note," Lute added, "I left it with the apron at the Chuckaway saloon there. Told me you always came there when in Dallas."

Kingdom poured another whiskey, but didn't down it. He sat broodingly turning the glass between his hands, speculatively regarding it. "You were looking for me, then."

"In every trail town from the Trinity to the Nueces. You were in that range somewhere; that was all I knew."

Kingdom sipped his drink. "You must have wanted to see me some."

"For a year now. You have a hell of a rep in this part of the world, fella."

"Do I now," Kingdom murmured. "And how are you thinking of using it?"

Lute blushed at the accuracy of this. He removed his horsethief hat and laid it on the table at his elbow, then leaned across the table in a confidential manner. "We can use each other, Doug." His merry little eyes were watchful and excited. Upon Kingdom's reply hinged his whole plan.

"Go on," Kingdom said, and then Lute saw his eyes shift to the door, which was at Lute's back. Because he was not usually so lax as to leave his back open, Lute mentally cursed his own carelessness as he swiftly turned in his seat. DeRoso was standing in the doorway, sullenly watching them.

"You put them horses back?" Lute demanded .

DeRoso nodded and stepped over to the table where his bottle of whiskey still stood; he picked it up by the neck and took a massive slug, squinting against the raw sting of it.

Kingdom stood up, nodding to Lute. "Obliged. I'll put my horses up, then come back and talk this over. There a livery or feed barn around?"

"On the south end of town, first building to your right as you ride out," Lute said. His voice was affable though he inwardly felt a sour irritation at this delay.

Kingdom nodded his thanks and walked over to the bar to pay Red, then strode out. Lute morosely reached for Kingdom's empty glass, poured it full, and tossed it down.

"He going in with us?" DeRoso asked.

"I don't know yet."

Lute noticed only now that darkness had settled over the town. Red lighted a wall lamp at either end of the bar. The murky saffron light burned in a sickly way to the corners of the room. Two drifters came in and bellied against the bar. Lute was facing the door, staring at the floor, when he heard the ring of a spur on the doorsill and looked up to see Kingdom standing there in the doorway.

Lute's face whitened; the glass in his hand shattered on the floor. "Huh?" said DeRoso.

Kingdom? Doug? Lute thought wildly.

This man was wearing faded levis and a tattered jumper and wore a gun. His face was that of the man to whom Lute had been speaking, but it was younger, holding an irrepressible gaiety in it. He was big, but still shorter and much lighter than the man in the rusty blue army trousers; and now as his face turned toward Lute, Lute saw the pleased recognition in the bone-white smile that flashed on the instant his bright gaze fell on Lute . . .

And this was Doug Kingdom.

But the giant stranger? Lute, recalling his suspicions, sank back into his chair, his mind dull-blank with the terrified shock of this moment.

## CHAPTER TWO

Doug Kingdom stepped forward, smiling, to grasp Lute's limp hand hard. "Lute, you damn jayhawker! When your note said I'd find you in Dry Springs, I knew that meant the saloon in Dry Springs."

DeRoso's mouth had slacked open in astonishment. He made a limp gesture at Doug and stared at Lute.

"You—got my note?" Lute said in a distant voice. He wondered obscurely if it was his own.

"At the Chuckaway in Dallas, sure . . . ." Doug glanced at DeRoso. "Friend of yours?" Doug's real attention was on the bottle of whiskey, and he slacked into a chair and reached for the bottle and a glass.

"Yeah," Lute said shakily. "Fred DeRoso, Doug Kingdom."

Doug barely nodded to DeRoso, drained a glass of whiskey, and set it down, wiping the palm of his hand across his mouth. "Washes the trail down," he observed. "Let's get down to cases, Lute . . . . What in hell's eating you?" Doug reached for the tobacco in his jumper pocket, looking curiously from Lute to DeRoso.

Lute said with difficulty, "Fella came in a few minutes before you did." He cleared his throat. "Looked like you —said he was you. . . ."

Doug's fingers froze in the shaping of a wheat-straw cigarette. Then he said slowly in a voice guttural with unnatural strain:

"Looked like me . . . ? How much like me?"

"Older than you—maybe ten years older. . . ."

"But big—a lot bigger than me . . . ?"

"Built like an ox," DeRoso said.

The makings fell unnoticed from Doug's fingers to the table; his deeply recessed eyes suddenly burned like live coals. He said in a trembling, almost inaudible voice, "Knew he'd come some day. Ma Kingdom's pride and joy . . . Hell!"

Lute leaned forward, gripping the table in his intensity: "Who? Who?"

Doug looked at him. Without seeing him, Lute thought eerily. "My brother Jim. Big brother Jim. Yeah." Doug squinted suddenly, almost painfully. "Give me a drink, damn you. . . ."

Lute silently handed him a bottle. Doug fumbled for

it without looking at it; tilted it up and drained what remained in it nearly empty before he set it down. He placed his hands on the table to steady himself till he could regain his breath. DeRoso gave him a silent, respectful regard.

Doug looked now at Lute, saying in a normal voice: "Where is he?"

"Went to put his horses up at the livery. Should have been back by now," Lute said, glancing apprehensively at the door.

"He'll try to take me back. He'll try to make me give up to what he calls the law and pay for my—misdeeds. Well, he can got to hell," Doug said softly. "He can go to hell. I'm not going back. . . . You hear me, Lute , . . ?"

"Yeah," Lute said, picking up his hat and jerking his head toward the door. Doug and DeRoso followed him out. They stepped along the narrow path worn through the rank weeds by the front wall of the building until they were a good talking distance from the bar; voices would carry far in the windless, still night. Lute paused then, turning to face Doug's dark form, voicing the thought which had been in his mind:

"Him being your brother, you wouldn't shoot him. . . ."

"How do you know I wouldn't?" Doug snapped out of the darkness. He paused then; a little drunk, Lute decided, and not altogether clear in his mind. Finally Doug said slowly, "You're right: I wouldn't shoot him. And the Almighty help you if you try to. . . ."

"Sure," Lute murmured. "But we have to get him out of our way. There's a way without hurting him—much."

"How . . . ? I can't bluff him with a gun. He'll know I wouldn't shoot. Think I'd trust either of you to hold one on him, without shooting? Think again, Lute-boy."

"Suppose we all jump him?" DeRoso put in.

"Hell, he could handle ten like us without trying," Doug said softly.

"Still, there's a way," Lute said insistently. "He'll come back along this way from the livery to Rhuba's."

"He would of left the livery by now," said DeRoso. "Must of gone to the cafe to eat."

"Maybe not," Doug said slowly. "You don't know him. . . . Likely to see to taking care of his horses himself."

"Listen," Lute said quickly. "Fred and I'll get in this alley. You stay here on the walk. When your brother comes by, get his attention. . . . I'll do the rest."

"Watch it," DeRoso whispered sharply. "Someone coming from the livery now. . . ."

Two men stepped from the livery stable down the street, and Lute saw a distinct tremor run over Doug. One of the men, holding a bull's eye lantern, was the white-haired hostler; the other, towering in the lantern glow, Jim Kingdom.

Doug watched hungrily, briefly, the brother he had not seen in six years, then gave Lute a long and sultry glance: "You tap him gentle, Lute, hear?"

"Sure, sure," Lute said irritably; he caught DeRoso by the arm and pulled him into the narrow, shadowed alley.

Lute waited, crouching against a wall.

Sweat broke on his face—he had forgotten he'd left his gun in his room. He heard DeRoso's hollow stertorous breathing behind him, and he reached a hand back into the darkness; it touched DeRoso's greasy shirt.

Lute whispered sharply, "Give me your gun," and waited till he felt it shoved into his hand. He wondered whether to grasp it by the butt or barrel for the blow, and decided that the stock would afford a more certain grip.

Lute could see the black hulk of Doug on the walk, leaning negligently against the building. Then Lute heard the booted steps of a heavy man crunching along the walk.

He heard Doug call softly, "Jim," just as the big man stepped past the mouth of the alley. He saw Jim come to a dead stop, leaning as though to discern the face of the man who spoke, and it was now that Lute moved one step forward, swinging his pistol savagely at the back of Jim's uncovered head. In the uncertain light, he nearly missed, and the heavy barrel of the .44 hit the big man only a glancing blow that staggered him, and brought him into a half turn as though to face his assailant.

Lute struck again, wildly, and the muzzle hit Jim Kingdom solidly over the temple. Kingdom's knees hinged and he fell forward. Doug had already moved to catch him as he fell; his brother's great weight dragged him down too.

Doug whispered, "Help me with him, Lute, damn you!"

"Where can we take him?" DeRoso asked hoarsely.

Lute handed DeRoso the gun and bent down to catch Jim around the legs, grunting with the effort as he and Doug lifted him between them. "My room—across the street —back of the store—Anyone coming—Fred?"

"Street's clear," DeRoso said.

Lute and Doug carried the unconscious man between them, across the deserted street and down the wide alley between a rooming house and a keno parlor. They skirted to the rear of the buildings. Once Doug swore as he tripped over a bucket and nearly fell. Guided mainly by the familiarity of association, Lute found his way in the moonless night to the very door of the tar-paper lean-to he lived in at the rear of McNamara's store.

"Set him down," Lute said breathlessly, "till I find the lamp. . . ."

He eased Jim's feet to the ground and opened the door. In the dark room, he located the lamp on the commode by the left wall. He struck a match, lighted it, and replaced the chimney. Light flickered uncertainly about the room. Besides the battered commode, the room was meagerly furnished with a straw tick on the rough-plank floor, just by the door, on which Lute had spread his bedroll.

He and Doug lifted Jim inside and lowered him onto the bedroll.

Doug went down on his knees by Jim and parted his thick black hair over the temple where Lute's gun had struck the second time. The skin was split, blood already thinly matting the hair. Doug glanced at Lute, his face gone white and bitter, his eyes like molten obsidian. He said suddenly, hotly, "I ought to shoot you, Lute."

Lute's own nerves were keyed to a breaking pitch. He said harshly, "Did you think of any other way?" He rubbed his aching arms.

Doug stood up slowly, his gaunt face drawn into a tired resignation. "I'm sorry, Lute," he said wearily. "I can't stand to see anyone hurt him at all." He met Lute's gaze fixedly. "You want to understand that, Lute—anyone. . ."

"Sure," Lute said, "sure." He looked back at the fallen man, and when he spoke, it was with hesitance because of his uncertainty of Doug's temper. "If you don't want to hold a gun on him, we better tie him before he comes out of it. . . ."

"*I'll* do it," Doug snapped. "Any rope?"

Under his straw tick, Lute located some long strands of rawhide for a riata which he had never gotten around to braiding. Doug tied his brother tightly hand and foot—the hands in front for comfort. DeRoso opened his mouth to protest this; Lute shot him a warning glance. Doug straightened to his feet now and began restlessly to shape a cigarette.

"Just why you want to see me, Lute?"

Lute set his back comfortably to the wall. "You've made yourself a reputation in the trail towns since you reached Texas. . . ."

Doug made a wry face. "And all bad. That have anything to do with it?"

"Everything to do with it," Lute said flatly. He was silent for a moment. Long ago he had planned what he would say to Doug when they met, and now he silently reviewed it before he spoke. "Kid, you're footloose. I'm footloose. We're both wanted. We've been running a long time, sleeping with one eye open and facing doors and windows and pulling penny-ante jobs for eats . . . ."

Doug regarded him quizzically. "Didn't know you were in Texas till I got that note in Dallas. You been living the hard way too?"

"I have," Lute growled, "and I'm damn well tired of it. After Bloody Bill and George Todd ran Quantrell out of Missouri, I lelt too. The outfit was falling to pieces. I lone-wolfed it since, but that's no good either. With Quantrell, there was at least safety in numbers. . . . You stuck with Todd, didn't you?"

"Till he was killed at the Little Blue," Doug said wearily. "Now will you spit the meal out of your mouth, Lute?"

Lute was about to speak when the unconscious man moaned softly and stirred on Lute's bedroll. Doug threw his unlighted cigarette away; he stooped beside his brother.

Jim Kingdom's eyes opened then; he lifted his head, squinting painfully against the light. He tried to move his arms and legs, and, seeing that they were tied, contented himself with swinging up to a sitting position, wincing at the pain it caused him. Seeing Doug squatting before him, he did not smile. Doug did, not very heartily:

"You made your loop too big, General."

"That happens," Jim murmured. His dark eyes shifted a little, and settled on Lute and then DeRoso. "So this is what you have taken to running with. . . ."

Doug stood up. He said dryly, "Did you come all the way from Tennessee to tell me that?"

"I didn't come to tell you anything," Jim said sparely. "Ma told me to find and see you're all right. I intend to."

"Well, you saw me—I'm all right."

Jim looked at him; he laughed softly; then, with an effort

raised his upper body from the blankets, his lips tight against his bared teeth in a noiseless grimace. The movement caused a livid trickle of blood down the side of his face. "Fool," he said quietly. "You're all wrong."

Doug paced across the room, slowly, and back. A soft, almost hidden pain worked soundlessly in his face. "How is Ma?"

"She's dead," Jim Kingdom said in an iron voice. "Last thought was of you. Find Doug. She loved you, damn you, more than any of us; more than me, Pa, or Polly or Jo or Jubal—more than any of us . . . You never gave a damn, though, did you?" He cruelly ignored the agony in Doug's face. "You killed her, sure as a bullet. You who couldn't come home because Pa would have killed you, knowing what he did about you; how you rode with Quantrell and burned homes and murdered women and children—you—oh, damn you to hell!"

"Stop it" Doug shouted savagely, then wheeled at the sharp metallic cocking of DeRoso's .44.

"I'll stop him," DeRoso suggested.

Doug did not hesitate; he took two steps to DeRoso and hit him in the face. DeRoso stumbled backward, crashing into the commode. He swayed there a moment, his face blank; then the hatred took it fully, and his gun came to a level on Doug's chest.

"Fred!"

The whiplash of Lute's voice somehow broke through DeRoso's rage. He swayed on his feet, his gun held rigid before him for a long instant in which Lute did not breathe at all; then the muzzle slacked, slowly. Doug eased his half-drawn gun back into its holster. Lute breathed again; he came erect and stalked to the commode, yanking it open. He pulled out a dragoon gun and belt and strapped it on.

Lute slapped it and looked at them. "I'll take no more," he said grimly. "Not off either of you."

"Don't threaten me, Lute," Doug said mildly, not impressed. "Just keep the kid away from me. He stinks." He swung back to his brother.

DeRoso turned white, a hellish fury in his pale eyes, but he was wholly in check now, any impulse further governed by the plain warning in Lute's face.

Doug was saying, "General, this is no place for you. You go home to the old man. I let you go, promise that."

"You know the answer."

Doug said patiently, "This's getting us exactly nowhere. Fella, I can't go back. The old man would shoot me himself; you said so. . . . What else is there for me?"

Jim looked at him fully. "You can pay up," he said flatly.

"Pay what? I got nothing to pay except my life. And that would rot away in a federal prison. Quantrell—"

"Appomattox was two years ago," Jim said savagely. "I mean since. Go off somewhere, change your name. But go on like this and you're lost."

Doug said in a tried and patient way, "Three years of this mark a man. No matter how far you go, you can't turn back. . . . Only you quit this damn foolishness and go home."

"No."

Lute said uneasily, "What are we going to do with him?"

Doug regarded Lute flatly and without compromise. "Don't know, Lute. Know what we're *not* going to do, put it that way. . . . Go on with what you were telling me."

Lute glanced at Doug's brother.

"What's the difference?" Doug said irritably. "If he was posing as me, he knows you're up to something. . . ."

Lute hesitated for an unhappy moment and nodded uncomfortably. "It's this, Doug. There's safety in numbers. Money, too. Bunch of us organize, we could strike back instead of running. Get some real loot into the bargain." He paused.

Doug said dryly, "I'm listening."

"You remember when we were with Quantrell—the James boys, Frank, Jesse? And Cole Younger? After the war they organized. Men like us. Paid off. Can for us."

Doug said skeptically, "How do we get these—men like us . . . ?"

Lute smiled meagerly. "I haven't just been riding back and forth across Texas to look for you. I've talked to men in dozens of towns and on the trail. Ex-rebs, ex-yanks. Spicks, breeds, men from fifteen to fifty. A lot of them think I got something. Small bunch of hard-riding men can do more for themselves than a hundred times that number sifted through the state."

"For instance . . ."

"Planned bank and train robberies. Jayhawking cattle. A herd is gold on the hoof these days. . . . Besides—I've got a system, Doug. Yes, a real system. . . ."

"Why you looking for me in particular though?"

"We'll need a leader," Lute said mildly, and watched the astonishment wash thinly across Doug's face.

"Me."

Lute nodded somberly.

"Your idea," Doug pointed out dryly. "Why not you?"

"Unh-uh. I can plan and I can organize, but I'm fat and I'm too cautious. I'm a slow thinker and I'm getting on the wrong side of thirty. That's young for anything else, but not for this."

"Put it this way, then," Doug said. "Why me?"

"For opposite reasons. Nerves, youth, fast as I'm not. You got the knack for handling men. Seen that back with Quantrell. These hard-cases know who you are, they'll toe the line. Don't know another who could handle them, see . . . ?"

Doug removed his hat thoughtfully and musingly fingered the frayed brim. "You say you have the men lined up."

Lute nodded. "We'll move around—pick 'em up on the quiet. . . ."

Doug glanced idly at DeRoso. "He an example?"

A glance at DeRoso's face told Lute that DeRoso would have-to go; he and Doug wouldn't mix.

"Listen to me, Doug," Jim Kingdom said coldly. "You're on the borderline now. Only start raking this fat boy's chestnuts out of the fire by letting him use your name as the head of this scum he's pulling together, you'll be a target for every man who recognizes you."

"Sorry, General. . . . What the man says makes sense. I'm tired of being told to move on. . . ." Doug watched his brother, briefly, sadly, then clamped his hat on tightly and moved toward the door. "We're riding out now. You make enough noise after we're gone and someone will find you. Only don't follow us."

DeRoso was standing at the far end of the room by the battered commode and he said now, his face a malignant saffron mask in the lamplight, "On the quiet, Lute, you said. . . . How's that tally with letting Big Brother go so he can tell every law in the country? We'll be broken before we're started. . . ."

Doug stopped. He said flatly, "You won't be along to worry about it. Damn if I'll have a trigger-happy sheepherder's pup after a fast rep dragging along for a chance to shoot me in the back."

He wheeled, starting for the door again. . . .

Suddenly, goaded beyond patience, beyond fear, DeRoso pulled his gun and shouted, *"Turn, damn you, Kingdom!"*

The breaking pitch of DeRoso's voice brought Doug around, but barely touching his gun, when DeRoso shot. Doug buckled in the middle and came partly erect, still on his feet, to get his gun pulled, when DeRoso shot again. Doug was smashed back, dropping his gun and falling half through the open door.

DeRoso swung his weapon on Lute. "You move, Lute, and I'll kill you!"

DeRoso's attention was pulled from the door; he didn't see that Jim Kingdom had already dragged himself to his knees and was working with a terrible concentration to keep his balance as he leaned forward to grasp Doug's fallen gun between his bound hands and maneuver it into one fist.

Jim Kingdom fired once. The rickety commode rocked with a shuddering crash against the wall as DeRoso was flung into it. DeRoso dropped to his knees, a blankness filming his eyes; he fought to lift his gun, failed, and fell on his face.

Lute was already diving for the doorway. His gun was out now, but even in the passion of the moment, he would not shoot at Doug's brother. Jim Kingdom, in a blind fury, shot at him as he reached the door and the slug missed by only inches, whirring like an angry hornet into the darkness.

He ran for the side of the building to cut around it to the street when he heard the pounding of footsteps on the boardwalk by Rhuba's. The shots, he thought, and veered away from the street, cutting back from the building at right angles and into the concealment of the darkness beyond. He stopped abruptly, hunkering down in the tall grass, making himself small in the night as men rushed around the corner of the building and poured into the open doorway of Lute's room.

Lute heard the flurry of their voices as he squatted there in the sage, trying to think over the pounding of his heart. Everything he owned, except his horse and the clothes on his back, was in that room, and he would have to leave—now—without it. His horse was in the livery, but his saddle was in the room, and for one panicked moment he couldn't think beyond that. He thought fleetingly of asking the hostler for the loan of a saddle and bridle and rejected this thought as it came. There would be questions for which he was too unnerved to conjure answers. . . .

Then he recalled that when he and DeRoso and Doug had left Rhuba's, Doug's stud sorrel had been hitched to the tie-rail. Lute could safely assume that the shots had by now drawn everyone off the street. . . .

Instantly, with fresh hope, he came to his feet and, skirting the building widely, started at a run for the street. The sorrel was there, he saw; and he slowed to a casual but hurried walk. He angled across the street by Rhuba's, coming up beside the horse and pausing there to cast a fleeting glance around. The saloon was empty and there was no one in sight on the street. He paused long enough to check the latigo, then took the reins and stepped into the saddle, wheeling the horse and starting him into a dead run downstreet.

It was a dark night, and once past the last building, Lute slowed down. There would be no pursuit at night, and he could make dry camp a little farther on; Doug's suggans were still lashed to his cantle.

Lute rode on, heading in a vaguely southerly direction, oddly dead to the passions that had driven him into the night, running again.

## CHAPTER  THREE

ON HIS KNEES, Jim Kingdom strained his eyes into the sooty blackness beyond the door where Lute had disappeared, but presently, distinguishing no sign of the man, he slowly, with a great sigh, dropped the gun to the floor. His gaze fell to Doug, sprawled across the threshold. The crazed fury of seeing his brother shot down before his eyes evaporated into a deadness that left him drained and tired beyond thought.

The rush of feet outside brought him to his senses, and several men came in; the first was Red Rhuba, in his soiled bar apron and carrying his shotgun in one big freckled fist. His blue eyes took in the scene in one scanning glance —two fallen men and Jim Kingdom on his knees tied hand and foot.

"Hell," Red said feelingly. "What happened, friend?" He saw the residue of blank shock in Jim's face, and saw that the big man was looking at him without seeing him.

Red cut Jim loose and helped him up. Silently Jim moved to his brother's side and went down on one knee beside him. The first bullet had hit Doug low above the groin; Jim could feel Doug's own pain as he watched his brother's eyes flick open. His lips parted, touched now with a thin lacing of bloody foam. Punctured lung, Jim thought, and something sank and died in him.

Doug recognized him and tried to speak, barely succeeding. "Different story with an even break, General. . . ."

"I got him, Doug."

"You? There's a hero." He actually smiled. "Funny, can't lift my head. No feeling. A hell of a way to . . ."

"Doug—"

"No, listen." His breath shortened. ". . . There's a girl. I married her. Melanie Hassard." He caught Jim's arm. "Runs rooming house—town of Boundary. Due south to Rio Grande. Tell her—tell Melanie—I'm sorry. Just tell her that. . . . Sorry . . ." He squinted. "Fella, you there?"

"Yes, Doug."

"Yes. Funny—I thought . . . Go home. Tell the old man —tell—" His voice trailed into a racking cough; he looked at Jim. It was odd, very very odd, how suddenly clear-eyed he was, with that sly gleam of well-remembered humor. . . . "You tell the old man I said to go to hell. He'll believe that—he'll believe—believe . . ."

It was ended. Ended so imperceptibly that it was a moment before Jim fully realized it. Only the sly humor had gone to leave the eyes varnished with blankness, and there was no more talk and there was no more coughing; and Kingdom lifted the body of his brother very gently in his arms and turned to face those who stood in the room watching him silently, expectantly; and he looked at them still without seeing them. Carrying his brother, he stepped noiselessly out the door and into the shadowed and formless night.

"All right, boys," he heard Rhuba say. "Get on back. Drinks on the house. It's all over. . . ."

Jim Kingdom, staring into the cobalt void of the night, vaguely heard the murmuring of the men leaving the lean-to. Yes, Kingdom said silently; yes, it's all over. . . .

He heard footsteps behind him and was presently aware that Red Rhuba had come to stand beside him. "There's a cleared spot back of my place we use for burying," Red said gently. He paused and cleared his throat. "I got a shovel."

Find him, Jim, Kingdom's mother had said. Find Doug and see he's all right.

*Yes. Yes, Ma. He's all right. Doug's all right now. The rest of it doesn't matter. He's all right. . . .*

Jim roused a litle. He looked at Red, trying to hold to Red's words over the throbbing ache of his head. At last he said in a dull, half-comprehending way, "Yes. Thank you."

Jim Kingdom rode out of Dry Springs before dawn.

The first thing was to find Melanie Hassard. Red had told him that Boundary lay due southwest; the simpliest way to find the town was to strike west until he hit the stage route, perhaps three hours' ride, and follow it south to Boundary.

Jim reached the stage road before noon, and by noon had caught up with the stage when it stopped at Ocotillo Station. Here, at the direction of the driver, a small spare man of vinegar-waspish temper, he tied his horse behind the stage. Without waiting to eat, Kingdom climbed inside, settled onto a horsehair-padded seat, and, in a stuporous exhaustion of more than twenty-nine strenuous and sleepless hours, was asleep even before his glare-strained eyes could become accustomed to the subdued interior of the coach.

He scarcely realized that there were three other passengers until the jolting of the stage awakened him two hours later. A small tattered tramp, unwashed, unshaven, and unfriendly, sat beside Kingdom. The young man across from the tramp was not especially garrulous, merely hungry for talk; his name, he said, was Jean-Paul Villon. He and his wife were traveling from New Orleans to live on her father's ranch near Boundary.

Kingdom had met one or two Creoles during the war; this slender, frail young man of middle height he judged to be one, with his queued black hair and his soft-voiced accent. His slender expressive hands were completely graceful, completely aesthetic. He wore the tight fawn-colored trousers of the fashionable of ten years before, a travel-grimed white sharkskin waistcoat, gold-embroidered, and a black frock coat. He had frequent and violent fits of coughing. In spite of his frailty and his quiet-seeming mien, there was an erect and fearless pride in his carriage that Kingdom found admirable in a man so little gifted physically, however handsome facially.

His wife was far less impressive at first glance; a small girl of good form but thinned down. She wasn't pretty; her mouth was too wide, her nose too short, and her eyebrows oddly sun-bleached so much lighter than her dark chestnut hair that they were nearly invisible against her pale skin. Yet her violet eyes held a childlike charm that seemed far from spurious, enhanced by the faint tracery of freckles across the bridge of her nose.

Character, Kingdom thought, was a poor and inadequate word for the compounding of pride and gentleness that he saw in this girl. Goodness was better. She was not yet twenty, he judged, though her husband was little under Kingdom's own age, which was thirty-one. Her dress was of plain calico with a short blue cape of better material and she wore both with a warm and human queenliness; but there was sweet and patient resignation in her face that made Kingdom think, She could stand to laugh a little.

"My father-in-law used to ranch on the Louisiana side of the Sabine," said Villon. "He heard there was good grazing land by the Rio Grande so he sold out and established a ranch down here shortly before the war. He wrote us at New Orleans to come and live with him. I was doing well at my portrait painting in Orleans, but my physician insisted that the bayau country is bad for my lung condition. I was glad to accept the invitation. I am bringing my savings too, which are not inconsiderable. I hope to go into partnership in cattle with him. I have heard that the business has potentialities. From your experience in this part of the country, what would you say?"

Kingdom shrugged sparely. "I only came West not long ago myself. Never been so far south as the Rio. Heard it's good for cattle. But cattle isn't always money."

"What do you mean, sir?"

"Question of a market," Kingdom said dryly. "You have to get a herd to a shipping center. In Texas, that means a trail-drive hundreds of miles. Missouri, Louisiana. Indians, border gangs, flooded rivers, dry water holes every mile of the way. Lot of ranchers hate to try it; those that aren't have to sell their souls to get a crew with the insides to make the drive all the way. If they do get through, they're likely lucky to have enough cattle left to sell to pay off the crew."

"Is Missouri the best way?"

"That's what they said in Springfield. But there was talk of the railroad pushing west into Kansas."

"Would a Kansas drive be better?"

"Couldn't say. There's bad country up through the Nations. You'd have to talk to—"

The entire coach seemed to half lift under the sudden violence of its braking; the shoes squealed savagely and trailed into silence as the stage rocked to a stop, creaking heavily back on the thorough braces. Kingdom pulled the leather dust curtains back and thrust his head from the window. Villon called in a shaken voice, "What is it, Mr. Hollister?"

"What the hell you mean by riding at us like that? Want to get run down?" came the driver's angry-strident voice.

"Just take it easy," the horseman said gently.

Kingdom could see the man now; he had reined close around to the side of the coach, a small young man in a baggy black suit. His smile was narrow and warning, yet the white flash of it was utterly good-natured and reckless; and mad flecks danced merrily in his black-irised eyes. The curly black hair, glossy as a cricket's shell, which tumbled carelessly from beneath his back-tilted gray hat, only heightened his uncaring air. His gaze moved to Kingdom looking from the window, and he smiled a little more and nodded cheerfully.

Hollister's voice softened and there was an almighty patience to it. "Son, if you don't move off, so help me I'll knock you clean out of your saddle with this popper."

The young man's heavy-lidded gaze moved almost idly away from Kingdom to the driver. "Don't push it, grandpa," he murmured, his smile gentle to the extreme. His slim hands were crossed negligently on the pommel. . . .

Kingdom quietly drew Doug's revolver from the waist

of his trousers and eased it up to the window, then stopped
in the act of laying the long barrel across the sill. A full-
size dragoon revolver had appeared as if by magic in the
stranger's slim hand. He held it loosely, but he smiled directly at Kingdom as he spoke.

"I wouldn't, friend. I really wouldn't. It wouldn't do,
you know. You're a big man, but a little bullet could stop
you dead. Quite dead."

The youth reined his horse in nearer to the rear of the
stage, grinning in at the passengers. He motioned with
his gun, his attention on the others: "Throw it out, friend."
Kingdom didn't move. The boy glanced at him, his voice
softening a shade. "Throw it out, friend."

Kingdom let the gun drop out the window. The youth
looked at Villon. "Now. You."

"I pack none," Villon said with a stiff and outraged
formality.

"You, then, grandpa. Both of them." Hollister threw
pistol and shotgun out in to the road; the bandit pulled
in close to the stage door and leaned from his saddle to
wrench it open. "Out, my children. Sit tight on your whiskers up there, grandpa."

Kingdom climbed out, helped Mrs. Villon to the ground,
and gave Villon a hand down. Kingdom looked around
then at the bandit.

"Throw your wallet up, friend. Reach for it slow. . . .
That's fine."

Kingdom threw the bandit the worn leather sheaf and
his free hand snaked it easily out of the air. Kingdom
watched him take out the solitary gold eagle inside. It
made a bright twinkle in the sunlight as he spun it into
the air with a laugh, caught it, and slid it into the wallet.
The stranger tossed it back with such fluid unexpectedness
that it hit Kingdom in the chest before he caught it on
the rebound.

"Buy yourself some champagne, friend," the youth said

merrily. He looked at the little tramp, Loomis, flicking a black lightning glance over him; he laughed. He motioned at Villon. "All right—you."

"I have nothing."

"Untruths, untruths . . . ! Throw your coat up here. Then empty your pockets."

He looked through Villon's coat, said "Hm" thoughtfully, and tossed it back. "Come on, the other stuff."

Villon passed up the articles from his pockets—cigar case, expensive gold watch case, and wallet. The youth examined the articles, looked in the fine Morocco wallet, then carelessly threw all three costly items back into the dust at Villon's feet.

"Nice, but not much compared to what you must be hiding somewhere," he said musingly.

Villon had said he was bringing a large sum from New Orleans and it was obvious he would not carry a large sum in the open. His prosperous appearance was a giveaway, though.

"You, grandpa," said the young man. "Get down and get this pilgrim's luggage out."

Hollister hauled all of Villon's bags out and opened and rifled through them at the youth's directions. At the end of this fruitless search, the bandit grinned and scratched his jaw, then looked idly at Mrs. Villon. "Your wife . . . ?"

"Yes," Villon said tensely.

The bandit's gaze moved down her, stopping at her waist. Instinctively, she half lifted a hand, then dropped it quickly. The highwayman smiled disarmingly, saying to Villon, "Money belt. And on your wife rather than you. Clever." He nodded to Villon's wife and waggled his gun barrel at her. "All right, lady."

She did not move; merely watched him without fear. "But it's under my dress," her voice not losing a jot of its soft calm.

A murderous rage blazed suddenly across Villon's face. "*Sacre!* You misbegotten beast! If you—"

The youth, some eager, savage impulse breaking through his indifference, swiveled his gun to cover Villon. "Want to say something?"

For a split second the naked urge to do murder danced madly through the youth's black eyes. Villon's mouth worked silently, then closed; his face was white, more with the pitifully angry knowledge of futility than fear.

The youth said, again mildly, "Get in the coach, ma'am. All I want is the belt. Only be quick about it. . . ."

Relief crossed Villon's face, but only for a moment. He said shortly, "Don't do it, Wanda."

Mrs. Villon regarded the youth composedly. "It's all we have," she said gently.

The bandit's voice was nearly a whisper. "Lady, I'm trying to be nice about this. Get in the coach. I won't say it again."

Kingdom, watchful and unspeaking, saw Mrs. Villon look first at Hollister, then at himself, and he read her thoughts: her husband was no coward, but physically incapable of preventing this; it must be to one of the other men that she look for help. She turned then, slowly, and walked to the stage. She stepped up, closed the door after her, and pulled the dust curtains.

Kingdom looked back to the robber to find the young man regarding him with idle interest.

"Haven't I seen you before?"

"No," Kingdom said.

"Dallas, say? Maybe El Paso."

"No."

"Funny." The bandit shook his head and looked at Villon, a merry grin touching his mouth. "You should have put a few dollars in your wallet, friend. Would have thrown me off. Only an empty wallet on a prosperous-looking pilgrim—" He chuckled, gestured aimlessly with his gun and let the barrel slack to the pommel of his saddle. "Just don't look right."

Kingdom acted then, almost without thought, in the second that the man's attention was off him and his pistol unleveled. Kingdom was standing close to the head of the fellow's horse; he swung one great fist in a short upward arc that smashed with pile-driver painfulness into the skittish beast's nose.

The animal reared high with a sound of pain. The robber's response was unbelievably swift; as fast as thought itself, his gun was leveled and it crashed out at the very moment that the horse flinched from the blow. But that initial movement spoiled the shot, and he could not shoot again because he was fighting now to get his plunging horse under control.

Kingdom tried to catch the reins and missed. The man, cursing, fought his horse down; then turned the beast into Kingdom with a savage wrench just as Kingdom caught his reins and reached up to drag him from the saddle. The horse's shoulder hit Kingdom in the chest, tore away his hold and knocked him off his feet into the dust. The bandit's gun arced up again, and this time Kingdom was an easy and helpless target; then Hollister's whiplash shot out like the head of a striking adder—a living part of its wielder, as unerring as a third hand—and with a flat explosive crack, the bandit's gun was torn powerfully from his grasp and flung away.

Kingdom hauled himself dazedly to his hands and knees and saw his own gun lying where it had fallen only two yards away. He floundered toward it on his hands and knees, got it, and started to his feet, turning it on the bandit. With the same lightning celerity, the man clamped the reins with an iron hand, and spurred his horse straight at Kingdom and into him; Kingdom, only half upright, was again knocked sprawling.

Because he was unarmed now, the bandit did not stop but

drove his horse on at a dead run into the desert. Kingdom was on his feet then, and shot after him twice; on the second shot, the horse collapsed beneath the man, throwing him far ahead.

Kingdom, unconsciously holding the gun pointed in front of him, started running without thinking toward the fallen horse. slowing with more caution as he neared it. He saw that the highwayman lay motionless beyond. The horse was kicking in death throes to which Kingdom put a stop with a third bullet.

Then with infinite caution he moved step by step over to the bandit, wary of any trick. It was not until he actually stood over the man that the meaning of the grotesque angle at which his neck was twisted struck fully home to Kingdom. His hand, fisted around the gun butt, fell loosely to his side and he shivered and felt cold in this desert heat.

As he walked back to the coach, Mrs. Villon stepped from it and with the three men waited in silence as Kingdom stopped in front of them. He saw how her face showed the strain of the past moments, the skin stretched tautly white and nearly transparent over the delicate bones of her face.

She took a step toward him, her voice barely audible. "We can't thank you. We can't begin to thank you."

Kingdom looked at her dully, only half comprehending her words. Somewhere in the back of his mind a wordless voice was screaming that he should not have shot. The man had been riding away with his back turned; he should not have shot. . . .

Hollister said in rough concern, "What's wrong, son?"

"Nothing." Kingdom drew the back of his hand across his eyes and looked at Hollister. "You'll have to help me. . . . He's dead. Neck's broken."

## CHAPTER FOUR

LUTE LIGHTED a huge black cigar and laid out a game of solitaire which he tried for five minutes to pretend he was enjoying, then threw down the card he was holding with an angry "Ah-h-h—!" of disgust, relighted his dying cigar and leaned back in his chair.

Now, in the late afternoon, Ab's Keno Parlor in Boundary was nearly deserted, the only sound being the keno goose to the rear, and Lute had taken a front corner table to be alone and think. He was wondering in the gray fashion which had lately come to color his thoughts more frequently what the future could hold now. It seemed that with Doug's death the last possibility of escape from this life was ended. Too, Jim Kingdom would likely, blaming him for Doug's death, be on Lute's trail.

Lute's musing was broken by voices and by spurred feet clattering heavily on the walk outside, and two men in the nondescript denims of cowmen pushed through the batwings.

The first one came to a sudden stop in the center of the saloon, looking things over. He was over six feet, under thirty, his lower face yellow-blurred by a week's blond beard. His bone-white teeth clamped like a bulldog's on the cold cigar in his mouth.

The second man was an unshaven puncher with the look of the colorless drudge who spends all his life working for a bigger man's petty wages.

The tall man took the cigar from his mouth. "Hey, Ab! You here?"

The owner raised his fat, balding head above the bar beneath which he was restacking glasses. He watched the two with no friendliness. "We don't sell booze to you any more, Hassard. Not after the way you wrecked the place last time. . . ."

"Yeah," Hassard said. "Bless you and keep you happy. Only I am good today regardless. Got a stage to meet. . . . Alf and I just came in for a game while we're waiting."

"I thought you were Santerre's segundo, not his errand boy," Ab said with heavy sarcasm.

A kind of tidal flush worked up Hassard's neck. He said softly, "Just take it easy."

Ab snorted in disgust and turned his back on him.

Alf and Hassard sat down at a table by the wall; Alf produced a pack of age-slick cards from his jumper, and they played for a while, lackadaisically.

"This is peanuts," Hassard said. "Double the ante."

"Then you drop me," Alf said with a shake of his head.

"Hell," Hassard said. He glanced over at Lute. "Want in, friend? Stud. Two-dollar ante."

Lute hesitated; he had planned to go to bed early to get a full night's sleep and still be out of town early in the morning. But it was still pre-dark and he could stand to kill another hour or so. And he could use some money.

"I'll sit in for a couple hands," he said.

Hassard dealt. He played with a hot-headed abandon which Lute judged might characterize his every action.

Hassard chewed the cigar. "Raise you two?"

"Sure," Lute said, but he watched their hands with a frown. Each had two cards, one face down. Lute's face-up card was an ace; Hassard's only a ten.

"Call you," Lute said reluctantly.

Hassard grinned and slid a third card across the table to him. Lute's hand hid it briefly as he reached for it; then he turned it up—an ace. He looked mildly at Hassard who stared at the card, becoming very white. So, Lute thought, he knew what to expect.

Hassard said at last, thickly, "I don't understand that ace."

"I know," Lute said. "You expected this. . . ." He threw a three seemingly out of nowhere to the table.

"You palmed it!"

"Yes." Lute stood up, pocketing his silver. "So I could find out what kind of a game I was in. Now I know, I'm out."

Hassard smiled, almost idly. "What're you saying?"

"That you're a bellystripper," Lute said quietly.

Hassard gently laid his cards on the table and leaned back in his chair. "I'm waiting for you to say that again— only I don't think you will say it. . . ."

Alf dropped his cards, his face turning faintly ashen under the dirt and whiskers. "Egan, let it ride. . . ."

"This whey-belly drifter worry you, Alf . . . Don't you let him. He won't say it. He won't say anything. . . ."

Someone laughed over by the door and said, "I think he will."

Lute looked swiftly in that direction. The man who had spoken was so little concerned as to not even glance at them. He and a companion were both walking toward the bar now, the batwings swinging to behind them. They signaled for whiskey and bellied up to the bar without a glance at Hassard.

A kind of baffled anger mounted in Hassard's face. He said thickly, "What did you say, Incham?"

Incham poured a drink, still not troubling to glance at Hassard, and said in a bored voice as though this were an old story to him, "I said I think he will."

"I'll argue that," Hassard said thinly, something bright and hot kindling in his face.

Incham's companion threw his head back and his long and clear-tinkling laughter lifted through the room, a mad and wild note of danger in it that made Lute's scalp prickle.

Hassard said sparely, "How would you like to learn manners?"

The man stopped laughing; he leaned forward a little, barely lifting his voice above a whisper. "You must make shift to give me a lesson, Mr. Hassard. Soon. Oh, very soon!"

"You are on the verge, Hassard," Incham murmured, "of making a very grave mistake. Tory is a little mad, you know. . . ."

Hassard said thickly, "This time we let it ride—"

"You're wise," Incham said.

"Next time," Hassard said. "There'll be a next time."

Tory clapped his hands. "Encore . . . !"

"Be quiet, Tory," Incham said irritably. He had turned back to the bar and was gazing absently at his drink, Hassard already forgotten.

Hassard pivoted on his heel and walked silently out, stiff with rage, Alf following.

Incham looked over his shoulder at Lute. "Join us," he said shortly.

Lute got up and walked over to the bar; Ab, behind it, said sourly to Lute, "You damn fool," and walked disgustedly to the rear of the room where he sat down with a two-months-old newspaper and ignored them. Tory threw his head back and laughed. Incham was sunk in brooding again and had apparentliy not even heard Ab.

Lute looked puzzledly at Ab, then at Tory. "What was that for?"

"Ab doesn't approve of us," Tory said merrily. "He thinks you're taking up with bad company. . . . Have a drink."

Lute poured one, regarding the two men with unslackened interest. Their utter fearlessness in spite of their small stature was all that they held in common. Incham was in his forties, his thinning sun-bleached hair gray-streaked as he removed his hat. He seemed listless and bored, and Lute felt that this was a pose; there was a flicker of wicked arrogance behind the show-nothing opaqueness of the deep-set eyes. He wore a frayed and dusty suit, the coat open to show a threadbare linsey-woolsey shirt, and the trousers stuffed into jackboots. He carried no gun in sight. Far from being all-over impressive; but Lute sensed that wherever this man went, he would be the leader.

Tory was an effervescent opposite; the wickedness fairly danced through his dark eyes. He was about half Incham's age, the coal-black curls spilling from under his hat in startling contrast to his teeth which constantly showed in a laugh. There was a kind of Mephistophelian handsomeness to his face and about the sober black he wore from head to foot. The story of him could be read in an instant in the tied-down Colt—butt pointed forward—at his left hip. It was somehow prominent, as through a part of the man; perhaps seeming so because it lay black against the unrelieved blackness of his clothes.

Tory had already had three quick drinks and was pouring himself a fourth. Incham looked at him suddenly, sharply. "You've had enough."

Tory paused in the act of lifting the glass and watched Incham with gleeful wickedness. "Who says I have?"

Incham's pale eyes fixed him. "I do."

Tory set the glass down and gave another burst of mad laughter. He substituted a cigar for the drink and was still chuckling as he lighted it.

Incham ignored him and turned to Lute. "I'm John Incham. This is Tory Stark."

"Lute Danning," Lute said and shook hands with both.

"I like your guts," Incham observed. "You're the first

man I've seen who'd tell Hassard to his face that he cheated you. That's why I stepped in," he added idly. "You have too much nerve to die for it. . . ."

Lute's throat tightened. "I'm new here. . . . I didn't know he was that good."

Incham shrugged as though the subject held no real interest for him. "He's good for a cowhand. Tory here could beat him. Knows it too."

"That's obvious," Tory said and laughed some more.

Incham looked at him with irritation. "I wonder if that brother of yours will ride in today? We've been waiting in town for two days now, and I'm sick of it."

Tory shrugged. "Maybe he's held up on business."

"No doubt," Incham said dryly, "seeing that his business is holding up."

Tory howled with laughter and banged his glass on the bar. Presently he sobered up enough to say, "You'll be glad we waited for him, Mr. Incham. Bob, he wants much to join us. You wouldn't regret it if you waited another day. Or two days."

"Or another week? Or two weeks?" Incham said sarcastically.

"He's hell on wheels with a gun," Tory persisted.

"Better than you?"

Tory smiled enigmatically, thoughtfully. "Like I told you, I don't know. He's three years younger than me, and we haven't seen each other much since the war ended. Got this letter from him awhile ago. First I heard of him in months. . . . Maybe . . . we'll find out."

Lute was beginning to understand now. This Incham was doubtless the head of a gang of wanted men; men from the backwash of the war years like Lute himself, cast up on the tidal beach of the raw frontier, a lawless frontier where they fell naturally into the guerrilla and bushwhacker ways which had characterized their wartime tactics. Men like this Tory Stark. Perhaps like Lute Danning too.

At this idle thought, Lute felt a sudden and mounting excitement as the seed of an idea came to him. The excitement, at least, must have been apparent to Incham who smiled faintly and cocked a tawny eyebrow.

"You look as though you have a mouthful of hot meal, my friend, and your tongue scalding to get rid of it."

Lute glanced at Ab, scowlingly absorbed in his newspaper, and lowered his voice. He talked quietly for ten minutes during which Incham said nothing, only giving him an occasional silent and appraising glance.

Finally, when Lute had ceased to speak and was watching the inscrutable Incham intently, expectantly, the man said thoughtfully, "Your idea, now, Friend Lute—nothing new in the idea itself. Organized outlawry is an old story."

"And it's paid off," snapped Lute. "It's the development of that organization. . . . Clockwork efficiency. Discipline. Military-type strategy and tactics . . ."

"You need officers, trained officers, to whip 'em into shape," Incham pointed out, and seeing the patient smile on his face, Lute felt withered. It was the same patient smile with which you would humor a child or an imbecile.

The gorge of anger rose in Lute; he drew a deep breath. "Look, Mr. Incham," he said quietly. "I know what I'm talking about. I only had a few years of schooling, but I always been a reader on field tactics. Books by military men. I ate the stuff. I used to read Caesar's Commentaries and Napoleon's Maxims over till the books fell apart."

Incham's eyes sharpened on him. "You mean it, don't you? You really think you've got something."

"I damn well know I've got something."

"All right, Napoleon. We'll see. . . ."

"You mean—"

"You're welcome to come with us. Put your ideas to practical use if you like. I believe that every man should have ample apportunity to discover how much of a fool he can be." Incham tempered his words with a faint smile.

" 'We must hang together or assuredly we shall hang separately. . . .' "

Tory laughed. "That's a good one, Mr. Incham."

"I didn't say it," Incham said dryly, then lifted his head sharply. "That's the stage horn. Would your brother be likely to come in on the stage?"

"He might stop it," Tory chuckled, "but not to get on it."

"Doubtless," Incham said. "Still, we'll look." He drained his glass, set it on the bar, and walked out, followed by Tory and Lute.

The westering sun softened in its last light the harsh and raw outlines of the sprawling frontier outpost of Boundary as they stepped onto the walk. The arrival of the stage was always a thing to hold the attention; a small crowd was already gathering. The big Concord had just pulled up before Decatur's Mercantile across the street, the roiled dust of its stop already settling. The driver threw the lines around the brake, swung down from his high seat, and opened the door. A young woman and man were first down, followed by a nondescript little saddle bum.

Then the giant frame of the fourth passenger blocked the door, and a sudden half-recognized fear touched a cold finger to Lute's brain. Now the passenger had stepped down and the last rays of dying sunlight struck down on him fully there in the street.

Kingdom! He followed me here! Lute thought, and for a moment could not think beyond that; then he half-turned to take the step that would carry him back into the concealment of the saloon. It was too late. Kingdom's gaze had already swept up across the three men on the walk opposite; yet the glance must have been an absent one, for it moved on, idly, down the walk. Lute took a sidewise step then that put him in back of Incham, out of Kingdom's direct view.

Lute saw that the young woman had turned and spoken to Kingdom, who replied briefly, touched his hat, and

walked past her to the boot to get his horses, leaving the
young woman and her escort looking after him in surprise. Lute heard the woman's soft laughter.

The driver was talking, handing Kingdom his reins;
Kingdom asked him something. The driver spoke and
pointed downstreet and Kingdom started in that direction
without a backward glance. Lute slowly, almost cautiously, let out his breath in relief and shivered in the fading
light.

Tory said carelessly, "He ain't on it," and turned to walk
back into the saloon, when Incham, staring intently at the
stage, said curiously, "Wait."

Incham stepped off the walk and started across the
street to the coach. Tory hesitated a moment, then followed
him, Lute trailing after. They arrived at the stage with a
few other onlookers, and Lute saw then what had attracted
Incham's attention: the soles of a pair of boots on the
floor of the stage, plainly visible through the open door.
Beyond the boots, the blanket-covered figure told its own
grim story.

"Dead man," grunted Incham and reached through the
door to draw the blanket away.

"A dead man," Tory said disinterestedly. He shrugged.
"There's enough in the world."

Lute caught the sharp, astonished jerk of Incham's
shoulders as he bent through the doorway to examine the
man, his body blocking the others' view.

"Why," he said in a soft, shocked voice which was, Lute
considered, peculiar to his usual dispassionate tone.

The sound of it pulled even Tory to attention.

"Why, Tory," Incham said, "he looks enough like you
to be—"

Perhaps he only then was struck with the significance
of his own words. Incham looked at Tory, then back at the
body; he reached out to draw the blanket too late.

Tory stood motionless for a moment, puzzling, his lazy

poise slowly sloughing from him. Then Incham's words hit him with complete understanding, and his sudden movement forward was as swift as that of a striking snake. Incham barely stepped aside in time as Tory sprang up through the doorway. Lute heard Tory's single choked exclamation as he bent over the still figure.

Then Tory bolted through the doorway. In two strides he confronted the driver "Which one . . . ?"

"Tory!" Incham said in a whiplash voice underscored with steel. Tory ignored him. The young couple, the saddle bum, and the driver looked at Tory in surprise.

"He kin of yours, son?" asked Hollister quietly.

"You can damn well see he is," Tory breathed almost inaudibly, "and if I have to blow the guts from every one of you to get the—"

"Tory," Incham repeated, altogether warningly. . . .

Tory turned slowly. He said icily, dangerously, "Mr. Incham—this is my business."

"And mine," Incham stated flatly. There was a long and tenuous pause. . . . Incham's bleached eyes were no longer bored; they were suddenly agate-blue-bright, agate hard. "And mine, Tory," he repeated, his voice flattening into the monosyllabic tonelessness of an Indian's.

Tory's black gaze fixed Incham's blue one; it seemed that time hung still in eternity. Tory relaxed then, barely, without lowering his eyes.

"Why don't you ask," Incham murmured, "how your brother was killed rather than rant about like the mad idiot you are?"

"I don't care a damn how he was killed! One of these people done him in; that's all I care," Tory said savagely. His eyes swept the driver and the passengers.

"Which one?" Tory said musingly. ". . . You?" He looked the young woman's escort over, measuring his frail frame —then gave a cold laugh. "No, not *you!*"

Tory's hot gaze raked on the the saddle bum; the little

man flinched instinctively; Tory's lip curled and he looked then to the driver who stood watching him with serene patience. "There was another one," Tory said. "A big fellow . . . Where'd he go?"

Hollister said wearily, "Picking daisies for all I know. Why don't you just take another look at the feller before you jump us any more, son? See how he died."

Tory frowned at Hollister for a long time, then turned and walked, still frowning, back to the coachdoor and climbed in. After a moment he said in a puzzled way, "He wasn't shot."

"Looking for the wrong thing," the driver said dourly. "Neck's broke."

Tory gingerly lifted the dead man's head, moved it, and lowered it gently. He said meagerly, "How?"

"He held us up. He rode off fast; horse stumbled, threw him. That's how. His gear's back in the boot if you want it."

"You sure none of you had a hand in it . . . ? You—that how it happened?" Tory looked at the frail young man.

The young man's jaw set. "Yes," he said coldly.

"Come off it, Tory," snapped Incham. "How else could it have happened?"

Tory didn't look at him. "Where's his horse?"

Hollister looked Tory in the eye. "Busted his leg when he stumbled. Shot him."

"Ah," Tory said softly. "Two fatal breakages. It must have been *quite* a spill. . . ."

"Are you through garnishing it?" Incham asked mildly.

Tory shot him a look of wrathful bafflement. "I don't know," he said, "but—"

"Then quit it! I damn well know what you're trying to do. Your brother's dead and you're looking for someone you can take it out on. Face it. It was his own damn fault. . . ."

Tory waited in a kind of hateful silence, and again looked

to Hollister. "I'm sorry," Tory said with no apology in his tone. "Will you do me the kindness of seeing that my brother is buried? And keep his gear."

"Thanks, son," Hollister said in a neutral voice. "I'll do that."

Incham, Tory and Lute left the group then and went without talk to the livery where they claimed their horses. Lute stopped at the hotel long enough to gather his scant belongings and check out. Rolling up his blankets, he congratulated himself on this windfall. He wouldn't need Doug after all, and Incham was an older and steadier head. Nor would he have to assemble men; the raw material was here.

As they rode out, passing the eating house, Lute glanced hugrily at it.

"We'll eat when we get to the home grounds," Incham said. "You'll like our little hamlet, Friend Lute. It's only ten miles' ride. After we eat, we'll talk plans—eh? I was halfway humoring you when I said we'd take you on, but the more I think about your military idea, the more I think you've got something."

Ten miles on an empty stomach, Lute thought morosely, and to take his mind off this depressing thought he asked: "What kind of work you been doing till now?"

Incham smiled wryly. "Mostly nothing. There's eleven of us in all. We're all wanted somewhere. Birds of a feather, you know. . . . If there's a leader, I'm him by understanding. That's about all there is."

Lute silently considered it a slovenly sounding outfit and was wondering if he could whip them into condition when Incham said with wry amusement, "I know what you're thinking. But it's a lean country right now, Texas, even for an honest man, and no one has enough to be finicky about."

Incham considered this briefly, then added, "Me now. I just don't give a damn." Incham shook his head. "It's a hell of a way to be, Friend Lute. You think you know what you want—money, a ranch, what-have-you—then you get it and you know you don't want it. . . ."

"This idea of yours now," he went on thoughtfully. "It's not the money you mentioned. It's a fresh toy now—something new, you understand. In a week, a month, the novelty will wear off. Hell of a way for a Harvard graduate to be, isn't it?" And at the look of surprise on Lute's face, he nodded, and said, smiling, "Oh yes."

Tory, riding till now in dangerous silence, spoke. "What are the men going to think about this?"

"Whatever I damn well tell them to think," Incham said gently. He jogged along in the gathering darkness in muteness for a while, then said in sudden anger, "Dammit, Tory, don't sound so cocky. I'm still top rooster on this dung-heap."

Incham swiveled his head toward Lute, his bleached eyes faintly luminescent. "You're the big brass, my boy, and it goes for you too. You're the general, but I'm commander in-chief. . . . Try to remember that. We'll all be happy. . ."

Lute marked something about Incham then—that only his lips smiled, ever.

## CHAPTER FIVE

LEAVING THE STAGE, Kingdom had been about to step to the boot to claim his horses when Mrs. Villon, at his side,

spoke: "There is no way we can begin to reward you for—
you know."

He shifted uncomfortably from one foot to the other
and didn't reply.

She went on with a hesitant smile, "Will we see you
again?"

He looked at her, a little wonderingly. "I don't know.
Maybe."

"But you will tell us your name, at least? You never
did, you know. . . ."

A meager smile touched the lines of Kingdom's face.
"Yes, ma'am. Davis," he said. "Jefferson Davis." He touched
his hat then, saw the surprise wash across her face and
her husband's, and turned to walk to the boot where Hollister was unloading. He heard Mrs. Villon's quiet laugh
behind him. Hollister looked up, grunted, and untied Kingdom's bay, handing Kingdom the reins.

"How much do I owe you?" Kingdom asked.

"This ride's on the line," said Hollister, "after the way
you made a hero of yourself."

"Thanks, only he would have gotten me without your
using the whip."

"Things work out," Hollister grunted, passing the saddle
to him.

"Which way to a place to sleep?"

"The Benton House's down the street. Next to last building on your right. . . . So long, son."

Kingdom turned his horses in at the livery, then regis-
tered at the hotel, paid for a night, and carried his gear
up to his room. He stripped off his shirt and washed; then
gloomily inspected in his palm the nine silver dollars remaining to him after breaking his last gold eagle. . . .

Putting on another shirt from his warbag, not much
cleaner than the one he'd had on, he sought the street.
It was early dark now and the first lights showed in rec-
tangular orange patches in the windows. He headed down-

street looking for an eating place he had seen on the way to the hotel. He saw it across the street and had stepped off the walk to angle across to it when he was hailed.

"You. Big fella. Hey!"

Kingdom stopped and squinted at the shadows under the mercantile gallery; a tall man stepped off the walk and came over to him, walking with a slight limp.

"Let's have the gun, brother," he said, extending his hand.

Kingdom caught the glint of lamplight on the badge on his vest, but did not move. "How come?"

"Town ordinance. No guns worn in the town limits. You check 'em at the jail from now on when you come in, pick 'em up when you leave."

"Since when?"

"Since an hour ago," the tall man said, satisfaction in his voice. "I finally got the city council to vote on it. Been after them a month." He snapped his fingers. "Let's have it."

Kingdom pulled Doug's Walker Colt from the waist of his trousers and passed it over. The tall man stuck it in his own belt and turned away with a nod. "Get it from the jailer when you're ready to leave." A light in the saloon across the street went on at that moment, a hazy illumination streaming out onto the street; it caught the tall man's profile as he turned.

"Pat Frost!" Kingdom said with a start.

The man turned to face him, a mild scowl touching his fine aquiline features. "I thought your voice was familiar, but where—"

"Spring of sixty-three—Leesville," Kingdom said, watching him, a slow smile coming to his face. "We were tent partners. . . ."

Frost snapped his fingers. "Jim Kingdom!" he rapped out, and grasped Kingdom's hand. "Sure, I remember. Never did see each other after that. . . . Leesville put me out of the war, Jim."

"Didn't know but what you were dead, Pat. Looked for you after . . . among the dead and living."

"Took a Minie ball through the leg. One of our own." Frost chuckled and shook his head. "Not so funny at the time, though. Spent the rest of the war in a half-dozen hospitals trying to save the damned thing."

"So now you're sheriff or marshal here?"

"Marshal. Headed west after I was able to get around. Was sort of absorbed into this community. City council figured I'd make a town marshal of sorts. . . . But you, Jim—what're you doing here? All you ever talked of was that family you were going home to. Something happen to them?"

"Nothing. much. . . . A long story, Pat. Tell it over a drink?"

"Never touch the stuff. How about over supper? Or you eaten?"

"No. Just going to."

"Good! I was going home. Come on—Laura can put on another plate. . . . Staying here long?"

"No. . . . You married? That's right—you used to tell me about your wife. . . ."

He's got something, Kingdom thought, and a bleak and indefinable loneliness settled in his mind.

They hauled up on a side street then, and Pat led the way up a sycamore-shaded pebbled path to a small lighted house. They tramped up on the porch, walking in through the propped-open door. The front room was small, the furnishings bright and comfortable.

Pat sailed his hat into a chair. "Laura!"

"In the kitchen, Pat."

"Come out here a minute. . . . An old friend of mine came in today. Want you to meet him."

She came out of the kitchen, a tall, red-haired young woman whose slim face, flushed from stove heat, was pleasant when she smiled. "Laura, this is Jim Kingdom. We were tent partners during the war."

Kingdom took off his hat, nodding self-consciously.

"Hello," she said and smiled. "Pat used to tell me about you. . . . You'll stay for supper, Mr. Kingdom? It's all ready."

"I already invited him. . . . Come on in the kitchen, Jim."

Kingdom had three helpings of beef stew, the first decent meal he'd had in months, and though he was never particular he appreciated the difference. He quietly envied Pat. The marshal said nothing until Kingdom had leaned back in his chair with a cigarette while Laura cleared the table.

"Anything particular bring you here, Jim?" Frost prodded gently.

This was business to Frost as much as friendly curiosity, Kingdom knew. He explained in a few words.

"Mm," Pat said thoughtfully. "Melanie Hassard, eh? I know the girl you mean. . . . She married some wild young fellow—a drifter. Damn! I remember. His name was Kingdom too—but I never thought to connect. . . . Well, she runs the rooming house. That's across the street from my jail. . . ."

Kingdom stirred in his chair. "I'd best be getting to see her." He stood. "Thank you for the meal, ma'am. Very good."

He walked to the front door, Frost following him, pipe in hand. At the door, Kingdom put on his hat and turned to shake hands with Pat.

"Good luck, Jim. Hope you don't come across this fellow Lute you're looking for in my town. Hate to run *you* in for something like that."

"I'm not looking for him," Kingdom said, "but if I find him, I think I'm going to hurt him."

Pat grinned. "Right. Come and see me before you leave."
Kingdom said he would, and they parted.

Kingdom paused outside the rooming house. It was two
stories, the warm light of the windows a comfortable and
homelike thing. He stepped up on the porch and knocked.
The door opened almost immediately. A young girl of about
nineteen in a beige-gray dress stood there. The look on
her face was wondering as she regarded him, and this altered suddenly into a wild happiness and she took a step
toward him and the happiness faded and some of the life
went out of her eyes. But the wonderment remained. She
stepped back, holding the door open.

"I thought you were someone else. Please come in."

He stepped inside, pulling off his hat and looking around,
then settling his gaze again to the girl before him. "Mrs.—
Kingdom?"

"Yes." She was not tall, was very dark, and had a strong,
earthy, almost coarse prettiness that held no appeal to him
though he judged that Doug would find it most attractive.

"I'm Doug's brother," Kingdom said. The puzzlement
left her face; a kind of welcoming warmth came to it.

"Jim," she smiled. "Of course. He spoke of you so much,
I always thought I'd know you right away. You do look
alike. . . ."

She led the way into an adjoining room. There was a
long dining table reaching the length of the room; it was
still uncleared as though the roomers had finished eating
shortly before. Melanie pulled out two chairs and sat down,
smoothing her skirt.

"I'm sorry Doug isn't here, Jim. . . . He's been gone for
several weeks. But he must have written you about us.
. . . Of course, or you wouldn't be here."

Kingdom mumbled something and looked at his hat
again.

"I haven't really seen much of Doug since we were
married. That was six months ago." A shade crossed her

face. . . . "He has to get out sometimes—to travel and such. But he'll tire of that. He . . ." The defiance crumpled suddenly and evaporated into misery; she said in a low, passionate voice, "I keep telling everyone that, Jim. . . . I don't care what they think, but I keep telling myself the same. It's no use to pretend to you—you know what he is. . . ." She bit her lip, tears starting from her eyes.

He played for time, time in which to gauge the saying of this. "How did—how did you happen to meet?"

She wiped her eyes. "I used to bring food to the prisoners at the jail. They had put him there over night—for getting drunk, he said. We wanted to get married almost right away, but—I have a brother too. . . . And what a brother he is." Her voice was soft and bitter-edged. "Since Pap and Mam died, he has delegated himself to tell me how to live—what men I can associate with, how to run my business. . . ."

"Your brother didn't want you to marry Doug? In his place, can't say I'd blame him. . . ."

"You don't understand. You couldn't—not unless you know Egan. He likes to ride rough-shod. Anything that he owns, or feels he owns, he has to break and crush. What anyone else believes or cares is nothing to him if it conflicts with what he wants. I used to do as Egan told me because it was easier to give in than to always fight him. Then he married a girl he couldn't control, and—well—I guess her example helped me to fight back. Poor Egan. Between the two of us, we nearly drove him crazy."

Melanie hesitated. "It didn't do him any good. He's . . . He's changed into something I can't name. He drinks and gambles away his wages and picks a fight on the least excuse. That's why his condemning Doug is so stupid. . . ."

Filled with a deep pity for the girl, Kingdom said gently, "But you and Doug were married after all. . . . Your brother bother you since?"

"He sees me about twice a week. Always to tell me that

one of the times Doug rides off, he won't come back. Egan says I likely won't see him again this time. Sometimes," she burst out suddenly, "I think he's right!"

"This time," Kingdom said carefully, holding back no longer, "he is."

Her eyes lifted; a fear widened in them. "Jim—what do you know . . . ?"

"Doug's dead," Kingdom said with a flat and nearly intentional brutality which he could not help because these things were utterly strange to him. "What I came here to tell you, ma'am. I've been looking for him two years. Finally caught him a couple days ago in a little town northeast of here—Dry Springs—"

"You—" she whispered. "You—"

"No!—I didn't." He looked bitterly at his hat brim. "I don't know what I would have done. But I didn't have time to do anything. He was shot by a trigger-happy kid. . . ."

Kingdom did not look at her after that, but he could not close his ears to her soft choking sobs. Vaguely, he was aware of the back door opening quietly, and he glanced up, seeing through the open doorway between kitchen and dining room that a man had stepped into the kitchen and was looking around. It was Loomis, the little bum from the stage. He must be boarding here, Kingdom thought absently, and, having missed the supper hour at some saloon, was entering by way of the kitchen in the hope of wheedling something to eat. . . .

Kingdom stood up, knowing that he must leave this girl in her grief; there was nothing, nothing at all, he could do for her. He turned wordlessly toward the front room, and had not taken two steps when Loomis' voice, strung like the twang of a tightened wire, came from the doorway to the kitchen.

"Turn around, you, and don't move."

Kingdom looked over his shoulder; Loomis had pulled his

gun and was trying to hold it on both of them, the barrel wavering from side to side in a ragged circle.

Loomis licked his lips. "I want all the money you got, lady. Get it."

Melanie slowly lifted her eyes and looked at the little man dully. She got to her feet with a tired and dragging movement. She faced Loomis directly—then began to laugh. She laughed with a wild unrestraint which mounted to a shrill note of hysteria. A primitive chill ran up Kingdom's spine at the sound.

Loomis stared at her; his jaw dropped. A gleam of fright touched his faded eyes. He had not anticipated behavior like this. His voice was panicked. "Stop it, lady! I'm telling you stop it!"

Melanie threw her head back; she laughed all the more shrilly; with a birdlike movement, she stepped suddenly to a highboy against the wall, opened it, and came out with a heavy pistol, which she swung to train on Loomis.

Loomis hesitated as any man will when it is a woman who threatens him, and his hesitation nearly cost him his life. As it was, the two guns crashed as one shot. The girl could not handle the heavy weapon's recoil; it bucked and the slug whined far to Loomis' right. Then she was driven into the highboy, bent half across it, and fell from there to the floor.

In one unbelievable moment of violence it was finished; too swiftly for Kingdom's slow and methodical mind to fully grasp, the girl's still form was lying at his feet, and he regarded it briefly in a kind of obscure horror. Then he looked at Loomis who stared at the girl, paralyzed into momentary immobility by the shocking enormity of what he had done.

Then Loomis, his gun falling loose in his hand, retreated backward to the door, making a whimpering sound in his throat. Kingdom came to his senses at the same moment and a white-hot wrath lifted in him, and he lunged after Loomis. Melanie's gun had fallen by Kingdom's feet and he did not even think of it, wanting only to get his great bare hands on this man. He reached the doorway and lunged through it without a pause, straight at Loomis.

Kingdom saw the panic in Loomis' face and then Loomis' pistol barrel swinging at his eyes in a wild, vicious arc; and Kingdom saw no more except mushrooming lights around a penumbra of blinding pain. The blow drove him to his hands and knees, and, sickened with the pain, he had to fight to retain consciousness. Catching the edge of a table in one hand, Kingdom hauled himself doggedly to his feet. The back door was open.

Loomis was gone.

Kingdom staggered to the door and leaned against the doorjamb for support. He could see only a dipping vale of prairie in the empty darkness out there; Loomis was swallowed by the night. Kingdom moved back into the room, putting his hand to his head. Where the edge of Loomis' gun muzzle had caught him, on the dirge of his forehead just over his nose, he was bleeding a little, not much. He wiped at it mechanically with his sleeve and walked slowly back to the dining room where the girl lay crumpled in a little motionless heap on the floor. Without thinking, he bent down and picked up the gun she had dropped. He looked down at her; her face, mercifully, was turned away.

He walked a few aimless steps away, to let the sick rage ebb from him, the gun still unconsciously grasped loosely in his hand, and became aware of voices outside.

Kingdom walked to the front door and was reaching to open it when it was flung open in his face. A tall, yellow-haired man charged through the doorway into him, almost knocking both of them down.

The man swore and stepped back, staring at Kingdom, "Well, who the hell—"

Pat Frost was in back of the fellow and pushed roughly past him. "What's happened, Jim? What—"

Kingdom nodded toward the dining room.

The yellow-haired man shoved Kingdom aside and pushed ahead of Pat into the dining room. Kingdom walked slowly after them. Before he reached the dining-room entrance, he heard the yellow-haired man's voice, soft with a note of pure horror.

"Melanie . . . !" A pause. "My God. She's—she—"

Kingdom heard Frost rap out sharply then, "Egan!"

The man was standing to face Kingdom suddenly as he reached the doorway. There was a sustained sheen of madness in his eyes that brought Kingdom to a dead halt. The man had opened his mouth to speak when his gaze fell on the gun still in Kingdom's hand.

"My God!" he breathed. "He used her own gun. . . ."

His hand whipped back his coat, closing with incredible swiftness on a holstered pistol there. Frost, anticipating this, had already moved to his side, his gun out. As the man drew, the barrel of Pat's weapon descended in a swift short arc across his skull. He pitched forward on his hands and knees. Pat picked up the gun and shoved it into his belt.

"I'd about talked him into handing it over when we heard that shot," Pat remarked. "Probably would have had to do this to get it regardless. Anyway, it was the only way I could stop him just now short of shooting him. . . ."

"This the brother?"

"That," Pat said dryly, "is the brother. A prize package, is he not?" His jaw set a little then, as though in shame of his unthinking levity in the face of what had happened.

Hassard was trying to push himself up, moving his head slowly, feebly, to and fro. Pat holstered his gun, bent down and caught him roughly under the arms, hoisting him to his feet and letting go of him. Unsupported on his feet, Hassard staggered off balance, caught at the wall, and leaned there. His eyes focused on Kingdom with a concentrated hard brilliance.

Hassard looked at Pat then and said bitterly, "He must be a friend of yours, Frost."

"He's my friend," Pat said flatly, "which is why I don't have to ask—I know he didn't kill your sister."

"You seem to have decided that already!"

"And you've already settled in your head he's guilty. What's that—the gospel according to Hassard?" Frost looked at Kingdom. "Let me see the gun, Jim?" He took it and broke it. "One bullet gone, all right."

Hassard snatched the gun from him and sniffed it. "Fresh fired, too." He lifted his hot gaze to Pat. "How much more you need, Frost?"

"She shot," Kingdom said evenly, "at the man who killed her."

"Then how come there was only one shot?"

"Be quiet, Egan," Pat said irritably. "How did it happen, Jim?"

Kingdom told him.

Hassard said with a deep long-ingrained bitterness, "So both guns went off at once. And the little man vanishes into the night. It's too pretty, dammit, Frost. Can't you see . . . Wait a minute." He looked for a long moment at Kingdom. "What happened to the bullet Melanie fired —if she fired it?"

"Where would it have gone, Jim?" Pat asked.

"In the kitchen, from the way they were standing, I judge . . ."

Hassard and Frost inspected the kitchen to locate the slug; Pat leisurely, Hassard with a fevered intensity. They found nothing. Hassard glanced at Kingdom, an acid comment ready, when Pat asked suddenly, "Did you open the back door, Jim?"

"No. The tramp left it open." Kingdom added dryly, "He left in a hurry."

"There's your answer, Egan."

"Answer to what?" Hassard snapped.

"The door to the dining room here and the back door are in line with where your sister was standing, over there by the highboy," Frost said patiently. "If the killer was standing in the doorway to the dining room like Jim said, and the bullet Melanie fired missed, it likely went on through the back doorway."

"It likely did," Hassard said with heavy irony. "Should we take a lantern and go out and look for the bullet? God, what a joke your law is!"

"That nick on Jim's head is no joke," Pat said, his patience on a fast down-wane.

"She probably gave it to him fighting him off," Hassard said, his frustrated rage carrying him beyond caution.

Kingdom shifted a little on his feet, his deep-set eyes burning on Hassard. Pat said dryly, "You ought to be nicer to him, Egan. . . . You're practically related." Hassard stared at him. "Doug Kingdom's brother."

"*His* brother . . . ? Yes, he looks like him." Hassard spat the words as though they were an anathema. "So he thought he'd take over where brother left off."

"That's just about all out of you, Egan!"

"Is it? What about now—he goes free, eh?"

"He stays at my house tonight," Pat said caustically. "We'll hold the inquest tomorrow. Suit you?"

"You better lock your doors and windows tonight," Hassard mocked. He turned his back on them and walked slowly back to where his sister's body lay. They left him then, Kingdom preceding Pat out the door. They started side by side across the street.

"I'll drop these guns off at the jail, then we'll get some sleep," Pat said wearily. "I don't have to tell you how sorry I am about this, Jim." He sighed. "I hope it doesn't upset any plans you have."

"No," Kingdom said absently, his mind weighted with all that had happened.

Melanie had wanted to die, Kingdom was sure. But

Hassard, with his vibrant and violent passions, would never see that. Nor would Hassard, carried by his own convictions, ever be convinced that another than Doug's brother had shot his sister. Looking ahead, Kingdom could see only trouble.

## CHAPTER SIX

FOR HASSARD, there was no warmth in the afternoon sun as he stood with his back against the tie-rail in front of his sister's rooming house, chewing on a dead cigar. He only stood, favoring the hurt of Melanie's death as a dog favors a bad leg. He scarcely looked up when fifteen-year-old Murray Ambergard, his youngest rider, walked up to him with the angular grace of early adolescence.

Hassard took the cigar from his mouth, frowning. "Why ain't you at the ranch?"

"Boss sent me in, Egan. To find out why you didn't bring his daughter and her husband in yesterday. . . ."

"The stage was late," Hassard growled, his gaze shifting to the marshal's office. "I carried their stuff over to the hotel last night. They stayed there. . . . Damn it all, kid—you know's well as anyone how Hollister keeps a schedule. So does Frenchy."

"I know," Murray said. "I already talked to Mrs. Villon

over at the cafe. She says for you to drive the wagon over
to the hotel and pick up their luggage so's they can go
out to the ranch right away."

"Does she?" Hassard said disinterestedly, still moodily
watching the jail. He wondered with a sudden anger if
Kingdom had slept well last night. A warm bed instead
of a cold cell for Melanie's killer, he thought. And this
morning, at the inquest, the coroner's jury had favored
Kingdom's story, absolving him of blame. The cigar was
tasteless; Hassard spat it savagely into the street.

Murray shifted from foot to foot, waiting, and when Hassard didn't speak, he said uncomfortably, "What should
I tell her, Egan?"

Hassard looked at him with the stir of a vast irritation
which heightened as he recalled Ab's words of yesterday
afternoon: I thought you was Santerre's segundo, not his
errand boy. . . . "Why," he said, turning the words with
slow relish on his tongue, "you run tell Mrs. Villon to go
to hell."

Murray's jaw fell; he became stilled in his tracks as
though rooted to the ground, staring at Hassard.

"Go on!" Hassard roared. "Tell her!"

Murray backed away, his mouth open; then turned and
broke into a trot, headed for the café. Hassard took out
a fresh cigar. Well, that does it. I'm through at the ranch,
he thought; and at the moment he didn't care a damn.

He pushed away from the tie-rail and was cutting across
the street toward Ab's when Mrs. Villon stepped out of the
China Café and headed down the walk to meet him. Oh
Lord, here it comes, Hassard thought tiredly. She stepped
off the walk and came up to him in the middle of the street.

"Mr Ambergard delivered your message, Mr. Hassard,"
she said very quietly. "I only wanted to tell you that if
you have any business here that is that important, we will
be glad to wait. . . . I'm sorry—of course it's your sister.
. . . You'll want to stay for her funeral."

"My sister, yes." Hassard stirred impatiently, wanting to get on to Ab's.

"I'm sorry the man wasn't caught, sir."

"Begging your pardon, ma'am," Hassard said bitingly, "they had him, then let him go."

"Do you mean—Mr. Kingdom? Oh, no. I heard of that, but you're mistaken. . . . At the risk of his own life, he saved my husband and me from being robbed yesterday."

"Shot the robber too. Heard about that. . . . Two killings in one day. . . ."

"Really, Mr. Hassard—you can't truly believe that he killed your sister? I am certain that Mr. Kingdom—"

In a sudden furious irritation, Hassard broke in, "You seem almighty concerned about *Mister* Kingdom, lady. . . . Maybe your husband would enjoy hearing just how concerned. Go on," Hassard taunted, a final shred of discretion falling from him. "Go tell that big bad husband of yours how the nasty man insulted you so he can come and whip me out of town."

"Yes," she said in a low voice, "and he would try." Her chin lifted. "You don't like women, Mr. Hassard." She did not question, merely affirmed.

"Not any."

"Yet you had a sister, and you must have had a mother."

Hassard said in a hard voice, "Drinking runs in our family. . . . She was never sober long enough to be a mother. Look, lady—if I'm fired, say so."

"Fired? For what?"

" . . . Saying things."

She laughed almost silently. "Fire you? What good would that do?"

"I know," grunted Hassard. "You'll wait till we're back at your old man's ranch, then tell him, and have the pleasure of watching me whipped off the place—or shot."

Her expression altered into one of open, scathing contempt. "No one will hear of it."

He frowned, watching her with wary suspicion. "Why?"

"Why?" she repeated, musingly. "Well, sir, insulting a woman seems to make you most proud. Now who would I be to spoil a beautiful ideal like that?" She turned away, walking back toward the café, her small back very straight. Hassard, watching her go, felt a deep shame, but it was only momentary.

He pivoted on his heel and walked on to Ab's. An hour later in the hot and muggy afternoon, he was still there, thoroughly drunk—not fuzzy-unsteady drunk; cold-ice drunk, the fury in him building and piling, tier on tier. The man who had killed his sister was free. . . .

With a quiet intensity he surveyed the scattering of loafers. His gaze settled finally on a small group playing stud at a corner table. One of the men was George Taine, a short wicked-tempered man in the disreputable dignity of a whiskey-soiled suit and neither washed nor shaven as usual. He'd had a good freighting business which he had mostly drunk and gambled away. But the fool still commanded an aura of respect, Hassard considered; at least among the crowd at Ab's who were his kind.

This was his man, Hassard knew.

Carrying his glass, Egan walked over to Taine's table, saying. "How are you, George," as he clapped Taine on the shoulder with one hand and reached for Taine's bottle with the other. " . . . George, you ought to get an apron and be your own bartender."

Taine brought his fist down with a crash on the bar just between Hassard's hand and the bottle. Hassard swore and jerked his hand back, though he was expecting this.

"Just keep your damn hands off my bottle," Taine said, working the words out slowly and thickly. "Nobody touchin' my bottle. . . ."

"That's right," Hassard said softly, "that's right, George. Sorry." Taine was in the state he had counted on.

"Another thing. I never wore no apron, damn you. You go round telling no one I wore no apron."

"I never said you wore no apron," Hassard began patiently, then broke off, looking intently into Taine's face. "Why, hell, fella—you need a drink." He sloshed Taine's glass full from Taine's bottle and poured one for himself. "On me, kid," Hassard said generously.

"Thank you," Taine said with dignity; they drank in companionable silence for several moments. The other men grinned to themselves.

"Heard about your sis, Egan," Taine mumbled. "That's a pow'ful sorry thing. Really is."

"Thanks, George," Hassard said somberly. An hour before, he would have hit Taine for mentioning his dead sister's name in a saloon; now it was only a prime excuse for the unfolding of his idea. Hassard smiled with drunken thoughtfulness and gave Taine a sidelong glance. "Hear how she died, George. . . ?"

Taine said he hadn't. Hassard told him his own version of the story. Several others became interested and listened.

"Fella who shot your sis is still running loose?" Taine asked with inebriate gravity, and when Hassard nodded, George clucked sympathetically and shock his head.

"If that ain't a pack of hell," said Taine. "What the hell is there a state of affairs like that for?"

"The law says he didn't do it," Hassard said sadly. "Man has to go with the law, George. . . . The law says so." He watched Taine slyly.

"Law, hell!" said a tough. "What good's your damn law for this . . . ?"

Hassard struck while the iron was hot. He said: "She had a big heart, Mellie did. . . . Many's the time she let some drunk sleep in her place when the jail was full up —you boys among others I recall."

"That's so, yeah," a loafer said.

"So she did," Ab said casually over by the bar, swabbing

it with a colorlessly dirty rag, "until Egan made her quit."

"Yes, I made her quit, "Hassard snapped. "Wasn't fitting a woman should be inviting men into her house to sleep off liquour, boarding house or not."

"Ain't fitting you should be talking about a lady, a dead lady too, in a saloon, your sister too," Ab said gently. It was a kindly hint that the discussion end here.

Hassard shrugged; he had only wanted to make these men recall the goodness of Melanie, to rankle a bit over the injustice of her killer going free. His part was done; from here on, he could depend on George Taine to take the bit in his teeth, and George was all the spur that they needed. . . .

Hassard bought everyone a drink.

"A damn fine girl," someone muttered.

Hassard bought everyone another drink.

Taine swung suddenly to Hassard, frowning and at least half sobered. "Damn it, Egan. We all liked Melanie. . . ."

"So did I, George," Hassard said, lifting a shoulder. "Only what can we do? Besides, he's innocent. Half a dozen public-spirited citizens said so this morning at the inquest. . . ."

Taine said with great gentleness, "Just show him to us."

"We're with you, George," a man shouted; a swift clamor broke out.

"Name the play, Egan," growled Taine.

"Get a rope," Hassard said, grinning. "I'll name it. . . ."

## CHAPTER SEVEN

"It's a shame, Pat, that's all," his wife said with controlled indignance, cleaning up the supper dishes with a louder clatter than usual. "I really don't see why Jim should leave so soon."

Pat took his pipe from his mouth, lifted a shoulder in a spare shrug and dropped it. "You can't talk to Egan Hassard, my dear. The coroner jury's verdict was a fraud to him. He will want Jim's head." His pipe had gone out and he irritably knocked it empty on the edge of his thick china coffee cup, then picked up the cup and moodily swirled the dregs aimlessly about, watching the ashes dissolve murkily into them.

Finally Pat set the cup on the table and glanced up at Kingdom. "You'll have to get out of town, Jim."

Kingdom pushed his empty plate back and stood up. "I'll make it early tonight."

"You will, like hell! Sit down. I'm not chasing anyone out at night."

Kingdom shook his head. "It has to be tonight, Pat. Hassard won't stop here." He'll burn your house down to get me. You've had enough trouble on my account. It'll stay light long enough for me to put enough distance between me and Boundary to make it worth while."

"Forget it, Jim. Hassard won't strike tonight."

As though in reply, a rock crashed through the single high little kitchen window and fell to the floor in a shower of jangling glass. Frost lunged for the door and swung it open; whoever had flung the rock was gone. Frost turned slowly back into the kitchen.

Kingdom watched him narrowly, saying quietly, "You see, Pat? It's started already. Hassard or another. It has to be now."

Before Frost could reply, there was a loud knocking at the back door. Frost opened it a cautious inch or so, then threw it wide; lanky Bud Casement, Frost's night deputy, came in, his long face rock-set.

"Hassard, Pat. He's been talking it up in Ab's He's got that bunch of saloon bums primed for a lynching. We can't stop it. They're set to string us up too if we try. Only thing to do is get him," he jerked his head toward Kingdom, "out of town."

Pat looked wryly at Kingdom. "Now you're in it, kid."

"So are you," Kingdom said grimly. "How can I get my horse? I can't show my face out there."

"A detail, James," Pat said. "You pack up your gear quickly, I'll go to the office to fetch your gun, and Bud here will go to the livery to saddle your horse. We'll both meet him there. Okay, let's go. . . ."

Pat was standing, as planned, in the archway of the livery, beckoning frantically to Kingdom, who lunged onto the walk and broke into a run for the archway, burdened with the gear. He had covered half the distance when there was a shout from the hotel and the crash of a pistol, and the ground between his running legs was ruptured violently, spraying his boots with exploding clods of dirt.

Kingdom reached the archway and ran on down the runway to the rear of the store where Casement was holding

his bay. Kingdom threw the saddle on and cinched it swiftly; he'd have to leave the packhorse. . . . He heard the
crash of Pat's rifle. Kingdom swung into the saddle as Pat
came running back from the archway, telling Bud to take
his place. Casement hurried to the front of the livery. From
his belt, Frost pulled Kingdom's gun and passed it up to
him, then grasped his hand.

"You'll have to ride out the back, Jim. They know you'll
be leaving that way; they'll try to circle and cut you off."
He paused, still holding Kingdom's hand. "My jurisdiction
ends where the town ends. Out there, Hassard can get you
without breaking any law. You'll be free game in an open
field. . . . So hyper like hell and good luck."

Kingdom raised a hand in parting salute and spurred the
bay lightly; he responded to the touch, heading out the
rear gate. There was another shot from the front. Kingdom
put the horse onto the plain, heading to the west.

He went at an easy clip for a mile, not looking back,
and when he finally topped a rise to pause and scan his
back trail, he felt no surprise to see the dust shroud of
pursuers just leaving town. They know his line of flight,
then.

Kingdom turned at almost right angles to his original direction, hoping to send them on a false beeline into the
desert. This hope dissolved into futility; the land was too
open, too rolling. He had not gone a half-mile before he
could see that the horsemen had turned off his original
route and were cutting at an easy angle toward his new
direction. He had done nothing except decrease his margin
of safety; his maneuver had only lessened the distance between his pursuers and himself. His only chance now, Kingdom knew, was to outrun them or outlast them.

He set the bay into a mile-eating pace onto a straight-
away course of hard-packed grassland rolling miles ahead.
The bay was a stayer, just getting his first wind. Kingdom
held him in.

The miles blurred past, the character of the land unchanging. Then the grass grew patchy and the face of the ground became raw and barren. Before Kingdom knew it, he was heading into brush. He cut quickly off and away from it. These men were familiar with this land; it wouldn't do to play hid-and-seek with them in brush country. But the move again severely narrowed the distance between him and those behind. He did not hold in now, but let the bay have his stride. Too late . . .

Kingdom heard the shots then and felt the horse's pace break. Hit, he thought, with a sinking in him. For all that he could do, the horse was slowing, the rhythmic beat of hoofs slackening, faltering beneath him. . . .

They thundered on. The time came when the riders were so near he could hear their shouts. Kingdom felt the ground dip beneath him and he raced down a gentle slope into a thinly timbered vale where the skyline cut him off from view of them.

The opposite side of the vale sloped up more steeply and at its crest was a dense wall of chaparral. Kingdom decided to find cover there, even if he had to leave the horse. It couldn't take him much farther regardless. He put it up the steep gradient of the slope now and was halfway to the top when the townsmen came into view, riding down into the dip. He was a plain target now, and on the first shot the bay reared back, mortally hit this time. Kingdom kicked free of the stirrups and jumped clear of the falling animal as its weight sloughed sideways.

Kingdom floundered on his hands and knees in the soft earth, then was on his feet, his boots digging hard at the loose dirt as he plunged on up the slope toward the chaparral. The chaparral was only three yards away. . . .

Then a rifle rashed out from the chaparral, almost in his face it seemed. The flash of it in the growing dusk washed into Kingdom's eyes and blotted out his sight for a moment. He stopped in his tracks, his first thought one of crushing panic, that part of his pursuers had somehow maneuvered in front of him and had ambushed him. Then Kingdom heard the owner of the rifle, crouched up there out of his view, call harshly:

"Come on, you damn fool!"

Kingdom began his running climb again, and as he went past two stunted Judas trees at the summit, found himself at the fringe of the chaparral. He dived unheedingly into it, landing with a wind-driving grunt on his side. He found himself sprawled beside the rifleman who shot again, and Kingdom heard the scream of a horse. He squirmed around on his belly to face into the vale and saw that the pursuit had reached the bottom of the slope on this side, that one of their horses was down kicking and that they had stopped, milling disconcertedly.

The rifleman shot again.

They turned their horses; one rider gave the unhorsed man a hand up behind him, and the entire body of nearly a dozen men turned and retreated. One rider alone hesitated, looking up toward the chaparral, his horse fiddle-footing beneath him; then he turned it, riding after the others. In the failing light, Kingdom could not have seen the man's face from this distance, but he knew that it was Hassard.

The rifleman eased himself slowly to his feet, looking after the riders. Kingdom stood up and watched too for a moment, then thrust his gun back into the waist of his trousers and looked at the man beside him. Kingdom felt a vague surprise at the grating sound of his own voice:

"I ought to thank you."

The man turned to regard him measuringly. "Not when you do it that way." He seemed to look at Kingdom more closely then, and Kingdom knew that his face, even in the growing darkness, must have showed the harried strain of these last days, for the man's tone was more kindly. "They laying a bounty for you, son?"

Kingdom felt a vast and weary irritation sweep him. "Ask my horse."

"Well, now, hard on a man."

"And on a horse. What place is this?"

The man's frosty gray eyes regarded him sharply. He was of about middle age, Kingdom judged; tall and gaunted, burned Indian-dark by years of desert wind and sun, his face weather-tracked like seamed mahogany. An untrimmed roan mustache hid half his mouth.

"You don't know?" he said slowly, and when Kingdom shook his head the man let his rifle, which he had been holding half leveled on Kingdom, slacken a little in his hands. "You didn't know this was Incham's valley?"

"Was I supposed to?"

"I figured so, seeing you came in with a posse salting your tail." The gaunt man waited a moment and when Kingdom did not speak, he said, "My name's Teal."

Kingdom nodded and said nothing.

Teal laughed. "Maybe you're right," he said. "Come on. You can talk to Incham then."

"Who's Incham?"

Teal had half turned away; now he looked back at Kingdom intently. "You never heard of Incham?"

Kingdom shook his head in negation.

"Well, this should be interesting," Teal said dryly.

## CHATER EIGHT

KINGDOM STRIPPED saddle and bridle off his dead horse and walked back up to where Teal waited.

"Watch out for the brush," Teal said, and started down a trail broken erratically through the chaparral. He must have followed it by instinct, for it was invisible in this light, and so nonexistent in some places that he had to force a way with his rifle barrel. Kingdom fought his way after Teal, stumbling, grunting, sweating, scratched and beaten by lashing, backswinging branches.

The chaparral ended suddenly, the trail breaking onto an open bank clustered with ocotillo clumps and greasewood. It dipped away and down steeply up here, sloping off gradually at the bottom and spreading away into a small, surprisingly heavily timbered valley. From here, one caught a panoramic view of the land: timbered with scrub oak and elm, hackberry, and where he caught a glint of water somewhere below, cottonwoods and perhaps willows. The water explained the verdancy, rare enough in this part of Texas to make Kingdom simply stand and look.

The valley itself was bowl-shaped, surrounded by the great ringlike dune on which they stood. The broad flat crest of the dune was, as far as he could tell, fringed all around by the thick and nearly impenetrable jungle of chaparral, as perfect a natural barrier as he had ever seen.

Teal let him look his fill, then remarked, "It got me the same way. Let's move."

Kingdom followed him gingerly, sliding and stumbling, down the steep bank. It was not until they were on the gently off-leveling lower slope that Kingdom saw the buildings thrown up here and there among the trees. As they started along a footpath leading into the trees, he saw that the dwellings were no more than patchwork shacks which seemed to have been carelessly erected from a few boards salvaged from some deserted settlement and whatever materials were at hand. Feeble and guttering lights showed behind the oil-paper windows.

As they neared the first shack, a door was opened and a man stepped into their path. "That you, Lampasas? Who's with you?"

"Me all right. Posse was chasing this fella. . . ."

"Heard the shooting. Thought you were practicing." The man stepped nearer to them, sizing Kingdom up; a small young man with the dark beauty of Lucifer. His black and merry eyes held a lively thrust of friendly curiosity. Somewhere, Kingdom thought suddenly, he had seen those eyes before, and not long ago. . . .

"I'm Tory Stark," the young man said, as though this were supposed to mean something. To Kingdom, it didn't, but the meaning was all there to read in the manner the fellow carried the heavy gun at his left side. . . .

"Hello," Kingdom murmured.

Tory laughed. "A man of few words. I like that. . . . I haven't seen you somewhere now, have I?"

Kingdom shrugged. He had heard this question somewhere before too, and could not think where. Then it came to him—the young stage robber he had shot had put these same words to him. And he knew with mild amazement that that man's eyes were those of which Tory's so strongly reminded him; in general features and build they were much alike too.

He had no time to consider the implications of this. Tory said, "Taking him to Incham?" Lampasas nodded.

"I think I'll go with you," Tory Stark said, "for laughs."

With Lampasas Teal leading and Tory bringing up the rear, they walked on down the footpath to the last shack, set just beyond a clump of cottonwoods.

Lampasas stepped by the door; he looked at Kingdom. "Just one thing. Don't get mad."

"At who?"

"Him. Just don't get mad."

Lampasas knocked at the door.

"Who is it?"

"Lampasas."

"Come in," said the man inside, bored.

They stepped inside. He stood in his shirtsleeves with his back to them, shaving with the aid of a shard of mirror propped on two pegs driven into the wall. He said without turning, "Close the door. What was the shooting?"

"Bunch of counter-jumpers were chasing a fella our way. I got rid of them. Brought the fella back with me."

Incham unhurriedly finished shaving. Then he turned around, and looked Kingdom up and down. "You're big," he said causally. "What're you running from?"

"What makes you think I'm running from anything?"

Incham sighed. "You wouldn't be here if you weren't. So you were being chased. . . . By whom and why?"

Kingdom said nothing. Incham flung the towel aside and picked up his coat from a rickety chair, shrugging into it. He straddled the chair, leaning his arms on the back of it. "That won't get you anywhere," he said pleasantly. "We don't have to be nice, you know. We can be just plain damn nasty and find out as much."

The skin tightened and smoothed over Kingdom's Indian high cheekbones. "I don't think you can."

Incham glanced at him shrewdly, one tawny sickle of an eyebrow lifting questioningly as though unaccustomed to such unco-operativeness "Damned if I don't think you're right. Only look at it this way." Incham idly pulled a cigar from the breast pocket of his shirt and gestured absently with it. "You come barging in here with a gang of town bums on your trail. For all we know you rigged it that way to jail our bunch. Just say you're a lawman—a United States Marshal or what-have-you—"

Incham smiled. "Oh, yes, it could happen. Most of us are wanted as deserters by the Federal army, or," he waved the cigar again, "if we fought for the Lost Cause, for failing to report for parole. Bluebellies have put towns all over Texas under martial law. Putting the whole state under military government this year, so I hear. . . . The army's just part of it. Many people for other reasons would like to nail our hides up. Anyway, suppose you stay with us long enough to make sure of us, go back and lead a troop of cavalry in here." Incham shrugged and smiled casually. "You see how it is. . . ."

"A mob in Boundary was trying to lynch me. That's all there is."

"Ah—no, not quite. Why?"

"They thought I murdered a woman."

Incham felt in his pockets and said mildly, "Damn. Give me a match, will you, Tory?" He thoughtfuly poised the proffered match, glancing at Kingdom. "Did you?"

"No."

Incham regarded him silently for a long moment, then struck the match and held it to his cigar. "I believe you. What's your name?" He chuckled then and the breath of it blew the match out. "I mean to say," he amended comfortably, "what do you *call* yourself . . . ? Give me another match, Tory."

Kingdom was silent as Incham lighted his cigar. Incham

glanced at him and sighed, throwing the match away. "All right. I'm John Incham. . . . Fair exchange?"

Kingdom was prompted to lie, but a wild and stubborn anger was carrying him now. To hell with him, he thought, and said aloud, "Kingdom."

He could hear a subtle outletting of breath from Lampasas at his elbow; before he had time to wonder at this, Tory said delightedly, "Ha! I knew I'd seen you somewhere before! Dallas, sure! More than once. . . ."

For a moment, only a blank puzzlement was on Kingdom; then it came to him. These men thought he was Doug.

Kingdom had almost opened his mouth to correct this when two thoughts came to him as one. One was that without their help, he was stranded on the desert on foot; he could not return to Boundary. The other was that he had no way of gauging the temper of these men. To give them the name of a nondescript would be to run a gantlet of suspicion which he was of no mind to court. But Doug Kingdom was a bedrock identity in the minds of these men. . . .

So when Incham asked idly, "Doug Kingdom?" he only nodded. "In that event, welcome, Kingdom. You were of course looking for us as I surmised."

"I heard about your place," Kingdom lied. "I only knew it was somewhere here."

"Of course. And have you decided whether you want to become a part of us, or have you lone-wolfed it too long?"

It was an invitation, Kingdom knew, and he nodded. "So long it got too rich for my blood. I like what I've seen of this place."

"Good. Come over here tomorrow morning. I'd like to talk with you, explain a few things that will get us off to a concrete understanding. . . . You can stay with Lampasas. I doubt he'll mind the company of another lone wolf like himself."

"That's what I had in mind," Lampasas said in his easy Texan drawl.

"A good thing for you Lampasas likes to prowl around." Incham smiled at Kingdom. "You didn't leave anything behind in your expeditious departure, did you? Any luggage? We can get it for you."

"It's all on my back," Kingdom said, "except my packhorse at the livery."

Incham nodded. "I'll have a man fetch it tomorrow. . . . I suggest we all retire early, gentlemen."

It held the flat finality of a dismissal, and the three of them left Incham's shack, stepping into cottonwood-scented darkness. They walked in silence for a way.

"First time in years," Kingdom mentioned, "that I've been spanked and sent to bed."

Tory laughed and slapped his thigh. Lampasas said dryly, "Leastways he's considerate. He didn't tell us to get the hell out."

"Not in as many words," Kingdom said.

"Still, he's king here," said Lampasas.

"And his word law," Tory said merrily. "You want to be nice to him, Brother Kingdom. Or he'll have me shoot you. And I kind of like you."

Kingdom was on the point of letting that pass, then remembered the role he was playing—of boastful Doug. . . . "You can always try," he said calmly. He felt an inward shudder at Tory's answering laugh—like the laugh of the young stage robber; an underplay of winter chill through it. . . .

At Lampasas' shack they parted from Tory and went inside. Lampasas trimmed the wicks of several beef-tallow candles. Lampasas' bed was a heap of springy boughs in one corner with some blankets thrown ever them.

Kingdom spread his own bedroll on the floor, thinking that his one danger now lay in the possibility that someone in the gang had personally known Doug, though Lute had known Doug and had been at least partly deceived. . . .

Kingdom did not trouble to look up from his blankets as the door behind him opened and someone hesitated on the threshold.

"What do you want?" he heard Lampasas say coldly.

"Just a candle. Just wanted to borrow a candle," the man said.

Kingdom's hands froze on the blankets. That obsequious snivel—it could not be—and he turned his head to look, and it was Loomis all right. . . .

Kingdom came off the floor on his hands and knees and before he was entirely on his feet was driving at Loomis. The little man saw him coming when Kingdom was almost on him; Loomis' mouth opened to scream and the scream never began because Kingdom hit him then with his fist— only once—and Loomis turned in his tracks and crashed face first into the wall. He began slipping to the floor like a tired child, and sprawled unmoving there.

Kingdom looked at Lampasas who was already staring at him. "I don't like him either," Lampasas said at last. "But what was that for?"

Kingdom gestured loosely toward Loomis. "Ask him," he said thinly.

"I think I better get Incham," Lampasas said slowly.

"All right," Kingdom said. Lampasas went out, and Kingdom, his breath labored with unexpended anger, stood looking bleakly down at Loomis and rubbing his knuckles. Incham came in followed by Lampasas. Tory was behind them; he stopped at the doorway and leaned there, grinning.

Incham looked down at Loomis, then glanced with an almost sleepy benignity at Kingdom. "You must have had a reason for that."

"I did. He did the job they were going to lynch me for."

Incham looked more attentive. "Woman-killing?"

Kingdom nodded.

"Well, well," Incham said; he stared at Kingdom, rubbed his chin and looked down at Loomis. He bent down and slapped Loomis twice across the face. Loomis groaned and tried to fight him off. Incham slapped him again. "Get up," he said. "So it was a woman you shot."

"Wait—" Loomis said, slack-jawed.

"It was a woman," Incham said gently. Loomis shut his jaws sullenly.

"You're under my protection or I'd let Kingdom finish this," Incham said. "But get out tomorrow. I don't harbor woman-killers."

Loomis stood looking at them, a small and helpless man seeming to shrink within himself even smaller, and even Kingdom could feel sorry for him in that moment. Moving slowly, like an old man, Loomis turned and walked from the room.

Incham turned to face Kingdom, saying apologetically, "He rode in this morning wanting to join us. I laughed at him. He showed how scared he really was then. Started babbling about robbing a store and killing a man. I felt sorry for him, perhaps. At any rate, I said he could stay."

"It was a rooming house he robbed," Kingdom said, "and shot the girl who owned it."

"A brave play," Incham said dryly, and added curiously, "How did you happen to become embroiled?"

"I was seeing that girl some," Kingdom said carefully. "I happened to be in her place when this fella came in and tried to hold her up. She pulled a gun on him and he shot her and hit me a lucky blow with his gun and got away. The girl's brother found me holding the girl's gun with one bullet fired and thought I did it."

Incham nodded thoughtfully. "I heard you were seeing some girl in Boundary. Even heard you married her."

"No. people talk."

"And hens cackle," Incham said. He smiled faintly and slapped Kingdom on the arm, a gesture from this cold,

remote man that surprised Kingdom. "I'll see you in the
morning," Incham said, and left the shack. Tory grinned
meaninglessly at Kingdom and Lampasas, and ambled silently out of the doorway and down toward his own shack.

Kingdom walked to the doorway and stood there watching Incham go, a small, slight man with an erect and unconscious assumption of a big man's size. Kingdom rarely
formed first judgement; when he did, they were tempered
with a cautious reserve. Still, he thought that he liked
Incham.

Tory Stark, in his shirtsleeves, eyes sleep-bleared, was
frying bacon for his breakfast. He was lackadaisically
turning it with a long fork while it spattered and bubbled
in the skillet set on a bed of glowing embers in the baked-
mud fireplace. A knock came at the door of his shack.

"It's open," he growled, not troubling to rise from his
squatting position before the fireplace. Dawn rarely found
Tory in the ebullient humor which characterized him, especially after a nightly bout with a quart of Mountain Brook.

His humor was not improved when he saw that it
was Loomis who stood at the threshold, fingering the reins
of his saddled horse who stood patiently by, a bedroll lashed
to the cantle.

"What do you want?"

"Talk," Loomis said, his voice nearly inarticulate in the
painful movement of his purple and swollen jaw.

Tory, forking his bacon out of the skillet onto a tin
plate, eyed him with mild curiosity. "What happened to
you?"

Loomis told him with curses.

"That what you wanted to talk about?" Tory asked with
mild amusement.

"No. I'm leaving now like Incham said." A sly and
malevolent gleam touched Loomis' red-rimmed eyes which
betokened a painfully sleepless night. "Only first I figured

you'd like to hear about your brother's killer. . . ."

Tory came upright and stalked wordlessly across to Loomis, doubling up the front of his shirt in one slim and trembling fist. "You know?"

"A course I know—I was on the stage that brought him in. Let go, dammit!"

Tory slowly released him and let his hand drop, staring at him. "I remember. You were on the stage. You, the frog, his woman, the driver. . . . Which of you was it?"

"None of us. It was the fourth passenger." Loomis paused. He grinned, relishing this. "Kingdom."

Tory chuckled softly. "It won't work, fella. Kingdom wasn't on the stage. Like me to finish him for you, would you?"

"Damn it, he was on it! He left the stage before you saw your brother's body. Your brother held the stage up out of Boundary and Kingdom shot him in the back."

Tory frowned; he recalled now that he'd seen a large man leaving the stage: it could have been Kingdom; the light had been poor, and he was not certain. Then he looked sharply at Loomis. "You're a liar. His neck was broken."

"Because Kingdom shot his horse and it threw him."

Tory said thinly, "Prove it."

"Ask him! Go ahead, ask him!"

Tory threw his head back and laughed, long pure laughter rising clear and pealing in the still valley morning. "He'd admit it, of course!"

"Why not?" Loomis said harshly. "He's the kind of damn fool that would."

Tory stopped laughing; he watched Loomis with a basilisk intensity. "A man who would shoot at another man from the back is not the sort to admit it if the admission would cost him his life."

"The hell with you!" Loomis said wildly, beyond caution now. "I'm giving you the name of the man. You don't want to do nothing about it, that's your damn business."

He turned and stepped into his saddle and was violently turning his horse when Tory stepped through the door and grasped the reins. "Just hold it," Tory murmured. He squinted a little against the sunlight as he looked up at Loomis. "There's an off chance this isn't a lousy saddle-bum trick. Yes . . . I'll ask him about it. If he says you're a liar, I'll track you down and blow your damn head off. Understand? Now you get the hell out of here."

Tory saw pleasurably the naked fear in Loomis' eyes as the little man wheeled the animal with a savage spurring down the footpath. Tory turned slowly, heavily, and stepped back into the cabin and over to the table, looking down unseeingly at the plate of bacon. With a sudden savage sweep of his forearm, he knocked the plate clattering to the floor. He stalked to the single rickety chair where his hat and coat and gunbelt hung. He clamped the hat on and buckled the gun on with sure, furious movements. Then he stepped out the door again, heading for Lampasas' shack.

## CHAPTER NINE

Lute Danning hunkered on the ground before Incham's shack, his back propped comfortably against the wall, letting the drowsing coolness of the wakening morning and the warm early sunlight work through him while he lazily watched Incham, sitting on a bench by the door and talking.

He and Incham had spent most of yesterday discussing military tactics and their various applications. Incham was widely read as the well-worn and dog-eared volumes on the shelf inside testified.

And Incham was now on a subject upon which he so far scarcely touched—the most interesting of all, to Lute: the enigma that was Incham himself.

"I'm a tidewater Virginian, born and bred," Incham said carelessly. "I was in Richmond on business in sixty-two when McClellan's army was laying siege to it. When I got back to my plantation, I found it burned to the ground. My wife and daughter, they—" he broke off momentarily, staring at Lute who felt chilled, seeing the full blackness of memory tide back into his thoughts.

Incham's voice was bitter and toneless. "Some deserters from McClellan's army, I judged. I found a blue kepi and a new Federal issue rifle on the scene. I never found the men. I just got a band of cutthroats and raided Yankee towns."

Incham shifted restlessly and looked at Lute. "I paid them back a hundred times over for my family and my home. I know now it wasn't the way. It wasn't the way at all. And after the war, it was too late. . . .

"My men were fired upon by some drunken U.S. Cavalry when we came in to give our parole to the provost marshal. I reckon amnesty did not include bushwhackers. We were cut to pieces and scattered. Tory Stark is the only man of them still with me; he and I became tired of dodging Yankee patrols and came West. . . . Ah! Here comes the fellow I was going to tell you about. Slipped my mind."

Lute idly turned his head to look down the path at the man coming toward them.

Kingdom! Kingdom again! Lute thought in numbed disbelief. Then he caught on to Incham's words, glad that

Incham had taken no notice of his agitation. Lute decided to play dumb, and see what would happen next.

"After you left for your shack last night," Incham was explaining, "Lampasas came to me with this fellow—said he'd been up on the rim when this fellow came riding up with a posse on his tail. Lampasas drove them off and brought the fellow to me. He said he hadn't been looking for us, but I suggested he stay. A cool customer. I think you'll like him."

As Kingdom came up to them, his eyes rested only briefly on Lute before they shifted to Incham. Incham greeted him genially, inquired how he had slept, and motioned toward Lute. "Lute Danning, Doug Kingdom."

Kingdom acknowledged the introduction with a bare nod, the stern lines of his fresh-shaven face not relaxing. Lute's mind was whirling insensibly. So Kingdom was posing as his brother. . . . But this made no sense. What could Kingdom be after?

Kingdom absently hunkered down against the wall beside Lute, and began thoughtfully to build a cigarette. There seemed nothing to say, so Lute didn't comment.

"Quantrell," Incham went on musingly, squinting at the sky. "There was a fighter."

"A killer," Kingdom said quietly. Incham's gaze flicked back to Kingdom; he smiled ever so slightly. "You're considering Lawrence, for example . . . ?"

"Over a hundred and eighty massacred," Kingdom said quietly.

Incham snorted. "Kansas freesoilers."

"They were people."

Incham regarded him closely, searchingly. "You talk more like a damyank than a Southern bushwhacker." His gaze strayed idly to Kingdom's Union Cavalry trousers. "I don't know, you understand. I heard, just heard is all, that you were a guerrilla under Quantrell."

Kingdom said coldly, "You heard wrong," as he stood up. "If that's going to mark against me here—"

"Oh, sit down!" Incham said crossly. "No one gives a damn who you fought for. I just want to talk. . . . I was curious; you sound like a Southerner."

Kingdom said, "I am" warily.

"Ah," Incham said, watching him shrewdly. "Can a man ask why?"

"Matter of principle."

"Oh, of course," Incham mocked. "Slavery issue. . ."

"I'm one of those damn fools who fought for what he believed," Kingdom said without inflection. "What did you fight for?"

Incham made a wry face, smiling. "*Touché,* Friend Kingdom. Still, it goes against the grain. I wrote back to Virginia recently and found they'd split my plantation up among a passel of negras. Can you blame a lot of Southerners for still fighting the war . . . ? Dammit, Kingdom, you've ridden through Texas. What have *you* seen? Men coming home from the war to find their stock driven off or running wild, loose cattle roaming over a quarter million square miles, land-grabbing damyankee carpetbaggers, ex-Redlegs and Jayhawkers prowling the trails, hard-scrabble brushpoppers slapping a brand on everything with horns. It's no more than a step from mavericking to jayhawking. If men like us don't live as we do, we don't live. War's bitter legacy, Kingdom."

"You might raise stock in a small way with all this un-branded stuff running loose."

Incham shook his head moodily. "We've got too many odds on us now." He added with dry humor, "Lute's the military expert here. Just full of ideas. On cattle stealing among other things. Only we'd need a market. Damn if I'd care to try a Missouri drive. . . ."

Kingdom said musingly, "I was in Kansas City not long ago. Kansas Pacific Railroad is building through there to

Denver. Talk was that a fellow named McCoy was starting a cattle-shipping center for Chicago at Mud Creek—stage station on the Butterfield Overland Line. They call it Abilene now. About a hundred fifty miles southwest of Kansas City. Cattle pens, stockyards . . ."

"Did you see these rails to Abilene?" Incham said skeptically.

"They'd gotten fifty miles west of Kansas City, almost to Topeka, last I heard. But they'd be to Abilene by this fall."

Incham murmured, almost to himself, "A Kansas drive . . . I wonder."

"Army freighter named Jesse Chisholm said the herds could follow the trail left by his wagons, through the Nations, maybe to the Cimarron," said Kingdom.

Incham spiraled out a stream of cigar smoke and considered all this in silence. Then he glanced suddenly at Kingdom. "Now, there's an idea."

"What?" asked Lute.

"There's a rancher out of Boundary—old Frenchy Santerre. He's got five thousand on the hoof and he'll drive to Nawleans in a week or less. Used to ranch on the Louisiana side of the Sabine. Moved to Texas during the war, built a new spread under his old Staghorn brand. This'll be his first drive since the war ended." Incham smiled at Kingdom. "Do you like trail herding?"

"Why?"

"That'll be your job," Incham said gently, speculatively. "To get a job with Santerre for this drive. He's found it easy to get men for the roundup, but getting them to drive is another thing. Likely be short-handed and he'll be hiring. He'll hire you."

"Why do I get a job with Santerre?"

Incham laughed. "It'll be your task to persuade him to make a drive to Abilene—instead of Nawleans."

Lute felt a mounting excitement as he listened to Incham

say, "And once the drive's under way, we raid him and take his damn herd off his hands—finish the drive ourselves and collect at railhead. And unless I miss the pattern, stock prices will be booming."

"What's the difference between Louisiana and Texas."

"I told you; Santerre shipped to Orleans before the war. His new brand's the same as the old; it'll be known in Orleans. The stockmen there know him; he always goes with his herds. What would happen if we tried selling his beef there?"

Kingdom was silent. Lute thought, He doesn't like it.

"You're new to these parts," Incham went on. "Santerre or some of his men know the rest of us by sight. It'll have to be you."

"They don't know me," Lute said.

"You're hardly built for trail driving," Incham said dryly.

Lute felt a cutting anger at this unveiled gibe at his stoutness. Incham, ignoring him, said, "Also, you had an argument with Santerre's foreman day before yesterday. . ."

Lute forgot his anger. "Santerre's foreman? Hassard?"

"Yes, Hassard," Incham said disgustedly. "You'll have to be careful of him. So damn suspicious, his own wife hates him. . . ."

"Anything else?" Kingdom asked dryly.

"Yes," Incham grinned. "There'll be a couple of women on Santerre's place, so keep your mind on the job. . . . Hassard's wife—she's hell on wheels—and Santerre's daughter. Don't know anything about her; she just came to live there recently. She and her husband came in on the stage the other day—h'm, same one on which they brought in Tory's brother, remember, Lute?"

Lute felt an envious irritation. "You know a hell of a lot about these people."

Incham smiled and waved his cigar carelessly. "I've had my eye on Santerre's herd for a long time—and I never go into anything blind. Drop a question here, a question there . . . Not hard."

Lute glanced at Kingdom, who was staring at the ground, and Lute wondered what subtle workings were going on behind his passive mask. Presently, to Lute's surprise, Kingdom said, "I'll take the job."

"Good," said Incham. "You can rest up today and head for Staghorn tomorrow. We'll thrash out the details between now and then. . . ."

Tory Stark came striding up the path then, and watching him come, swinging along with the cockiness of a small man and the headstrong self-assurance of a big one, Lute had a sudden premonition of trouble.

Tory stopped before Kingdom and said very gently: "Did you shoot a man whose body was brought in the stage day before yesterday, Kingdom?"

Kingdom regarded him deliberately. "And if I did?"

"He way my brother. . . ." In the dead stillness that hung over his words, Tory said softly, "I asked you a question, Kingdom?"

Kingdom said matter-of-factly, "When I'm shot at, I shoot back. He tried to rob us; he took his chances and lost."

". . . His life," Tory said hotly.

"That was the stake and he paid it. Should have, too."

"You *did* shoot at him from behind?"

Kingdom didn't reply for a moment. He looked down at his hands speculatively, then back at Tory and murmured, "Loomis?"

"You shoot him in the back?" Tory demanded savagely.

"Shot at his back. Hit the horse."

Tory shook his head in his wrath, as though baffled at finding this stolid integrity in a man who would backshoot.

Kingdom said: "He shot at me first. When he started to get away, I got him."

Tory let out his breath, settling his weight on his heels, watching Kingdom. "Will you meet me?" Tory asked in a shaking voice.

"No."

"Well, I'm not surprised," Tory said with a deep malice. "It would take a lot of nerve. . . ."

"You're a fool, Tory," Incham said, yawning. "He's not afraid of you."

Tory swung on him blazingly. "Then why won't he meet me?"

"For the same reason no one would give a loaded gun to a baby," said Incham in a hard low voice. "Now hear me, Tory—I'll have no trouble in this camp. We need Kingdom, and your damn brother got his coming-up. . . . Get out!"

Tory spoke to Incham, but it was at Kingdom that he looked. "I don't like being baited, Mr. Incham. This isn't finished. Remember it."

"We'll try to remember," Incham said dryly.

Tory spun on his heel and stalked away, a dark little shape of menace.

Incham said lazily, "He meant it, you know, Kingdom. He isn't finished and not even I can stop him. If the whim strikes him, he'll kill without reason, and now he has a reason. He has only one answer to anything, living by the gun. . . ."

"One of these days he's going to die by it," Kingdom said.

"Quite," Incham said moodily. "The war taught Tory to place a shallow premium on human life. All I ask is, don't hate him. He can't help the way he is."

"I don't hate a fool," Kingdom said shortly.

Incham dropped his cigar butt and thoughtfully ground a heel on it. "So you shot Tory's brother? Then you must have been on the stage with Santerre's daughter and son-in-law."

"I kept them from being robbed."

"Just what I was thinking. And Frenchy should be duly grateful to the man who helped them. Yes, he'll be glad to give you a job, Kingdom. . . ."

Kingdom said nothing to that. He stood up, grinding out his cigarette against the wall; said, "I'll be seeing if Lampasas has breakfast ready," and walked back down the path.

As he disappeared among the trees, Incham turned to Lute. "What do you think?"

"A good man," Lute said cautiously.

"I was thinking so, yes," Incham mused. "Too good, maybe, for this game. A quiet man, with the look of an honest one. No judging by looks of course, but somehow he doesn't fit his reputation. Still, I like him—perhaps for that reason."

"So do I," Lute admitted.

The conversation became desultory, and Lute took his leave for his own shack, one of Incham's well-worn volumes under his arm, anticipating a pleasant forenoon of reading. Heading down a sycamore-shaded footpath, he stopped abruptly, seeing the mirror-still surface of the stream ahead through a screening of bushes and Kingdom on the bank dipping up a bucketful of water.

Lute hesitated, having no inkling of the man's temper or intentions. For a moment he stood irresolute, then thought, The hell with it. I'll face him out. He stood, watching Kingdom straighten, come to his feet, and start back up the path to Lampasas' shack, the bucket of water swinging at his side. Then, stepping around a crook of the path, he saw Lute and came to a dead stop. Lute could see his fist gently tighten on the bucket handle; he gave no other hint of expression, only stood and silently watched Lute.

"I'm not looking for trouble, Kingdom," Lute said in a dry voice.

"You found it, seems," Kingdom said. His voice was

chilled and dogged, every word distinct and spaced.

"Think back some, will you?" Lute paused, and when Kingdom said nothing, only waited grimly, Lute said: "I could have brought you down after you shot DeRoso. I could have shot you in the back a minute ago. . . ."

Kingdom still said nothing, and Lute said angrily, "Damn it, I liked Doug."

Kingdom said with the bite of a cold wrath, "You had a damn odd way of showing it, friend."

"All right," Lute said angrily, "I was going to trade on his name, and what of it? He was as tired of this life as I was. If a man sees maybe the one chance out of it, he'll take it. What happened, it was an accident—I'm sorry about that. . . ."

"You're sorry. That will make my brother feel very well."

"Dammit, it wasn't as though I pulled that trigger . . . ! The worse thing I did was wanting to make some money."

"If it meant spreading Doug's name across every wanted poster in the West."

"Listen, once we had a stake we could have gone to South America maybe, maybe up to Canada. Canada. There's a nice peaceful country. . . ."

Kingdom was shaking his head before Lute was done. "You're finished, Lute. You don't know it, but you're finished."

"Not by you, though. You make a pass at me, and Incham—"

"Yes, Incham," Kingdom broke in. "Going to use him the way you would have used Doug?"

Lute smiled with no humor. "No one 'uses' Incham—but you'll know that before long. . . ."

"I'm not interested," Kingdom said coldly.

"You come here looking for me?"

"Not for you, Lute. But I'll be seeing you. . . . Now step out of the way."

Lute moved out of the path and Kingdom walked by him

without another glance at him. Lute sighed and was about to go on to his shack when he heard Tory Stark's voice so close at hand and so sudden that it unnerved him; Lute froze in his tracks.

"Stop there, Kingdom!"

Lute gingerly parted some twigs without exposing himself. He saw that Kingdom had come to a dead stop, facing Tory Stark who stood squarely athwart the path. Tory was smiling over the sun-glinting pistol poised negligently before him.

"I said it wasn't finished, Kingdom—drop the bucket."

Kingdom dropped it; it struck the ground woodenly, tilted over on its side. The only movement for a long moment was the water runneling muddily back down the trail, long wet serpents creeping to coil into little hollows and distend in small gleaming pools. . . .

It was Kingdom who broke the nerve-strung silence. "What about Incham?"

"I can handle Incham," Tory smiled. "This is my affair and none of Incham's mix. . . . Where's your gun?"

"In Lampasas' . . ."

"We'll get it, then," said Tory, and stepped off the trail, motioning Kingdom to move on ahead of him, then swinging into step behind.

It was then that Lute made his decision and moved. Pulling his gun, he eased out silently into the path and said sharply, "Stand still, Tory, and drop it."

Tory came stock-still, and for a moment in which Lute's breath hung still in his lungs he wondered if Tory would obey. . . .

He did not drop the gun or turn—only spoke without looking around. "We ain't been bad friends to now, Lute. Don't mess it."

"Tory, I'm telling you, drop it. . . . That's better. That's fine. Now walk away. Incham needn't hear a word of it."

"You haven't heard the last of it," Tory said meagerly,

"what's more important," and was out of sight down the path.

Lute holstered his pistol and walked heavily on to meet Kingdom who had bent down to pick up Tory's gun. Without expression he handed it to Lute. "I'll give it back to him when he's ready to behave," Lute said. ". . . How does the Dry Springs incident set now?"

"It's not forgotten," Kingdom said shortly.

Lute could no longer fetter his curiosity. "Why're you here? Why'd you agree to handle the Staghorn thing?"

"You're damn chatty for changing the subject."

A sudden anger flared in Lute; his patience was gone. "The hell with you!" he said wrathfully. "I was Doug's friend. I want to be yours. But you make it so damn almighty hard for a man to like you with that sulky bear way you got to you—" He broke off, shaking his head in a baffled way. "I still like you and damned if I know why. . . ."

Lute turned violently and headed for his shack.

## CHAPTER TEN

EVEN BEFORE a pastel dawn-flush softened the raw outlines of the Staghorn main house and outbuildings set comfortably in the gently rolling vale, Emilion DeLorme was down at his slope-roofed blacksmith shed, hammering with his sledge at a wagon felloe. When true dawn did come, Emilion, with a deep appreciation of these things, left his anvil, filled his stubby, blackened pipe, and stood watching the roseate firstlight seep across the land.

Full dawn was on the earth now, bright and clear and sharp, and Emilion threw back his gray-shot thickly black mane of hair with a toss of his leonine head and filled his great chest with the clean early air. Looking down toward the cookshack, he saw with no surprise that Wanda, in a faded crinoline dress, was already up with the dawn, moving between the rows of the cook's scanty garden with a rapt and childlike attention. Emilion's weather-troughed face softened a little. . . .

She had seen him now and came lightly up the incline to his workshed. The young sunlight ran a fitful auburn tracery through her dark chestnut hair, caught the light dust-spangling of freckles across her nose, and (ran Emilion's thoughts) danced in eyes which were the tranquil infinity of a summer dusk. . . .

Wanda came to his side, her smile warm for him, and was about to speak when her glance fell toward the house. "Look," she said. "There's Inez. Inez!" She waved to the tall woman who had just stepped onto the back veranda.

"*Sacre*, that termagant," muttered Emilion.

Wanda protested. "Why, she's lovely."

Emilion was too French not to admit that Wanda was unquestionably right; Inez Hassard was beautiful of both face and form, even though *enceinte*, heavy with child, as now. A complexion, Emilion thought, as warm and clear as a summer sky, hair like ripe grain, eyes as gray as morning mist, a tongue edged like acid, and—ocasionally—the temper of a thousand devils. Hassard had brought her to the ranch nearly a year ago. *Le Bon Dieu* only knew what she had been before that.

Hassard and she—they are a prize pair, Emilion thought sardonically.

Inez reached them, even this slight climb an obvious exertion to her. Sweat brightened her upper lip; her eyes were dark-circled. And not from too little sleep, Emilion thought disgustedly. *Ma foi!* but it was strange that the iron-handed Hassard made no effort whatever to regulate his wife in the way he did all else—or at least to hide her bottle. Not that, being married to that *cochon*, she was entirely to blame. . . .

"You are up early," Emilion said slyly.

She shielded her eyes from the sun, as though it hurt them. "You're altogether humorous this morning, Emilion," she said tiredly.

"You shouldn't have walked up here," Wanda said, watching Inez' face anxiously.

"What's the difference," she said tonelessly. "If I could sit down—"

Emilion swept out a crate from behind the forge and placed it against the shed wall with a flourish. Inez sank onto it, putting her back to the wall and closing her eyes without thanking him.

Emilion restoked his pipe. "The small one comes soon?" he asked conversationally.

Her eyes opened, the sudden gray of them pouncing on him. She looked down with distaste at her body. "What do you think?" she said irritably. Wanda looked embarrassed; Emilion unconcernedly lighted his pipe.

"A baby," Wanda smiled in her little-girl way at Inez.

"I'll cut it out and give it to you," Inez said, her face settling into a cast of utter bitterness.

"Inez!" Wanda had met Inez only two days ago; she could not yet reconcile the shocking venom of this beautiful woman's speech to her appearance.

"It's *his*," Inez said tonelessly. "I am bearing *his* child. . ."

"But to say—" Wanda faltered.

Inez looked at her slowly; to Emilion's surprise, her face gentled inexplicably as she watched the younger girl.

"Forgive me, my dear. You don't understand. Some-times"—she sighed—"I wonder if I do."

Emilion's brooding gaze roved out lazily to the heat shimmering plain beyond, then snapped to sudden attentive focus on a distance-tiny rider. He watched the horse-backer come nearer, wondering idly what the man's errand was at this early hour. Wanda and Inez presently followed his gaze, watching in silence.

Not long afterward, the stranger reined his blaze-face sorrel down in by the harness shed fifty yards distant and looked about the deserted ranchyard.

"I wonder what he wants!" Wanda murmured.

Emilion's voice lifted in a mild bellow. "Ho, friend! You are looking for someone?"

The man's head swiveled swiftly, his gaze moving up the slight incline to the smithy's shed. He pulled his horse around and rode up toward them. Emilion's eyes widened in astonishment as he came nearer. Name of a name, but here was a man. He was fully as great through the chest and shoulders as Emilion himself, and inches taller. Emilion measured his face as well; it was somber and for-bidding, with a be-damned-to-you look walled behind a still, black reserve.

Emilion's fingers began to twitch with a primitive excite-ment as he measured the lofty stranger's girth against his own. "*Sacre bleu!*" he murmured happily, the light of battle in his eyes.

The stranger, dismounting, heard him and his glance was unfriendly. The temper of him was edgy to the eye of Emilion. Then he heard Wanda say, "Why, Mr. Davis!" in a tone of welcome that caused Inez' eyebrows to arch gently and made Emilion nod sagely and smile thought-fully. There was more to this than the eye met.

"I knew I'd seen you before, sir!" Wanda said, extending her hand. "Even with the change, I knew it!"

The stranger took her hand gingerly and gave a faint

reluctant smile as though her delight were infectious to even his black mood. He said, "You saw me before? With fur maybe?" He rubbed his clean-shaven chin.

"Yes," she laughed. "Yes Mr. Davis. With fur. Lots of fur." She turned swiftly to Emilion. "Oh, Emilion—this is the man I told about—who saved Jean-Paul's money on the stage. . . . Mrs. Hassard, Mr. DeLorme—Mr. Jefferson Davis. . . ."

"Jefferson Davis!" said Inez with a slow smile.

"That's what he told me," Wanda said merrily.

"So *he* is the man!" said Emilion delightedly, his great hands closing and unclosing. "Ah, *mais oui*, a fighter, this one! Ah, *joi* . . . !"

"Oh, Emilion," Wanda said.

The stranger settled a cold and appraising look on Emilion.

"What, my friend," inquired Emilion, hugely grinning, "is your true name, seeing that the other must be a *nom de guerre?*"

The stranger looked Emilion over with great care. "That," he said very gently, "is none of your business."

Emilion's delight heightened. "*Nom de Dieu!* You do not disappoint me!"

"Stop it, Emilion," Wanda scolded. "Shake hands with Mr. Kingdom."

"Kingdom?" Emilion scratched his head. "That is a name?"

The stranger smiled faintly. "It's not a common one," he said, "but this time it's real."

Emilion swept out a hand, grinning wickedly. "Pardon, M'sieu Kingdom." Kingdom regarded the hand for a long moment in a neutral way, then took it.

They struck hands and Emilion felt the stranger's hand tighten under the bone-crushing grip he deliberately applied. For a moment they strained and there was no perceptible give on either side. Only Emilion's smile faded slowly to a look of mounting puzzlement and slow-dawning bewilderment; Kingdom's face was expressionless.

"By gar, end it!" Emilion said suddenly, and they broke free. "Brother," Emilion said in awe, "you should watch your strength. To this day, no one made Emilion DeLorme cry quit."

Kingdom gingerly massaged his right hand, regarding Emilion with a grudging respect. "You hadn't, I would."

"If you're through making muscles, Emilion," Inez said sweetly, "let's not delay Mr. Kingdom's business any longer."

"I'm sorry," Wanda said, laughing. "Do you have business here, Mr. Kingdom?"

"I was looking for a job," Kingdom said. "Heard you were starting a drive in a few days."

"Why, Father said he had all the men he needs, but —oh, surely he can find a place for you. . . . Come, he should be at breakfast."

She set off down the incline with Kingdom, he leading his horse. Emilion, curious, knocked out his pipe against the forge and started after them. He paused by where Inez sat and extended an arm to her with the finesse of a courtier of Old France. She hesitated, unaccustomed to such courtesy, then nodded her thanks and stood with his help. Afterward, they followed Kingdom and Wanda to the veranda of the rambling house of hand-hewn timbers. Etienne Santerre himself had just stepped out the back door as Emilion and Inez reached it.

Seeing Santerre, Emilion felt his customary swell of inward pride that he worked for this tall, imperial-looking man. Like Emilion, of French-Canadian extract, Santerre was an exceedingly distinguished picture of a man, his coal-black hair and trim, precisely clipped Vandyke set off by threads of gray above the temples. His kindly eyes were the dark violet of Wanda's. Yet he affected nothing; he dressed as shabbily as the sorriest man of his crew in homespun jeans and a much-washed linsey-woolsey shirt with an old-fashioned stock, once white but now a dishrag gray. His one concession to dignity was a clawhammer coat, rusty-black with age.

"Father, this is the man of whom I told you—from the stage—Mr. Kingdom."

Santerre came off the veranda. He did not embrace Kingdom or kiss him on the cheeks; he grasped his hand and measured him with cool eyes that saw much. "*Mon ami*, you saved my son-in-law's bankroll, so I understand. I am in your debt for any favor you may request."

"All I'll ask you for is a job," Kingdom said.

Santerre raised a finger and smoothed the point of his beard thoughtfully. "You have struck me for the initial favor at shall we say an unpropitious time, monsieur. I have in very fact as many men as I require for the trail drive. For you, however, I think we can use an extra hand."

Kingdom thanked him.

"My son-in-law is ill abed," Santerre said. "The tedious days on the stage . . . He would be glad to see you, I know. . . . Have you breakfasted yet . . . ? No . . . ? Then please join us in the kitchen. You will want to wash up, of course; the wash bench is at the back. . . . The corrals are beyond."

Emilion, more or less a privileged character on the ranch, ate with the family, together with Hassard and his wife, as often as he ate with the crew, and he followed the others into the kitchen, pausing at the door to watch Kingdom leading his horse up to the corrals. Him I must fight at all costs, Emilion thought contentedly, knowing that he would know no satisfaction until he had matched his strength against Kingdom's.

"Julio! Set the table," Santerre called. "Set an extra place. Sit down, my children. . . . Is your husband up, my dear?" he asked Inez.

"I'd hardly know," she said indifferently, sinking listlessly into the chair Emilion held for her. Santerre looked at

the table, somewhat embarrassed, doubtless recalling that
Mr. and Mrs Hassard did not sleep in even the same part
of the house.

The house cook, a slender Mexican boy, had set the
places and was bringing in the food when Hassard appeared in the doorway leading off the kitchen to the sleeping quarters. His eyes were bloodshot; he was unshaven and
shirtless, his cotton underwear, above his trousers, dirty.
"Breakfast already? Can't you wake a man?"

"That might be possibe," Inez said tartly, "if you'd tuck
your bottle in a separate bed nights."

Hassaerd laughed. "Oh Lord, listen to that! The blind
leading the blind."

"You don't see me groaning about waking up, do you?"
she snapped.

Hassard snorted. "I don't see you drinking out of a
teacup evenings, either."

"Bless you," Inez told him.

Emilion roared and banged a fist on the table, saying,
"Family felicity, by gar, amity and accord!" being very
proud of his command of words, and never losing a chance
to demonstrate it.

Santerre rapped a spoon sharply against his coffee cup.
"Enough! We are civilized human beings, not barbarians.
Eat; be silent."

Hassard pulled a chair out from the table, scowling
blackly, and had begun to sit down when Kingdom came
through the back door into the kitchen. Hassard stopped
in midmovement as though turned to rock, his eyes on
Kingdom. A tremor shook Hassard; he caught at his belt
for a gun which he recalled too late wasn't there.

"Oh for heaven's sake!" Inez said in exasperation. "Now
what?"

Hassard looked wildly about; he saw the heavy Sharps
buffalo gun mounted on its pegs on the wall behind Emilion's chair and lunged around the table after it. Emilion

leisurely, effortlessly swung a leg in front of Hassard as he came past Emilion's chair, tripped him, and sent him sprawling headlong. Emilion reached up then and plucked the rifle from the wall, turning it in his hands judiciously.

"You wanted this, m'sieu," he observed innocently to Hassard. "But why? Is it perhaps that you perceived a snake?"

Hassard got up slowly. He said, his face white with rage, "I'll remember this, DeLorme."

"I did not intend that you should forget it, m'sieu," Emilion said smoothly, giving Hassard his most beamingly tranquil smile. "But come. Apprise us of the reason for this display of truculence."

"Yes, the reason, Egan," Santerre said sharply. "Mr. Kingdom is a guest under our roof, and as such is immune to unwarranted acts of violence. You have shamed us with this; now, explain yourself."

The words dragged thickly from Hassard's tongue. "Ask him. He shot my sister two nights ago . . . Killed her . . ." The last words tore from him in a violent whisper.

Every eye swiveled to Kingdom who stood in the doorway, watching Hassard with a guarded wariness.

"Why did I not hear of this?" Santerre said angrily.

"You might have asked me," said Inez wearily. "I've heard little else for two days. He came in drunk the other morning and harangued me for hours about it. All he'd say was some gunman shot Melanie. I couldn't get more out of him."

Wanda said coldly, "He had to have a scapegoat on whom to fix the killing, and chose Kingdom."

"Mr. Kingdom," Santerre said quietly, "you owe us a word."

"I'll tell—" Hassard said thickly.

"Be quiet, Egan," Santerre said. "Let Kingdom speak."

Kingdom let his breath out slowly. "I came West to look for my brother after the war ended. He'd ridden with

Quantrell and had been outlawed. I followed him to a town north of here. He was shot by a trigger-happy boy and died telling me about his wife here in Boundary. I came here to tell his wife of his death. She was Hassard's sister. . . . While I was talking to her in her house, a tramp broke in and demanded money. She pulled a gun on the tramp and he shot her. Hassard came in, found me there, and blamed me for the killing."

"But what of the man who committed the crime—the tramp?" demanded Santerre.

"No one saw him," snapped Hassard. He glanced at Kingdom, his voice edged with hateful mockery. "No one —except Kingdom. . . ." He added wickedly to Kingdom, "How are your friends?"

Emilion watched the big man stiffen all over. "My friends?"

"Yes! The ones who shot at us and drove us off when we caught up with you the other night. . . ."

"You're mistaken," Kingdom said gently. "I was the only one shooting at you."

Santerre said in a puzzled way, "What of this?"

Hassard said hotly, "I got some men and ran him out of town. We'd caught up to him and dehorsed him and he dodged into some chapparal. There was shooting then, and we were driven off." He scowled. "I don't know. I could've sworn someone besides him was shooting at us. Maybe not. . . ."

Emilion guffawed. "Hassard merely hates to admit he was driven off by one man! My congratulations, M'sieu Kingdom!"

Wanda said angrily, "Ran him out of town, indeed! Tell about the lynching, Mr. Hassard! You forgot that!"

Hassard eyed her uneasily and looked away. Santerre groaned softly. "A lynching now! What else?"

"Let me tell you, Father," Wanda said quickly. ". . . Hassard incited a group of men to lynch Mr. Kingdom and shot at him on the street when he attempted to escape. Marshal Frost and his deputy helped him get away, but Hassard and his gang pursued him out of Boundary. That was the last I saw of them until Mr. Hassard came back hours later and drove Jean-Paul and me out to the ranch that night. He was drunk and quite offensive."

"He's that first half the time and the last all the time," Inez observed.

Santerre said wrathfully, "Why did not you not tell me of this before, my dear?"

"I—did not want to make trouble for Hassard. But I could not stand now and let him condemn Mr. Kingdom."

Santerre swung on Hassard. "So! I wondered why it took you two days to bring my child and her husband to the ranch, Egan. Your excuse was thin, I thought, and I was right."

Hassard watched Santerre; now that the die was cast, a kind of patient resignation had come to the segundo.

"Egan," Santerre said in a surprisingly gentle voice, "this is a bad thing. I have not heard you deny what has been said against you. But you have been a good man to me, and I wait for you to speak in your own defense." When Hassard said nothing, Santerre went on, still gently, "Did it not occur to you, Egan, that were Kingdom truly your sister's killer, he would scarcely come seeking work at the ranch where you are segundo?"

Hassard said thickly, stubbornly, "I put it down to gall. He came in here trading on the friendship of your daughter and her husband—maybe to wait for a chance to get back at me."

Santerre smiled and gestured at Kingdom. "Would a man so big be capable of something so small, Egan?" When Hassard was stubbornly silent, Santerre said tiredly, "It would not be fair to discharge you, Egan. Your service has been good."

"As a damn errand boy?"

Santerre's falcon gaze sharpened on him. "I sent you after my daughter and her husband for the same reason I made you my segundo—you are my most trustworthy man. That is why I keep you now. Neither could I discharge you with your wife in her present state. But Kingdom stays. And if you stay, I must have your word that there will be no conflict between you."

Hassard was silent so long that Emilion wondered if he would answer. He saw Hassard look at Kingdom and at Inez and back to Kingdom, finally to say tonelessly, bleakly, "It won't be started by me."

"Then the matter is closed," Santerre said with finality. "We eat. Ho, Julio! More coffee."

Kingdom and Hassard took their seats and began to eat without looking at each other. The silence over the table was constrained and tense. Emilion, bent over his plate, cast an occasional glance at Kingdom or Hassard.

The matter closed, he thought scornfully. *Voila!* but look at them. The match and the powder keg . . .

## CHAPTER ELEVEN

KINGDOM WAS down by the wagon shed where he had the spring wagon up on blocks, the wheels off, when the coming night forced him to quit work. He would finish tomorrow. He went up to the bunkhouse and cleaned up at the outside wash bench. He could hear the crew inside, bantering back and forth. Because it better suited his solitary nature, he walked away from the bunkhouse off into the quiet of the growing night toward Emilion's smithy.

He rolled a cigarette as he walked slowly, thinking—something he had assiduously avoided through hard work in the two days since he had come to Staghorn.

This is a fool's game, he thought. I should have kept on riding when I left the valley. . . . But he had not, and Kingdom could not say why. And now he could not turn back. Somehow he must find a way to help Santerre, whom he had come to like. . . .

Kingdom paused by the rear of the house to light his cigarette. As its orange flare washed up in the cool dusk, and he bent his head to it, the door to the rear veranda opened, light falling softly into the yard. Mrs. Hassard stepped into the doorway. He came to a stop, hoping that she wouldn't see him in the poor light, but her silver tinkling laughter spilled into the night.

"Come over here, Kingdom. Come over here or I'll scream." She waggled a finger at him. "Better come. I could say you were molesting me and ol' Frenchy would have you horsewhipped off Staghorn. . . . You don't think I'd do it?"

"I have no doubt you'd do it," Kingdom said grimly.

"You are right," she said in a grave and tipsy voice. "A drunk will do anything. And I am drunk, Kingdom. Quite. Come over and help me sit down."

He hesitated and she smiled warningly; he stepped over and assisted her to sit on the edge of the porch. "You too," she said. He sat down warily at a distance.

"Now," Inez said, "what is your opinion of me, Kingdom?"

"I had heard," Kingdom said dryly, "that you were hell on wheels, Mrs. Hassard. I believe it."

She laughed genuinely. "Who said that?"

"A man who loves beauty. Good night."

"Oh, sit down . . . !" Inez regarded him speculatively "You didn't come to this ranch for nothing. . . . Was it t make trouble?"

He said warily, "Why that?"

"Because you knew Egan would try to shoot you o sight. Knowing that, you had the gall to ride in here an touch old Frenchy for a job."

Kingdom said carefully, "I had no way of knowing tha your husband was segundo here."

Her lips half curved. "I don't believe a word you'r saying. I saw the way you looked at Egan the other da when you surprised him at breakfast. *You* weren't sur prised. You were ready for trouble was all. And you looke it."

"My reason?" Kingdom asked tightly.

"Reason? Oh, yes. . . . Well, there's Wanda."

His throat tightened; he started at her, his heart a pul sing drum roll in his ears. "I—don't—"

"You needn't pretend, Kingdom," Inez said carelessly "I've seen the way you look at her. I know you met he before you came to Staghorn. And she's why you came.'

"You're seeing things," he said thinly.

"Am I then, Kingdom? But I couldn't be seeing thing two-sided." She laughed quietly. "You see, she's been look ing too. She's a very fine mother to her husband. . . .'

"About her, you're wrong," he heard himself say.

"You men make me sick!" Inez snapped. "You shove us women up on pedestals and expect us to stand there all our lives like painted little puppets. You've built a nice pretty halo around her head, and it's going to fall off the first time she sneezes. Sure she's sweet and innocent, but still a woman. And if you don't walk in and take her away from him, you *are* a damned fool."

"And what about him?" Kingdom asked dryly.

"Oh, stop trying to sound ironic, Kingdom. It fits you like a glove with ten fingers. He doesn't give a hoot about his wife as a wife. . . . Don't look so surprised. Villon's a Creole gentleman, the last word in courtesy—But how many small attentions does he give her . . . ? Oh, he doesn't realize it. Not at all. Down in him, though, he thinks of Wanda as nothing but a backwoods girl, just a cornfed calico sweetheart. The sophistries of New Orleans society are under his skin, and for all he's a fine fellow, he doesn't give a damn for all the innocence in the world. . . ."

She smiled faintly. "Am I boring you, Kingdom? No . . . ? Well, that's about it. They shouldn't have been married. And she, at least, knows that."

"Did she tell you?"

"She didn't have to."

Kingdom said nothing; he felt with utter certainty that Wanda would never be disloyal to Villon, however mismated they were. Riding him still was that sense of wrongness.

"Actually, she's no more than a girl . . . much too young for you, Kingdom. But too young for Villon, for that matter. . . ." She yawned, seeming to lose interest in the subject. "I'm going to get a drink. Join me?"

Kingdom felt his brief rapport with her vanish. "No."

"Don't be righteous. You'd drink too, married to him."

"It's not Hassard," Kingdom said irritably. "You drink because you're afraid."

To his surprise, the smooth composure of her face crumpled and shrank. "Don't say that," she whispered. "Don't ever say that. It's ugly."

"Fear is seldom pretty," said Kingdom wearily. "I'm sorry."

"No—you're right. It is my only reason; I really hate liquor. I've told myself for a long time I'll quit—now, perhaps I will. . . ." She looked at him with a strange gentleness. "Thank you, Kingdom. You're a big man in more than one way. . . ."

"We'll forget that," he said in a gruff voice.

She fingered a pleat in her skirt thoughtfully. "Egan's a good man. He took me out of a job as gambling shill in El Paso and made me his wife. We could have been happy. But he tried to run me as he tried to run his sister Melanie, and it was no good. He has to twist and break everything he thinks he owns. I wouldn't take that. One night he found me taking a sip of brandy and became violently angry.

"I understood then how I could best defy him—by drinking—so I did."

"I think I understand."

"I really think you do. Bless you for that, Kingdom."

"Bless him?" said Hassard, so near at hand in the soot-black darkness of the yard that both started. He stepped into view in the lamplight then. Kingdom wondered how much he'd heard. He had been drinking; his step was unsteady. They watched him warily. "Bless him?" Hassard said sardonically. "Bless is not your customary term—not the one for me."

"Oh, stop shooting at the sky, Egan," Inez said disgustedly.

Hassard's gaze flicked to Kingdom. "How did you get here?"

"I was able to walk."

"You're a purple fool, Egan," Inez said coldly. "We were talking."

"Just so, my dear. . . . About me. I want to talk to you, Kingdom." He looked at his wife. "Go inside." She did not move. "Go inside, I said!"

"I'd go, Mrs. Hassard," Kingdom said quietly.

"I'd better." She stood with Kingdom's help. She looked at Hassard then, her voice very clear. "Don't worry for me, Kingdom. He hasn't sunk to wife-beating—yet."

She stepped into the house then, pulling the door to behind her, and the veranda was in complete darkness. Kingdom spoke into it: "The matter deserves a thought before you jump."

"Never mind that," Hassard's voice said between his teeth. "I long ago quit noticing what my wife does, and much less care."

He's lying, Kingdom thought neutrally, and waited for him to go on.

"What I wanted to talk to you about," said Hassard, "was this drive." A match flared in the darkness; he looked at Kingdom over the flame; and Hassard's face was suddenly wolfish in the wash of ruddy light. He lighted his cigar and threw the match away; the cigar tip bloomed brightly, cherry-red against sable night. "You went to a peck of trouble to persuade the old man to make the drive north. Why?"

"Let's say I like progress."

"Let's say something stinks. Why should you give a damn where we drive? Still, you do. . . ."

"The market," Kingdom murmured. "Up to twenty dollars a head, maybe. Santerre did me a good turn hiring me when he had enough men. My turn."

The disbelief in Hassard's voice carried to him in the darkness. "Twenty dollars a—? Now I know you're lying."

"You think so?"

"I don't believe the railroad's reached Abilene yet," Hassard snapped, "if there is a place called Abilene. . . . Let's say for the sake of argment there is—how far is it?"

"About a thousand miles. Up through the Cherokee Strip and the Nations. Good grass. Buffalo've foraged there for ages. So can cattle."

"That's three months and more on the trail. And the Nations—border gangs, Indians, desert, floods, quicksand, Lord knows what. I don't like it. . . ."

"You're breaking me all up," Kingdom murmured.

"That's not a bad idea!" Hassard snapped. His cigar was flung to the ground with a brief fiery arc and an angry shower of sparks in the night. "I'm not done with you, Kingdom."

"And your promise to Santerre?"

"That applied as far as the ranch." Hassard's voice softened. . . . "We'll be on the trail soon. A hundred days on the trail. A lot can happen in that time. A great deal can happen on a drive. Yes. . . . It can even happen to you, friend."

Kingdom heard him turn, begin to walk away; then suddenly he came back. ". . . And by the way, Kingdom. There *was* someone in that chaparral the other night, shooting at us. . . . Someone besides you. . . ." Kingdom could hear the bitter smile in Hassard's voice. "I recall now, I saw your dead horse. And your rifle was still on the saddle; you didn't have time  to take it with us almost on you. Well, whoever shot at us was using a rifle."

Kingdom did not answer.

"So you have friends, Kingdom. And I'm wondering if that has anything to do with your being here . . . ? Sleep on it, Kingdom."

With a laugh, Hassard walked off into the darkness.

And Kingdom did little sleeping.

## CHAPTER  TWELVE

HASSARD STOOD in the cold half light of pre-dawn near the bunkhouse, rolling a dead cigar from one side to the other of his mouth, looking restlessly across the stirring hulk that was five thousand head of massed, horn-tossing cattle. Nearly gaunt, string-muscled cattle. Soup stock, Hassard thought contemptuously, and half wild, the lot.

Today, at any rate, the drive would begin. He could hear the shouts of the riders hazing the distant edges of the herd. Two ox carts had been drawn up before the bunkhouse, piled high with the warbags of the crew. Some of them were at work at a branding chute a hundred yards distant, searing the road brand into the last bunch of longhorns brought in.

Villon, in rough-jeans and a much-washed shirt—a far cry now from the *bon mot* of New Orleans—was at the chute gate, working the bar that opened it. Kingdom held the running iron in gloved hands, drawing it now down a steer's flank. The beast bawled and lunged for the gate which Villon swiftly opened for it. Young Murray Ambergard waited there on his chestnut gelding, and he paused briefly to exchange a friendly word or two with Kingdom and Villon before he hazed the steer toward the herd.

Seeing Santerre coming down from the house, Hassard ground the cigar beneath his heel and walked to meet him.

"Really letting your son-in-law come on this drive, are you?"

"You object, Egan?"

"A drive is no place for a sick man."

"He cannot become well by sitting at home. He wished to accompany this drive, and while he may well regret it later, I did not refuse. He can at least drive a wagon. . . ."

Hassard sulked in silence and looked restlessly away, over toward the branding fire, whose smoke lifted and furled and was one with the thick dust as another steer went into the chute. One of the hands, Harve Soberin, had just come from breakfast, relieving Kingdom at the iron, and Kingdom went down to the cookshack for his own meal.

Hassard saw Villon's wife, a shawl thrown about her

shoulders, stepping off the veranda up by the house and coming on down toward the branding chute to speak with her husband. Hassard's mouth tightened. Inez would not do as much for him; she would not even be up by the time they left.

He saw with some puzzlement that Villon and his wife did not embrace, that there was great constraint in their parting, and he was wondering about this when Wanda left her husband and came over to where he and Santerre were standing.

"Have you seen Kingdom, *mon père?*" she asked. There was high, excited color to her cheeks. And not because she's cold, Hassard thought cynically.

"*Dieu de Dieu, mon enfant*—Kingdom! But I thought you would be desirous of spending these last moments of parting with your husband."

She blushed deeply in a way that lofted Hassard's tawny eyebrows in sardonic speculation. "Of course with Jean-Paul," she murmured. "But I want to say good-by to Kingdom. Where is he?"

Santerre said, regarding her with a deep trouble in his face, "I saw him go to eat but a few moments ago."

Taken shyly aback by what she saw in her father's face, Wanda said hurriedly, "Thank you," and walked toward the cookshack.

Watching her go, the troubled sadness grew weightier on Santerre's features. He was French, and far from blind to the pattern that these things made. This thing that was coming to his daughter was very bad. All this Hassard could read in his face.

"Doesn't look so good, does it?" Hassard murmured.

Santerre settled a wintry gaze upon him. He said icily, "I have never known Wanda to be indiscreet, Egan. And I advise you to look to more discretion in your own actions— and speech."

Hassard smiled with great thoughtfulness. He did not reply.

Sheep Dip, the cook, complained stormily as he left off packing grub and utensils in his wagon to dish up food for Kingdom—beans, biscuits, and coffee which he had been keeping warm in the cookshack for the crew's morning meal. He was a small, balding and unshaven man who, in the fierce tradition of trail chefs, found an excuse for irascibility in the most minor awry detail. Kingdom knew it to be his apex of contentment and turned a deaf ear to it as he carried his food to the long table while Sheep Dip, cursing him bitterly, stormed back out to his wagon to finish loading.

Kingdom was alone now and he ate slowly, with the solid content of a man of solitary nature. The door opened at his back and he glanced over his shoulder to see Wanda there. He came to his feet, almost spilling his coffee.

"Please sit down," she said. "If I bother you—"

"Why should you?"

Some determination fought with her shyness. "Because you really like to be alone—don't you?"

"I would reckon so, but it's only a habit."

"No. It's a part of you. It really is. You're a quite complete man. Kingdom. Sufficient unto yourself."

"Not that complete. Like saying a man can't be lonely."

Her violet eyes widened. "You, lonely? You, Kingdom?"

A heavily self-conscious embarrassment swept him and he thought with anger, How did we get off on on this? This personal talk must be guarded. His feelings were deep-buried; he would keep them so. He said patiently, as to a child, "You would not understand."

"Perhaps."

"No."

"That is to say that a woman can't be lonely."

"You have a man," he said roughly.

He was surprised by the fleeting shade of pain crossing her face. "Perhaps," she said, "perhaps you think I am lying to sympathize with you."

Kingdom let his breath out tiredly. "It's too bad you're not," he said. "Only you're not. No one lies about being lonely."

Her head was tilted back to watch his face; her eyes dilated briefly, and she looked away from him. She said, "Good-by," almost inaudibly, and was out the door at the same moment.

Kingdom settled on the bench to finish his breakfast, and could not finish. He washed down most of what remained with his coffee and stepped outside as a crewman's bawl lifted into the rose-pearl dawn: "We're moving!"

Kingdom hurried to the corral where some hands were assembling a picked remuda of nearly three hundred of the countless lean mustangs which grazed Staghorn range: cutters, ropers, broncs. Wrangler Porfirio Montoya, a dashing Mexican youth in greasy buckskin *chivarras* and an ornate charro jacket, cursed enthusiastically horses and men alike in the tongue of his fathers as he rode back and forth, bunching the remuda, in which, somewhere, was the blaze-face sorrel Incham had given Kingdom.

He asked Porfirio for a horse. Porfirio cursed him and cut him out a mount. Kingdom saddled up at the harness shed; he was placed in the drag with the green riders by a curt word from Hassard.

Santerre sat his horse by Hassard, his dark eyes roving the faintly stirring bulk of the herd. He looked at his riders at their postions; he raised his arm and let it fall.

"Yip-yip-yeeowee!" This was the rebel cry from the drag that set the herd in motion. An imperceptible movement at first, beginning around the outer periphery of it. It swelled and moved; it seemed to breathe, as though a couchant monster with an integrated life of its own. The cry was taken up. Irresistably, the herd shifted north.

The drive had begun.

Hassard and Reeves Gayland, on point, swung the lead steers out, lining them at the end of a slowly forming crescent, guided and built by flankers and swing men. The cattle assumed the form of a strung-out trail herd five hundred yards in breadth, an immensity of life shaped by the prompting of thirty riders.

Sullen dustclouds billowed chokingly about the drag-riders in the wake. Through the haze, Kingdom could see the others assigned to the drag. He knew a few by name: Breen, the drag-boss; Granger, Lovelace; and off to his left, young Murray Ambergard, dwarfed in his mackinaw and barrel-leg chaps. Murry saw him now and grinned whitely through the shrouding dust-pall: "Hi-hah, dust-eater!" Kingdom lifted a hand in reply and headed in to cut off a mulberry steer who had angled back among the stragglers.

He had leisure now to wonder when Incham would strike. He would follow with his crew of human scavengers . . . and wait . . . and wait. Kingdom had had no opportunity to take a count of Incham's men back in the valley, but he guessed them to be ten or a dozen. Even outnumbered three to one, a formidable handful in a surprise attack. Incham had said he would warn Kingdom before the raid and apprise him of his part in it. He must make his plans to help Santerre pending that warning. . . .

## CHAPTER THIRTEEN

Night camp was made on suitable bed-grounds near a grove of the scrub oak called blackjack. A thick ground fog gathered through the ocean of night, becoming ruddy-misted about the campfire, a half-mile from the bed-grounds. The men sat about the fire, wolfing their grub and too tired for much talk. Santerre was pushing hard these first days to make the herd trail-wise swiftly.

Porfirio, scheming how to break the apathy, walked with his empty plate and cup over to the wreck pan on Sheep Dip's wagon and dropped the dishes with a clatter that made everyone look up.

Porfirio winked at them, then looked soberly at the cook. "Sheep Dip, boy, know what we need?"

Sheep Dip paused suspiciously in the act of loading a plate for himself. "What?"

Porfirio delicately picked his teeth with the tip of his Bowie knife. "We need a cook."

Sheep Dip used bad language. There were grins; this was life's own spice to cook and crew alike. Sheep Dip damn well knew how to cook with the best, he said; he had been twenty years practicing.

"What did he say?" yawned Lovelace.

"He said he's been practicing spoiling grub for twenty years," Porfirio said tranquilly.

"No wonder he's so damn handy at it," said young Overmile.

"He ain't practicing on us," said Lovelace. "Get a rope."

"Let's have him fight Emilion," said Granger.

"Bah, I fight big game," said Emilion. His gaze settled slyly on Kingdom. "Like him."

"Fight him, then—fight Kingdom." They took up these words and passed them about.

"*Regarde,*" boomed Emilion. "He sits; he does not speak."

"Man's taken with himself, isn't he?" Kingdom murmured.

"Ha? You fight?" Emilion asked, grinning, his hands twitching.

"Do you want an engraved invitation?" Kingdom asked dryly.

A ripple of talk ran over the group; they cleared a space in the pool of firelight. Despite the chill, Emilion and Kingdom flung off coats and shirts and rolled the top of their underwear down tightly around their waists.

"Boots too," Emilion said. "We wrestle—eh?"

Kingdom was no wrestler, and he suspected that Emilion knew it; still, he nodded and pulled his boots off. The men murmured; they made bets. Another fight might have been only a pleasurable break in the monotony of the trail, but this . . .

They began to circle in, arms half before them, hands poised. The soft wash of firelight set their thickly muscle-coiled upper bodies palely agleam, the deep brown of face and hands startling by contrast. Emilion's Indian-dark eyes danced with the purest of happiness.

Kingdom would not strike first; he waited for Emilion to make the opening move. Emilion was very patient. He kept Kingdom circling for a full minute, then sprang in, his right hand closing over Kingdom's left shoulder. Emilion tried to close, but Kingdom wanted to avoid closing. He ducked under Emilion's arm, and when Emilion tried to lock his neck, he lifted his shoulder into Emilion's belly and heaved massively. Emilion nearly left his feet, then caught his balance. More warily now, he circled again.

Emilion grabbed at his shoulder again. This time Kingdom could not avoid closing, and they strained powerfully together. For the first time, Kingdom felt fully the awesome strength of the man. Then he left Emilion hook a leg around his left one and throw his weight into him. To keep his feet, Kingdom instinctively tried to fling his left leg back for support, found too late that the leg was immobilized by Emilion; and the blacksmith's weight carried him backward and onto the ground, the breath driving from him with the impact.

Emilion sat on him, beat his arms aside, and caught his throat. Emilion's fingers tightened powerfully; Kingdom, his wind already broken, found Emilion's strength resistless. He fought to break the hold, and with all his effort, could not. Then some boyhood wrestling trick came to him. He wedged his fingers beneath Emilion's thumbs and twisted them back hard against the joints.

A roar of pain lifted from the blacksmith; he came off Kingdom in his wild effort to loose his thumbs. In the moment that he was free of Emilion's weight, Emilion straddling him, Kingdom wrapped his arms around the giant's legs and heaved upward with all his strength. Emilion's feet left the ground; he was lifted clear off it, arms thrashing helplessly. Kingdom came to his knees, still lifting, and then to his feet, Emilion's great weight held unbelievably helpless above him.

Then Kingdom dropped him. The blacksmith landed on his face. While he was still dazed, Kingdom came on to his back, hammerlocking Emilion's right arm up behind him. Emilion resisted it silently, and with all his strength, which was such that no ordinary man could have held him so. It was all Kingdom could do to hold Emilion's wrist as far as the small of his back. But to the thickly corded thews of Emilion's huge arm, even this was uncomfortably painful. . . .

"Enough," grunted Emilion, his face in the ground.

Kingdom let go and came off him. There was a moment of awed silence around the fire. Emilion stood, shaking himself like a great mastiff. He gave his hand to Kingdom and powerfully wrung Kingdom's; his enthusiasm was boundless. "The first time!" he roared. "The first time!"

And Kingdom, about to remark that if Emilion had been twenty years younger, wisely concluded that Emilion would not take kindly to this.

Emilion looked about at the men, grinning hugely. "*Vive le roi,*" said Emilion DeLorme.

No one contradicted him.

The bets were paid and the talk died away as the men unrolled their suggans. Kingdom, carrying his bedroll off behind Sheep Dip's wagon, overheard Santerre accost Hassarrd over by the tailgate. Kingdom came to a dead stop and listened, their voices carrying through the fog.

"Kingdom is a top rider," Santerre said, "even a natural stud-horse man. Point would not be too good for him, green though he may be. Yet you make him eat the dust of the drag. Are you still taking out your petty revenge upon him?"

"Takes years of experience to make a top hand, don't give a damn how good he rides," Hassard snapped. "I reserve point for my top hands. Kingdom's raw, and he rides with the raw men."

"If he will be of more advantage other than in the drag, place him there."

"I'd send him away," Hassard said coldly. "Do you know how jayhawkers work? I do. They send a man into camp to size the situation off." He told Santerre briefly of the incident at the chaparral where a rifle was fired at the posse when Kingdom had no rifle; obviously the man had friends. . . .

"Anyone might have fired on you, you and the other drunken idiots in that mob," snapped Santerre: "Or you were so full of whiskey, you were seeing things. This is folly. Have no more of it."

"Folly, sure. Who decided this fool drive to Kansas? Not you and not me—Kingdom."

Villon's quiet voice broke in then: "I pity you, Hassard."

"What? Why you damn' lily-fingered snob! You pity me!"

"Yes, pity you," Villon said, and Santerre's sharp reprimand of them both was lost on Kingdom as he walked on, head bowed, into the fog. He heard footsteps after him then, and turned to see a slim silhouette merge out of the milky haze.

"Kingdom?" a voice called. The word was followed by a raw racking cough that left no doubt of identity.

"Here," Kingdom said, and came to a stop. Villon came up, blanket drawn around him.

"You heard it," he said.

"Yes."

"He is a damn cruel man, Hassard," said Villon, an edge of anger to his voice.

"Doesn't matter."

"You are charitable, Kingdom. Still, one day Hassard will make you truly angry. If he carries no gun then, I will name the corpse."

"Thanks," Kingdom said dryly.

The sick man turned away, back toward the fire, then stopped as though caught up by a thought. Villon turned back to Kingdom. He said levelly: "A matter comes to my mind of which we should speak now, rather than let it run its course until harm is done."

Wariness touched Kingdom. "Yes?"

"I don't know whether my wife knows her own mind," Villon went on evenly, "but I fancy that you know yours well enough, Kingdom. I fancy that you know what you want—even if it should be another man's wife. . . ."

Kingdom began to speak; Villon cut him off with a raised hand. "Hear me out, Kingdom. It may be that you are playing a game with my wife which she may regret. However; I doubt that; I have taken your measure as that kind of man who can never be less than sincere. I wish to establish that to show you that your sincerity or lack of it makes no difference. I am appealing to your honor to stop the matter before it goes further." He paused. "To a point, I have been a blind fool. However—well, I was strolling by the house last night and on a still night, voices carry. . . ."

Kingdom thought of last evening on the rear veranda; he chilled a little.

"I'm sorry," Villon said in a wry way. "Though I heard only one side of the talk . . . Mrs. Hassard, you will own, does not exercise the softest voice in the world. . . ."

Kingdom said simply, "I'm sorry."

"No. Don't be sorry. Then you make me feel as though I am in the wrong to take this stand. And I do not think I am. I am only trying to keep my wife's name from tarnish. . . . It may be that someday she will need someone—but, if so, you must wait till then."

"I don't understand," Kingdom said slowly.

Even in the fog then, he caught the strange ghost of a smile on Villon's mouth. "It is in my mind, Kingdom, that I have come to this land to die. . . . Good night."

Kingdom, a frown deepening on his face, watched Villon vanish in the fog toward the wagons. Standing in the mist bound night, it came to Kingdom that all of them were like tornado-driven chaff, drawn into the vortex of something greater than they were.

## CHAPTER FOURTEEN

LUTE MOVED warily through the blackjack timber toward Santerre's camp. The night was utterly still; there was only the crunch of his boots as he passed the dreary, spectral march of trees in the cold mist. He moved to the very edge of the timber and paused there, hunkering down in the brush, straining his eyes to single out objects in the fog. Gradually he recognized the shadows pooling darkly on the ground around the dying fire as the forms of sleeping men.

His heart was pounding; his breath caught at his throat as he heard the sound of horses moving invisibly toward the wagons far to his right. They came dimly into view, horsemen merging out of the mist as though part of it, dismounting by the wagons and uncoiling their riatas. In these first days on the trail, there was no offsaddling, no slipped bridle. Every man slept with his riata about his wrist, the end looped on the saddle horn.

Nighthawks, these, Lute thought. It was time for their relief. The men straggling into camp, ground-tied their horses and moved forward among the sleeping men, waking some. One bent over a man not five yards from where Lute crouched. The rider shook the sleeping man's shoulder. "Kingdom."

Kingdom! Lute thought—a stroke of luck finding the man he sought so easily. . . .

"Time for your watch," the rider said in a low voice.

Kingdom rolled out of his blankets. He had only to put on his hat and he was ready. The rider's cigarette glowed ruddy contrast to the unrelieved shades of variant gray in this fog-shrouded night.

"Still," the rider murmured. "Real still. I smell a storm. Bad one. And that." he added wryly, softly, "might be all we need to set them off."

"How are they?" Kingdom asked.

"Skittish, some. Can make trouble maybe. No saying."

The other reliefs had already stumbled sleep-drugged to their horses, stepping into their saddles and heading out toward the herd. Here was luck; it would give Lute the opportunity he needed to speak to Kingdom. He stood and moved soundlessly through the timber, paralleling Kingdom heading through the ground mist toward his horse. Kingdom had a hand on the horn, one foot in the stirrup, when Lute called his name softly.

Kingdom stiffened, turning, eyes straining at the black-jack.

"Me, Lute. Over here."

Leading his horse, Kingdom moved carefully into the shelter of the grove, coming to stand before Lute.

"It'll be tonight," Lute said flatly. When Kingdom didn't reply, Lute massaged his chin with a hand and said wryly, "You won't like it."

"It's too soon. First night on the trail."

"Not what I meant," Lute said irritably. "Incham means to stampede the herd over Santerre's camp. Wreck the wagons and carry away the remuda—"

"And maybe kill a few men," Kingdom said quietly. When Lute was silent, he gibed, "What is it, Lute? Weak stomach?"

"Dammit, yes, if you must know," Lute snapped. "I've seen enough killing."

"You're ambitious, Lute. There's the price for it. That's part of what you pay."

"Incham's going up," Lute said harshly, "and I'm going with him."

"You're going down with him, then."

A sickness and a shame gorged up in Lute. Then, with a mildness that astonished Lute, Kingdom said: "You won't go through with it, Lute. You know you won't."

There was this sudden ease between them, the tension gone. Lute said bleakly, "You're right. And neither will you."

"No," Kingdom admitted.

"What do we do, then?"

"What was my part supposed to be?"

"At midnight Incham means for you to take care of the nighthawks—the ones likely to be dangerous. Do it quiet. You get a gun on 'em, and cold-cock 'em. Signal us with a shot then; we're waiting behind the herd. We make it noisy—start the herd moving over the camp."

"This is too quick."

"He don't trust you. He likes you, but he don't trust you."

Kingdom said thoughtfully, "Go back to Incham. Tell him it's set."

"What'll you do?"

"Warn Santerre. Tell him all of it."

"Lord. He'll likely shoot you."

"He likely will," Kingdom agreed dryly. "He'll be warned though. He'll be ready. Have a care of yourself—it'll be hell out there." He scrubbed a hand across his jaw; the stiff rasp of whiskers grated along Lute's surcharged nerves.

"Hell, why worry," he said half angrily.

"The war's over, Lute," Kingdom said wearily. "I'm through fighting it. Believe that or don't."

Lute argued silently with himself for a moment, then said, "I'll believe it, Jim," and extended his hand. "About Doug—he never took part in the worst at Lawrence. Or Olathe, Paola, Shawneetown, or the other bad places." He cleared his throat self-consciously. "Neither did I."

"I wouldn't have guessed you had, Lute. Thanks for that—about Doug. Be easier on his family."

"Sure."

"Funny," Kingdom said musingly, "I liked Incham. . . ."

"Ah, the business tonight," Lute said quietly. "Don't blame him. He's a husk. War burned out the best in him."

"An empty man," murmured Kingdom; "but the I-don't-give-a-damn way he's got to him—why, it's a pose."

"He puts on quite an act," Lute agreed dryly. "But one thing he needs, always: to feel that he's best. . . . He needs power and he needs to feel that he has it, and he won't stop for anything in his way. . . . Like tonight."

"Like Hassard," Kingdom murmured.

"What?"

"Nothing. . . . You'd better get back."

"Right away. . . . What about Tory? Sooner or later, you'll have to meet him."

"Let it be later, then. See you, Lute."

"I doubt it," Lute said gloomily. "Watch yourself."

They shook hands and Lute turned, took a step, then looked back. "Curious. Why tell Incham you were Doug?"

"Health."

Lute considered that, nodded thoughtfully, and forced a grin. They parted then, Kingdom to find Santerre, and Lute to work back through the timber to where he had left his horse. He mounted and cut out of the timber, making a wide circle around the herd. He headed down into a meadowlike vale where the shapes of men and horses took form out of the fog.

"You, Lute?" It was Incham's voice. Lute replied, and rode in, stirrup to stirrup with the leader. The fog gathered so thickly in the low vale that only dark outlines of men and not their features could be discerned.

"He knows his part," Lute said.

"When's he on watch?"

"Right now."

"We'd better get into position, then," Incham said. "Lute —you, Lampasas, Valdez, take the left flank of the herd. Tory, take right flank with Woodring, Tremaine, and Herschel. I'll take the rear with the rest. Lute"— Lute could imagine him smiling —"has grilled you on the details of your postions with military precision. . . . You flankers will hear Kingdom's signal shot, but don't make any noise until we in the rear start the herd moving. Understand . . . ? You know your jobs. Any questions?"

"One, Mr. Incham."

"Tory?"

"Why don't we all make it noisy at once?"

"The ones behind the herd will start it moving in a certain direction—toward Santerre's camp," Incham said patiently. "We don't want you on the flank messing it by shooting too. Your job is to keep the herd guided that way once we've got it moving. Any more questions?"

There were none, and the group split up into three parties which moved in on three sides of the herd, disembodied wraiths in the mist, keeping well beyond the easy perception of Santerre's nighthawks. Distantly, dimly, by straining his eyes, Lute could barely distinguish the bulk of the herd, the guards circling it, riding in pairs, their soft and lonely crooning to the cattle carrying obscurely to his ears.

A tingling raced up and down Lute's spine, prickling the base of his neck. The blood pounded thickly at his temples. Kingdom would have warned Santerre by now; Santerre would be planning a counteraction against the raiders. He tried to think how that counteraction would go, and could not. He had to be careful, was all. Let Incham and the others watch their own necks. A man had to take the cards as they fell.

The crooning of the night riders had died away. Lute became attentive, every nerve straining for sound and sight; but the fog had thickened and even the outline of the herd was barely visible. He could no longer make out the riders; that meant that Santerre's counter offensive was in motion. He would pull his men in to make Incham think that Kingdom had taken care of them. Thank the Lord for the thickness of the fog. If Incham even suspected . . .

Lute stiffened. He could hear a vast movement out there in the herd, and he thought, Midnight. It is immemorial with cattle in herds that they come erect at midnight, step restlessly about, and again bed down. Of all the moments which a drive could bring, this was, Lute knew, one of the most dangerous: the moment when every night guard tenses to the restlessness of his wards, the moment when an untoward incident could break all hell loose. . . .

So Incham had scheduled his attack as nearly as possible for midnight.

It would come any moment now. . . .

Lute looked over his shoulder at his men, strung out behind him at loosely measured intervals, paralleling the body of the herd. "Ready," he called softly, and they began to move in slowly toward the herd. He could see the dark forms of Lampasas and the others moving in unison, and it was odd to think that before the night had finished, some, perhaps all, of them would be dead. . . .

The signal shot fired by Kingdom—or one of Santerre's men—came suddenly. Lute heard the shots and shouting as Incham's party converged on the herd from behind. Somewhere out there a steer snorted in fear. There was a violent concentration of motion through the herd. As one it surged. Lute's Spencer was out of its boot; he shot into the air, and his men closed in at the flank of the suddenly onsurging cattle. He heard the heavy roar of Lampasas' ancient Sharps over the tumult of sound. At the opposite flank, Tory's men were peppering the air with pistol and rifle, and their rebel cries reached even here. Lute's men had taken up the shouting. The flanking parties pulled alongside the herd, racing on fleet cow ponies that no steer could distance.

Lute could hear the outbreak of shooting from some-where ahead—Santerre's men at the forefront of the herd, attempting to turn it away from the camp. It was the best they could hope to do now; it could only be diverted and not stopped, for in its momentum it must run itself out until it could be milled. Nor could the flankers guide it now; it was out of their hands. Give your horse the free rein; let him run.

And then, from ahead, riding to meet them, what Lute had been watching and waiting for—uncertain shadows in the fog, quickly taking the forms of horsemen—a half dozen of Santerre's men. . . .

Lute twisted in his saddle and shouted a warning at his men which must have been lost in the flood tide of heav-ing backs and tossing, clicking horns and the thunder roll of twenty thousand hoofs.

Lute turned his horse before he could meet the Staghorn riders head on, turning off at right angles to the path of the herd, to freedom in the cover of the night. Then San-terre's men opened fire, their guns winks of rosefire in the gray obscurity. Glancing back, Lute saw Lampasas pitch from his saddle. Lute was stunned. Lampasas. . .

He lost sight of the others in the confusion.

Then Lute's horse crumpled under him, suddenly hit, and Lute flung himself sideways from the saddle, landed on his shoulder and side with a grunt, rolled over twice, came upright unhurt, and started running on foot. He had lost his rifle. The tumult was well behind him now. He was safe.

Then he looked back and knew that he was seen and

that this was the showdown after all: one of the Santerre riders had cut out of the fog in pursuit of him.

He reached for his pistol on the run. His holster was empty; he must have lost it when he left his falling horse.

He put his head down and ran, hearing the sound of the horse bearing down on him. The cold mist was on his face; he felt his feet running, running beneath him. Good-by, California. More dreams. Good-by, Oregon. Funny, you thought you didn't care a damn about living, but when it came to it, you were an elemental animal groping wildly for life, and all you could do was run.

Every sobbing breath seared his chest; Lute thought as though in a dream, hearing the thundering hoofs almost on him, Why doesn't he shoot?

He looked back to see why, and he saw the horse and rider towering blackly over him, and he saw the rider's arm lift, and there was a flash of bright bursting flame in his eyes. Something smashed him in the face and that was all.

## CHAPTER FIFTEEN

KINGDOM HAD had no difficulty with Santerre whose quick mind was receptive to the information he had to offer. A few swift questions; and Santerre roused out his sleeping men. In seconds, the men were mounted and ready, rifles in hand, their gear assembled and pitched in the wagons which were driven out of harm's way. Santerre snapped out his directions: wait for the raiders to close in, then hit them with half of his men. Hit them before they hit us, some said. Santerre overrode this; wait, he counciled, and possibly they could surprise the enemy. The stampede would come regardless of any preventive measures when shooting started.

Santerre split the men; half to hit the enemy, half to turn the stampede. Then he divided the first fifteen again, taking command of eight himself to attack the raiders on one flank of the herd, assigning the others to Emilion, who would hit those on the opposite flank.

Santerre had placed Kingdom under Hassard who would take the remaining men and attempt to divert and mill the stampede.

Kingdom was among those who pulled far ahead into the probable path of it. "Watch it, men," Hassard's voice carried to him. "When that beef comes through, it won't stop for hell or high water. Get in front of it and it'll run over you like a river. Try to turn it from the flank. . . ."

Kingdom heard and felt the throbbing ground-pulse of numberless hoofs before he saw the black mass of the herd grow out of the fog.

The Staghorn riders whooped and shot into the air. Hardly able to make out the cattle yet for distance, Kingdom was already awed by a sense of the irresistable force of this massed hurtling juggernaut. He saw too that he would be caught in the outfringe of the herd's passage unless he pulled his horse farther to the flank; recalling Hassard's warning, he reined quickly that way.

Then, a careless shot by a rider—Kingdom felt the smashing impact all through his left arm. For a stunned moment, he lost control of his horse; the animal turned toward the very head of the oncoming herd.

In a panic, Kingdom wrenched the horse's head to turn him back toward the flank, and in the violent movement

the horse stumbled and pitched sideways, throwing Kingdom partly from the saddle. Kingdom might have held on,
but he fell on his wounded arm, and in the blinding hot pain
of it lost his seat wholly.

By the time he had reached his feet, his spooked horse
was gone.

The millrace of steers drowned all other sound now, and
Kingdom, in its direct path and helpless, did not hear the
rider; he did even see the rider until the horse was almost upon him.

The man motioned Kingdom up behind him. Kingdom
tried to swing up, but his wounded arm would not take his
weight; he could not do it one-handed. The rider dismounted impatiently, assisting Kingdom into the saddle,
then swinging up behind him. And Kingdom saw in
astonishment that it was Villon. . . .

The stampede was almost upon them; it would reach
them before they could get beyond danger if they attempted
to cut out of the herd's path at right angles. Instead, Kingdom turned Villon's mount in the same direction the herd
was running so that they traveled the route of the stampede, but well ahead of it. Gradually, then, Kingdom
turned the horse's head toward the flank, hauling them out
of danger slowly but with a broad margin of safety.

Kingdom jumped the horse high over some brush, and
hitting the ground again the animal kept on with no break
of pace.

But Villon was gone! Hanging tightly at Kingdom's back
on the slippery rump of his horse, Villon must have been
unseated by the jolting.

With a frantic hand to the rein, Kingdom hauled the
horse up short. And even then, with a single backward
glance, he knew that it was too late: Villon was swallowed
and lost somewhere under the roar of hoofs. . . .

Slack with pain and tiredness, Kingdom rode into camp.
The wagons were drawn up a few yards from the fire;

horses were ground-hitched close by, their heads low, sweat-frothed, thick-drawn breath sighing audibly from their lungs. Ten' or a dozen riders sprawled around the fire where Sheep Dip had the coffee boiler going.

Santerre stood at the tailgate of Sheep Dip's wagon, the sleeve 'of his shirt torn open. The cook was tying up a flesh wound in the owner's forearm. Santerre looked up as Kingdom slid from his horse's back. There was no rancor in his face; he lifted the cup of inky, scalding brew he held in his good hand in pleasant salute.

"Ah, *mon ami*. You make twelve. I fear not to see some others."

"You hit?" Sheep Dip asked as Kingdom stepped wearily over toward them.

"Yes."

"Hurt bad?"

"No," Kingdom lied, wanting to talk to Santerre alone. Santerre, seeing this, waited till Sheep Dip was finished with his arm, then walked off a short way with Kingdom.

"Didn't have time before," Kingdom said. "You'll want to hear the rest of it."

Santerre did not answer; he did not stop looking at Kingdom while he explained fully everything he could remember of the past week. "If I hadn't said anything to Incham of Abilene, this would not have come about," he concluded.

Santerre snorted. "If not this way, then another way. What of that? What of this of tonight? You saved my herd, possibly the lives of many men, with your warning. As for the man Incham, you were forced into his association by circumstance. No other has heard what you have told me; no other shall. Let us lay the incident aside; it is ended."

Kingdom shook his head impatiently. "Not ended. You don't know Incham. We beat him tonight, and he can't take being made second best. He'll strike back any way, anyhow, he can."

Santerre said slowly, his dark eyes searching Kingdom's face, "With what may he strike back? We wiped out his band this night."

"Not all. Some scattered into the fog. He'll round them up somehow—if a man can do it, he can." He looked intently at Santerre. "There's—there's another thing. . . ."

Something in his face brought Santerre alert.

"Villon," Kingdom said. "He's gone—fell into the path of the stampede."

He saw the shock wash across Santerre's face, but before the owner could say a stunned word, a horseman rode out of the darkness. It was Murray Ambergard. He grinned at Kingdom as though relieved to see him all right.

"Mr. Santerre," Murray said, "Egan said to tell you the herd's stopped. We turned 'em and milled 'em; you can't tell the lead steers from the drag now."

"The men are all well?"

"Egan took a count. Everyone's there, 'cept Villon and Kingdom, and Kingdom's here."

Santerre nodded wearily. "And all mine are accounted for. . . . I shall ride with you to where you're holding the herd." And almost under his breath, Kingdom heard him add, "Ah, Jean-Paul. Poor Jean-Paul. Never the land for him, this . . ." He set his jaw and headed for his horse.

"Wait a minute," Kingdom said sharply.

Santerre turned back to him with an impatient gesture. "Incham and his men will not strike again tonight. There is no need to worry of them."

"Not here, no," Kingdom said slowly. He was trying to think of something—what Incham's strange mind would carry him to next. . . .

Impatiently, Santerre turned to his horse, and in that moment the full horror of realization came to Kingdom; he caught Santerre's arm and whirled him about as though he were a child.

"The ranch," Kingdom said fiercely. "The ranch!"

"What?"

"He won't hit here again. He knows we'll be ready. But one way or another, he knows he must get back at you. He'll ride back to your ranch and . . ."

"This is madness!" Santerre said. "*Folie!*"

"His, then. He runs to a pattern."

Santerre shook his head incredulously. Rage beat high through Kingdom, hot wave on wave, a painful heart pulse in the fevered pain of his arm. He thought of Wanda at the ranch—she and Hassard's wife alone save for two half crippled crewmen Santerre had left behind.

A kind of madness came to Kingdom. Wordlessly, he turned and ran to his horse; his hand clamped on the saddle horn, and he swung up. He threw his weight on his bad arm and the pain nearly caused him to cry out. He kicked his horse around toward Santerre who stared up in amazement at this big, black-haired man with a bloody and useless arm from whose fevered and wild eyes every trace of brooding calm was suddenly gone. Kingdom had taken too much in these last days; his seemingly fathomless and passionless patience had plumbed its last depth and had broken.

"Do I take it alone?" he asked harshly.

"Get down, Kingdom! You're sick!" Santerre took a careful step forward, then lunged suddenly for Kingdom's rein.

Kingdom reined the sorrel hard; the horse lunged in against Santerre, his shoulder hitting the rancher in the chest and staggering him.

With a violent hand, Kingdom turned the sorrel into the fog in a run that jolted his shoulder into a heightened crescendo of agony. He heard Santerre shout after him once and then the camp was behind him.

## CHAPTER SIXTEEN

THE FOG had lifted and a fine drizzle had set in. Incham sat his horse at the summit of the rise overlooking Staghorn. His men—four in number now, including Tory Stark—were about him, their horses head-hung with exhaustion. Around them, the gray dawn, a less murky gray than the fog of the night, lifted silently.

Incham said, "Come on."

They rode down into the ranchyard.

A man on a crutch was limping out from the bunkhouse to meet them, quartering across to cut off their advance toward the main house. He carried a rifle. They pulled their horses up as he stopped before them.

"I know your bunch," the man said. "Get out."

"Suppose you get out of our way, friend," Tory said.

"Yeah," the man said without moving.

Tory, with a single spare movement, shot the man down in his tracks before he could lift his gun. As the echoes of the shot died into the dismal dawn, Incham reined in his prancing horse and looked inscrutably at Tory. Tory was happy. He was very happy now. He slid a fresh load in his gun, his face full of soundless laughter.

Incham shook himself. He said irritably to his men, "We'll see if there's anyone else in the bunkhouse. . . ."

They found another crippled crewman, helpless on his back with a broken leg. Incham knocked Tory's gun up be-

fore he could shoot this man. Incham told Andre and
Caples to take their horses to the corral, to rub them down,
water and grain them, and tie them there in readiness. Incham and Tory and Delaney walked on to the house. Two
women were waiting on the porch. One, Hassard's wife,
had a rifle; the other, the small one, was holding a six
shooter.

As Incham started up the short flight of steps to the
veranda, Mrs. Hassard swung her rifle to train on him. Her
face was pale, her hand steady. "Are you feeling brave?"
she asked.

Incham halted, his foot on the top step, and looked at
her. He said dispassionately, "I'm taking over this house
—for a while. I don't intend leaving until I'm good and
damn ready. Keep your guns if you like, but keep the hell
out of my way."

Then he said he didn't want to be disturbed, walked
on through the back door without another glance at any
of them, and found himself in the kitchen. He started a
fire in the stove, brewed up a pot of coffee, and sat at
the table, drinking black coffee, and idly musing.

Now that he was here, he asked himself, why didn't he
burn the place and get out? Santerre might fear something
of the sort and send some men back. . . . But why should
Santerre suspect?—he had no grounded reason to fear such.
Unless Kingdom gave it to him. Whatever the case, Incham
decided, he had a few hours' grace here while Santerre
was too occupied in taking toll of any ravage of the stampede to worry of other things.

But all this was merely a sop for excuse in his own mind,
Incham knew. He would delay the burning of Santerre's
ranch as long as he dared, simply because he wished to
sit here and savor the power of destruction which lay in
his hands. In the next two or three hours, he could destroy
or spare this ranch and no one could stop him. It was almost the very taste of deity. . . .

Once he had admitted this to himself, Incham felt better. He walked to the stove and refilled his coffee cup. As he set the pot down, a door opened behind him, the door of the corridor leading off the front room. Incham turned swiftly, defensively, some of the coffee spilling from the cup to scald his hand. He swore under his breath. It was Hassard's wife, he saw with a glance. She must have seen him spill the coffee; her face held a distant amusement. She carried the rifle in her right hand, the stock nestled in the crook of her elbow.

"May I have some coffee?" Mrs. Hassard said dryly.

"Go ahead," Incham said irritably, slacking back into his chair at the table. "And put that gun down. No one's going to hurt you."

Mrs. Hassard leaned it against the wall, fetched a cup and poured it full, then carried it to the table, saying ironically, "May I sit down?"

Incham's wise and sardonic-cynical eyes lifted to survey her for a long time. What the hell was she up to? "Go ahead."

Mrs. Hassard sank into a chair, sipped coffee for a moment, looked at the table and said nothing. He didn't encourage her. Finally she said, "Would it be too much to ask who you are and what you want here?"

"It is," Incham said shortly. "It's none of your damn business."

The remark did not disconcert her in the least as he had suspected that it would not. Mrs. Hassard put her elbows on the table, crossing her arms. "I think that it is."

"You might be right," Incham told her, rather liking her coolness. "My name, then, is John Incham. Does that mean anything?"

"Incham?" Mrs. Hassard said thoughtfully. "Oh, yes— you run a wild bunch of army deserters, don't you? Well . . . what's the rest of it?"

Incham was nettled by the almost contemptuous note

of her voice, but his admiration was mildly aroused. "Las
night I raided Santerre's market herd. But they were wait
ing for us. . . . The upshot of that is that I have fou
men left out of eleven."

Inez sat erect, saying softly, her eyes on his face, "Wer
any of Santerre's men hurt?"

"Ah," Incham murmured. "Worried about your no-goo
husband."

"I am not worried about him," Inez said dispassionately
"I hate him."

Incham smiled idly, searching his pockets for a cigar
"You are a beautiful liar, my child, but a liar neverthe
less."

The woman looked down at her distended body and shud
dered. "I hate him," she repeated.

Incham's agate eyes sharpened. "Because you will bea
his child? That is your mission in life."

Her calmness broke. "No! That's not so—how can yo
say it? I know; you're like all men. A woman is for one
thing, to be broken and used for that. What she wants o
thinks does not matter."

"If you believe that, you're a fool," Incham said coldly
"With any decent man, the happiness of his woman is firs
and last. Bearing his child is only part of it, and it he
highest privilege as well as her grestest duty."

Mrs. Hassard watched him, a pathetic note in a voic
which had lost its distance, its contempt. "Do you believ
that? Really believe it?"

"I do." Incham knew with surprise that this woman wa
asking him for assurance—the first time in her life, doubt
lessly, that she had asked anyone for anything. . . .

"You're an odd one, do you know?" Inez murmured
"You don't fit your place in life, Incham. . . . What hap
pened?"

"The war mainly. Other things. Doesn't matter." Incham
dismissed this flatly and stood restlessly, walking to the

window and staring out into the driving rain. Mrs. Hassard stood and came over to look too. A dark and rain-pelted shape 'lay out there. . . .

She said: "You killed that man."

"He was ready to shoot. It gave us some right."

"That much?"

"Afraid?"

"You have that effect," she murmured.

"He had his warning," Incham said irritably. "He was in my way."

Mrs. Hassard said slowly, "You're a sick man, Incham."

"And you're a little fool. You're like all women; your mind is finite, limited. We come from dirt; dirt is our destiny. Why hang on to a thing like life anyway . . . ? Your hell is here on earth and of your own making. Probably did that fellow a favor. If I didn't what difference to him? We live our little egotistical span of years, they weep for us, then forget us. I say the hell with mankind and its petty inhibitions."

Inez stared at him, startled by his bitter and scalding vehemence. Incham ended then, his eyes snapping into focus. Something was out there—something coming through the rain. . . . A man on horseback rode ploddingly over the summit of the dune beyond the blacksmith shed. The horse did not seem to be guided by the man; it merely drifted slowly down toward the ranch. Incham saw now that the rider lay limply across the neck, his head bowed into the mane. The man had a death grip on the saddle horn with one hand, the other hanging limp, as though useless.

Incham flung his cigar away, threw the back door open, and sprinted out into the rain. He caught the horse's bridle and led him to the veranda, tying him to a wooden column supporting the roof, and turned his attention to the rider. He knew from the man's great size, even before he caught a handful of thick black hair and turned his head to see his face, that it was Kingdom, his eyes glazed and nearly closed.

Incham saw the blood-saturated bandanna bound tightly above the triceps of his left arm and swore. He tugged at Kingdom's dead weight until it left the saddle. He tried to support it, but it was too much for his meager frame; Kingdom's whole weight came down limply into him. He slipped and fell with Kingdom on top of him. With a hard effort, he rolled Kingdom away and came up cursing, his face and clothes covered with mud. Inez stood in the doorway, hand braced against the doorjamb, staring. He snapped at her, "Help me."

They tried to pull Kingdom erect; his great weight was too much for a woman and a small man. Incham slapped him. "You'll have to help us, Kingdom—hear me?" He slapped him again. "Put your feet under you—push up."

The last words must have come through to Kingdom; his legs straightened under him, and they could feel him lifting his weight though his head did not raise. His chin lolled loosely on his chest. They had only to support him on either side as he pushed himself erect.

"Walk," Incham said. "One foot after the other. . . . That's it. . . ."

They had some trouble getting up the steps; Incham cursed Kingdom until he lifted his feet laboriously up, one after the other.

They were in the shelter of the veranda now, out of the angle of downbeating rain, just as it began in earnest, slanting down in pale slashing sheets which churned the yard into a chocolate sea of mud.

"Where can we put him?" Incham shouted at Inez.

"My husband's room . . ." She nodded toward the corridor leading off the kitchen.

Hassard's room was small and cramped and had a look of barren meagerness and hard, Spartan simplicity. They eased the big man down on the bare cornshuck mattress;

Incham pulled his mackinaw off. Kingdom's clothes were damp from hours of fog and mist. Incham, seeing the gun in Kingdom's belt, took it.

"Boil some water," he told Inez. He drew his pocket-knife and cut away the sleeve from the unconscious man's shoulder, then the blood-sodden bandanna bound around it. The cloth was dried on with the blood.

When Inez brought a basin of hot water and strips of clean material for bandaging, Incham soaked the fabric and blood away from the whole arm until the raw angry lips of the wound lay clean with fresh blood welling a livid trickle as fast as it could be washed away. The bullet had not gone through. From its angle, Incham judged that it had gone on into the bone and splintered it—perhaps lodged there. . . . He shook his head. This would require a doctor's care. Little wonder that Kingdom had been nearly unconscious—doubtless with the pain of this as much as loss of blood.

Incham tied the wound up as best he could. Standing, then, he frowned down at Kingdom. Then he produced a cigar and lighted it, passively regarding Kingdom's still form through the pale curling smoke. "Can you hear me, Kingdom?"

Kingdom's eyelids twitched and draggingly lifted, his eyes deeply recessed mirrors of obsidian. His gaunt and pain-ravaged frace turned slowly to Incham.

"Hurt some?"

"What do you think?"

"Ha! Nothing much wrong with you," Incham said, hesi-tating. He wanted to know for a certainty of Kingdom's per-fidy, and yet he didn't. Why ask? Yes—why not fatalistically accept last night's fiasco as a bad cast of the gods of chance?

He started at Kingdom's sudden question: "Where is she?"

Incham's gaze snapped into focus on his face with quick shrewdness. "Where is who?"

Inez said quickly, "They didn't hurt her, Kingdom. I'll fetch her. . . ."

Kingdom's great frame seemed to lose tension, as though in a sudden excess of relief.

"Well, well," Incham said. "Mrs. Villon, eh? Why Kingdom!· And you the idealizing moralist. . . !"

A wicked glint struck Kingdom's bright dark eyes in a sidelong glance at Incham.

"Still the moralist," the leader observed cheerfully. "Else you wouldn't get salty over it." He stepped to the door, looked back, and grinned. "Yes . . . I thought there was a reason you rode back here even if you were half dead in the saddle. I'm afraid my reputation has gotten considerably out of hand. . . ."

Kingdom watched him silently, burningly. Incham grinned again and stepped out into the corridor. Mrs. Villon came hurrying down toward him, saying breathlessly, "Is Kingdom—"

Incham pointed at the door with a tilt of his chin and she went in, closing the door after her.

Incham paced through the house like a caged beast. He found his men sitting in the front room. They already had the floor littered with cigarette butts; they looked keyed to hair trigger pitch.

Tory Stark came to his feet as Incham entered. "I am an easy man, Mr. Incham, but not this easy. What are we doing here? When do we leave? This is no place for any of us."

"Shut up," Incham said absently, not looking at him, not looking at any of them. No one else said anything; they were too familiarly keyed to the occasional dangers of the leader's shifting moods.

Incham stepped out onto the front veranda and started pacing, trying to come to a decision.

He must burn Staghorn to the ground immediately and clear out. He had reached the end of the veranda in his pacing and now he turned decisively back toward the front room—then stopped. . . .

The room where Kingdom lay was at one of the front corners of the house; its single high window opened onto the veranda, and Incham started, then halted, as the voices of Kingdom and Mrs. Villon came suddenly to his ears. Only then he realized that the window of that room was about a foot above his head: the voices of its occupants came clearly to him—actually Incham stood no more than a yard from them with only the thick wall of hand-hewn timbers between.

"That's why I had to hire out to your father," Kingdom said in a low voice. "Incham thought me my outlaw brother. Best thing to do seemed to play along and wait for a chance to help your father. . . ."

"It's all right. Please rest. . . ."

"Your husband—sorry I had to be the one to tell you."

"Go to sleep, Kingdom," she said gently.

"Wait. It isn't the time, but there may never be another chance. . . . I—I love you. That part didn't fit in. I—oh, damn it to hell!"

There was a flat hopelessness in his voice. No man of words, Kingdom, thought Incham wryly.

"Kingdom, Kingdom, you utter fool," she said in a soft, strange voice. "Can't you see it? Or won't you?"

Kingdom must have understood finally. Incham heard his soft curse.

Mrs. Villon said gently, "I know, Jim. You're trying to hurt yourself now because you feel you're wronging the memory of Jean-Paul so soon after his death. . . ."

Kingdom said miserably, "That. Also he lost his life trying to save mine."

"No. Jean-Paul was a dying man. His case was incurable —the doctor said so. Jean-Paul knew it, and so did I. Only it was a point of pride with him to pretend that it was not. But dying to save someone else—he'd hold that a fair exchange. Dying bravely and worthily—this was a matter of honor to Jean-Paul, and far preferable to the lingering death that was coming to him. Don't you see, Jim?—it's not dirty. It's what can give us strength, if anything."

"But"—Kingdom struggled for words—"you take it so easily. Doesn't his death . . ." His voice trailed off.

"As the death of a friend. Maybe that sounds terrible, but it's only the truth. Jean-Paul and I—at the first—were in love with something in each other that never was. When we found out, we could only make the best of it. . . . Jean-Paul would never have consented to a divorce; he could not brook an admission of personal failure to the world. Perhaps that was a wrong kind of pride, but it was in keeping with the honor that caused him to save your life. . . . Jim, look at me. It was never a real marriage. Believe that."

Incham stepped off a short way, to the edge of the veranda, staring into the rain and not seeing it and listening to the steady thrumming of the rain on the roof and not hearing it. It was a strange pleasure to know what the man and woman beyond the wall had found. He tried to remember how it had been with him once, and another, and he could call up only a dim sad memory.

Too full until now of his personal embitterments, he looked beyond himself with a new-found insight: he knew that he could not destroy this ranch—this home—and what it might mean to these people and their children to follow.

Incham stepped into the front room. Three of his men sat smoking. Tory was standing at the north window, hands rammed in his hip pockets, staring out at the drenched plain with his back to the others.

"On your feet," Incham told them. "We're leaving."

Tory turned slowly from the window, the old mad devil dance of laughter in his dark eyes. "Why, Mr. Incham, you waited too long, sir."

Incham looked sharply at him. Tory was smiling delightedly; he nodded toward the window. Incham was at his side in a moment. He looked and saw nothing through the driving rain, then caught movement at the brow of the long slope which rolled gently down toward the outbuildings.

Santerre had come, and a rough twenty of his crew rode with him.

## CHAPTER SEVENTEEN

IT HAD BEGUN to rain. Slowly at first; then the sky seemed torn from horizon to horizon. Hassard, gigging his horse after the others, put up his face to the rain, welcoming the beating and coldness and the wetness of it. The dawn was a dismal gray neutrality of storm-lashed wasteland and roiled murky clouds banked darkly over the land.

Hassard hunkered miserably into his saddle, shivering shoulders slouched against the slant of the rain, water runneling down in a tiny cataract before his face from the trough formed by the rolled brim of his hat.

This riding back to the ranch was another of Santerre's brainstorms. Santerre had been nervous and irritable for hours last night after the stampede. Hassard had attributed this to the after tension of the night's violence; but this morning, after stamping back and forth restlessly before the fire for a while, Santerre had turned suddenly, decisively, to his men and ordered them to saddle.

He'd left ten to stand watch over the herd and hold them at the spot; the remaining nineteen, including Hassard, he ordered to follow him and rode off without a word of explanation. All Hassard could tell was that they were heading on their backtrail, toward Staghorn.

Hassard, numb with weariness in body and mind alike, sat slack in the saddle, rolling loosely to the gait of the horse. He had himself started the turning of the cattle during the stampede. He had directed the rebunching of the herd. He had taken a cursory tally of their losses when it became light enough to see, riding ceaselessly to and fro throughout the night, expending the tremendous reservoir of nervous energy which lay untapped within him and which he had never fully plumbed.

The losses were small, in weak steers that went down, unable to hold the pace, to be tramped beneath their fellows. They found Villon—enough to recognize him. Hassard felt a wry disgust for himself, recalling his open contempt for the man. They found as well the bodies of three outlaws, shot down in Santerre's surprise counterattack. One of them Hassard had recognized with surprise as the short fat moonfaced fellow with whom he had played poker in Boundary not long ago and who had accused him—and rightly so—of bellystripping.

So suddenly that Hassard scarcely realized it, they were at the crest of the rise beyond which they could view the sprawling Staghorn house and outbuildings. Santerre did not even pause; he swung his arm, motioning them on, spurring his mount savagely into a run down the slope, the crew sweeping after him.

Then the shots crashed out from the house. Hassard pulled his horse up with the others. Santerre swung his arm again, directing them to cut off at right angles rather than ride into the teeth of gunfire. They headed in a body toward the wagon shed. Bullets kicked up the ground under them.

Hassard thought in bewilderment: The old man expected this. But how the hell?

They offsaddled at the shed, and at Santerre's direction took up positions behind fence and building. He commanded them to hold their fire; there were women in the house.

Hassard moved to Santerre's side behind the shelter of a wagon. "What the hell is this?" he asked. "Who're those fellows in the house? How'd you know they'd be there?"

"The ones that attacked us last night," Santerre said grimly. "Incham's men. Kingdom warned me that they would come to the Staghorn, perhaps to burn it in retaliation. He told me so last night. I did not believe him. Only a short while ago was I able to persuade myself that he was right."

"How did Kingdom know?" Hassard asked, eyes narrowing. "Was he with Incham? Where the hell is Kingdom, anyhow?"

"Never mind that," Santerre said shortly. He stared through the steady rain at the house. "Your wife and my daughter are in there with those men."

"God!" Hassard looked wildly around as this bore fully home to him. "I've got to get to the house. . . ."

"Do not be a fool," Santerre said sharply. "You would be in the open all the way."

Hassard whirled on a crewman at his side. "Alf. Give me a hand. Lay a hold to this spring wagon."

Santerre opened his mouth as though to speak, then closed it. He watched as Hassard and Alf tugged the wagon out away from the wagon shed. Hassard hauled it around to face the front of it toward the rear veranda of the house; then he found an old piece of rope and lashed the tongue down. There was a slight incline from the shed down to the house. Hassard judged that with a litle impetus the

wagon could roll that far by itself. He climbed into it and
flattened himself on the bed. He could depend on the low
walls of the wagon as partial shelter from bullets.

He told Alf, "Give it a push."

"You are mad!" Santerre snapped. "What can one man
do down there?"

"Be all right once I'm up by the house," said Hassard.
"Getting there's the hard part. Lend Alf a hand."

Santerre shook his head, but he put his shoulder to the
wagon with Alf, and they heaved together. Hassard felt
the wheels stir creakingly, then fall into motion and roll,
rocking and jolting, picking up speed on the gentle gradient.
Through a crack in the front, his face pressed to the rough
boards, Hassard could see the veranda pillar. With a mild
scraping bump, it came to a sudden rest there.

Hassard lay on his belly, scarcely breathing, his Paterson
in hand. The wagon had been seen from a rear window; the
shot proved that. Whether they knew he was in it was
another question. He had to get inside. He waited, watching the back door, every fiber of his body straining. . . .

The door burst open suddenly; a man came out, lunging off the veranda not two yards past Hassard flattened
on the wagon bed. He was making a break for the corrals,
Hassard saw; must have left their horses there . . . Hassard lifted himself a foot or more, lining the Paterson on
the man. But the fellow's back was to Hassard now; he
swore and lowered his gun.

Then Santerre's men opened fire from the wagon shed.
The jayhawker went down, sprawling headlong. He tried to
struggle up, coming waveringly as far as one knee; then
sighed as though in great weariness and slid back on his
face in the mud.

Hassard's attention swung back to the open door. Someone else going to make a break. A cold terror took him
then. A big black-bearded man came through the door, gun
in one hand, the other holding Inez—his wife—before him,

her arm wrenched up behind her back, holding her helpless. . . .

Santerre's men could not shoot without endangering Inez. But Hassard was close and the big man hadn't seen him. If he could draw a bead from the side . . .

The jayhawker edged across the veranda, slowed by his struggling hostage. When his right side was presented fully to Hassard's view, he raised himself again, laying the barrel of his gun along the top of the sideboard and drawing his aim with minute care.

The slight movement drew the man's attention; he swung, his gun blasting at the wagon. Inez wrenched free and threw herself down. A bullet smashed the top edge of the sideboard by Hassard's face, tearing off a foot-long splinter which flew away, the raw jagged wood hitting Hassard between the eyes, the pain blinding him. He squeezed off his shot and rolled flat against the wagon bed, claws of panic fixing in him.

Blood was running in his eyes, but he could see again. He was still and rigid for a moment, then realized unbelievingly that he was unhurt, and saw, raising his head again, that his one blind shot had found the mark. The jayhawker lay loosely spreadeagled on his back on the veranda, one arm trailing limply over the edge in the mud.

He saw Inez running toward the wagon then, and he came to his feet, caught her under the arms and swung her up into the wagon, pulling her down flat within its shelter. A woman in a million. No hysterics; no incoherency. Only her body trembled a little against him. He shook her by the arms, looking at her face.

"All right?"

"You're not."

"Nothing. Piece of wood hit me."

They lay for a while in silence on the rain-sodden boards. Inez said, the words seeming drawn at great length from her, "What brought you back, husband mine?"

"You're my wife. Is that enough?" Hassard could feel the old constraint falling back between them, and he knew suddenly that he could not, must not, let this happen. "It was like something screaming in me," he said slowly. "I wanted to break you and hurt you, but it was beyond me. . . ."

"My fault," she said almost inaudibly. "I married you to get out of that gambling hell."

"I knew it," Hassard said. "I took you out because I cared for you. I'd hoped—in time—" He ended it there.

Inez said nothing for a moment; then, gently: "You weren't very patient."

"Never been my way," he said. "Lower my horns and charge into it, that's my way: Always. I never thought— till awhile ago—that that could hurt other people. Hated myself for what I'd done to us both, and that's no good either. . . . Forget that. You're free after this."

Inez didn't move. "Is that what you want?"

He looked up at the sky. The rain, slackening off now, streamed off his face. He said simply, "Answer to that is, I'm here."

"Egan—look at me." He turned his head back to her, and it came to him that for the first time the hard and beautiful mask of the percentage girl was softened in all its lines and the woman was there. She said very clearly, "I don't want to be free. . . ."

Hassard looked at her intently. He said in new-dawning wonderment, "What changed that?"

"A man—a little man named Incham. . . . Don't talk. Hold me."

## CHAPTER EIGHTEEN

WHEN KINGDOM heard the shooting, he hauled himself painfully off the bed onto his feet, and motioned Wanda to a corner. Then he took a step that carried him behind the door.

One of the outlaws stepped warily into the room, barely opening the door to edge through; he saw Wanda standing in the corner and started toward her. Kingdom smashed his fist with all his strength into the base of the man's head. He was hurled forward, half off his feet, crashing face first into the opposite wall and falling, doll-limp, to the floor.

"Always look behind you, Kingdom," Incham said in a lazily reproving voice. Kingdom turned; Incham stood in the doorway, a little gambler's pistol loose in his hand.

"I would reckon this ends it," Incham said conversationally. "Really too bad, Kingdom. I liked you."

Shots sounded from the rear of the house. Incham tilted his head. "Delaney and Andre making their break," he murmured. "The fools. They'll not make it." He looked back at Kingdom. "It was a hell of a thing to do, Kingdom."

"All right."

Incham chuckled softly. "No nerves. . . . What we couldn't have done together. You and Lute and I—a lot alike. Only I'm on one side of the fence and you're on the

153

other, and Lute—Lute was straddling the fence and didn't know which way to jump." Incham smiled faintly. "Funny. I was about to ride out just before Santerre's men came down on us. Well, nothing for it now. . . ." He motioned at Kingdom with his gun. "Turn around." Kingdom turned slowly. Behind him, Incham spoke again: "This has to be. You played me false, Kingdom. No man will ever do that to me again. . . ."

The shot crashed; Kingdom felt his whole body shrink together. Then, imperceptibly, disbelievingly, he found that he was erect and unhurt, and some horror in Wanda's face made him turn.

Incham was stretched on his face on the floor, arms outflung.

He had shot himself in the head.

Kingdom stood and looked down at him, a shabby little man unimpressive in death.

Kingdom took Incham's gun and, Wanda behind him, maneuvered carefully down the corridor toward the front room, reaching it just as Santerre and three crewmen came charging through the door.

Wanda was in her father's arms then. Presently Santerre released her and stepped over to grasp Kingdom's hand, saying, "Well, Kingdom, as you see, I was not entirely a fool."

"I'm wondering," Kingdom said, "if there are any more of them."

"There were five altogether when they rode in," said Wanda.

"We shot down one who made a break for the corrals," Santerre said slowly. "Hassard got another who was using his wife for a shield. . . ."

Kingdom jerked his head toward the room he and Wanda had just quitted. "Incham is dead in there, and one of his men is cold-cocked on the floor."

"Then," Santerre said slowly, "there is one man still

in the house. . . ." He glanced at two of his men. "Get the unconscious one of whom Kingdom spoke, tie him, bring him out."

They left the house, Santerre waving his arm to the men who waited by the wagon shed, guns at the ready. "It is finished," he called, "save for one man. Surround the house so that he cannot escape. But do not get too close."

The rain had stopped. They slogged through the mud up to the shelter of the wagon shed. Hassard was there, his wife close beside him, and Kingdom knew that something had happened here, and, without knowing what, that it was good. Emilion was there; he boomed a welcome to them.

Hassard, somehow looking beaten and victorious at once, stepped over to Kingdom. "Won't discourse on this. Say I admit I was wrong. Let it go there."

Taking Hassard's hand, Kingdom felt the last burden of the past week lift ponderously from his shoulders. "You had to take the hand that was dealt you."

"But not like that," Hassard said: "You too, Mrs. Villon. My apologies."

Shooting broke out down at the house; they all turned to look. Lovelace and Granger came running up the slope, Lovelace favoring a wounded arm. "He wants Kingdom," Granger said, out of breath.

"What?" Santerre said.

"Fellow in the house. He's barricaded himself in your room. We tried to get close to the window and he got Love, here. He yelled out to us he wants to see Kingdom. And you."

Santerre glanced at Kingdom. "Shall we go?"

They left their guns and side by side set off down the slope, past Santerre's men, crouching behind whatever cover they could find, stopping a hundred feet from the house.

"You wanted to talk," Santerre called.

The man inside raised himself into plain view in the window, and Kingdom went cold.

It was Tory Stark. . . .

"I have a word, Kingdom," Tory called, smiling recklessly, utterly insentient to the odds against him.

"I'll hear you, Tory."

"A deal," Tory said. "You hear me too, Mr. Santerre. If Kingdom meets me now, you won't have to lose a lot of men, which you sure as hell will if you try to rush the house."

"And if Kingdom meets you?"

Tory's laughter pealed out bell-clear, tinkling chillingly. "One of us will be killed. If me—then that's what you want, isn't it . . . ? If Kingdom—then you call off your dogs and let me ride out. Only I say this: I won't leave without I meet Kingdom first. . . . What do you say?"

"I'll take it, Tory," Kingdom said, not looking at Santerre.

The rancher wheeled on him. "More madness! You are no gunman. You will stand somewhat less chance than an icicle in hell."

"More than me to think of," Kingdom said quietly, and Santerre was silent.

Tory said gleefully, "I've been wondering if those yellow stripes on your pants are in the wrong place, Kingdom."

"That's all, Tory. You'll pay the piper."

"You'd better get a gun first," Tory taunted. ". . . You should have stayed home, Yankee boy."

They turned and headed back up the slope, his mocking quicksilver laughter floating after them.

"Why does he want you?" Santerre asked puzzledly.

"I shot his brother," Kingdom said briefly.

"Ah—the stage incident of which I was told."

They reached the shed. Santerre told the others of the proposal.

"Let me meet him," Hassard said meagerly.

Kingdom said in an iron voice, "It has to be this way."

He looked at Wanda's white face and looked away.

Hassard took off his gunbelt and handed it to Kingdom. Put that on and draw once."

Kingdom did.

"Oh, Lord," Hassard groaned softly. "I seen running molasses that was faster. . . . First of all, pull the damn belt higher. Never mind that low-slung business; it doesn't have to be hanging from your kneecaps."

"Use two guns," suggested Emilion. "Twice as good chance, *hein?*"

"No," Hassard said flatly. "Hard enough to be accurate with one. Look here: bring your gun up natural. Take your time. You can't get your gun out first anyway, so take your time. Just remember that. . . . Tory's hot-headed, and you killed his brother. He may get wild, shoot too fast. . . . May give you your chance." He measured Kingdom's size with a gloomy eye. "You can outlast him, for certain."

Kingdom turned without a word to leave. Wanda blocked his path. He looked at her. "Move aside, Wanda," he said. She did not move.

"It's no good," he said gently. After a long moment, she stepped aside, and he would never forget her face then.

He walked on, every foot seeming a mile. Down the slope, past Santerre's men, starting across the stretch of mud-choked yard to the house.

In a fluid movement, Tory climbed over the window sill and dropped like a cat to the ground.

He was smiling. His coat was off, showing the black butt of the gun buckled at his left hip for a cross draw. . . . He began walking across the muddy yard.

Kingdom took three more steps, then drew his gun. Tory's hand moved with the blinding sweep of heat lightning. His first shot was off before Kingdom could finish the movement of hand to gun he had begun before Tory had even moved.

Tory's shot was too hasty, a clean miss. It was as Hassard has said: facing his brother's killer, a temper mastered Tory, and his skill had left him. Kingdom's gun was out; it swung to a level. *Take your time.* Tory's second bullet smashed Kingdom's left shoulder only a little above the other wound.

Kingdom drew back a step; the Paterson, pointed low before him, went off in the pure reflex of this second numbing blow. The pain came then and for a moment he was blind with it.

When Kingdom could again see clearly, Tory was on his knees, sinking forward, his hands pressed to his belly. He was still smiling when he pitched on his face.

Kingdom turned; he walked blindly back toward the shed, thinking: It's finished. Really finished . . .

He got three yards. Two Staghorn riders, running to meet him, caught him as he fell.

"What a mess," Dr. Flamsteed said cheerfully as he packed his bag. "Two damndest subborn bullets I ever took out. . . . You ought to rest now, and since you damn well won't, here's your shirt."

Kingdom swung himself off Hassard's cot and pulled on his shirt, buttoning it around the bandaged arm. It was late afternoon of the same day.

"Good of you to ride out from Boundary, Doc."

"Thank that damn Hippocrates. Take it easy on that arm now."

Kingdom said he would and followed the little doctor out to the front porch. Wanda was there, and her father, and the Hassards.

"What the hell you made of?" Hassard asked Kingdom. "You're supposed to be dead to the world."

"An ox is so tough, nothing but an ax drops him," said Doc. "How's the arm, Santerre?"

"No difficulty."

"Good. So that's it." Doc had just stepped off the veranda when Inez said faintly, "I think I'm going to have a baby. . . ."

"Oh, my God," Hassard said. "Doc!"

Hassard carried his wife into the house, followed by Wanda and Dr. Flamsteed, Doc muttering, "Rest for the wicked—a hollow dream, dear friends. . . ."

After a while, Wanda and Dr. Flamsteed came out. Wanda said happily, "A girl."

Flamsteed mopped his brow with a big silk handkerchief. "My God," he said. He set his black bag down, opened it, and pulled out a near-empty flask of J. H. Cutter. He drained it with a final pull and flung it away. "You know," he said conversationally, "I think nature slipped. *We* do all the suffering."

After Flamsteed had gone, Santerre turned to Wanda and Kingdom to look gravely from one to the other and to see what he had expected. This was the frontier, a land of quick death and of quickly accepted change, and Santerre took in without comment what he saw. It was right this time, it was good; and he had never had this feeling about his daughter and Villon.

"You will not feel Jean-Paul's death between you?" Santerre asked gently.

Kingdom looked at Wanda and she shook her head soberly.

Santerre smiled and nodded. To Kingdom, he said: "So. A pat hand. Play it. . . . *Sacre!* I have a drive to finish," and left to gather his crew.

They stood in the dying light and he took her hand in his good one, but nothing more, because all this was too sudden. There was a strangeness to all of it that would pass.

"Look," she said. "The sun is showing at last."

The golden warmth sped across the land to them, shadow sweeping away before it; it fell on them and held them.

Watching, they knew that it would rain again. But the sun would be there, and that was enough.

# ABOUT THE AUTHOR

**T.V. Olsen** was born in Rhinelander, Wisconsin, where he lives to this day. "My childhood was unremarkable except for an inordinate preoccupation with Zane Grey and Edgar Rice Burroughs." He had originally planned to be a comic strip artist, but the stories he came up with proved far more interesting to him than any desire to illustrate them. Having read such accomplished Western authors as Les Savage Jr., Luke Short, and Elmore Leonard, he began writing his first Western novel while a junior in high school. He couldn't find a publisher for it until he rewrote it after graduating from college with a bachelor's degree from the University of Wisconsin at Stevens Point in 1955 and sent it to an agent. It was accepted by Ace Books and was published in 1956 as *Haven Of The Hunted*.

Olsen went on to become one of the most widely respected and widely read authors of Western fiction in the second half of the twentieth century. Even early works such as *High Lawless* and *Gunswift* are brilliantly plotted with involving characters and situations and a simple, powerfully evocative style. Olsen went on to write such important Westerns novels as *The Stalking Moon* and *Arrow In The Sun,* which were made into classic Western films as well, the former starring Gregory Peck and the latter under the title *Soldier Blue* starring Candice Bergen. His novels have been translated into numerous European languages, including French, Spanish, Italian, Swedish, Serbo-Croatian, and Czech.

The second edition of *Twentieth Century Western Writers* concluded that "with the right press Olsen could command the position currently enjoyed by the late Louis L'Amour as America's most popular and foremost author of traditional Western novels." His novel *The Golden Chance* won the Golden Spur Award from the Western Writers of America in 1993.

Suddenly and unexpectedly, death claimed him in his sleep on the afternoon of July 13, 1993. His work, however, will surely abide. Any Olsen novel is guaranteed to combine drama and memorable characters with an authentic background of historical fact and an accurate portrayal of Western terrain.